BODY OF
EVIDENCE

By the same author

LINCOLNSHIRE MURDER MYSTERY SERIES
Dead Spit
Seaside Snatch
Once Bitten
Dead Jealous
Or Not To Be
Twelve Days
Sacrificial Lamb
In Plain Sight
Tissue of Lies
Final Whistle
Reasons Why Not
Best Served Cold

You can contact the author by e-mail at:
carysmithwriter@yahoo.co.uk

AN INGA LARSSON NOVEL

BODY OF
EVIDENCE

Cary Smith

BODY OF EVIDENCE
Copyright © 2021 Cary Smith

ISBN: 9798486823398

PublishNation, London
www.publishnation.co.uk

1

2021

As tall Freddie Curran brought his blue Ford Tourneo slowly to a halt outside the gate to their new property, his partner Kirsten in the front passenger seat stretched her arms out in front of her.

'Been great having a break, but you know, there's no place like home.'

'You call this home?' Freddie sniggered as he applied the handbrake and uncoupled his seat belt. 'Back to the hard graft more like, I'm afraid missus,' he said as he opened his door and stepped out. 'Brilliant!' he gasped as his partner emerged from her side. 'Mitch said he'd empty the bloody skip. That's a great start to come back to.'

'You know what he's like,' she shrugged away.

'Don't remind me it's why he's cheap.'

'Can't have it both ways.'

'Look at the bloody front door!' he almost shouted. 'Said he cut the damn ivy back for God's sake.'

This was their new property, but not one for them to enjoy in exactly the same way the previous three had not been home either. This was a teacher and an IT manager who for the best part of three years had become used to living in virtually one room and sleeping in another in their struggle to progress up the property ladder.

Just one more after this and then Freddie says they'll look for somewhere bigger and better to settle down properly and permanently. A place to truly call home was what Kirsten dreamt of for years.

The great adventure had all started off with that old former council house terraced place in the city they'd completely re-modelled, revamped and refurbished. Then the first two-bedroomed semi in a slightly better part of town. From there it had been onto three-bedrooms with a garage and quite a decent garden. Now number four, appropriately four bedrooms in a quiet village close to Lincoln.

Nestled at the end of a country lane but not too close to other villagers. Chosen on purpose as they were both well aware how some sad folk with the location mantra will one day pay well over the odds to gain bragging rights over so-called friends. All of which they planned soon to make financial gain out of.

Therein lay the problem. With the property market in the doldrums for ages both pre and post Brexit and Coronavirus, selling was always a frustrating and tediously lengthy process. Now the market had become far more buoyant they hoped to gain from.

Kirsten opened the white gate in the low fence and headed off key in hand along the fairly straight flagstone short path bordered by rose bushes to the red front door.

Freddie lifted the tailgate of their Tourneo and lugged out two big travel bags he plonked on the grass verge. He then repeated the action humping out three back packs. With the door slammed shut he opened a rear door and lifted out two white paper carrier bags containing the set meal for three they'd just purchased on the way in.

The process had become a ritual over time. In this particular case on the Friday before they headed south once all the packing had been done to Kirsten's satisfaction, and they were ready to go, off they'd gone to find somewhere for a meal.

On this occasion they'd been to Windmill Farm and enjoyed the carvery. Freddie had chosen the beef and Kirsten turkey. Now on their return the process was repeated in that on the way back they'd stopped just as they had done previously at the end of holidays and short breaks, to pick up a take-away. This time it was her choice and she'd gone for Chinese.

In a home with as yet only a basic microwave and no dining table they could not go to any great lengths over cooking a meal even if they wanted to.

As he headed away from the car Freddie knew they were both looking forward to enjoying Kirsten's choice of meal comprising Shrimp Chop Suey, Tomato Beef, Roast Pork Chinese Style, Sweet and Sour Chicken, Barbecued Spare Ribs being Freddie's favourite and Special Fried Rice.

Freddie trundled up the path with the meal bags in one hand and two others in his left he placed carefully in the hall and strode back to the metallic car once more, and the first of their heavy bags. Tall Freddie had just gripped hold of his navy blue holdall containing their dirty washing his mother would deal with for them, when he heard a scream.

'Freddieeee!' from inside the house told him it was Kirsten. 'Help Freddie! Please, oh my God!' he heard her shriek as she clattered noisily down the wooden stairs in front of him and ran sobbing straight into his arms now free of the load he'd just dumped down. 'Think he's dead!' she gasped her shout.

'What?' he exclaimed. 'Who?' he pushed her away at arms-length but retained hold of her shoulders. 'What you on about?' he implored.

'Up in bed...in our bed...a man, Freddie there's...a dead man up there!'

'You bloody what?'

'God, it's awful!' she shouted. 'For crissakes Freddie!'

'Stay there,' he snapped, released his hold and was indoors and scampering up the stairs two at a time as she bent over to wretch onto the path..

'Fuck sake!' she heard him shout. 'Get the cops,' he said on the stairs as he scampered down. 'Stay there, get back in the car, lock the doors,' with Kirsten still stood there white with fear and shaking. 'Now!' he hollered as he pulled out his phone and tapped nine three times too hard. 'Police,' he waited as Kirsten scampered for the car. 'I want to report a dead body,' he said. 'In our bedroom...my name?' he shouted. 'For God's sake. Freddie Curran.'

2

'Exactly what were you doing sir, when you claim your wife first discovered the body?'

'Partner,' he corrected unnecessarily. 'I explained this already,' Freddie Curran pushed out a breath of frustration leant back against the bonnet of his blue Tourneo.

'Away from the car please, sir.' Jake Goodwin knew from experience he needed to speak clearly and precisely wearing a mask, although this man'd not bothered.

'What?' he grimaced as he moved slightly.

'May well need to be forensically checked.'

'What you on about?' this Curran sighed deeply and shook his head. 'Go on don't tell me, you're bloody taking it. For shit sake you lot really are the bloody pits. What d'you imagine is wrong with the damn thing? Just driven it all the way from bloody Cornwall, or haven't you been bloody listening?'

'That's why we'll be taking it,' he was told. 'You were just about to tell me what your partner was doing, and I'd rather you calmed down, sir.'

'Once again,' he sighed. 'Kirsten'd gone in to open up while I'm unpacking the car,' Freddie said as he stepped nonchalantly almost absentmindedly away from the vehicle. 'Dropped off a few bags in the hall and I was back here at the car when I heard her scream. Dropped what I was carrying and she came running out the front door.'

'You were actually planning to spend the night here, were you sir?' was smiled sarcasm.

'Yes. Of course. Why not?' he grimaced. 'Is that a problem officer?' he demanded.

'There's virtually no furniture.'

'And?' he scoffed and shrugged..

'Would you mind explaining what's going on?' Detective Sergeant Goodwin decided this guy with attitude must be in his thirties but looked younger. Tall and thin with rimless glasses and an uncombed lump of hair on the top of his head.

'Tonight you mean?' Goodwin did not respond to. 'Apart from the fact we'd just got back from having a few days away you mean, and picked up a Chinese on the way in?' he sighed again to explain his mood. 'Guess once we'd eaten, probably leave the unpacking having driven all the way up from Cornwall and we'd have just gone to bed. I'm bloody knackered me.'

'In the bed currently occupied by a dead body you're talking about are you?' Jake Goodwin considered amusing but refrained in order not to annoy this Curran bloke any more. 'That the one you mean?' Probably not a good idea to mention the weather Cornwall had suffered that week.

'Yeh.' he shook his head at the thought of it.

'Would you mind telling me why the whole place is almost empty, sir?' said Goodwin scanning the house. 'If as you claim you live here?'

After he'd seen the body and handed it over to the pathologist and CSI, Jake Goodwin had Googled North Carlton. Knew it was a small village about five miles from the city. Wikipaedia told him there were less than 200 residents at the last census and pictured the big church he'd passed.

Most of the front of the property was covered in ivy. Something which'd put him and his Sally off for a start. Even the red front door was partially hidden by the growth.

'We're developing the property. S'what we do. Virtually live in the bedroom and spend all our spare time working on the house. It's how we progress up the property ladder. Number four this one. Work and sleep here when we're not at work.'

'And work is what exactly, sir?' sounded a trifle sardonic.

'Sorry?'

'I said. What do you do for a living?'

'Be bloody easier of you took your mask off. We're outside.'

'Sorry sir, protocol.'

He sighed. 'Teacher,' then replied with stiff politeness. Goodwin just looked at him without a flicker of emotion or comment aware now why he had an attitude. 'Economics.'

'Why is it unfurnished?'

'We're never going to live here, it's being made ready for sale, or weren't you listening?'

'Made ready?' Goodwin chuckled. 'When would this be for?' Even he could see the house itself couldn't be more than a century old. Not as if it was some run-down, falling-down wreck of a place.

From what he had seen Jake thought it might need more than a bit of a paint job, but the house itself was not inspiring.

'Two, three month turnaround at the outside.'

'Can't be that much to do surely.' *Apart from getting rid of that awful ivy which'll leave marks.*

'Not that you'd notice,' he snorted. 'Too many closed-off rooms to be fair. Has to be open plan living in this day and age so there'll be a few walls coming down, new high-spec kitchen and wet room.' Then he just stopped as if deciding how much of his plans he should reveal. 'Got an en-suite to fit in and the garden's just a shambles out back,' he looked left and right. 'Needs a complete bloody overhaul and we're hoping to go somewhere for a hot tub round the back of course, depending how the finances go.'

Jake Goodwin was pleased he'd never been the sort to be desperately in need of such trendy, soon to be out of vogue and forgotten phases. Temporary fads such as quaffing an obscure gin to impress was not for him or his wife.

'Do you live somewhere else, or are you actually saying this is where you plan to live for now…just in one room?'

'Sorry?' this tall Curran managed, seemingly appearing to be more interested in the comings and goings around him.

Across at the white CSI van a technician appeared to be scouring about for something they were in need of, as arc lamps were being assembled in readiness for a long stay to give better vision to the front and rear of the house.

'Are you saying this is where you plan to live, in just one bedroom?' Goodwin pressed again.

'We've done it each time,' Curran conceded and Goodwin sensed the polite smile coming with it was in fact a smirk. 'How we operate.'

'Eating, drinking and simple things like cooking Sunday dinner, having a shower and relaxing in front of the telly. What about those everyday aspects of life?'

'We're not into retro scoffing,' provided the beginnings of a clever-dick smile around the corners of his mouth, Goodwin found annoying. 'Doing the major works, mostly be oven-ready meals we bung in the microwave in the kitchen to be honest. Use that on a day-to-day basis and we shower at my parents place. If we're ever desperate to watch some reality nonsense we can get that at their place too or on my phone,' was sarcasm Goodwin recognized as part of his way. 'Not that we do, but anyway broadband's going in any day soon.'

Jake knew he'd be there for ages and knowing his luck he'd miss the Olympics round-up later.

'And you'll live like that for how long?'

'First couple of months, then life gets better as we progress. Live in it finished for a bit then sell it on and move on. Not take long now the market's picked up.'

Jake had already bumped into one or two sorry souls who were proud of not having watched the Euros football with the way it turned out. Bragging as if they knew what was coming all along. He just had the feeling this Curran was of that type.

As strange as some he knew would think, for Jake England losing to Italy in the final was to some extent a good thing. Particularly as this was the first major event of its kind he had been able to share with Tyler. England losing was a good life lesson for his son.

The racial abuse, hooliganism and mindless violence that followed was not, but to a degree he was able to protect his son from the worst.

'I've got to ask,' he said looking left and right. 'Why buy here specifically?'

'Good price always helps, plus extra kudos for where it's located.' Goodwin glanced again for inspiration. 'Village is listed in the Doomsday Book as Nortcarltone. Henry VIII stayed in the big hall locally when he visited Lincoln once upon a time.' Goodwin knew he'd tack on another ten or twenty grand for such provenance. Trouble was, somebody with more shady lucre than sense would pay over the odds in order to boast at dinner parties. *"Henry VIII stayed here don't you know."*

'You've got a problem then.' Goodwin paused momentarily to allow it to sink in. 'You'll need to find somewhere else to do all your lesson planning,' was more of Jake making light of him. 'You'll not be going back in, at least not for a day or two. Apart from anything else, CSI have a great deal of forensics to carry out, as you can imagine.'

'You are joking.'

'No sir. This is now a crime scene,' Goodwin said as if he was on road traffic duties catching him not wearing a seat belt. This was not open for discussion. It had to be locked down, and speed he knew was of the essence. Local GP, Pathologist, Forensics, witnesses, CCTV, neighbours and teams to start a search.

Jake thought the front aspect looked good. In the centre aligned to the front door overgrown with ivy was an open sturdy wooden white gate with a thick hedge either side covering the whole width of the front of the property. To the right poking out slightly from the drive was an overladen skip. The flagstone path to the front door however had not been well tended for a while. Somebody had most surely stopped caring for the property before this pair turned up.

'Tell me. Why here, why a small village like North Carlton?'

'Urban living is all last century,' forced Jake Goodwin to keep his smirk to himself. 'Folk moving out in droves and place like this done up'll fetch a fair price.'

'What about facilities. Shop, pub? Is there a bus service?'

'People I'm targetting don't use buses,' he grinned and chuckled with. 'Use bars in town, Just Eat, Amazon and Waitrose delivering is all our todays.'

'That'll all be for another day,' was Goodwin working hard to avoid being rude.

'None of this is our fault...we didn't put the bastard up there for crissakes. You'd better not start blaming us for all this, let me tell you,' he said pointing at Goodwin. 'What about all the stuff I plonked in the hall and I need clothes for work?'

'Sorry sir, you'll just have to make do as best you can for now, but anyway if you really are a teacher, surely you're on holiday?'

'What is it you don't seem to understand?' Curran shot back.

'Oh we understand, sir.' More questions than answers was always an edict Jake followed by naturally.

'We're on a tight schedule here and I've made arrangements. Stuffs being delivered, subbies arranged, things have gotta get done. Plus,' he said pointing at Goodwin again. 'With all the Covid business we've got kids need extra tuition in the holidays. Got all that to deal with as well.''

'Very busy yet you still found time to have a holiday.'

'Give us a break. We didn't bugger off to the Maldives or Cape Verde Islands or some place the Red list.. When Boris said he'd be getting rid of lockdown I booked a week, think it was in February with my aunt and uncle. They've got a holiday cottage on their farm outside Truro. Bloody Coronavirus stopped us doing anything last year. Have you any idea how hard life was teaching in school and organizing on-line learning plus that cock-up with exams? Eh? It's been a steep learning curve with no extra pay remember. Plus we were not first in the queue for the vaccinations like we damn well should have been. Got all this work to get done on the house, it's why we took a few days away so we can come back refreshed and get stuck in for five weeks or so.'

Working twelve hour shift, savings countless lives seven days a week time and time again all wrapped up in all that PPE, Jake kept to himself.

'Your partner off all that time too is she?' Jake Goodwin asked rather than give this selfish individual a lecture.

'No,' but he guessed more was required. 'She's gotta work in a week, but free evenings and weekends.'

'Have you had any tradesmen in here recently?' Goodwin asked in a calm manner he knew would annoy this Curran. From his exasperation hopefully the truth would emerge.

'What?'

9

'Tradesmen. Who's been in there?'

'Two weeks we've had this place,' this slim man insisted loudly. 'Plan was to strip the whole place before we went and get the skip emptied.' He sighed noisily. 'Or somebody should have. All the walls need skimming. Brickie and the plasterer haven't been in at all as yet but soon will be. Walls coming down early doors...got windows guys booked for later on and I'm helping do all the floors starting in a couple o'weeks. This is non-stop, this is full on let me tell you. Time is seriously money.'

'Be next week I should imagine, sir.'

'Old folk we bought it off tried to hold out for more cash.' He shrugged. 'Cost us a few weeks, but they gave in, as they always do.'

DS Jake Goodwin had seen the results of a ferocious, vicious attack with gashes across the cadaver's head just below his receding hairline and the encrusted globules of blood covering what remained of the left side of his face when he'd looked down at the body upstairs in the house before CSI took over.

None of which quite took his attention as much as the rabid smell and state of the whole bedroom.

Dull, faded slightly in places, beige lightly patterned wallpaper on all four sides the manufacturer would no doubt describe as some sort of smokey blush. Yellowing white skirting boards and woodwork, stained pale sanded wooden floors with a tassle ended fawn mat either side of the bed.

'Well, when?' Freddie demanded.

'We'll let you know,' said Goodwin as thoughts were streaming around his head.

'Sorry but letting me know is nowhere near good enough. I'll say again, none of this is our fault you know,' was him shifting the blame. 'I've got contractors booked, got no bloody clothes apart from these,' he said and looked down at his mustard shirt and jeans. 'And my bloody Chinese'll be cold by now.'

'Time to reschedule the work. Couple of weeks I suggest'll be your best bet, wouldn't you?' Goodwin knew the sight in that bedroom would outrage the local community and give the media something nasty to get their teeth into.'Good chance to watch the Olympics.'

'You're bloody joking!' Jake was a swimming and athletics fan but had enjoyed the Mixed Triathon he'd stayed up for to see GB get gold. 'Why d'you not realize none of this cock-up is down to us?' was him back to the blame game.

'If it's not your fault Mr Curran, why might I ask is there a dead man in your bed right now? Not quite the sort of thing people normally discover when they get home from holiday and not what we expect to be faced with every day when we're called out, I can assure you.'

'No good asking me. Nothing to do with us, we've bin in Cornwall. Walls gotta come down this week, whether you like it or not. That happens or the whole damn schedule turns to dust.'

'But we will continue to be asking you, sir. You and your partner are the very people we will be needing answers from.'

Jake Goodwin from his years of experience knew it was always possible the man in front of him was the murderer. It was also distinctly feasible the reason for the body being where it was, had absolutely nothing whatsoever to do with him or his partner chatting with DS Nicky Scoley behind her car.

Always good at the end of a case when it's all nearly packaged for CPS, for Jake to reflect on just how he perceived things from his perspective on the first day and in this case in the first hour. What are the innocent getting up to at that very moment and of course who are the guilty and what alibis have they been busy cooking up?

'Where is she anyway? Where's Kirsten?'

'Being interviewed round the back of one of our cars,' he gestured to two bedraggled scrotes stood just the other side of the blue and white tape. 'Unless you want them taking selfies.'

'She's like me, she doesn't know anything. We just came home and by chance Kirsten happened to be the one to find him, scared the living daylights outta her I can tell yer.'

3

Goodwin could imagine how this guy's partner had felt facing that upstairs, although he had seen a darn sight worse at many unexplained deaths. Usually more blood and certainly more signs of frantic activity.

The bed itself had looked fairly new and modern acting as a vibrant highlight just as if somebody had chosen his resting place with considerable pre-planning. The delightfully patterned and highly coloured duvet with a patchwork design printed all over was the absolute highlight of the room. His wife Sally would no doubt be able to quote chapter and verse about the design and designer responsible for the subtlety.

Such sights of peace and tranquility with that vivid splash of colour blue, green, mauve and purple paled into insignificance the moment he had fully white suited-up, stepped into the undisturbed room and taken his first breath.

Goodwin had this nagging picture in his mind of somebody just taking the time and trouble to smooth down the duvet before they left. Almost as if it was a woman's last gesture before heading off on holiday.

He had faced the smashed face of a middle aged man peering from under the duvet. No splattering, no drips or streams trying desperately to escape the body. Just this one main area of destruction.

A sleeping caved-in face in a near perfect tranquil setting.

'Tell me about Kirsten. Happy are we?'

'Yeh. Why?'

'What about your love life?' made Curran scrunch up his eyes. 'Kirsten had affairs by any chance?'

'Of course bloody not! What you on about now for shitsake? What in God's name's the matter with you people?' was loud. Jake was tempted to ask this teacher the very same question.

12

'Whereabouts have you been in the house since you got home?' was the change of subject deemed to insert a tad of confusion.

Another big sigh. 'After Kirsten told me what she'd found I went up there to have a look and came back down,' he said pointing to one of the three windows upstairs.

'D'you know who he is?'

'Don't actually know him but know *who* he is.'

'How would that be, sir?'

'By reputation more than anything else when I happened to be involved in looking for a car from him. Obnoxious sod.'

'In what way?'

'All stereotypical. Looked my mate's old car up and down, kicked a tyre, sucked in noisily, all the usual car salesman bollocks and said it'd not be easy shifting a green car. What tosspot sort of nonsense is that I ask you?'

'I take it you didn't buy one.'

'No chance.'

'When was this?'

'Year or two back. Ages ago. Not for me, went with a mate.'

'Do you know his name by any chance?' Goodwin prayed for an answer

'Me mate?'

'No, sir.'

'Morgan Hallam,' was very useful and a name he'd heard of.

Why, Jake Goodwin was still asking himself had somebody gone to all the trouble to make the setting so good. So calm and serene. Almost as if people were to be invited in to queue in dignified silence to view a lying in state.

What was wrong with a wood some place, having him tossed in a beck or down a drain? If he'd got his geography right Jake was sure the River Till was not that far away plus plenty of ditches and dykes. Was that a clue and was the man stood in front of him somehow involved? If so in what context?

'Where else?' Goodwin asked. 'Have you been indoors?'

'In the hall, up the stairs, along the landing, in the bedroom.'

'That it?'

13

'Had a piss,' he threw back. 'Been driving for bloody hours remember,' was his reasoning.

'Where?'

'Upstairs. Where d'you think?'

'You'd be surprised, sir.'

'My parents are just down the road there trying to get to us,' Freddie pointed. 'But apparently your lot won't let them through.'

'Cordoned off, sorry. As I said, this is a crime scene.' DS Goodwin glanced across at the CSI team unloading more equipment from their van. 'Did you touch the body?'

'Sorry,' was grimaced.

'I asked if you touched the body.'

'Don't talk daft,' and he looked back at what was going on along the road to the first house in the distance. 'Haven't moved in yet, but this bloody lot'll soon know all our damn business, and what they don't know they'll make up.'

'Thought you weren't moving in?'

'You know what I mean.'

'Either you are or you aren't, sir. It's one thing or the other.'

'For God's sake!' exclaimed Freddie as he stamped his foot. 'This would've been our first night sleeping here. We set everything up before we went so we could just kip here and get working first thing in the morning.'

'Where were you before this? Where d'you move from?'

'Staying with my parents and we've got a load of stuff in storage.'

'Thought you said this is your fourth.'

'Sold number three.'

'And your parents, they live where?' Curran gave the DS their address in Branston. 'Your wife's a teacher as well is she?'

'Partner,' he retorted emphatically as if it was all important. 'No, she's not.' DS Goodwin waited again. 'She's the Senior Client Services Manager for E-Quilibrium,' Jake guessed meant she was some sort of IT techy woman with one of those fancy dan places with bean bags.

'So she'll be going to work, will she?'

14

'On Monday morning for an hour or two that's all, then back here to get grafting.'

'When did you set off for Cornwall?'

'Last Saturday early doors,' was a phrase to seriously irk Jake. 'Had our breakfast on the way.'

He was no doctor, no pathologist though he'd watched a good few at work on bodies or a member of the CSI team, but Jake knew almost immediately this poor guy had been dead some time. Killed elsewhere no doubt and brought to his rest and placed with considerable care into such a calm situation.

'Might be an idea if you head off,' Goodwin suggested with his mind still elsewhere, up in that room. 'But before you go we'll need your mobile and your parents phone numbers.'

Freddie pulled out his phone and began to recite his number.

'No sir, not the number, the phone.'

'What d'you want my phone for?'

'Our eTeam will need to check it, sir.'

'What in God's name for?'

'To check your calls.'

'How bloody long's that gonna take?'

'Won't be too long, sir. You'll need to keep in touch,' the DS handed Freddie a business card. 'Call me on this number and we'll get you back in as soon as we can, but there will more than likely be further interviews depending on what we discover.'

Jake Goodwin wrote down the information Freddie Curran told him on the reverse of one of his own cards.

'What do I do for a phone? I've got all sorts to sort out with all this business going on.' he gestured towards the house. 'Insurance for one thing,' he exhaled obviously. 'And how do I get in touch with them, tell me that?'

'Your parents have a phone,' was Goodwin's turn.

'What a bloody cock-up!'

'If by any chance you decide to move from the address you've given me, please make sure we get to hear as soon as possible.'

Kirsten Wroe walked up to the pair of them. 'Guess what. They've taken my bloody phone,' also unmasked she told her

15

taller partner. 'Now what d'we do?' she said as she linked his arm and rested her head into his shoulder.

'You bastards. You really are aren't you!' he moaned as one of the CSI team all clad in white walked up to the three of them. Jake Goodwin moved to one side. The pair spoke briefly before he returned to Curran and Wroe.

'Keys. How many keys are there to the house? And how many have you got?' the DS queried.

This female had to be in her thirties at most and at around the same height as Nicky Scoley. Short fairish hair and had it been darker it would have reminded Jake of a public schoolboy. Without a coat she sported a good healthy bust and athletic hips under a thin jumper tucked into her jeans.

'Estate Agent handed me two front door and two back door keys. When we walked in we found all sorts just chucked in a drawer in the kitchen. Took us an age to work out what they were for.'

'Two front and two back. And where are they now?'

The couple produced keys, him from his jeans pocket and Kirsten Wroe from her shoulder bag. 'Front door,' he held between forefinger and thumb. 'Back door,' he did the same, 'and car key.' His partner just laid hers out in the palm of her hand.

'Any others?'

'Not that we know of.'

'What about your parents?'

'Why would we?'

'Just asking. You've just sort of moved in and you've been away.'

'Nothing to nick is there. Why would anybody want to break in?'

'Except squatters,' Kirsten offered.

'Somebody has.'

'Broken in?' came with an incredulous look from Curran.

'No,' Goodwin insisted. 'Made legal entry by the look of it. Certainly no suggestion of forced entry. I'm going to need the estate agent and the people who lived here before you.'

'Old couple moved to the coast somewhere few weeks back.'

16

'Do you have their details?'

'Name and address for forwarding mail that's all.'

'If you'd be so kind.'

'On my tablet in the car, you say I can't go near,' Curran grinned sarcastically.

Why? He asked himself for the umpteenth time. Why there of all places was a repeated unfathomable screeching across his mind in search of answers.

By now Jake knew how Shona Tate the Crime Scene Manager and her team would be using Bluestar Forensics to detect traces of blood in the house. The body bleeding out looked as though it had happened elsewhere. To the senior Detective Sergeant that had to be extremely significant.

'Thank you sir, one of our team will obtain the details from there,' he said as Curran gestured to move towards the car. 'We'll need to get our tech lads to check the system over, which we can do at the same time. Password's not desperate but would save them a bit of time.'

'When'll I get it back?'

'Few days, sir. Password, if you wouldn't mind.'

'Shtam two Pi,' he said. 'S-H-T-A-M in caps plus 2-Pi'

Jake Goodwin knew he was expected to ask for an explanation but the distinct possibility of being made to look ridiculous so kept the request under wraps.

4

36 year old DI Inga Larsson head of the Major Incident Team sipped lukewarm coffee from her red mug with 'Guv' printed on one side. Given to her for no particular reason, other than a kindly gesture by Raza Latif's wife who'd seen it in a shop on holiday in Wales. She was fairly pleased with Ghada's choice, as the 'Ma'am' alternative was to her nothing more than an annoying colloquial shortening for somebody who had never been anybody's *madam*.

It was everybody's opinion amongst the senior more permanent members of the team that Raza left the job at the door when he went home. Perhaps the mug meant it was not quite as his wife saw it.

Sat at her desk on a dull damp morning waiting for her troops to settle down out in the Incident Room There was as ever the all too familiar buzz of her assembled detectives and extras waiting on her every word. They'd be ready soon enough for her to start the tried and tested process of opening the initial proceedings by commencing the Sunday morning briefing on this Operation Thanatos.

The computer generated names had now landed once more on Greek gods and in this particular case it was this Thanatos, conveniently, the personification of death.

She would start when she knew all those who could find one, had taken their seats and were as settled as they would ever be.

Inga Larsson was well aware whole categories of crime were not being investigated due to a serious lack of resources. As far as she knew since she'd been away she'd not been hit badly but her team were becoming care worn around the edges.

She'd lost staff in the past with more than one being seconded to an investigation covering three forces into people trafficking and exploitation. 'Tigger' Woods she could call on if desperate, was now working on intelligence gathering and she'd lost another to financial crime linked to the web.

The Detective Inspector had always found it particularly useful to be able to access the crime scene in order to actually see the body and the situation. Two things were missing in this case. She'd not been to the house where Hallam had been found all tucked up in the comfy bed and she'd known almost from the outset it was not where he had been killed. She did however have an extensive array of photographs from Connor Mitchell the CSI photographer, DS Scoley's partner.

Inga kept reminding herself she was a long way from being at home caring for young Thérése, aware her daughter was in good safe hands. She knew her team were all doing whatever they felt would make them appear busy.

When Inga walked from her small office out into the Incident Room they all turned to face her mindful of Hallam's body having already been moved into Lincoln to the mortuary with CSI getting on with their work back at the house.

'God morgan,' the Swede opened with and grinned.

'Ey up, mi duck,' was Jake Goodwin's good natured response he'd used before with a good accented Lincolnshire phrase, despite his mother being French.

'This cadaver,' she said when they'd stopped chuckling. 'Turns out as you know to be one Morgan Hallam who's been on the misper list for about a fortnight,' the blonde told the gathered silent attentive team. 'Before you ask, the storm call cards have been checked.'

That morning the throng in front of her was made up of her regular team plus what some of the lads called the 'comeovers' always drafted in the moment Code Red for murder or 'unexplained' gets a mention.

'We're all in this canoe, which means we all need to paddle. We're treating this as a Cat A murder.'

Jake Goodwin as her number two had introduced all the extras before the briefing started.

If the Detective Sergeant had a fault it was his tendency to hide behind too many principles. His wife Sally was convinced therein lay the reason for his lack of career progression. Living strictly through his adherence to right and wrong, being at odds with the low life's view coupled with a degree of inflexibility.

Sally knew Jake's formality was often seen by their friends as stimulating. They were married because in Jake's eyes that was the proper way to illustrate commitment. Tell her man about people being partners and he'd immediately retort about not realizing they were in business.

'Thought we'd been given extras to ease the burden,' she shrugged her shoulders in a new pale blue blouse. 'There you go,' Inga sighed. 'We'll come back to the whys and wherefores of him being missing,' an annoyed Inga went on. 'But first let us start with the discovery of the body, about which we do know bits and pieces. Jake, if you'd be so kind.'

'Frederick Curran owns the property. Four bedroom detached out near North Carlton, has a tendency towards being the angry young man,' said Jake Goodwin on a Sunday morning he and wife Sally had planned to visit friends for lunch out at the coast. 'Which I can understand to some extent, but I kept getting all this "not our bloody fault, nothing to do with us," as if he was trying hard to convince himself as well as me. Frustrated might be a better option. Told him, don't look at us son we're the cavalry. Came back from Cornwall or so he claims, picked up a take-away on the way in and while he's unloading the car his missus opens up the house. Finds the body and comes screaming down the stairs. Phoned us. That's it pretty much.' Before anybody could react he commented. 'Plus he's a teacher.'

'Sarge. Are they really living in one room?' one of the add-ons borrowed from the Prisoner Handling Unit checked.

'Not only that,' Jake smirked. 'Allow me to explain. They buy run down cheap as chips properties, but not to build some sort of buy to rent chain of doss houses like some do, but to enable them to move up the property ladder step by step. Each one so he reckons, better than the last. They've done it I think he said three times before, and he plans to carry on with more. Not at all sure she's up for it,' he queried with Nicky Scoley.

'All his idea pretty much,' the neat blonde DS responded. 'Seems to me anyway. Not sure she really wants to move again let alone carry on for donkey's ages.'

'Forever and a day,' Jake translated the colloquial phrase for his Swedish boss. 'Keep on and on.' Inga nodded receipt of his translation.

'You English,' she sighed. 'Worse for me has always been words even you lot can't pronounce. Apropos, awry and facade half you people get wrong. When you're trying to learn the language it's all a bit much.' She grinned and shook her head. 'Worst still is this Cockney slang business. She tumbled down the apples,' she smiled with. 'How can anybody be expected to know that's stairs? Right, where were we?'

'Somebody say they got no furniture?' Jamie asked going back to what Jake was on about.

'Just a bed, bedside cabinets, chest of drawers and a couple of mats. We didn't get round to all that, but I think he mentioned storage somewhere.'

'At his parents I reckon she said,' Nicky offered.

'No signs of false entry, which means a key, copied, begged, stolen or borrowed.'

'Nothing's stolen remember, because there's virtually nothing there,' said the Detective Inspector.

'I meant the key.'

'Two weeks they've had the keys, and according to him two front and two backdoor keys,' Jake advised the gathered MIT. 'Come Monday morning we can double check all that with the estate agent. Got the keys on Friday 16th,' he continued from his screen. 'Started ripping out straight away according to him, reckons it was all out by the Wednesday. Chopped it all up. Filled three or four skips already and most of what was left has filled another one still sat outside.'

'Surely he was at school all week.'

'Broke up on the Thursday and went off on Saturday 24th for a week. According to him they worked all weekend, couple of evenings then three or four days. More than likely he got a few mates to give a hand.'

'Curran mentioned to me somebody was supposed to get the skip emptied while they were away.'

'And it's a big bugger.'

'What do we know about her?' was aimed at Nicky Scoley who had interviewed Wroe on site.

21

'All to do with Cloud technology apparently, and I'm not talking Cumulonimbus here,' a grinning Nicky looked back at her screen. 'Kirsten Wroe has a Masters Degree in computing of some sort and works for stupidly named E-Quilibrium which is written as, e hyphen quilibrium,' she said slowly to get it right. 'Works on contract management and I quote from their website. Simple, intuitive and yet very flexible solutions for all your contractual needs, involving complex data reporting. Her actual job title is Senior Client Services Manager. According to her she is out and about two or three times a week visiting clients' sites to provide hands-on training and advice.'

The DI blew out a breath at the end of all that.

Nicky had taken the trouble purely out of personal interest to have driven past E-Quilibrium's glass fronted building that morning on her way in. She was sure one half of the complex had been one of those places at one time with a name made up of a few letters but with no indication of what they might be involved in.

Accountants, pension advisors and all sorts of financial firms she'd never heard of. always seem to occupy such buildings for a year or two and then disappear almost overnight.

'I've warned the eTeam her phone might be all fancy dan showing off.'

'Right now it's about gathering intelligence and fast. Time is always our enemy, so we'll allocate tasks,' said Inga to get the system up and running. 'Sandy's still out on scene co-ordinating and I can find him a job or two depending what he and CSI come back with. I'll deal with forensics as they come in and I'll do the Post Mortem.' She spotted the look from Jake. 'Jake, can you carry on synchronizing all aspects as you have been doing, please?' she hoped would appease his concerns as she peered at her tablet in hand. 'At the same time if you will, concentrate on this Freddie Curran and Nicky will you keep Jake onside with what more you discover about his partner. Between you, look at their employment, their oddball life together moving home and this holiday. Have they really been to Cornwall? I thought these IT wizz kids like her headed off to Phuket and Cambodia to do good deeds.' She scanned the room. 'Oh Jake, nearly forgot. Message from Dexter Hopwood one of the eTeam Digital Forensic geeks. Curran's password is Maths backwards and something they think to do with Pi and the square root of 2 and he has an iCloud account they're into.'

'Thanks,' he said grinning. 'Just what I thought!'

'Said something about...irrational numbers if that means anything.'

'Of course, how stupid of me not to realize that. Don't you just love cocky sods?'

'Holiday?' Nicky asked to remind. 'Based down on a farm in Cornwall,' she went on. 'According to her the pair went about a bit sightseeing including a trip or two up into Devon, and headed back up on Saturday setting off mid-morning.'

'Thank you. We have Alan Westcott to thank for the cadaver's name which this Freddie Curran says he's had brief dealings with. Our Morgan Hallam owns the Brough Barn Motors group of garages or did. Need to check who will own it now he's gone. If you will please Ruth. Could very well be an important aspect.' She looked at Raza Latif. 'One for you Raz and take Jamie with you please. Two things. Need everything you can lay your hands on about Hallam's motor business. People getting their head bashed in is not an everyday occurrence around these parts, especially topping somebody just because they sold you a lousy car. Plus, we need to ascertain from them what his movements were prior to him disappearing off the face of the earth. Must be a secretary or someone who ran his appointments. Where do they think he was and why? Another thing you might try while you're at it is, doing a check around the force here or get one of the lads to see who's bought a car from him recently. See what they make of the set-up, customer service and all that.'

'Will do guv.' Inga knew dusky Raza would be thorough. Lacked interpersonal skills quite often and was never a self-starter but she knew he'd ferret away for the very detail she was after. He for some reason always had an issue with shirts. He somehow never quite managed to tuck into his waistband, probably due to being according to her standards, slovenly when off duty by allowing tails to flap free.

'Family Liaison,' Inga thought for a moment. 'Have already informed the family, but they've not been given any detail so far or given the body location although the media seem to have added two and two together according to the *Lincoln Leader* website.'

'His Jaguar was discovered abandoned in a small car park in Horncastle apparently under false plates, a few days ago,' Jake advised from his monitor. 'Somebody from Brough Barn Motors will be collecting it or has already done so and we assume return it to his missus.'

'Not to mention a hefty parking fine no doubt.'

'Pity,' said Inga. 'Could have done with having Forensics going over it. Raza,' she spoke to again. 'Another one for you. Find out where they took his Jag and have a word with Shona Tate about her team giving it the once over. Ruth,' she said and glanced down. 'Social media search, please.'

'Mate of mine calls it anti-social media.' Her complexion was almost bleached as if she's stayed well out of the sun on purpose. Something she dabbled in herself but Ruth knew she dare not miss a trick with the social media remit in such a case as this. Her tried and tested system was to start with the biggies the Facebooks and Twitters of this world. Then progress onto the Snapchat, WhatsApp, Tumblr, Instgram, Flickr using access systems Nicky Scoley had somehow arranged with Dexter from the eTeam to provide. All of which alleviates the need for her to actually join and give away emails and passwords. Head down, mug of hot chocolate and get stuck in.

Ruth Buchan was still annoyed at Scoley having been chosen to work with the nerdy eTeam on digital forensics for a month or two. A world she wanted an intro into. Social media was a start and it was office based she greatly preferred rather than getting stuck with knocking on the doors of the half-baked, oddballs and weirdos.

The business of the boss and Scoley going out and about together for coffee and cake also really got her goat.

'Go after all of them,' was Inga. 'This Hallam and his wife,' she had to check the name again. 'Frances. Plus this Freddie Curran and the IT woman Kirsten Wroe. Include all the stuff on her profile. Plus any other names anybody comes up with. Link anything you find into Jake and Nicky.' She looked across at the latter. 'Depends what Michelle comes up with we might need you to delve deeper.'

'We know there's a wife do we?' Ruth queried. 'If she's only a partner do we have a name?'

'Family Liaison confirm and I was just coming to that,' and Inga was back to her notes and was tempted to ask why from time to time the chestnut haired divorced DC let herself down by not checking for example the overnights first thing. 'Frances Hallam answered the front door.' She hesitated. 'Obviously pregnant according to Deanna from Family Liaison.' More than one sucked in a breath noisily. 'But remember, she reported him missing nearly two weeks ago. Claimed he'd gone away on business and not been seen since, phone goes to nowhere. Not heard hide nor hair of him since. PHU have been dealing with it as a misper except he's no longer missing, so we'll leave them to that aspect for now with all this we've got on.'

'Talking of PHU,' said Jake. 'They're also giving a hand with house-to-house, but out there where Curran and his woman plan to live is a dead end and close neighbours are a good fifty, hundred yards before you get to their place. And they're unlikely to know them, remember,' he added. 'Only moved in two weeks ago, not been there for a week of that, but somebody might have seen or heard something.'

'We ever that lucky?'

'Waiting on the PM of course, but it looks more than likely he has been somewhere dead or alive before he was tucked up in Curran's bed. Be easier to configure when we know rough timing.'

'What d'you make of this Curran then Jake?'

'As I said he kept on about it not being their fault, how he'd got a lot to do. Got a bit stroppy when I told him CSI had priority. Did ask if he'd fallen out with anybody, and he said not. But oddly enough he did volunteer the fact he'd not fallen out with any of his pupils which is a strange thing to say when I'd not mentioned them. Said he wasn't on social media as if that was the only way to have a dispute.'

'Say that again.'

'Asked him if he'd fallen out with anybody and he said no and from memory he then said something like "but then I'm not on social media" which was a bit strange.'

'Agree, but we are talking feral schoolkids,' she offered with just a hint of a smile.

'Just have to hope that mobile ban for schools comes in. Leave them at home,' was Jake's obvious firm opinion.

'Right team,' Inga said louder. 'Time now to get busy. Actions stations.'

Inga had wondered just how toxic this case might well turn out to be. Online abuse about Hallam was something to keep an eye on.

With so much of the world's activities being online these days she knew there were probably thousands of keyboard warriors claiming to be in the know. What joe public would get to know through this multitude of platforms would be a great deal more than in the olden days.

Except of course as she was fully aware it was not always the truth, whether that had come from part-time pundits on a coffee break, people in it for a few bob or pucker journos pretending to be trolls to incite another story.

In truth nothing changes. Once upon a time according to biographies Inga'd read at uni, it had been freelance stringers, planting stories, half-truths mixed with political leanings and folk being tipped off in exchange for a few quid or a pint. Now millions had the opportunity to add their two pennuth along with trolls, bloggers and naive social justice wallys.

'Yes Jake?' she said to her senior man when he tapped on her door and walked in.

'Word of warning.'

'Yes sir,' she quipped and smiled.

'I'm being serious,' he insisted. 'Appreciate you coming back early for this, but better to be safe than sorry. We've got this sorted, so if you need time off just take it, stay at home with Terése for a few mornings if you like. Nobody's going to think the worse of you for doing so and Terése deserves your support.'

'Thank you Jake.' The Swede hesitated momentarily. 'A word if you wouldn't mind,' Inga suggested and sat at her desk.

'Is there a problem?' she asked up to her DS once the door was closed.

'No.'

'Problem with this Curran, you've kept to yourself?' Jake was a matter of just a few months older than her.

'Just attitude. He was at me from the get go. Body in his bedroom and it was nothing to do with him. Unwilling to understand why they had to move out of a crime scene. Intelligent as they often are, but lack common sense.'

'How d'you mean as they often are?'

'Teachers. That all?' he shrugged.

'Fine, thanks.'

What Jacques 'Jake' Goodwin had never discussed with anyone except his wife Sally was how he had been treated by teachers at school, and one in particular. Born of English and French parents Jake was fluent in French by the time he reached the big school.

Looking back now, stick thin Miss Greenway his French tutor was obviously not at all happy with his ability. At one point she had marked his homework wrongly and on his mother's insistent he pointed out her errors to crabby Greenway.

From then on to stop her picking on him to score points he allowed the French lessons to pass him by, but soon realized how three or four other teachers had sided with her to assume an attitude towards him.

To his mind that Curran had a similar stance. Only knowing how to handle children, his ability to deal with a more aware adult he struggled to cope with.

5

Kirsten Wroe

I was just hoping and praying when we finally got back after stopping off at the Chinese, Freddie wouldn't get all truculent about going into the house first, insist he was dying for the loo and beat me to it.

All the way home I was telling myself there'd been a change of plan and when I got there the house would be empty. Whatever it had been used for, good, bad or indifferent I wrongly assumed would show no sign whatever of what had been going on in our absence. Particularly in a place we'd already almost stripped bare.

One of the things I get annoyed about all the time, is driving the car or rather, not being able to. For some reason when we are together Freddie insists he drives. Not actually insists, just that he always jumps in the driver's seat even though I actually passed my test first time and he took two apparently, so his pals tell me.

I drive myself to work every day and with my job I need to travel all over the country. In an average week all he manages is to drive to and from school. All in all I'm far more experienced than he is but no, he just never suggests I take a turn at the wheel.

Not something I've ever asked him about, but I'm guessing it's one of these ridiculous man things some of them tend to get fussed about. I wonder, does he feel he'd be less of a man if he was sat beside me? Is there an air of him feeling compliant and obedient were I to take the wheel? Does Freddie somehow imagine his pals would take the piss out of him if they see him being driven about by a mere woman I wonder? Is that what he does if he sees a mate of his being driven by a partner or sister?

Watching the Euros had been a delight, but fat men taking their shirts off was something I've never been able to understand. I can only assumed it has to be another proving I'm a man thing and too much drink.

No drink involved, but now we have wall-to-wall Olympics I'm really not bothered about.

No doubt some of these feminism junkies would make more of him always driving, even if he never took his shirt off for no good reason. It was more annoying than anything else and I'm better than him with IT and probably hog the laptop. Swings and roundabouts of a good relationship, not marching down Whitehall in sandals carrying a placard demanding more steering wheel time.

What a shock to the system it was arriving home and facing what I walked into. Suddenly in the twinkling of an eye all our plans were shattered: nice cup of tea and enjoy our Chinese before we got a bit of shut eye. Fat bloody chance.

What a waste that turned out to be. By the time we got away from those coppers, met his folk and got to their place it was just a cold congealed mess and I was starving.

Typical of his mother of course, she offered up a bloody paste sandwich and a packet of crisps because according to her eating late is bad for the gut. Stuck it all in her microwave but it was never quite right. At least we didn't have to suffer her lecture for once about weight gain, diabetes and heart problems such late eating creates, which is often the case.

At times I feel guilty because of our circumstance I'll be unable to cook something nutritious and healthy for months on end. That is of course alongside being jealous of friends who have the life I yearn, they are already thoroughly enjoying. I dare not even contemplate the sheer joy of simple pleasures such as a glass of something chilled and a box of dark chocolates, all relaxed and at peace.

Whenever such life experiences come bubbling to the surface I have to remind myself how a much better and grander life awaits around the corner. Problem with Freddie is, which corner.

Children are another constant thought to infest my mind with increasingly regularity as the years roll by. The closest

I've ever managed has been a bit of spot of child minding and babysitting for friends and colleagues.

I know there are people who would suggest that is me punishing myself unnecessarily. Steering clear of close contact with babies and young children would most probably reduce the anxiety and frustration I feel.

Last thing I ever imagined facing was Morgan of course, dead as a dodo peering out from under my favourite duvet. A cold dead body of somebody I knew, offering up a revolting putrid stink of rotting flesh was something which had never crossed my mind. Why would it?

Even if Freddie had beaten me to it and he'd not gone into the bedroom, the smell as it turned out would surely have raised his alarm bells. I know a lot of blokes are not good in picking up the senses, linking with unusual smells, but even so, what I walked into was a whole different world of stench.

I just never imagined a body would be lying there and would go off that quickly. I do have to wonder what they do in funeral parlours? The place must reek of it.

I know it's not their fault and they're only doing their job, but to be honest the police were a bit of a pain with all their questions, and those forensic people all dressed up in their white suits with pretty blue covers over their shoes and gloves I've got to say looked pathetic. Sort of thing you see on the news sometimes, but up close they looked bizarre and reminded me of those horrid Covid hospital scenes we endured for months on end.

All in all it must have been a good hour and a half we were stuck outside, before they allowed us to leave to stay with Dick and Penny. Good job they had turned up as it happened, with our car being driven onto a big transporter lorry and taken away all covered over as if we were guilty of something.

Wondered how Frances was feeling being told late on a Saturday night her husband had been found dead; and with her being pregnant too. That'd be a real shock to her system and I hope she has somebody with her, being that far gone could be too much to take.

Of course as much as I would have liked to I daren't even try to make any form of contact with her.

She just happens to be a 'friend' on social media although we do have a history. With the cops having my phone, keeping our relationship secret could prove to be a bit of a bummer. Even though of course I've got app-specific passwords along with two-stage verification. Chances are they'll still manage to find bits and pieces I've not bothered to hide.

Bet cops love all that, poking their noses into folks business.

Soon as the news gets out my phone'll be full to bursting with messages from all and sundry, many from people I'd never heard of I bet.

It had certainly been a good break away down west despite the bad weather at times, before all that business spoilt it all. Eaten too much of course but with all the work coming up over the next few weeks I'll soon burn that off. Not something we'll be doing for a few months, dining out. Not that we have hardly at all for eighteen months. Be back to the ready meals, the microwave and eating off our laps. To be fair the supermarkets these days do some pretty good stuff. Lost count of how many different flavour ice creams Freddie scoffed in a week while we were away even in the rain.

I tried one or two, but drew the line at bubble gum flavour along with Rum and Raisin and Guinness, but not together!

Wasn't just him, no siree. We had great meals every evening out in restaurants, plus cakes with our coffees, pasties at lunchtime which down in Cornwall were pucker and in my case scones with jam and clotted cream of course. Don't care about the argument, for me its got to be jam first.

Got to say the ones his aunt made were really scrummy and cream from their own milk was something else.

Yeh, it'd been really good till we got back and all hell broke loose and I'm now stuck with Freddie in one of his moods.

This wholesale cock-up reminded me in many ways of how politicians frequently behave. They tend to go overboard on one particular subject in the vain hope it will become beneficial at the ballot box.

To say Freddie abandoned his career is overstating the matter, but it is true this buy cheap, do up and sell business with property has taken over his life. That is until events transpired to knock his plans on the head.

It happens with the politicians. David Cameron as an example came unstuck with the shock of Brexit and was forced to resign. Others have taken subjects like the NHS as their focal point by forcing media attention in that direction. Everything is fine and dandy for the party in power until just before an election there is a flu epidemic and their struggles are never out of the news. The pleased as Punch opposition clean up at the ballot box.

Law and order is another bandwagon some have jumped on from time to time with success, when out of the blue there's a terrorist event to bolster the argument for more Police on the streets.

That Matt Hancock just snogging his lady friend probably stopped a by-election win. Freddie despite all the angst at work thought he was doing a good job.

Now Freddie found himself in a similar situation. Suddenly he's at the mercy of an event over which he like these politicians had no control. Now my partner has all our eggs in one basket - an empty house he cannot access, contracts he's had to cancel without his phone or car and with the school holidays just whizzing by.

6

Detective Inspector Inga Larsson's decision to return to work as soon as her daughter Terése had recovered from a sickness had nothing whatsoever to do with her loyalty to the force, the Chief Constable or the dear Home Secretary.

She was aware how more than once it had been suggested the nation should have a squad of maternity workers.

People who will take over a role while the pregnant women are off on maternity leave or when a young child is sick. Save the burden being placed on the loyal staff and especially on people who have no children or sadly cannot and therefore are unable to enjoy the experience or all that time off.

In addition Inga had her mother on Skype reminding her all about the Swedish system of child care. A constant prompt about how things really should be.

Christal considered a child in the UK appeared to her to be a carrot to gain votes by politicians, with little or no interest in making it an essential part of the British psyche, a way of life for a modern society in the same way her countrymen and women accept as the norm.

Back home Inga was fully aware how work life balance is aimed at supporting the dual-earner model family. Flexible leave and working hours are paramount. A given.

For the sake of the overworked and put upon Major Incident Team she headed, the blonde Swede had returned to work as soon as she felt able. Why on earth should her colleagues be the ones to suffer through no fault of their own? They too had lives to lead, families to support and care for in most cases.

There were those around her of course who had her best interests at heart – in particular husband Adam.

They were the ones who made flexible working possible. The very same good people who continue to ensure the British police remain the envy of the world.

Inga had been warned the moment she announced her pregnancy back in 2019 how police career advancement can be severely damaged by maternity leave as it can in many areas of society.

Inga knew how a move up the ladder would involve management, all about shuffling paper, attending boring pointless meetings, being forced to drink crap coffee and eat free biscuits. Free to her of course, but not free for the public who ultimately pay for them.

Crime detection is her reason for being a policewoman, what she joined for and now combined with a good life with her physiotherapist husband Adam and their young addition, gave her the best of all her worlds.

It had been Jake who had phoned her at home late on Saturday evening, with what she expected would just be one of his cozy updating calls.

'Thought you'd like to be made aware. We've got what looks like murder of a slightly notorious used car dealer. Most certainly an unexplained death. That's where normality ends. His body tucked up in their bed was discovered this evening out near North Carlton north of the city by a couple returning home from holiday.'

'Interesting,' and she thought for a moment about what Adam would say. 'Morning do?' Larsson had said as her man close by rolled his eyes.

'Up to you ma'am.'

Inga Larsson felt a tiny bubble of excitement in her stomach.

Larsson's early afternoon briefing on Sunday with her Detective Superintendent boss turned out to be exactly that, brief.

He's never consistent, when the balloon goes up. To be fair he always makes contact, but it's never along the same lines. She can sometimes receive a simple recognition and suggest she briefs him as soon as operations allow.

Next time, out of the blue Inga'd find him turning up at the scene. With Operation Thanatos maybe because it had been Saturday night with Olympics and cricket on the telly the team had not seen anything of him at North Carlton and it was after lunch when he deigned her with his presence at Lincoln Central.

As part of her re-introduction Inga Larsson had not been involved in dealing with the couple or the crime scene, being as yet not back on the call-out list since her daughter had been taken ill.

Her Detective Sergeant Jacques 'Jake' Goodwin and DS Nicola Scoley had taken on her lead role as they had done during her maternity absence. They'd been on the spot shortly after her Crime Scene Manager and the first of the CSI crew had turned up all dressed in what look like plastic blue and white onesies.

Monday after feeding Terése Danielle and having her own breakfast Inga had arranged to meet Jake out at the house. It was the location and situation which had intrigued her enough to want to return to service. Some drugged-up found dead down an alley would never have had quite the same effect on her curiosity.

The DI knew immediately there was certainly something not quite right about the place. Nothing she could put her finger on or maybe those few days off had ravaged her brain.

At least it meant she could get on organizing things in her own particular way, and go through the format her team are conversant with and have modelled for themselves to some extent.

 What little Jake Goodwin already knew or had been made aware of by the rest of the team, was all on the system. The Detective Sergeant was co-ordinating receipt and entry into the Murder Book, adding to the crime board and constantly updating the on-line version in order for people higher up the ladder such as 44 year old Det Sup Craig Darke could read it all at their leisure in a wishful thinking attempt to keep him out of their hair.

Forensic strategy was progressing and they were working on victimology.

'Understand he had a bit of a bad reputation by all accounts,' Darke said when he and Inga Larsson were discussing this Morgan Hallam character on Sunday. 'So I hear.'

It was first pickings of this new major inquiry he was asking about. 'But then other people so I understand, talk very well of him. Probably depends whether you got a good deal trading in your old car I suppose. Think the fraud lads have tried to pick his pocket a time or two all based on urban rumour they tell me. So far they've not managed to make anything stick.' Inga Larsson sat there watching DSup Darke tapping his iPad and wondered where he'd got all that business about Hallam from. 'Talk to Paul Lomas, I'm sure he'll put you straight on this Hallam fellow,' could well have answered her question.

'To be honest Paul gave Jake Goodwin a bell when the name Morgan Hallam popped up on the system. You'll find his father's name on PNC though,' she told Darke. 'Harris Hallam is on there for VAT fraud about twenty years ago. According to what Paul said, he created false invoices and just made up the figures for years before HMRC caught up with him and he was concealing cash payments from customers. He was jailed for fifteen months back then and this would be when Morgan, named after the car, would have been in his early twenties, and he was forced to take up the reins when his old man was sent down. Paul says they are always aware of the sort of thing old Harris might still be up to.'

'Austin Healey and now Morgan named after cars, eh? Can't see somebody being called Qashqai or Sportage though'

'These days, anything's possible. Better than being called 3 Series!' made Darke chuckle. Larsson hadn't a clue who this Healey chap was.

'His son must have upset somebody,' Craig offered. 'Is Harris still involved in the business at all do we know? Might be a line of enquiry for one of your team.'

'Apparently he potters about doing odd jobs, delivering cars and the like but spends most of his time galavanting off on cruises all over the place.'

'You seen those giant cruise ships?' he asked. 'Five or six thousand people, can't imagine anything worse.'

'Sort of holiday we've considered,' Inga admitted. 'But never done anything about. Got a friend who says she's been there, done that but never again.'

'Any particular reason?'

'Who you can easily get stuck with was the big moan apparently,' she smiled. 'Get lumbered with a second-hand car salesman and all the bullshit you get coming from people like that.'

'Don't talk about Hallam like that!,' he joked. 'When Jillie and I hear remarks about *everybody* doing something or other we know for sure that's exactly what we need to steer well clear of. We've had friends blathering on about cruises and from what they say confirms we're best to stay put.'

'Adam always sees being on trend as a real warning.'

'Might just tip the wink about all this to a few I know with the HMRC investigation teams,' was Darke back to the business in hand. 'A bit of their forensic accounting might not go amiss.'

It had certainly all been a great deal more than she had been expecting when DI Inga Larsson volunteered to dip her toe back in the police world of murder, mystery and mayhem so soon after   Terése Danielle's health had stabilized.

As was often the case, her form of celebration was not to join the lads and lasses to down pints in the now closed local hostelry as they'd have done decades back. Instead the team would discuss the outcome over her provision of Swedish baking, something husband Adam had certainly got used to.

Jamie Hedley had done what he had been taught when his temporary boss appeared. Start of the day coffee organized, although it was close to lunchtime by then. In a proper cup, not cardboard and not too strong would put him in her good books, he hoped. That for him had been after a quick check of the overnights on the system. All what a colleague down in PHU called the 'curly wurlies' – all the dross incidents reported involving the brainbdead and logged in the small hours.

Being moved from the Prisoner Handling Unit to upstairs, Jamie knew this was a real opportunity to impress. A murder had to be as good as it gets, and having a crack at another one was certainly a long way from patrolling the streets of Gainsborough when he first started foot slogging.

Inga Larsson took heed of what Adam had said about too much too soon and Jake Goodwin another of her carers had mentioned more than once out at the scene. He and Nicky Scoley were well up for dealing with this issue, particularly with the dark boss hovering.

Scene visit, briefing Darke and in receipt of one from her two Sergeants, a slice of cake and a weak coffee was as much as they would allow her for day one.

First Monday morning in August after the crime scene visit, Inga Larsson head of the Major Incident Team didn't head for Paul Lomas as the dark boss had suggested when he had finished with her on Sunday, but she went up one floor to the weird world of the eTeam, lorded over by Detective Chief Inspector Luke Stevens. He of the pure cotton shirts, hand-made brogues and frequently gawdy socks. To his credit here she soon discovered was another concerned for her welfare.

Luckily he had already gleaned most of what she had to tell him from the system.

'Reason I've popped up about this case sir, is concerning the wife who actually discovered the body. She's some sort of computer Client Services geek for those E-Quilibrium people, so we may need your lads' assistance to point us in the right direction should she become a person of interest. Can't see a link to be honest with Hallam being a bit of a wide-boy in the motor trade, with her into all her IT business and her partner an economics teacher.'

'Difficult to see a connection with three like that. But,' he shrugged slightly. 'In this business as we both know nothing ever really surprises us. But all the same, be sure to let me know what assistance we can offer and I'll put one of my team on it for you,' Stevens assured her. 'You think this is linked to her work I take it?'

'Shouldn't image so, but you never know with her working in IT it's more likely anything involving her will have been done on line.'

'Don't see a school teacher being up to all this sort of nonsense, but you just never know. Over the years the most unlikely of characters have been sent down for the most dreadful crimes. Sort who wouldn't say boo to a goose are often the worst.'

That booing a goose bit she just didn't bother trying to begin to understand. She'd try to remember to check that phrase with Adam.

'Sutcliffe the Yorkshire Ripper was an HGV driver, Steven Wright was a steward on the QE2 and of course Shipman was a GP. I'll look up teachers for you when I've got five minutes.'

'No need, sir. Thanks.'

Back down to the busy Incident Room DC Ruth Buchan had already discovered the wife of Morgan Hallam was exactly as she always describes the social media self-indulgent: 'look at me, look at me.'

Inga couldn't imagine the amount of time Ruth must spend on her chestnut hair each day. At work her hair was pulled over to the side and plaited before being drawn back across her head and pinned in place. With a babe in arms a quick brush was all the DI managed these days. Pity Ruth'd never concentrated that much on her work.

All this Hallam woman's messages concerned little more than socializing, handbags and shoe shopping silliness. Meeting girlfriends for a gin lunch and bragging about her new white car and their next foreign holiday.

To her credit there were no soppy messages to a long dead grandfather, photos of her meals or ghastly selfies.

Ruth knew immediately what was coming when she had to admit to the team what she had found out about the woman, and in particular had expected ribald remarks about this Hallam going on about relaxing in the luxury of her giant hot tub.

It appeared for some reason to be a collective team decision to deride anybody wishing to have a pleasant soak, and with her mother having bought one a couple of years back she knew never to mention using it. Ruth had made that mistake once too often. One or two of the team were obsessed more than anything with the amount of faeces the average bather puts in the water.

Yes, she was in agreement that this indeed was a self-centred female in constant support of the pursuit of pleasure in all its forms, but to Ruth some of the comments were really uncalled for. She put it down to jealousy, and bet if big Sandy had one in his back garden he'd not try to deride them.

Two things stood out however. Firstly this Frances Hallam had a name with flashing lights amongst her 436 'Friends': one Kirsten Wroe. The very person who had discovered her husband's body in her new virtually empty home.

Last but not least was her habit of interspersing her social nonsense with opinions on society and in particular tragic teenage stabbings and murders, with gangs of menacing youths on the streets.

Inga Larsson was back up to Stevens and his e-Team who would on her behalf contact Facebook for detailed information and transcripts if possible of historical messages between the two main women.

7

Kirsten

That blonde and annoyingly attractive young Detective Sergeant phoned me on Sunday afternoon would you believe, and insisted we... No sorry, let me start again. When she phoned she became tiresome by demanding we meet to discuss what happened on Saturday night, all over again. Can you honestly believe that?

Freddie and I had no choice on Saturday but to go back to his parents place out at Branston to sleep and I would have liked him to be there with me when I met that annoyingly good-looking copper.

Alas, Freddie being Freddie his absolute sole priority despite everything going on, was the work he was desperate to get started on the new property. All of which he had of course now been forced to re-schedule. His selfish master plan on one of his spreadsheets would dominate our lives for weeks. Again.

Part of my own displeasure is my annoyance at Freddie's attitude. He knew I've offered to have a constructive, cost-effective and proportionate system produced for him by one of the programmers at work. We do this all the time for major companies.

No. This is his project, done his way. He'd hate me for saying this, but it really is just about what you'd get if you gave the task to his 6th form pupils.

I'd had to pop into work Monday morning which took far longer than expected, with everybody being desperate to hear my side of the story bouncing around the internet and particularly on the *LincolnLeaderLive* website.

I agreed to see this DS Scoley female on my own at his parents' home and we sat together that sunny afternoon on the old rickety bench at the bottom of the garden under one of the apple trees which Freddie frequently reminded me had been planted when he was at Junior School.

Penny said she didn't want the police traipsing around indoors poking their noses into things that don't concern them, which of course is so typical of her.

The property had at one time been a string of three terraced houses, probably workers cottages which somebody in their wisdom back in the 80s had converted into one long residence. Depriving two young locals of somewhere to live of course.

Hidden away off the beaten track it was an ideal quiet almost idyllic place to live in moderate to good weather. Living off Earslfield outside Branston snow in winter as they had discovered more than once in recent years, could become a real pain which had seen them marooned for a few days. Much to Penny's chagrin of course which amused me no end.

Getting up and down Canwick Hill into Lincoln can be a pain at the best of times, but in winter a real must to avoid.

Freddie's mother is a great one for putting the kettle on whether visitors want a drink or not, but not I have to say for this Detective Sergeant Scoley woman. Therefore under the limited circumstances we just sat there together on the old bench as she flicked through a notebook.

'Kirsten, let us start with Saturday night shall we? I know we've been over this before, but I have to ask. Did you know Morgan Hallam at all or come into contact with him prior to Saturday?' she asked all masked up although we were out in the fresh air, just as she had on Saturday stood outside our new property. Why was I not surprised someone like her couldn't get it right first time?

'No,' I had to lie again. She was wearing a tailored suit, too bright a blue for me but it did suit her. Linked with a very pale purple blouse and black shoes it was somehow not what I'd expected.

'Have you ever say, bought a car from him?' I thought was a bizarre question when I'd already said I didn't know him.

Somewhere in the back of my mind lurked something I'd learnt from a detective series on television. How they ask you virtually the same question from a whole range of different perspectives to see by your answers if there is any chink in your armour.

'I've never even bought a car.'

'Then whose is the Nissan out in the lane?'

How on earth did she know it was mine? Sort of smart remark you see on telly which thick drugged-up criminals often fall foul of when being brow-beaten into submission by some cop with a failed marriage or a drink problem.

'It's sort of mine if you like, it's a company car. Like I've already said, I've never purchased a car.'

'Your partner's car, what about that?' She was doing it to me. Just like their training manual said I bet, keep on the same subject and consider the answers carefully or more than likely read something into them.

'He bought his own car.'

'You have your own money then, is that what you're saying?'

'What's that got to do with anything?'

'And you weren't involved?' Butterscotch blonde DS Scoley was used to being part of a full-on pucker partnership with Connor, not one of these wishy-washy snowflake coming togethers with him insisting on retaining his own money to enable him to up sticks and clear off at a moment's notice.

'Why would I?' told Nicky Scoley even more about their relationship and why they had as yet not married. The big Cs of compromise and concession zooming at her. 'When the job required me to travel about they then provided me with transport.'

'How did you get to work without a car?'

'Same way many people do. Bus.' Then it came to mind. 'In the summer I rode my bike in the early days.'

'And the holiday you've just been on. What can you tell me about it?'

By now I'd decided it would be a process of one stupid question after another all over again. The silly woman already knew any info I had on the holiday was in my briefcase which at the time I assumed would more than likely still be sitting in the hall at the house, they still wouldn't allow either of us to enter.

'Stayed with Freddie's aunt and uncle in their holiday cottage they rent out on their dairy farm. Sort of did Cornwall first then went up into Devon a couple of times, before we headed home early Saturday morning.' I stuck up a hand to stop her going on before I forgot what I'd pieced together with Freddie. 'First three days we were in and around Truro plus the city itself of course. Did Exmouth and Dawlish and one or two other places. Had our evening meals out in restaurants in and around Truro and Falmouth. On Saturday and Sunday traditional roast as I recall, because we hadn't sussed anywhere by then and Sushi on Monday I think it was.'

'This what you do is it Kirsten, just go aimlessly from place to place even in bad weather?'

'Sightseeing you mean?' Why on earth did she suggest sightseeing was aimless? Our schedule had been put together by Freddie of course, months in advance. But I was never going to admit that for her to make something out of it. Yes, the rain had forced us into slight changes but so what?

With her perpetually using the name Freddie, Nicky guessed this was what some dum dums these days call a byname. Be Frederick in truth she guessed.

'Wondered about sunbathing,' this blonde copper with next to no make-up and clear skin suggested and then it made sense. 'Laid out by the pool in your bikini, glass of Prosecco in hand. All the usual.'

'Not us. Sorry. Never been near Prosecco, my boss's mother reckons it used to be called Babycham. Not at all sure how true that is.' Why'd she said that when she knew full well the weather had been off? Where the hell was this going, what had sunbathing in Polperro got to do with dead Morgan Hallam in my bed?

Got to say I wondered what she did on holiday. Maybe one of these cheap holidays where you spend your time fighting the Germans over a plastic bed by the pool. What's the betting she's one of those who go on a booze cruise with a group of like-minded coppers chasing anything and everything in long garish shorts with a tanned chest and vigorous tattoos.

'Never understand why folk fly off to goodness knows where and just laze by a pool getting sunburnt. Where's the fun

44

in that?' I asked. 'You can do that on a sunbed at a fraction of the price just off the High Street. Know people who've done that in places like Egypt and never bothered with the Pyramids or Valley of the Kings, all the must see fascinating history. Seems to me most of them just want to see the bottom of another glass.'

'Sunbathing is what most people do I'm afraid to say. And drink of course.'

Reckon I'd guessed right. I can just see her getting up at lunchtime in Majorca with a sore head. Sun all afternoon by the pool and alcohol all night again. Repeat.

'Not us I can tell you,' I was adamant. 'And we don't get drunk every night on some cheap plonk either,' I felt was necessary to add before she started to build entirely the wrong picture or thought I was like her. 'I've never been drunk in my life and I think Freddie has four times. Just once since I met him he's been a bit tiddly on red wine. But that's all.'

Nicky Scoley was experienced enough to understand how this woman would be feeling. Brand new abode she had never lived in, yet she would still feel violated and vulnerable. In most cases of intrusion people feel poorer but apart from their inability to get on with all the work they had lined up, nothing was missing.

'Truro the same was it?'

'More aimless sightseeing,' unfortunately she didn't react to my attempt at sarcasm. 'Including trips to places like Mevagissey, having lunch by the harbour. Been there before in the sunshine. Then there was almost a whole day at the Eden Project of course,' which I doubted would impress somebody like her.

'It really is magnificent,' was a surprise. 'We've been twice,' the blonde copper admitted.

I'd been petrified from the outset what she was going to ask me, but all this so far had been just easy stuff. Me telling her what had happened that I could remember, and where we'd been even if most of it probably didn't meet with her approval.

Spoke too soon.

'Can we get back to Morgan Hallam, please?' she asked as she scribbled a quick note. 'You claim you don't know him, in which case how do you explain he was discovered by you in your own bed in a house you and your partner claim was locked? This by sheer chance you think? Somebody chose your new house at random. And just out of interest, who else had keys to your new property?' She looked at Freddie's mother pottering about in the garden. 'We're checking the estate agent didn't retain a spare key by the way. Your in-laws have a key do they?' this detective gestured towards Penny. 'Makes sense with you away of course.'

'What's the point? There's no reason for anybody to break in, there's nothing there. It'd all been cleared out before we went. Microwave, bit of tea and coffee.'

'Not insured then?'

'House insurance but not contents. Don't think you can insure what you've not got.'

'How do you imagine a burglar would know that?'

'Look in the windows you can easy see.'

'Perfect for squatters.'

I was pleased Penny kept her distance even if she was all ears, I could have done with Freddie beside me and a decent coffee or a shot of something, but I certainly didn't need his mother poking her spiky oar in and pleased she'd not offered to put the kettle on for once.

Later she became a bit high handed when this Detective Sergeant woman advised her they needed to take a swab to establish her DNA. Went on about protocol and what guarantee did she have it would be destroyed eventually.

She calmed down to some extent when this Scoley woman explained it was part of their process of elimination as both her and Dick had both been inside the cottage. Freddie and I had already been through the process of having our mouths swabbed on Saturday evening when one of their forensic women in her funny white suit had taken ours.

'You were at work this morning, is that right?'

'Yes I was and you know I was.'

'All I know is what you told me you were going to be doing this morning. Why might I ask, when I thought you are supposed to be on holiday?'

'Clients are not on holiday, and a couple of hours cuts down on the backlog.'

'You always do that, pop into work when you're on holiday?'

'If at all possible. Anyway I can link up on line anytime if I have a need.'

From Nicky's perspective this Penelope Curran was a hovering pain quite obviously doing her level best to earwig. This interview was as important as the one on Saturday evening. Being well aware how away from the glare of immediacy it is surprising what people remember they'd not given a thought to previously.

'How much longer do you think you'll be house hopping?' I was asked by the copper. 'This buying and selling property business.'

'I'm hoping just one more after this.'

It was Freddie's grand scheme. The pair of us to be fair have good salaries and we'd have coped with a mortgage for a fairly substantial family home, but no. He'd seen these people on TV, and was keen to join them in climbing the property ladder faster, make giant leaps up to a level we'd no doubt not normally be able to achieve, in the same time frame.

My big worry is he just might once we are settled, look to carry on the process and take on a run-down place like our first one and start to create a chain of buy-to-rent properties.

I'm not at all sure that's all it's cracked up to be. Seen programmes about landlords with clients not paying rent for months on end and others who just trash places. We most certainly have no need of all that sort of hassle and expense. Be better off saving our money to my mind. Interest rates are pretty shitty still but it's better than nothing.

'You don't sound too sure.'

'That's the plan at the moment,' I admitted but knew Freddie would find it difficult to stop. My concerns over our future prospects being sidelined by his plans were none of her business.

'But it could change?'

'Anything's possible,' I shrugged sat there beside this Scoley in the sunshine with me desperate for her to get on with it all and clear off. It was always possible Freddie could jack in his job and do all this full time.

'Am I right in thinking your partner knew Morgan Hallam?' and suddenly the name was back.

'Not knew. No.'

'Either he did or he didn't, because we already have it on record your partner Freddie telling one of my colleagues he actually knew him.'

'Think he'd be talking about how one time he went with a friend of his to look at cars, and one of the places they popped into was his place out at Horncastle, I think it was.'

'And met Hallam.'

'Apparently he happened to be there, the salesman was busy with a customer or something so he asked if he could help.'

'What was that look for?'

'Freddie took a dislike to him, he was a stereotypical car salesman and came out with some nonsense about how he'd always struggle to sell green cars.'

'Frances Hallam,' shook me rigid. 'I understand she's a friend on Facebook.' Shit! Just knew this'd come up.

'Could be.'

'Either she is or she isn't.'

'You say she is, so maybe you're right.'

'Are you telling me you don't know who your friends are?'

'People can just get on as Friends on social media sites somehow. I'm never going to go through them all and ask for their ID am I? What's the matter with that anyway?'

'I'd have thought an IT expert would be more circumspect than that. After all it was her husband who was discovered in your bed.'

'And?'

'Dead as it happens. Dead in a fully made up bed when you've tried to suggest the house was empty.'

To be perfectly honest with you, I really have no idea how I managed to get myself through that weekend. I knew what I was letting myself in for to a certain degree. I was aware the chances were I just might come face to face with something when I opened the red front door.

48

Be something they'd forgot or had spilt to leave a mess with whatever they planned to do. What I hoped against hope I'd spot when I walked in and deal with it before Freddie started asking awkward questions.

Nobody had even hinted at anything like a dead body, certainly not bloody Morgan's and most certainly never mentioned the smell that would smother me.

It was just the most appalling stench, and the state Morgan's face was in I was most certainly not prepared for. How I didn't vomit all over the floor or him goodness knows. Looking back now maybe I should have, made it all more authentic.

Survive I did despite everything else going on. Then being harassed by the Police was a nightmare but to be fair Freddie parents were worst, with their endless questions and at times I felt as if Dick his father knew something the way he asked the same things time and again. I got more of a grilling from him than from Scoley the copper.

And as far as I'm aware I somehow seem to have managed to survive the grilling from those coppers somehow, let alone Freddie's old man. That blonde Scoley was so pleasant and understanding when she first took me to one side on Saturday evening. I thought how good it was of her showing the caring side of law and order, not something most of us come across day to day.

I quickly discovered another ruthless side to her and reckon she could easy be a right nasty bitch. It was as if she seemed to me to be thoroughly enjoying the way she toyed with my emotions and threw question after question at me, and picked up on every tiny detail as a way of hounding out the truth.

Told her I didn't know who the man was I'd found dead in our bed.

All I could think every time Morgan was mentioned was I'd have to dump everything there was, up in what we planned as our bedroom. Not just the duvet, sheet and pillows, but the mattress would have to go and I was concerned about the bed itself. The one we take to bits, shift from property to property and put back together would over time become a constant reminder of the horror of it all.

Early on during that first interview on Saturday night it suddenly dawned on me we'd have to go back to living with Freddie's parents at least for a few days which is not much fun at the best of times.

I know it's a small thing, but not having stuff of our own around us tends to get to me from time to time. I know what we have accumulated is in storage, but by now we should be enjoying the fruits of our labours not storing it all away in another bloody pink container.

One of the downsides of this refurbishing properties the way Freddie wants us to go about it, means there are often times when we need to move out completely and put up with Penny's poor cooking, all her fussing about and her objectionable friends.

Can always remember being out with Penny and bumping into one of them looking at a ghastly alarmingly expensive ornament in a store, saying how great it would look beside her gin and tonic trolley.

I know we don't eat well with making use of take-aways and only having a microwave, but some of her experimental concoctions really are abysmal. Got to throw in some of these pointless so-called super foods. Super they are not and I'm not even sure they are real food some of them.

Having spent a good amount of time being interrogated by that Detective Sergeant woman I can now fully understand how some people just confess to things they've not done.

On Saturday she demanded to know exactly when we'd left home to go to Truro and had to remember it was the Cheltenham North West Premier Inn we stayed at on the way down. Could have given her chapter and verse but she wouldn't let me back into what she kept calling the crime scene to check out the emails I had detailing our booking.

Where had we been, what had we done? To be honest after the shock of discovering the mess of Morgan just laid there I was in no fit state on Saturday evening to answer question after question I can tell you. I said to her, can't some of this wait, I'm in no fit state. Where we went and what we did I told her will still be the same whether I try to recall it all now or next bloody week.

50

"We need to make the most of the moment" was what this copper woman said, whatever that is supposed to mean. 'While it's still fresh in your mind,' she suggested.

'The horror of finding that body's what's fresh in my mind, not what we had for breakfast a week ago on blinking Monday!'

I wondered after that episode on Saturday evening if the police by nature love to gossip, enjoy sneering and snooping at anyone not conforming. Is that part and parcel of what the bigwigs look for at interview?

After that visit I then had to relate it all first to Penny when she made a pot of tea after the policewoman left and then repeat it all again for Freddie and Dick, the name everybody knows him by. Except that is for soppy Penelope who has to call the poor sod Richard like she's his mother.

8

Stocky Detective Constable Jamie Hedley found it far more interesting visiting a number of different motor trade retailers as he had done with DS Latif as part of their brief, than tapping keys and answering the phone to the world's most obnoxious all morning back at base.

Having been tasked by the boss with investigating the Brough Barn business run by the dead Morgan Hallam he had been fully briefed of the rumours about the man. Even a couple of mates back in Gainsborough had told him about this bullshitter.

With the boss only undertaking some actions herself, he was enjoying the extra responsibility she'd thrown his way.

Listening into the conversation about this Hallam's wife he guessed the poor fella had probably been forced to become so insincere in his attempt to keep his wife's needs satisfied, in particular in regard to her credit card.

As the Lincoln branch of Brough Barn Motors happened to be situated in amongst a row of different makes of car retailers all together in one area off Doddington Road, the pair decided on what they would purport to be looking to purchase, in order to gain a solid comparison.

Some were too quick of the mark when a young guy with gelled hair, grubby shirt collar and awful tie approached them the moment they stepped onto the forecourt. At another place the one they assumed to be a salesman appeared more interested in gaining a tan as he leant up against a Fiat and ignored them

After visiting them all Jamie did consider returning to three of them, asking for the Sales Manager and explaining exactly why he would not be making a purchase. Nothing whatsoever to do with the product on offer or price, just abysmal last century customer service.

Three in a row had been the stereotypical car salesman full of bluster and dressed scruffily in a way to make fashionistas cringe. The too tight trousers, cut away collars, garish ties with the top button undone, together with the ignominy of shirts hanging out. One crap spouting dibbo even had his shirt collar done up with no tie.

Based on what they'd been told back at Lincoln Central before they set out, Raza and Jamie decided that was just how Morgan Hallam would have been.

One they came across was pleasant enough but another appeared to be quite unwilling to leave them to their own devices and just kept banging on about this week's special offer. Jamie wanted to ask him what commission rate he was on, and what did he drive.

The fifth Raza recognized immediately as being ex-military. Not because of his bearing or a tendency to march rather than walk, to him it is always to do with their inability to dress properly. Something Jake Goodwin had once pointed out. On this occasion it was things such as a striped tie and checked shirt with a decades out of date pin-striped dark navy suit. Smart when in uniform issued from the stores no doubt, ironed by a steward, but always lost when they've to use their own initiative in order to create an acceptable mufti combination for themselves.

Then, the next place the pair visited was just too good. This smart properly dressed pleasant man making eye contact introduced himself and provided an immediate opportunity for the pair to take their time viewing the range available on their own.

As it turned out Brough Barn was not the best in their considered opinion but a long way from the bottom of the ingratiating pile. Time then to head back to base and investigate the company further.

DS Nicky Scoley's actions on her return from Branston had been to check with Devon and Cornwall their actually was a dairy farm where Kirsten Wroe claimed to have stayed in the West Country.

As it turned out Big Oaks Farm where they stayed was known to the local beat bobbies, simply as a good place to stay. The Retallacks who owned it were well known to them but for not any spurious reasons.

Because she had spent some serious time working upstairs learning with the techy e-Team in the past it was normal for Nicky Scoley to use the knowledge and skills she had learnt for internet investigations to take it all back down to MIT.

With her being involved in other important issues relating to interviews carried out for the boss, Ruth Buchan had in the meantime been tasked with low key scanning through social media for clues to any of the people involved.

Before she began Nicky Scoley nipped upstairs to have a word with DCI Stevens as the force's Child Sexual Exploitation Team was since stringent cut-backs, now within his remit of control.

Nicky was very aware of the likelihood of Ruth coming across a bewildering array of photos of children on the internet put there by stupid parents and in particular in many cases by doting out of touch grandparents.

That people would even consider allowing photographs of innocent children to be placed on the internet for ever and a day always amazed her. But then so did the numpties telling the world they're off on holiday, even messaging photos of the pints they're downing at the airport, thus leaving their property open to any skulduggery the low life want to throw at it for a whole fortnight.

She knew Luke Stevens had dealt with indecent images of children and teenagers and at one time working undercover had been responsible for cracking a serious major child abduction case.

His present team were using warrants two or three times a week to raid residential properties and seizing computers. In some cases using covert human intelligence sources (Chis).

Nicky knew they all had to be aware in this day and age of what somebody like Ruth might come across, the deeper and deeper she delved.

DCI Stevens, who Nicky had worked with before on cases, briefed her on current trends she might spot the potential of.

Now fully up to date with what red flags Ruth might recognize she returned to MIT to brief her colleague on signs to look out for.

The 'Freddie Curran' search came up with just a few candidates but not who she was looking for. Ruth managed to discover one who turned out to be female but not updated for years, and one who was a Crystal Palace supporter and it appeared from reading his messages nothing else in his life mattered.

She'd tried Frederick and Fred but all were next to useless through their stated location more than anything else. The first three Freds had no photo and one actually bizarrely wore a mask. She did come across a Freddy she'd not considered, but he showed very dubious unsavoury pictures but no photo of himself which was hardly a surprise.

Frederick Currant Bun was sad and to her mind slightly odd and reminded Nicky when told why she hardly ever went on mind-numbing social media. At least he was male but lived or so he claimed in Dinas Mawddwy she had to look up to make sure was real.

"Morgan Hallam" was really no better. Lack of photos, wrong locations she skimmed through but Ruth did come across one in America, but again turned out to be female.

Frances Hallam was most certainly there in full bloom, and the first one to really annoy Ruth with an overwhelming narcissistic attitude running amok through every message. Her profile picture had quite obviously been professionally taken and posed with specialist soft lighting. No selfie for her. When she was pictured with her brand new white BMW complete with personalised number plates it came as no surprise and Ruth knew such images would really annoy the boss.

Then this Hallam woman was to be seen dressed in a tailored cream suit with crimson red blouse, posing next to an AGA in her claimed new £17,000 kitchen.

Her friends appeared no better with names such as Tee-Paul (a woman) and Shawneey. There was no Anne, Clair or even a Shaz and their holidays or so they claimed had all been taken in places you'd need a good world atlas to locate.

The IT wizz Kirsten Wroe she found quite easily but her presence on just Facebook was very subdued and from that one site Ruth Buchan reported back to Inga Larsson how you'd struggle to learn anything much about her, if at all.

Raza Latif and Jamie Hedley had managed to obtain a print out of Morgan Hallam diary over the period of his disappearance which told them precisely nothing. Almost every entry was work orientated, but there were also a number of letters which according to the administrator who provided the information, often meant nothing to her either.

'Think they're personal,' she offered. 'To my mind if he fancied a couple of hours off he'd enter something like that so nobody'd gave him any appointments. Some of them I know of course.'

'How many people had access to his diary?' Jamie asked. With her wearing a mask as he was, it was difficult to read her face.

'Everybody who had what Mr Hallam called Executive Access, or EA,' she added ironically. 'But then as I say he always used letters, bit like the military.'

'Was he?' Raza slipped in. 'In the military I mean?'

'No. Sure he wasn't. Just his way.'

'And these,' Jamie said pointing to the print out, 'mean nothing to you?'

'One or two do I've worked out over the months. BM is board meeting, CP was when he had private meetings with Mr Pritchard, usually at his home or the golf club when it'd be CPGC.'

'Mr Hallam played golf?'

'No,' was firm. 'But Mr Pritchard does. Used to meet there for lunch sometimes,' this Jessica Cooke went on. 'Probably once a fortnight. Then there are things like HC for haircut,' she sniggered slightly. 'Always used the same barber in town as Mr Hallam was particular about his hair, said one's crowning glory was very important.'

'What about NS here,' Jamie pointed to and the brunette shook her head. 'WY or DRD?'

'Sorry.'

'Thanks for your help,' he said having enjoyed her company no matter how brief. She couldn't help but smile and made no further comment.

If this Hallam had been worried about his hair Raza wondered how long it would have lasted as from Connor Mitchell's photographs he was losing it, particularly at the front. Be long time since he'd sported a quiff.

9

Kirsten

One thing I knew right from the start having seen the body was, I must really do my level best never to admit to my relationship with Morgan Hallam's wife.

It has never been one of those the young tend to go in for these days, where they are in each other's pockets on a daily basis, having to text all the time and all the moronic nonsense that goes with it.

We meet up very infrequently and indeed there have been times when we've not met for lunch or even snatched a quick coffee for months on end.

Not something I've ever done to any extent to be honest with anybody, and these days what with one thing and another I'm just too busy. Probably another part of me I can put at the door of my parents. To be honest I don't think I can remember them ever having folk round for a cup and a chinwag. Not the sort of thing mother did, buy special biscuits for when friends pop round. Meet up with a couple for coffee some place. Always had to be about Fellowship business, always far too intense.

I've never introduced Frances to Freddie and she's never been to any of our properties over the years. Well, not that I know of.

Her husband however is a different story. Keep this to yourself if you will, but I've been intimate with him. Yes, you heard me right, me and the late tubby Morgan Hallam.

Just the once mind, and there was a specific reason why and I promise you, there has been absolutely no other contact apart from that one solitary encounter in a posh hotel room down in the smoke.

I'm getting a bit of a flush on just talking about it. Mind if I take a short break?

Now then, where was I? Oh yes, it always seems to me how each time Frances and I have met up over the years there have always been pinchpoints to ensure I can always recall the event with utter clarity.

First of those must have been getting on for two years after she and Morgan got married. I'd not been to the wedding as it just so happens I was unfortunately or from my perspective fortunately, away in California in the sunshine. I'd been on a fact finding mission for work and all in all I spent a whole fascinating week over there at that time.

Frances and I have always had the sort of relationship built around one amazing incident and as a result in the main these days, we keep in touch through private messaging on social media. A birthday greeting and all that sort of thing. One of those pop-up things to remind you it's somebody's birthday today so you can add a few words and send. We have never exchanged birthday or Christmas presents and all that yesteryear business; just a message here and there.

We met for coffee one time and had gone through all the normal business of bringing each other up to date when it was time for her confession.

Looking back now it was as if she stoked herself up on coffee to give herself a boost. I'd already had a Cortado, my drink of choice at that time, and when she suggested a refill I went for a Latte. I know they're not good for your waistline, but hey ho. Life's too short to get fussed about such stuff. Those special Hazelnut ones they have at Christmas really are a delight.

To be honest at the time I didn't know why she should mention her marriage format at all, but one has to assume with hindsight it was in some way her desire to clear the path for what would be heading my way further down the line.

To be honest I sat there glued to my seat, and my drink was little more than luke warm by the time I got round to it, so mesmerized was I by what she had to say.

People nearby were probably wondering why I was sat there with my mouth open!

Frances and Morgan, her successful businessman and entrepreneur hubby she announced in a low tone sat in that fairly busy branch of Starbucks with women and babies left and right, have an open marriage. She actually used a word I can't quite remember now. Polysomething.

By that she means they both have other lovers. Other lovers each of them know about, each of them talk about in truth.

'Please understand,' Frances had said carefully. 'The home we have built to our taste is our home alone and neither of us would ever consider bringing our lovers back there. Crossing the threshold is something only the two of us ever do together.'

'These others,' I said, agog with what I'd heard. 'Are you saying you know their names, you know who they are? He's with women you actually know?' I almost demanded from her.

'Of course,' she smiled and nodded as if that was a given. 'Some of the women Morgan has intercourse with are very good friends of mine. I lunch with two or three of them quite often actually. We also tell each other how important that other person is to us, what part they play in our lives.'

'But what if you fall for some guy?'

'Sorry, that's not what this is all about. I've never dated anybody other than Morgan who I would consider I have been in the slightest bit romantically linked with. The men are all dear, dear friends of mine and I'd not see it any other way.'

'I don't understand,' I had to admit. 'What is there to gain by all this?'

Frances took a moment to answer. 'He's never going to cheat on me in secret, no clandestine relationships, no adultery. Anyway his business can't afford a scandal.'

'How on earth can you know that? How can you be sure what he's up to and with whom?'

'Firstly there is no pressure on me to be everything and everybody for Morgan,' she continued. 'If you stop and think about it, that's an impossible concept. I am who I am and nobody else. I cannot possibly pretend to be another person, act out a part or fantasy in the same way another woman can. You'll not catch me dressing up as Wonder Woman,' she tittered before downing more coffee. 'I have no worries about being forced to take part in all his sexual desires. If he is looking for something different, then we discuss it and he arranges if and when he can, to meet up with somebody who can satisfy his in-built manly requirements. The sort of drive we all have inside us, and to be honest the way men have been created and for good reason.'

'Why be married? Why not just remain single and he can become one of the numerous lovers you meet up with from time to time as a vital component of your bed hopping policy?'

Frances shook her head. 'In that case I would just be one of his conquests if you like. The way it is with our rock solid marriage we are the primary partners and we return home to each other every night. Since the day we married, we've hardly ever been apart at night, all night. In most cases when that has happened, he has been away on business.'

I'd always known about her Morgan having a reputation as a "ladies man" - how my mother would describe his sort, and I wonder if in fact Frances was just one of his conquests who somehow managed to get him to the altar.

Since that amazing chat over too much coffee I have frequently wondered if she had at one time caught him misbehaving with women he came into contact with, and she had decided if you can't beat them, join them.

I do know I would feel threatened every time he went out with a cheery wave and a "see you later, darling" to jump into a tart's bed or shove some woman up against a wall.

According to Frances who claims she has none of the worries associated with many relationships, her Morgan showed his love with small gallant gestures of kindness and generosity she claims he would never consider to be part of his other relationships.

That she knows of.

Having a glass of wine and her favourite expensive chocolates waiting for Frances on her return from bedding one of his customers, is I guess what love and marriage is all about to her.

I want to marry one day, but I can assure anybody listening that there is no way I'd ever consider entering into such a bizarre relationship. This really is a case of having your cake and eating it, or in her case a lemon drizzle muffin, Victoria sponge *and* a Dundee.

I reckon she justifies all this to herself by being happy in the knowledge she is the only person who actually sleeps with Morgan each and every night.

As an aside I often wonder why people say so and so is sleeping with somebody, when sleep is the last thing on their minds.

10

Pre post-mortem it had been suggested by both the CSI team and the doctor about the body having been dead for more than a fortnight. As it turned out they were not far wrong.

Dr Dean Parish the newish Home Office Pathologist on the block removed the blue sheet from the body on that Tuesday morning to commence his procedure. Blonde, attractive DI Inga Larsson in attendance was pleased she'd remembered her Bergamot oil to rub under her nose. Even so, the decaying stench had been there all along, mixing with the disinfectant smells but from that moment the pong became more pronounced.

All his staff were in regulation scrubs, caps, gloves and masks. Parish with his goggles sat on the top of his capped head had his mortuary technician fussing around him with implements, bowls and a variety of specimen pouches, Inga was not looking forward to being used.

'First thing I have to state is how the perpetrators of this crime have taken great consideration for his welfare. Where he was placed, made comfortable and generally looked after. Strange,' he screwed his eyes shut. 'To say the least.'

'Any reason for that?' the woman in her needed to know.

'He bled out somewhere else, which we do know from the scene. He's been washed post-mortem. As to why? Your guess is as good as mine. My only thought is somebody most certainly felt sorry for him.'

'Had second thoughts?'

He shrugged but made no immediate comment. 'In his forties,' Parish then suggested from behind his mask.

'Forty four,' Inga advised and they shared a momentarily smile beneath the masks.

'White,' he said for the microphone above his head as he went through a visual examination of the whole body laid out in front of him. 'Overweight,' he said as his assistant rolled the cadaver over. 'Back scar, could be anything from a Nevis to something more serious. Check medical records,' was a message for later.

'How long?' Inga needed to know as Morgan was laid back face up.

'Couple of weeks. Not accurate until all the tox results come back, but at least two I suggest.' Was him hedging his bets. 'Massive severe head injury to the facial parameters more than anything else, as you can see. Has a look of hate behind it, looks unnecessarily vicious,' Parish said as he moved the head to check both sides.

'Early days I know Dean, but any idea what with?' Larsson enquired.

'First signs and initial indications lead me to think something like an axe possibly but don't quote me.' Parish peered up over his glasses. 'He was what?' was unanswered. 'What was he involved in?' he asked, pointing at the head and moving away to allow the photographer to concentrate. 'What did he do for a living?' was more abrupt.

'Owned garages, motor repairs, bought and sold cars.'

'Be tools they'd use I guess,' said Dr Parish with arms folded. 'Easy do that to him in the right hands. Two blows but it'll be better when I get in there and have a closer look.' Inga didn't really want to look too closely with maggots rife.

From what the pathologist went on to say it was obvious even to Larsson the damage to the right orbital ridge and cheekbone would have certainly taken a degree of force not to mention a considerable amount of rage.

'Protective anger, jealous rage which is often the worst,' Parish advised.

She made a mental note for MIT to keep an eye out for somebody with anger management issues.

When Dean Parish got down to delving into Morgan Hallam torso Inga made her excuses and left. She had no reason to know what might have been going on inside him. They knew what killed him, they'd always known the basics.

If she'd stayed on there was very little she'd learn by watching him saw the poor sod open, weighing his heart and liver like the butcher does. As ever in the end it'd all be down to the toxicology and forensics. People handy with a microscope rather than a sharp saw.

Inga always wondered what little gems she might pick up from post-mortems. Once her friend Dr Bronagh O'Connell's had explained the need to always wash rice when cooking, as the levels of arsenic discovered in rice is high.

No such gems from Parish that day.

Michelle Cooper had been tasked by Inga Larsson with tracking the movements of Freddie Curran and Kirsten Wroe for the two week immediately prior to them heading for the West Country. It had been a year or two since she'd first been called upon to help out in MIT. Out of the blue Inga Larsson wanted her to join the team with a Code Red, with pregnant Gillian having had leave to give birth to her third child.

Her then deciding to remain at home as a mother had provided Michelle with this great opportunity.

With Curran's presence on social media being almost non-existent, there was nothing more she could do than visit the school before she dared tackle him personally for his version of events.

Cooper had found obtaining information from the school difficult as it was holiday time. In the end she managed to arrange to visit when one of the support staff and the headmaster would be present to advise her.

Lanky Freddie Curran, Head of Economics had been in school every day for the month prior to end of term before then heading off to Cornwall. She spoke to the estate agent who confirmed they engaged in phone conversations with him about the house purchase three times leading up to handing over the keys which they arranged for during a school dinner break.

Dick Curran readily confirmed the couple had been living with them for almost three months prior. Names of friends provided by Freddie confirmed they had worked with him out at the house in North Carlton, to strip it bare of all character, from the moment he had been handed the keys.

Doing the same with Kirsten Wroe was tediously more complex and frustrating. E-Quilibrium were very reluctant to divulge where their Senior Client Services Manager had been to give talks to staff, deal with practical issues with regard to software and generally service their client's enquiries and procedures. Other that is, than a meagre willingness to list the days when they claimed she had been at her work station in Lincoln.

Despite trotting out all their client confidentiality nonsense saying they were unwilling to disclose information and data on their clients' service arrangements, in the end under threat of a warrant and suggestion by DCI Stevens about his team invading their systems, they relented. That simply provided Michelle with further headaches she was more than happy to cope with.

This was certainly a further step up from working with the Family Liaison crew and the agonies she'd had to deal with.

Now a move in the right direction away from the Personal Handling Unit with all the shabby berks and gobby tossers she'd dealt with shoplifting for their latest fix.

In addition to visiting three companies within close proximity to Lincoln, they claimed Kirsten Wroe had visited Worthing, Hereford, Pitreavie and Hendon in north London during the week before Hallam disappeared and the two weeks between then and her joining Curran on their trip west.

Some of the local locations the Detective Constable was obviously able to visit. Others had to be dealt with over the phone and by email. These as it turned out she eventually discovered had meant Kirsten making an overnight stay usually in a Premier Inn and in the case of Worthing and Hereford for two days and Pitreavie she was away for four days staying in nearby Dunfermline.

It took Michelle more than a day to obtain emailed and telephoned confirmation of Wroe's presence at all sites on all dates.

Investigations about Morgan Hallam were being carried out among the force personnel; with his high profile locally there had to be coppers who knew him or knew of him.

It soon became pretty obvious from the in-house reports of people's opinion, how this vulgar man had a reputation not only as a creepy bull shitter, but also for chasing and to some extent harassing women.

One disappointing aspect was no comeback from women in the force other than the suggestion he was a smooth talking chunk of a man with they understood, quite often an element of touchy feely about him.

Gift of the gab when selling cars probably at rip-off prices had stayed with him in his private life. All tedious and annoying bluster alongside quite unnecessary hugs.

There had been very little unusual about his wife Frances Hallam's reports of him being missing. According to her, during initial conversations with Lincoln Central she explained on the Monday morning Morgan Hallam had by then been missing more than the requisite 24 hours having set off around the county on business on the Friday but had never returned home. All confirmed by a recording of her call.

Frustration was building for Inga Larsson with every question her team were asking having a return of another.

A major puzzle was trying to fathom how it was Freddie Curran knew when the house purchase would be completed in order for him to book accommodation on the farm in Truro months earlier? And allow enough time to rip the place apart in between?

Under the circumstances Family Liaison were already at the Hallam' big home when DI Inga Larsson decided to despatch DS Nicky Scoley to carry out a brief, fact gathering but sensitive interview.

Out at the Hallam big home in Osbournby near Sleaford even with masks no longer mandatory, would it not have been good manners as well as safer in her condition if she'd worn a mask. But no.

'Your husband Morgan was last seen by you on that Friday,' the trim blonde repeated from her brief. 'You reported him missing on the Monday around lunchtime?'

'Yes.' Nicky Scoley knew it was 12.39.

'When did you first realize Mr Hallam was missing?' she was asked in her kitchen accompanied by deep brown haired slim, trim DC Lucy Needham.

'Saturday morning it must have been.'

'That's Saturday 17th is it?' the Detective Sergeant asked.

'Yes.'

The maternity dress looked expensive and Scoley guessed that was the purpose behind her wearing it. Fiery red and orange blooms on a deep maroon background.

Hardly the demure look of a mother-to-be and the fit-and-flare sleeves to her mind were somewhat inappropriate as were the high heels indoors.

'What initially alerted you?'

Frances Hallam perched up on a stool just stared at the Terrazzo tiled floor, and spoke without lifting her head. 'Empty bed.'

'Is that you saying he'd not been there the previous night? He'd not come home. That what you're telling me?' Scoley loved the kitchen, but would not be at all happy living in such a barn of a place all on her own.

'He does come home late at times, but we pretty much know what each other has planned. I knew he'd be away on business all day like most days, but as far as I knew he had nothing organized for the evening.'

'When you went to bed there was no sign of him, then on the Saturday you began to worry. Did you get in touch with anybody?'

'Rang the office, they told me where he had been heading on the Friday.' She sucked in a breath and sighed it out. 'Rang them, they confirmed…' the breath was pushed out again. 'I've been through all this before with your people, you know.'

'If you wouldn't mind.'

'They said…'

'Who said?'

'Pentangle Motors. Chris Selvey and Morgan have been pals for years. Played football together decades ago.'

'And?'

'Chris said he'd left his place around three, three thirty, said not to worry probably had a few too many bevvies and was holed up for the night to sleep it off.'

'But he hadn't.' All young Lucy Needham, having another temporary stint with Family Liaison, and Nicky Scoley received in return was a sullen shake of the head. 'If you were in our shoes Frances, how would you link your husband's disappearance with him turning up in Curran's new home?'

'How would I know? I've no idea where he'd been. Isn't that your job?'

'Had he fallen out with anybody?' trim Needham asked.

Scoley had spotted as they walked in a county-set glossy magazine, and their research told her within the pages would undoubtedly be photos of Hallam all done up to the nines. At some charity dinner pictured with the full range of do-gooders on the make in all their regalia. Part and parcel of her projected superficial image.

'What?' she pulled a face. 'Like had a bit of a tiff with someone in the queue at the bank you mean and got himself killed for it?' she chortled about.

'What about on going? Had he had a feud with anybody long term you know about? Does the company have any financial worries for instance?'

'If you think this was all over money you can think again. Brough Barn is in the black, despite the hard economic times that damn virus caused the industry. We came out the other side in as good a position as possible and a great deal of that's down to Morgan. New car sales in March were better, much better.'

Nicky knew others were looking into the company's finances but as yet there had been no hint of anything untoward despite Morgan's reputation as a wheeler dealer. Her mentioning new cars he had no dealership for, was an odd noted comment.

Frances Hallam has stuck pretty much to the party line by simply confirming information they already had to hand. There seemed little to be gained by continuing just for the sake of it. Time for the pair to find a café some place, and having said goodbye they headed in Nicky's Mini for Sleaford.

11

Kirsten

I can remember as if it were yesterday. Our paths hadn't crossed for quite a long while when out of the blue there was this voicemail from Frances. I immediately got this feeling, you know how it is, how she was after some act of kindness, a favour.

Why else would she call? I'm not part of her close social circle, not that I'd want to be quite frankly. All her overblown nonsense is simply not what I'm used to at all.

Could I give her a lift somewhere, claim she'd sprained her ankle when she'd only slightly twisted it and needed to get to the doctor. Some sort of emergency or what I often get of course from people, is a cry for help concerning IT and their damn broadband.

Frequently it's a case of people's laptop not working properly and can I spare a few minutes to have a look at it. How many times have I simply had to turn off the whole system and switch on again?

Sort of thing happens to all of us in life from time to time. It never crossed my mind that she might well be wanting a sub with Morgan being so successful, it was never likely to be a "can you lend me fifty quid" sort of request in between sips of her chocolate sprinkled cappuccino.

To be honest she didn't say what it was she wanted over the phone, but we arranged to meet for afternoon tea yet even half way through the twee sandwiches with the crusts cut off I was still in the foothills of understanding what she was after.

In truth the sandwiches were odd. Rather than being asked which we prefer, white or brown bread, each small finger of sandwich had white on the top and brown underneath. .

It was at that point, after the last cucumber and cream cheese offering as we sipped our tea before moving onto the scrummy cakes when I should have simply got up, got out onto the street and just strode away.

I didn't as it happens. I just sat there in a sort of mesmerized state listening to her heart-felt saucy yet disturbing plea. Had she guessed, was it something I had said or hinted at in the past that made her assume my purity status?

'Look, I know it's a lot to ask,' she'd started head down looking at and twisting her apostle spoon between her fingers. 'But you did say if I ever need a favour…and to be honest, I'll not ask for anything like this ever again.' She sighed and peered up at me. 'Will you sleep with Morgan, just…?'

'Pardon?' I very nearly shouted loud enough to wake up all the old dears supping their camomile tea and struggling to nibble a salmon sandwich with their false teeth.

'Just the once, only one night, you'd be doing me a really big favour. Please,' has to be the nearest she'd ever come to begging as her warm fingers just nestled on mine across the table.

'What's going on?'

'I need to save him from himself,' was the sort of phrase I've never understood. Like people confirming their status as complete bozos by saying they've found themselves which I have always considered to be preposterous nonsense when the world is full of mirrors.

'Really?' I gasped. 'Sorry but, Morgan's actually not my sort.' In truth he's exactly the type of man I have always steered well clear of, gone out of my way to ignore as much as I am able. I come across his type quite often with my work, travelling as I do to clients' sites being on their territory some seem to think gives them certain touching and stroking rights. Frequently have to endure all their immature nasty remarks, shameful sexist innuendos and jokes they and they alone think are amusing.

'Part of my role in life as a good wife is needing to keep my man satisfied, to deal with any little quirks which might appear in our marriage,' she went on. 'Ones likely to if they are

71

allowed to fester, eventually do untold damage in the long term.'

I'll be honest I thought she was going to say she'd become bored with the ethos of this open marriage business. All this chopping and changing blokes had become more of a chore and the thrill of it all she had at one time appeared happy with, had maybe gone sour. I was going to say bottoms up but that's a bit silly under the circumstances!

Anyway. My second thought in rapid succession was the likelihood of Morgan having fallen for some long-legged young bimbo who had turned his head. Not the youngster herself but the concept.

'You know how it is these days,' said Frances with her white cup held in both hands. 'All these once pretty young women becoming all wrinkly and going to fat and finishing up desperate to blame their ills on that first young love.'

I sat there satisfied that I'd got it right, there was a young sprog with a short skirt and cumbersome uncontrollable bust causing issues.

'Morgan,' she said barely more than whispered. 'Really is a good man, you know.' Was she trying hard to convince me or herself? 'Just has these….things…desires…' she struggled. 'Desperate for a virgin,' she rushed out after what seemed a lifetime of deliberation.

I ask you. What was I supposed to say or do? Look around the tea rooms for a nymph who might fit the bill? Search out an app? After all there's one for pretty much everything else these days.

'Why?'

Frances grinned. 'He's a man. That's the way they are. In-built need to procreate, in their DNA all that biological stuff. Bit like us and babies I guess. At least in my case I know what he's doing. We discuss who he's going with and why in the same way as he does with me.'

'Are you saying he can't find one, none on the internet maybe?' I somehow managed to say without a snigger.

Frances simply gave me no answer and headed onwards. 'If there was anybody else I'd not ask, you know that,' didn't actually make sense when she said it, but I did recognize the inference, the *"if there was anybody else"* was a critical part of *"I once did you a huge big favour, now it's your turn,"* emphasis, without actually coming out with it.

Should have given her a straightforward no and hopefully that would have been the end of it and none of this would be haunting me now day after day.

'Not following you,' I said before I took a good gulp of my breakfast tea.

'Only be one night, and he's clean of course,' she chuckled with. 'Not as if he's a complete stranger, and he's a good man you know that. Plus he really likes you, says you're good for me,' she said as what she was asking of me began to wander all over my emotions.

It had all come as a real shock, to the extent I was so nonplussed I quite forgot all the about the miniature cakes I'd looked forward to. Pink macaroons and tiny Battenburg slices.

Frances Hallam wanted me to have sex with her husband. Not some good looking, young tasty hunk of a man off *Love Island.* We're talking about her husband, the tubby oaffish unpalatable self-imposing car salesman. To be fair he was in truth facially fairly attractive and I'm guessing he showered regularly and cleaned his teeth, but that wasn't the point.

It had been years previous I'd said to her that if I could do her a favour she only had to ask.

Now this. Really not at all the sort of thing you can see coming no matter how hard you try.

Time for the background story.

Just happened out of nowhere to be honest. Carole Gumbrell a friend of mine from work and I were out one evening eating in a recently opened restaurant we had decided to try.

I was told later how out of nowhere as I began to choke this woman just appeared and took control of the situation. I became desperate to breathe and very soon I felt as if my life was ebbing away when she told me to cough and despite the proximity of other customers started giving me abdominal thrusts to no avail. And when she started on back blows between my shoulder blades I had by this time become terrified. This was it, this was my dying day the one you dread, all happening in a strange public place in front of strangers and I wanted my mum.

Then this woman placed her fist right at my belly button and suddenly pulled inwards and upwards and just as my life was close to ending, it was over.

Tiny piece of chicken still attacked to a thorn like bone had shot across the restaurant floor and landed between this woman's feet who screamed as if it were a hand grenade.

Daft bitch reacted as if she was the one with a problem, not me, the one who very nearly breathed her last.

Without this Frances Pritchard I'd not be here now, not telling my story. I owed her everything from there on.

There we were years down the line, and it's her asking me to do her a big favour.

It was a Brazilian restaurant that much I remember, where they kept bringing meat to the table. It's not there now, but so many of these new eating places seem to last no time at all. I can't imagine my nasty experience had anything to do with its demise.

On that evening in the dimly lit restaurant when we first met properly, it was quite a few minutes after the chaos of my near death experience had subsided and things had almost returned to normal, when I was actually introduced to her.

At the time I was in no fit state to understand what was happening who had grabbed hold of me to thrust that damn chicken out, let alone be in any state to say a proper cohesive thank you.

'This is Frances,' said my pal Carole I'd gone for the meal with. I'd thanked her with pure appreciation and honesty for behaving the way she had towards a total stranger. 'She's the one who saved your life.'

Now further down the line of life I'd once almost lost, it was time to pay my dues.

12

Larsson was still waiting for the main toxicology results from the lab but some localized info had been punted through by the CSI team, although a great deal in this particular case had gone to higher authority in Leicester.

A lack of information would never mean they could just sit back and bide their time, when Inga Larsson always had an exhaustive list of actions for her team to undertake.

People who had visited the property or close neighbours were on her list as in this precise case the circumstances were most certainly different from the norm. DC Michelle Cooper their stocky copper had been tasked with interviewing a couple of the more likely candidates. Ruth to her displeasure was packed off to the coast.

Wednesday morning, with more medals won in Tokyo it was time for Peter and Audrey Merrikin the nearest neighbour to give their side of the story which Michelle carried out in their home close to a hundred yards along the lane back towards the village. A real step up in authority for her.

She had decided to start with the one she perceived to be the weak link by addressing her initial questions to the dyed brown haired skinny woman. Peter Merrikin being somewhat antagonistic from the outset had made the decision for her.

Like her husband Audrey was of average height, but his cheeks, florid and veined bore testimony to more than a casual taste for whisky. They were sat masked-up side by side on a sofa like matching bookends, both dressed in a mixture of boring dull fawn and brown.

'Have you ever been inside your neighbours' property?' Audrey's nervous eyes darted left but her head remained quite still.

'They new ones you mean?'

'We can start with that,' was an essential ingredient of the tedium Cooper was used to which was always associated with such interviews. Introduced herself, shown her warrant card to this Peter to examine and explained why she had called.

'We've already been asked that,' said Merrikin abruptly.

'Mrs Merrikin?' Cooper asked without acknowledging her husband.

'Not been in a day or more afoor they was off,' she said then glanced at her husband for confirmation, or was that her seeking permission to speak?

'Filling them skip things umpteen to the dozen seemed to me.'

'What about when the previous owners lived there, did you get invited in at all?' was Cooper still with the wife.

'Of course we did, what d'you take us for?' he answered instead.

'But not since your new neighbours moved in?' Cooper checked.

'Hardly habitable from what we've been telled. Can't see why they clever clogs had to do all that. Lovely place when Cynthia lived there. We'll miss them now they's done a flit that's for sure, won't we Peter? Be a good twenty year or more they were there, always were a yon decent couple of souls.'

'Be thirty,' was thrown in from beside her.

'You've not been inside since the new owners took over then?'

'Lovely couple,' was no answer. 'Roger and Cynthia, good friends too, mind.'

'Did either of you hear anything while the young couple were away?' Cooper asked.

'What sort of thing?' Peter queried with a grimace as if it was a difficult question.

'You tell me. Cars, van, unusual noises?'

'They was away. Still a damn skip there though. Can't be right surely, has to be a limit how long they things can be there making the place look untidy.'

'Just wondered if any strange traffic might have gone past you noticed.'

'Skip lorry made a reet mess o'the grass out front.'

76

'While they were away was that?'

'Mebe, mebe not.'

'Apart from that?' the pouted shake of his head from Merrikin heralded the end of that line of enquiry. 'I take it you've had your Buccal swab?'

'What?' he pulled a face again as he asked.

'You've given a DNA sample?'

'Why not say so?' this Peter Merrikin sighed obviously and shook his head.

'Owd police chappie yesterday said it'd be in all our interests,' said Audrey almost apologetically for her husband.

'It's part of our elimination process. Our CSI team will have established what DNA is present on site, and from these tests we can eliminate people such as yourselves from all those we collect. The alternative is for us to be stuck with a whole raft of unknown DNA samples.'

'We've already told you, we've not been in the place.'

'Even so.'

'What d'we have to do then, duck?' Audrey checked.

'I'll arrange it. Are you due into Lincoln at all?'

'Bank in morning.'

'Building Society,' he corrected.

When in the past Cooper had become concerned about the lack of a man in her life, this sort of situation starkly reminded her she was probably better off without.

'Same thing,' was a surprise remark.

What a pity Michelle thought to herself. Freddie Curran could seriously have done with a pair of nosier neighbours. The over eager stroppy opinionated folk who quite often make such enquiries a real pain or go on and on about dog poo on the pavement.

DI Inga Larsson was slowly but surely getting used to delegating more than normal, to save her having to undertake interviews. This meant she had no need to be at her desk from the crack of dawn or arrive home after Terése had been put to bed.

Ruth Buchan had been tasked with obtaining DNA swabs from the three pals who had worked with Freddie over that first weekend by helping him to rip the place apart. She also had Dennis Luxford on her list who had supplied the filthy dirty battered old skip which was still sat outside, full to overflowing with his name plastered all over it.

He was seriously the source of some moaning and groaning when she visited his yard. He claimed he'd been too busy to collect the third full skip during the time Freddie had been away. Now he was bitching and moaning about the CSI team not allowing him access, as everything in it had to be double checked. He was not a happy bunny and nor were Shona Tate's forensic team having to go through it all piece by piece.

First thing that morning Ruth had already been across in Chapel St Leonards on the coast swabbing the mouths of a Mr Roger and Mrs Cynthia Teesdale who had previously owned the property Freddie and Kirsten had bought to do up. She guessed the couple must have made a tidy sum after living back up close to Lincoln in their four-bedroomed place for well over thirty five years.

For their retirement they had for some reason purchased a bungalow at the coast as so often people do. A trend so many later regret, but seem never to learn from others mistakes.

The name Cynthia seemed very old fashioned. Ruth wondered how many babies would be given that name nowadays. Be like others the world had dismissed. Mabel and Ada, Hilda and Daphne all replaced by the likes of Dafne, Mabes or Hylde.

'Did you see Mr Curran and his partner at all in the two weeks prior to them going on holiday?' Ruth asked the pair sat out in the back garden in fresh air they had insisted upon.

Annoyingly this Roger had insisted in going through every medal won overnight, when Ruth mistakenly said she'd not heard the news. She kept her general disinterest to herself. Sleeveless Fair Isle jumper over a checked shirt and fawn trousers, he looked as if his wife had dressed him.

'Nah,' was as much as he could manage for an answer.

It looked to DC Buchan as if she'd turned up after they'd had breakfast and a follow up cup of tea had almost been drunk, as two daisy patterned empty cups and saucers were sat on the rickety wooden table in front of her. Their choice of everyday crockery spoke volumes.

From what little she had seen it was a trim and very tidy home they'd bought. Just a pity there was no sea view and they'd not bothered to tidy the garden and mow the lawn back at their old place.

'Did you ever meet them?' she asked this Cynthia with faded greying hair straggling to her slender shoulders. 'Curran and Kirsten. Kirsten Wroe.'

'Nah,' said Roger, grimaced and shook his head.

'Problem?' Buchan sensed to add to what she was suffering..

'Sorry,' said this Roger. 'Be honest we're never happy with people not being married these days.' A bitter retard on her lips was as far as she got.

'Just out of interest,' came to Ruth's mind instead. 'Have they by any chance bought it jointly do you know?'

'Doubt it these days,' he said as if her suggestion was ridiculous. 'Got no sense seems to me. Anything happens to him and she'll be up Queer Street eh?'

Ruth was not at all sure the PC brigade allow you to say that these days.

'The woman phoned, and one of our old neighbours called to say they was setting about knocking the place about,' Mrs Teesdale offered and looked clearly glum at the thought. 'Upset me quite a bit, got to say when she told me. All we'd done, all the care we'd taken. Years we'd spent…' For a moment Ruth thought the grey haired tidy woman might burst into tears.

'Took early retirement mesen,' considerate thin Roger took over peering over the top of his glasses. 'With me on-going back and hip problems, so there's no way we could contemplate what they plan to do even if we had a mind to. Should've had me hip done ages back but that Covid business put a stop to that. Well-built property you know, not like some of the squat nonsense you get these days kids reckon they can't afford. Shame, such a shame really it is.'

'We're both a bit upset,' Cynthia admitted. 'We just couldn't tidy up the garden more's the pity, but at our age we're not as agile as we once were and Roger's not been good for a fair while. Got a problem with one of me knees,' she tapped her right one. 'On the list, but these days...eh?''

'You saying Kirsten Wroe phoned you?' Ruth Buchan asked the woman. She'd cleaned her teeth and swilled mouthwash round before she left home, but the taste of last night's Onion Dopiaza takeaway just kept coming back.

'If I remember rightly she phoned to say they'd found a load of keys in a drawer. Be all sorts we accumulated over the years, thought it best to leave 'em for them. Be no good to us now will they?'

'Other than a phone call, no other contact I take it?' they were asked.

'Terrible business all this, terrible for them,' was not an answer and she annoyingly mumbled behind the pale blue mask. 'Imagine coming home to that, doesn't bear thinking about.'

'Do you by any chance know of anybody else who might have been to the property they might have forgotten about with everything that's been going on? Like a window cleaner?'

'Estate agent has to be the only one. Did all the viewings. Cancelled Tom doing windows few weeks back.'

'My colleague is dealing with the estate agents and the guy who'd shown others round.' Buchan looked at her notes. 'Is there any chance you knew Morgan Hallam?' she asked the pair.

Roger pulled a face. 'Knew his old man,' he eventually offered. 'Did a year or two in jail I think it were, a good while back now as I recall. It were all in the *Leader* and the *Chronicle* at the time, seem to remember.'

'You knew him, Morgan that is?'

'Not really,' he chuckled. 'Knew of the father, all in the papers and that at the time. Never knew the son.' He stopped to lick his lips. 'Sort I've always steered clear of, you know the type with their sharp suits and gift of the gab. Crooks the lot of 'em seems to me.'

'People have said as well,' his wife offered with a brief nervous smile.

'Full of all the usual nonsense.'

80

'Thank you both,' said Ruth Buchan moving to stand up. 'One last thing. You say you left a load of keys in a drawer. By any chance was there a front or back door key amongst them?

'No,' was expressionless. 'Just odds and sods really. Ones what fitted cupboards in the garage that sort o'thing, bits and pieces we'd got rid of, old padlocks and all sorts. Old shed key we had at one time I'm pretty sure was there.'

Ruth was all set to leave but Roger Teesdale he of very little useful to say about the Merrikins, Curran or Wroe then had a good chunter about Covid. Repeated almost verbatim what she had heard the previous evening about infection rates being on the wane, save for a big spike in Lincoln. He went on and on about nightclubs and bars needing to be closed to halt the whole shebang being caused by the young..

Shown out the back gate by the cautious pair and from there it was time to head off in search of a decent coffee, enjoy an Americano if possible with an extra shot and a couple of rounds of toast with marmalade.

As much as she enjoyed the sustenance and the break from the mask, she was acutely aware that particular scenario was becoming a habit. Eating alone. Overlooking the Beach made a pleasant change and had proved adequate for her needs at the time.

Breaking that lonesome pattern from time to time would mean being with friends and with them inevitably the name Marty would pop up.

When she felt really down she would tell herself it was all done on purpose. Talk of how well Marty was doing in his new job, where he'd moved to and how happy he was.

Sat there that day looking out to sea, Ruth couldn't help but wonder about Cynthia Teesdale. Guessed the poor woman was locked in a controlling marriage a long way from her family and friends most probably, living in a place he insisted he wanted to move to.

A scenario she of course could relate to having suffered herself with that short lived so-called marriage. She had felt dejected of late and was considering the idea of buying a dog as company. Nothing as snappy and over excited as her gran's Tramp the mad Springer Spaniel and the problem was, living in a flat was not conducive to easy access and leaving the mutt couped up for hours on end was never a good idea.

That and the thought of coming home at the end of a long tiring shift on a rainy night or one with snow on the ground, she'd be faced with taking the creature for walkies no matter what.

Difficult scenario to ignore with that Cynthia woman when the signs were there she could spot a mile off. There was a degree of sadness in the thoughts of the chestnut-haired policewoman who'd been there, suffered within a bad relationship and got out.

Ruth was no good at small talk and when this woman wanted to chunter on about the weather and what they planned to do tomorrow if it was sunny as if she was desperate to make a contribution, her mind had drifted.

Drifted to scan a photograph on a shelf below the TV. Was that them? Was she looking at the Teesdale wedding photo and next to it was that their children?

At least before she'd plucked up the courage to get the hell out of it, she and Marty fortunately had not had children to complicate the scenario.

Ruth knew from those she'd come across before, such places were great for a holiday or for a few days in the sunshine. Week in, week out in February on your own was a whole different ball game altogether.

Anything happened to him and this poor woman would be stuck on her own just like thousands before her.

Trundling her way back to Lincoln later, Ruth Buchan felt somewhat despondent. Whenever she was tasked with these interviews of people on the fringes of a major incident she was in receipt of a fillip of responsibility, but then somehow always came up short. Left with little more than she had arrived with.

Why was it she always appeared to be lumbered with the wrong people to ask questions of? It was almost inevitable the boss's star pupil Nicky Scoley would come back with vital information or crucial detail to please her no end.

Was it her, Ruth wondered of herself? Because she always asked the wrong questions or did the boss only send her to interview the unimportant dimwits?

At least she's had a decent breakfast, wasted half an hour sat with her coffee and obtained their DNA swabs so all was not lost.

13

Inga Larsson was meeting with two of her Detective Sergeants explaining the content of a new edict issued by boss man Craig Darke.

DC Sandy MacLachlan knocking on her door cut Jake Goodwin's astute considered suggestions short and Inga waved him in. Sandy is a big man but somehow has the ability to walk almost silently. Certainly not somebody any dork would welcome creeping up behind them when up to no good. A proud Scotsman and sports enthusiast to boot.

'Sorry to disturb you boss, but Jethro Bennettt off the cars', he gestured towards the dark fully kitted and uniformed policeman stood almost to attention behind him out in the Incident Room. 'Has information you might be interested in.'

'Show him in,' she said and smiled at the young man all kitted out stood in front of her.

'Morning, boss,' the bulky PC said for openers. 'Might be nothing, but with all this Morgan Hallam business going on something caught my attention this morning. Told my sergeant all about it when I got back and he said to trot up here and see you, like. Over the weekend we all learnt about a Lexus being stolen out at Mabo in a Millenium, you know a two-in-one burglary. That one in particular caught my attention with the reg plate.' Inga stayed silent but really wanted the young man to get on with it. 'See, the last three letters are JRB,' she tried to fathom. In much the same way she always wondered what was to be gained by having personalized number plates the meaning of being known only to the owner. 'Jethro Robert Bennettt,' was the answer she was looking for. 'Then this morning out near Faldingworth coming back along the A46 heading into town I came up behind this white transit towing a trailer with a silver Lexus on the back. Guess what?' he smiled.

'Somebody'd stuck false number plates on it, but one side had sort of come unstuck and dropped down to reveal the one underneath.' He grinned again. 'Sure enough it was JRB.'

'You stopped it I take it.' Jake offered.

'Radio'd in and me Inspector told me to follow, see where it went. He reckoned chances are it'd not be the thieving gits taking it some place. Get the car back yeh if I stopped it right enough, but driver could be some poor foreign sod got nothing to do with nicking it.'

'And then?' was a sighed hurry up.

'Pulled down this road a piece heading towards Buslingthorpe and he goes off down side o'this house.'

'And you reported that in?'

'No. Phoned a friend,' Nicky Scoley sniggered at the look on Jake's face. 'Reckons its some bloke called Rumbold who has this workshop tagged on the back of his house like with a yard and a bit of a smallholding on the end. Does up old crocks and flogs 'em and does repairs locally, cos there's no actual pucker garage in the area.'

'And?'

'Still there I imagine.'

'No,' said the DI shaking her head. 'What I mean is, what's the connection with Morgan Hallam?'

'Me mate said.'

'Said what?'

'People round that neck of the woods like, reckons it's linked to the Hallams' business somehow, probably doesn't own it but reckons this old boy could be his old man's mate or som'at. It's this Rumbold what runs it they reckon, but think Hallam' got his fingers in the pie sort o'thing. Could always be one of these urban myths people quote of course. Kev seems to think the old boy got into trouble few years back and Hallam bailed him out and that. Lads reckon he's a bit shifty too.'

'Why would Hallam be involved in a run-down place like that sounds, when he's got five fairly decent places?' Circumspect Jake queried.

'Why's a nicked Lexus being taken there,' was a good answer.

'Can I just say,' said Jake once Bennettt and MacLachlan had left. 'He reckoned this Rumbold got into trouble and Hallam bailed him out. Think somebody's got their knickers in a twist. Hallam's old man was the one who got himself into a bit of bother with the tax man surely.'

Inga Larsson's first thought had been to hand this all over to PHU (Prisoner Handling Unit) who dealt with the aftermath of all manner of roadside arrests, shoplifting, burglary and all the other acquisitive day-to-day criminal offences.

DS Raza Latif who had been investigating the Brough Barn Motors business had taken a few days off work with his wife going into hospital for a minor operation.

Persuaded by Sandy and Jake not to wait for his return, Inga agreed in the end to assign the former along with Jamie Hedley driving, to pay this place a visit with Jethro Bennett showing them the way initially.

When the pair turned up, there was nothing untoward. The big white house had net curtains at all the windows and when nobody answered the front door, they both trooped round to the rear while Bennettt headed back to hunting down traffic offenders heading east towards the coast.

At the rear were big grey roller doors with a single door on the right. They knocked to be polite and not cause too much disturbance. Within thirty seconds it opened inwards and they were greeted by this balding guy of medium height with three or four days growth of beard dressed in overalls who invited them into his large workshop.

The only vehicle inside up on a ramp on the right was a metallic blue Kia Pecanto with a wheel missing and in that corner a rickety old desk with paper strewn all across it, with a calendar of countryside views hanging on the wall from a nail.

Jamie's eyes had been immediately drawn the moment they'd walked in to the far wall covered entirely in a series of colour pictures which looked for all the world like pages torn from motoring magazines. They all depicted F1 cars and drivers from decades past plastered from top to bottom as a very bizarre and unusual form of decoration.

There was no sign of the four month old silver Lexus they could see. The left hand wall had two old batteries and a dented fan heater shoved in the corner by the entrance door and the floor hadn't seen a broom in ages. Above which hung tools all too neatly displayed, Sandy reckoned had not been used in many a long day. The rest of the wall was just brick with bits of dirt, dust and grime, two filthy dirty plastic containers, litter and detritus somebody had just tossed to one side and failed to pick up. Three huge barrels of oil appeared to have just been plonked down in the empty space and left.

The right hand side from their perspective was altogether completely different. It looked like a proper serious workshop, just the sort he'd been to many a time when he had his car serviced with all the equipment and tools. Spick and span metal tool cabinets and a workbench as expected made the two sides like chalk and cheese.

'Guid morning, sir. Masked-up Detective Constable Sandy MacLachlan,' the big copper said by way of introduction. 'And this is Jamie Hedley by the way. We've just popped in on the half chance to see if you cannae help at all. We're on the lookout for an eleven reg 3 door Renault Clio Dynamique,' he said detailing his wife's car sat back in Lincoln. 'Wondered if by any chance somebody's popped it in here for a bit of work. Been nicked and involved in a guid old shunt. Think it's probably got a damaged off side wing and wheel arch. Could be the wheel's a gonna too.'

The un-masked balding mechanic just blew out a breath, then proceeded to casually pull a tin from his pocket, take out a roll-up, lit it and took a drag despite the likelihood of petrol present.

While they waited Jamie was still looking at the wall in an attempt to recognize as many cars and drivers as he could. The inimitable look of James Hunt was easy to pick out, as were Niki Lauda and Nigel Mansell who did battle for a while, but none were current as far as he could see.

'Be long time since I seed one of they old Clio things,' he managed before another lung full of smoke went in and out again. 'They be nobbut trouble them, let me tell yer.'

'Why's that?'

'Problems with sunroofs leaking and rattling. Done my fair share of a few o'them I can tell yer.'

'And you are, sir?' Jamie slipped in easily.

'Dez.'

'Is there anybody else local who repairs motors?' Jamie enquired casually as he scanned the workshop without being too obvious.

Sandy was looking at the photos and recognized an old Brabham he'd had a toy one of many moons ago back home in Dumfries.

The unshaven shook his head. 'Not int village, son. Next nearest gotta be Jacko's place out at Rasen.'

'He do repairs does he?'

'Sure does.'

'Aye. Thanks for that,' said Sandy as he turned. 'Might just poke our noses in there. Thanks a lot.' He'd noticed hairs sprouting from the man's ears, something his wife had told him to look out for about himself. Since then Sandy had always looked at others for such signs of decay.

Jamie handed over a card. 'If you see this Clio give us a bell, please. Deep red it is, almost plum coloured.'

'Aye righto, sonny.'

'Thanks for your time fella,' was said before the guy followed them out. 'That yours?' Sandy enquired pointing to a worse for wear black Mitsubishi Shogun.

'Belong here, son.'

'Still run okay?'

'Sweet as a nut.'

'Thanks again,' Sandy said memorizing the registration numbers as he turned, what were more than likely sus vehicles, gestured to Jamie and together they strolled away and heard the door rattle shut.

The pair strode off together down the concrete drive past bits and pieces. Old tyres, two batteries and even a rusty exhaust just sat amongst weeds to their left before they reached Jamie's Corsa sat on the drive by the house. The workshop appeared to have been tagged onto the house where anybody else would have a nice patio and a rear garden.

'This is like a back to front Tardis. Smaller inside than outside.'

'First half's an extension, don't look now in case he's watching,' said Jamie. 'But there's a house extension going way back and then it appears that workshop we've just been in they tagged on the end.'

'I reckon something's not quite right,' he said the moment he'd pulled the car door shut and they both jotted down registration numbers. 'Why's the extension got no windows?'

'All a bit weird.'

'You can say that again,' Sandy responded. 'What's with all those pictures? Some o'them go back a bit.'

'Recognised Damon Hill, John Surtees and one or two early Williams' cars, but some of the others go too far back for me. Think one was a Swede we can tell the boss and Senna I spotted. Knew a place once had Ferrari models on shelves in the showroom, made the cars they had for sale look at bit tatty.'

'No right,' Sandy muttered as Jamie reversed out back onto the road. 'Cannae put my finger on it, but it's very much right hand fine, left hand suspect somehow. Very suspicious and what's the chances he's one of the bad guys?'

'To my mind it's all too tidy when you see the state of him. One side'd pass any inspection for health and safety, eat your tea off the floor. Tother's just old bits and pieces of litter and stuff, few barrels and needs a damn good sweep.'

'Nobody'd take their Lexus in there.'

'Not if they've got any sense but still, worth a try.'

14

Kirsten

I do have to say I simply hated myself for months after I'd been with paunchy, boring, petrol-head Morgan, but at least I knew Frances was happy and to a degree I felt at long last my debt had been paid in full.

Used and abused was my new found status. They say every woman remembers her first time with great clarity. What on earth have I got to reminisce fondly about?

Of course I cannot give you marks out of ten for his performance, because at that stage in my sexual experience development I had no benchmark to go by.

I can fully understand how women fall for his charms and the lavish use of his wealth. The restaurant to which he took me happened to be the sort of place I've seen on the telly, read about in magazines and passed a time or two when in the capital, but had never previously entered. Michelin starred of course and I chose traditional roast grouse simply because I'd never had it before. Plus a bottle of Cabernet Sauvignon Morgan just had to mention cost more than £200 a bottle. A ridiculous amount just for wine, but who was I to argue? I had more than one glass with my nerves on edge and not looking forward to the afters at all.

I didn't ask and Morgan didn't explain why both the restaurant and the lavish hotel were well away from Lincoln. In fact all the arrangements had been made by Frances to coincide with a trip I'd had to make for three days to Croydon just south of London for work with a client. He was obviously keen, as he had travelled down especially for the occasion or should I say, event.

Only once have I sort of lost control in the presence of Frances, in that an invite to her big gorgeous home ended up with us downing far too much wine.

During that session it turned into confession time by her. Looking back now I wonder if she used me as a sounding board to admit her marriage issues and problems despite this polyamorous business she claimed they were both entirely happy with.

Frances admitted after we had started on the second bottle of red, how her Morgan had revealed he had these sexual quirks a sort of bucket list of conquests he had to deal with. She just openly sat there and admitted how she'd somehow managed to see him through his sexual encounters with among others a Muslim and a black girl he'd been chasing for months and months apparently.

Me? I've got a Duck It list. Things I aim to avoid. Nonsense like Hang Gliding, those awful zip wire contraptions. Bungee Jumping, eating Snails and going anywhere near a hot tub.

Tiddly Frances had explained how there was a disabled woman on his bucket list, but then as he had worked his way through a number of varieties one stood out he craved for. A virgin.

Guess what?

Unbeknown to me at the time, further down the line of course was where I'd come in. I'd never for the life of me imagined such a scenario would ever have my name on it.

It was a long time before I worked out what had first attracted Frances to Morgan, when in truth he's the sort of fellow who can probably have his pick of any woman. To so many females he has the volume of disposable income he can and will splash out. never really for their enjoyment but always to his distinct advantage.

I had just never ever imagined the prize at the end of his personal rainbow was a tick box on his bucket list.

My friend, my life-saver has never come out and said it in so many words, but I sussed their getting together involved this list of his again. Not sure of course she had been among his original listings but my guess is, when he was first introduced or saw her with her father he made a note to add her.

You see, Frances suffers from Alopecia and I have to give her so much credit for how she sees herself when she looks in a mirror before her wig goes on.

"Beauty is only skin deep," is what she will say to people who stare at her and wrongly assume she has cancer when she goes out bald with a scarf wrapped around her bonce from time to time.

Of course the world of weird shaped eyebrows and all this plucking business has helped her no end. She just looks like another dollop to have them removed but at least she has more savvy than to have penciled in crooked replacements you see too often.

Frances chooses sometimes as her way of throwing her attitude right slap bang into other people's laps, by deliberately going out without a hair piece or hat or scarf. There are of course plenty of trolls about even off the internet who enjoy shouting rude and abusive comments. Frances knows full well they'll do it if she goes out bald, but it is her great way of throwing it all back at them, back in their faces none of which to be honest can ever be as clean, clear, and pure as hers.

She never apologizes for who she is or how she sometimes appears and I've got to admit truly proud of her being.

They do say it was most probably a reaction to the stress of university and taking her finals that brought about this amazing change in her, to result in Morgan making a bee line for a bald woman. Another box ticked for him, and possibly without her knowledge at the time she believed it was love at first sight.

15

'Please Sandy, let me stop you there,' was the forthright Swede. 'If this is to do with what you believe you've found out near Faldingworth, which as it turns out was next to nothing, might I remind you about the HMRC investigation discovering absolutely zilch at Brough Barn. In fact they said it was squeaky clean, and you know why that is?'

'Boss...' the subject still uttered but ignored.

'His old man got sent down for fiddling the books, and my guess is Morgan Hallam has gone completely opposite, he wanted nothing to do with slopping out, being buggered in the showers and visiting times. I know you say the place you went to didn't seem right, but I see people in the street every day who don't look right, but we can't go round invading their space on any passing whim. Numpties in trainers and black socks, skurks walking the streets in flip flops, women struggling to stay upright with their ankles crossed. We can't go around arresting every cack-handed oddball.'

'Guv,' MacLachlan insisted again. 'It's because HMRC found absolutely nothing is why I think more than ever we need to go in heavy handed and find out what is really happening out there.'

'Half good, half bad,' Jamie said. 'Why would you sweep one half of the workshop and not the other? Why wallpaper the end wall with old photos of racing cars, and only that wall. Why bother?' he shrugged. 'It's only a workshop. The left hand scratty wall is only breeze blocks. Not even had a coat of whitewash.'

'You know what I ken?' Sandy said turning momentarily to look at Jamie sat at his work station behind him. 'That was all aboot making us zero in on the pictures. Friend of mine who knows a thing or two about psychology reckons it's to do with transfer of focus or words to that effect. It makes you look at the pictures and not at the wall. Why's there no tools on that wall, no shelves, cupboards, nothing? Just these tatty pictures cut from papers and magazines. Everything is on the right hand wall as you walk in. Exactly as you'd expect with the ramp, all the tools, all the cabinets for tools, all the equipment you'd need to fix cars, like in every garage I've been to. Why is the opposite side...?'

'Enough!' stopped him, then Inga took a moment to check her team's reaction and Jake as ever offered one of his skeptical looks. 'Tell you what I'll do Sandy, if you type it all up in a report, list all the odd-ball things...'

'The wan wi' met is a bloody odd-ball for starters!'

'If you'll let me finish,' said the determined DI. 'This is what I'll do. Come up with a full report with facts and thoughts of you both, punt it over to me and I'll send it through to the boss, see what he makes of it. But, and it's a big but in this day and age, how much will it cost? How much will he need to fork out based purely on your notion? If say we send in, what shall we say, four or five of you, two cars and forensics probably with their van? That's where he'll be coming from, what he reminds me about all the time. He'll not risk a penny on a frivolous guess. Could just do with proper substantial evidence to back up your theory.' She looked hard at Alexander MacLachlan. 'You with me? You'll do that?'

'Just now. Nae problem, boss.'

'Fine. Now, can we please move on?'

Whatever it was the boss wanted to move onto went in one ear and out the other with Sandy. He'd planned to do more investigating on his return, but the moment he walked in DI Larsson was at him which he could understand. Facts and figures were still thin on the ground and he guessed she was hoping for something she could pass onto the dark boss to keep him quiet.

Inga Larsson's pathologist friend Dr Bronagh O'Carroll would always converse about a cadaver in such a way she could understand the intricacies of her work.

Not so Dr Dean Parish in his green scrubs and fancy bandana that Thursday morning. His full autopsy report landing on her desk minus the final toxicology tended towards the dramatic use of medical terminology.

The same thing annoyed Inga about some gardening programmes on television with some old fool pontificating with pompous and irritating talk about Lonicera Periclymenum rather than common Honeysuckle the average viewer knows them by.

What the DI had taken from the report was the pathologist's opinion that Morgan Hallam would apparently have been facing his attacker. Reference to his frontal lobe told her that, but it had been visually obvious even to an amateur.

The Dr Parish however had no superior words for blunt force trauma which had resulted in half his face being caved in, nor the blunt instrument which could have been just about anything. At least he had confirmed death to have been at least two weeks earlier than the date of discovery which aligned with the weekend his wife reporting him missing.

'We've got the basics we all suspected from Connor Mitchell's photos,' said Inga to those in her team who were present that morning. 'Hallam certainly took a good smacking a fortnight before we came across him, but we still have no idea why or by whose hand.' Inga looked down at her iPad in hand. 'Toxicology will take time as ever, so we all carry on our merry way and hope the final report comes up with more clues than we have so far. This was no accident, this was foul play and we don't know where he was for at least the first week or more. Was the Curran four bed chosen as the dumping ground completely at random due to its location? If it was, why? How was access obtained and who had a spare key?' She grinned at them all sat there listening intently. 'Enough to be going on?' she asked and clapped her hands.

'Pal works for the estate agent.'

'And?' Inga queried.

'Just saying. Not me. How about our killer has friends working there. They'd know about keys and access, when and where, probably knew Curran was off to Cornwall. Easy get a copy made.'

'Off you go,' she told Jamie.

'Been a few cases involving estate agents,' Michelle suggested. 'Suzy Lamplugh for one.'

'She was the estate agent,' Jake reminded.

'But it means they have access, can easy get spare keys cut.'

'Guy in the office overhears chatter about the North Carlton house being exchanged, just in time with that Curran bloke off on holiday.'

'Wonder what checks estate agents do?'

Sandy MacLachlan got his head down once he'd taken all that on board and quickly returned to his scribbled notes about the workshop. Made a quick check with DVLA and then a phone call on his mobile downstairs outside and he was back up to face the Detective Inspector again.

He was full of enthusiasm about the new information he had gleened but whether on purpose or not, she made him wait.

'Back to the workshop,' Sandy started and Inga Larsson looked less than impressed. 'KIA Pecanto he had up ont ramp actually belongs to a Derek Rumbold at the workshop we visited. The guy we saw told us his name's Dez. Assume Derek. Just phoned said I'd got an issue with my car and asked for Dez Rumbold and he came tae the phone.'

Larsson shrugged. 'Playing devil's advocate. What if I were to suggest he just happened not to be very busy when you two called and he was repairing his own car? Big Deal, so what? Chances are it happens all the time,' she grimaced as she tried to keep the impatience out of her voice.

'There were nae other cars save for that one, except for a Shogun he said belongs to yon business and a van outside he reckons he owns. Where was the Lexus? And more than anything else, the workshop's gotta be less than half the size of the whole building. I'm damn sure there's something cracking off out there.'

'Jamie says the first half of the building is actually an extension of the house and…'

'Same brickwork I agree. But getting on for big enough to play five-a-side footie in!'

'Allow me to finish if you will,' was sharp. 'The second half according to him is the workshop you both went into. Did you

95

actually go into the house? How do you know that's not one of these huge country kitchens they go on about with an island, an AGA, a walk-in pantry and all that utility room business so you can let your mangy dog in?'

'Want me to see if I can get in the house? There's nae sign of life anywhere, net curtains at all the windows.' Sandy sucked in a breath. He had no plans to give in that easily. 'Seen cannabis farms looking like that, boss.'

'You're not…' Sandy shaking his head stopped Inga. 'You've certainly got a bee in your bonnet with this one.'

'Neither of us got a whiff of anything, but it's just nae right. How's about I pretend I'm Amazon delivering maybe and knock on the front door?'

'Now that's not a bad idea at all,' she gestured to her big DC. 'Sit down,' she told Sandy which he did. 'Can't see the boss agreeing to a raid without due cause. I appreciate you're suspicious but we have no real evidence, and it's difficult to see how that fits in with Hallam's death. But to be honest that's not a bad idea of yours. It'd need to be somebody else though,' she said looking out into the incident room. 'How about somebody like Bill Knapp downstairs?'

'Okie doke.'

'In the meantime keep developing the intel.'

16

Kirsten

What I didn't realize at the time was there would be more to come, more demands from Frances, but this time loaded with threats.

You know when you see or speak to someone and the situation or conversation raises an important issue you need answers to. That is exactly what happened when I met up with Frances, the penultimate time before Morgan's death.

I'd been putting her off and putting her off, but then bold as brass she just turned up at E-Quilibrium reception asking for me. It was probably the state of her made me give in, as this was seriously a case of curiosity killing the cat.

She was pregnant, well pregnant. My question bearing in mind her admitted string of bedmates was not how, but who. As it turned out I never posed the question, just gave in and went off with her to a scruffy caravan parked on a bit of rough ground near where I work. Place the guys rush to for a bacon roll on the way in or an egg sarnie at lunchtime.

By this time rays of sunshine had broken through the fluffy clouds again. We sat down in the sun with white polystyrene cups full with what the old geezer with a triple chin behind the counter claimed was coffee.

In truth we know nothing about other people's lives if we're honest, do we? What goes on behind closed doors is always a mystery. Take this crap coffee being dished out. How does he keep going, I'd like to know. Surely people are used to better than that, so why do people ever go back? Or is it in truth just like the own label garbage they get dished up at home?

In case you're asking, from my point of view it was convenient and there were no big ears about. The fat guy running it. my work colleagues call Dod. No idea what that's about. Haven't got a clue if it might be short for something or just a weird surname. Could be Billy Dodd of course.

Half way through chastising me for not meeting up with her two or three weeks earlier when I could sense what was coming, I began to shake my head.

'Hear me out,' she insisted. 'How's Freddie these days?' she opened with.

'Fine,' I think illustrated my mood.

'What's the situation with the new place you're buying?'

'Exchange contracts and get the keys in a week or two we hope. Why?'

'Like to use it,' but before I could ask what on earth for, she went on. 'D'you still do that business of living in one room sort of thing when you get in?' she queried with more than a hint of a smell under her nose.

'Yes why?'

'Like to borrow it.'

'What d'you mean borrow it?'

Frances raised a penciled in eyebrow. 'Want to store a bit of stuff.'

'Don't be ridiculous!' At that point I came very close to tossing the excuse for coffee onto the ground, chucking the cup in the bin and walking off.

'Listen to me,' she said firmly. 'Summer holidays are coming up and you've said before how Freddie always wants to take a break to get the horrors of teaching feral kids out of his system. We could use it while you're away.'

'No thank you,' I shot back as Frances then gave herself a contented smile akin to a pat on the back.

Right there and then almost as if this was to be never ending I got the message in her look. The don't forget I saved your life, you're sitting here in fresh air and warm sunshine because of me, not just a pile of bones rotting in the ground or ash sprinkled at the Crematorium the rain has turned to mush.

'Freddie know about Morgan does he?' was a question I just could not answer so gob smacked and helpless was I at her audacity. 'Know about all the others I lined up for you, does he?'

'What in God's name…?' A familiar knot of worry had tied itself tightly in my stomach and not for the first time.

'Just you listen here. I've got all the dates and times all listed down and every one of them will confirm.'

'How dare you?' I shouted loud enough for Dod whatshisname to hear. 'I've never ever been with anybody else and you effing well know that!'

'But can you prove it? What will you say to Freddie when he storms home once the letters start arriving addressed to the Head of Economics with a copy to the head teacher?'

'You wouldn't dare! You…'

'Try me.'

'Tell me if you will. How many people will be rushing to buy cheap cars off Morgan when they know about his list of targets?'

'Don't be ridiculous. What list?' She pointed at me. 'Now sit down!' I refused to take notice of her demands and once again wished I'd just said no and left, like I should have done before. 'We need to store stuff while you're away, just for a few days. All I need from you is a copy of your front door key to the new place. Freddie won't even know we've been. Easy as.'

'I didn't even know Freddie back then.'

'Assume you've told him though.'

'Yes,' I lied. 'And if I say no?' I said down to her as I stood there hands on hips with the ragged fat git leering at me from the grubby caravan.

'That's easy,' Frances said and continued after a slight pause. 'The police will just happen to hear about this woman who arranges for women and girls to perform for middle aged men for money. All bit strange of course be all sorts, things Morgan loved. How long I wonder will Freddie hang about when all that comes out on top of stories of you shagging Morgan for fun on one of your work trips down the smoke? What will he think next time you say you have to go off somewhere eh?' She laughed at me. 'What I'd give to be a bloody fly on that wall!'

'You loathsome bitch!' I screamed and the chins looked across at the pair of us.

'It's that or the key,' she said as I just spun round and walked off. 'Choice is yours!' I tried to ignore as I strode away. 'Hey!' she shouted after me. 'And don't think I won't.'

I felt sick to my stomach and going back to work was the last thing I wanted. Some of the lesser lights bragging about what they were doing and where they were going at the weekend. I sat on a street sign shaking and thinking of my Freddie and what I'd say. What on earth could I say?

I'd been happier working from home until we sold our old house which put paid to that. Back to the offices socially distancing and all that. I'm never going to work from the Currans' place with Penny poking her nose in and making weak tea.

My Freddie's had such an awful eighteen months what with all this pandemic business and the rotten government forever not making up their minds. Some schools closed and some were open to start. Then a nationwide lockdown, then they opened and before you could turn round a resurgence shut them down again. On top of that nonsense he had to suffer that cock-up with exams adding to his stress. Some privileged kids were in class he had to teach, and others home schooling doing their best with the work he had to stream on-line.

Then there were all those others parents he'd had to deal with. The boozed up, drugged up element of society. Too busy spending their benefit cash on a new iPhone, take-aways and gambling on line to bother about a laptop or the wi-fi to go with it for their kids.

Then on top of all that hassle, he was in the front line and did they give him and his colleagues priority with that vaccine roll out to protect him? No of course not. Dished it out to a load of old biddies who were never going to party or bump into anybody anyway.

With everything's he's been through I couldn't take the risk could I? With the wonderful gift of hindsight I should have come clean with Freddie about that dreadful business with her damn Morgan early doors. But, you know how it is. I didn't because at the time I thought it was the right thing to do and I just never imagined it would all turn out like this.

If any of those dozy women at work were in trouble they'd speak to their dads, an option I didn't have.

I just wanted to go home and make it right with my Freddie. But how?

In the end I just trudged back to work hoping none of them said anything sarcastic.

I got her a front door key. In fact I'd had a client to deal with down in Colchester a couple of days after we'd got the keys. Got a copy made down there, and with all this business going on I never gave a thought to ask her for it back.

And to think when I first got to know Frances Hallam I thought she was proper nice.

17

Three Detective Sergeants trooped into Inga Larsson's small office each with a mug of coffee. Raza Latif back at work returned out into the Incident Room to lift a chair in and once they were all seated and the door closed, their boss with biscuit in hand, began.

'Operation Thanatos, as if you didn't know. Geeks upstairs in Steven's eTeam are still ploughing their way through the dark net investigating the world of Morgan Hallam. On their way through the jungle Dexter up there came across an email offshoot,' she slid a single sheet of paper in front of each of them. 'This has been re-written by Hari up there in Word because somehow Hallam's had a lock put on all his work stopping anybody printing off copies or attaching it to a file. It is specifically read only.' Raza after scanning the sheet went to speak. 'Reason it's all so long winded is due to these locks they're trying to break through, all of which take time,' stopped him. 'I've had this,' she waved her copy. 'For an hour trying to fathom what it all means and so far I've only come up with one idea. The top piece is the equivalent of an email and the bottom half is a one page file.'

'Who is Super Snipe?' Raza managed to slip in at last.

'He must be in the motor trade, or rather he was,' Jake smiled. 'My guess is if there is a motor trade connection with a reference I reckon to an old car called a Humber Super Snipe conceivably, he's using as a moniker.'

'Not a person?' Jake looked at his Asian colleague. 'He's Morgan and that's a car.'

'Humber's a river.'

'And the list? What do we all make of that?' Inga asked before she took a sip of her coffee and bit into her coconut biscuit.

'Dear me,' Nicky Scoley sucked in her breath noisily as she pulled a face. 'Is this what I think it is, a hit list?'

'Sexual predator's list more like. Do the NCA know things like this are going about?'

Jake read carefully. 'You could very well be right and can I say what I think this is?' He didn't wait for an affirmative. 'What's the betting, this is Morgan Hallam's shag list, excuse the expression. Like some goons go in for all that bucket list nonsense,' was typical Jake. 'Looks to me as if this is a list of those he's had his grubby mits on already and those he was still seeking out.'

'How d'you make that out?' Inga queried even though she was thinking along exactly the same lines as she set down her red mug.

'Well, it's not a list of people he needs to recruit for Brough Barn are they? Ticked ones are slightly easier than the unticked. Well to me they are,' he grinned when he looked at the boss.

'Do people really behave like this?' Inga asked and sighed then answered her own question: 'Yes, of course they do. Some of the things I came across in my previous life tells me this is real.' The DI looked back down at the list in front of her. 'To do list is all in bold. What's that all about?' Inga queried.

'Box ticked as I said?' Jake offered. 'Top section is his yet to achieve list all in bold. He's always had a reputation so we understand and my guess is he was a lot worse than that, he was a sexual predator who managed to shall we say, avail himself of the services of ...a Blonde, Brunette, Redhead and the Schoolgirl, which has to be the most worrying. All of them are in the bottom half, with Bold removed makes then less visible is the way I see it.'

'My thoughts exactly,' The DI admitted and her hand went up to stop any comment. 'My reckoning is the Muslim for example could be more to do with an attack on religion and the hijab than her actual colour or ethnicity.'

'Tells us he's racist or was, if this really is him.'

'Black is on the done list though if we've got it right.' Nicky offered.

'So, when he says,' Raza read: 'Can anybody help me, those in bold at the top are our greater concern.'

103

'One's he's after seems to me.'

'Was after,' Jake corrected.

Raza peered up. 'Having a list like this is one thing, but asking folk for help…' he blew out a breath.

'At least I'm not in bold!' blonde Nicky quipped to lighten the atmosphere. 'But a Dwarf and a Nun? Wow!' she sucked in and expelled a breath and drunk more coffee.

'Why are we going down that avenue?' Inga asked Jake throwing in a negative. 'Why have we all assumed this is a sex list?' Why are we suggesting these are women he once targeted and those he was still after? How about it's merely a list of women he's sold cars to?'

'Alopecia's there,' said Nicky immediately. 'His wife Frances has Alopecia. She's not in bold and she's in the second batch along with pregnant woman.'

'Two for the price of one.'

'Where'd that Alopecia come from?' Jake pounced.

'It's right,' Inga confirmed. 'Snippet from Family Liaison. Until now it was completely irrelevant, but having seen it on this list,' she pulled a face.

'Not bold.'

'Thought something wasn't right when we interviewed her. Trawling through social media it's been mentioned once or twice.' Nicky pulled a face. 'Until now as the boss says, it was a case of so what, like getting all fussed if she was left handed. One that worries me more,' she went on glancing out into the Incident Room, 'is Policewoman not being in bold,' she tittered to herself.

'Don't look at me!' was the boss's retort.

'Doesn't have to be from Lincoln Central,' Jake offered. 'If that's any consolation.'

'Who's got themselves a new car?'

'In exchange for…?' Jake threw in. 'Surely not.'

'Already taken action with that,' the DI advised as two pulled faces. 'I've had a message put on our system just before you walked in asking if anybody, male or female has ever had anything to do with Hallam prior to his death. I've also taken the liberty of doing the same with the local NHS Trust's internal staff memo system, asking any nurses to get in touch if they've had untoward contact with him. Anonymity is promised.'

'Trouble is, there'll be a few I should imagine who've bought a car off him.'

'Realize that.'

'Blind, Muslim in Hijab, Dwarf, Amputee,' said Nicky one by one as she read down. 'Beggars belief all this.'

'Appalling and sick, but be careful,' said Jake. 'Visually impaired I think you'll find,' he chuckled. 'Three blind mice has been outlawed remember.'

'Oh Jake,' said Inga. 'D'you hear on the news? They reckon the French'll never return to their silly cheek peck nonsense.'

'Bozos here'll carry on. Too much hugging already.'

Goodwin was a good man and the women were of one opinion regarding his obvious ability to be a cracking good husband. Inga Larsson called away, off on a course or holidaying and Jake would simply take over any current investigation without sight or sound of a join.

'Any other theories?' Inga posed, mug in hands shaking her head at such incredulity

'Apart from height impaired is it?'

'Restricted growth,' Raza knew.

'Just call her titch then,' Nicky slotted into the discussion.

'What's the chances as an alternative this has nothing whatsoever to do with predatory sex? And why are all these women doing it with him?'

'How about as I said, this is just out of interest he simply created an innocent list of women he's sold cars to?'

'Be serious!'

'Gift of the gab?' Raza asked, as he lifted his mug away from his mouth.

'People say he's just all bullshit.'

'It's possible, but at this stage we're not ruling anything out. You tell me what else this list might be.'

'Still say the Alopecia is a clue and coincidentally she's the very one who reported him missing, remember. Plus if you think about it, she has no hair, her wig is deep red and she's pregnant. Three in the second list, Alopecia, Pregnant and Redhead. Not one in bold. All done and dusted to coin a phrase.' Nicky chuckled when the others immediately started checking their list.

'It's true what Jake says. The easier ones are below the line.'

'I could tick Nurse,' Jake joked and they all found amusing. 'Nun, Vicar and Old Woman they'd not be easy even if he was a Bishop.' Momentarily Jake considered making a remark about one living in an old shoe, but refrained.

'What chance have we got of tracking any of these down?'

'Policewoman and maybe a nurse, if they're willing to admit to it. How many Chinese are there for crying out loud?'

'Two billion!' produced smiles.

'Why Chinese and not Japanese?' Raza asked. If he was hoping one of his colleagues would explain a reasoning for the difference he was mistaken.

'Disabled not easy, lesbian won't admit it and foreigners could be just about anybody from the Welsh to a Bangladeshi.'

'So, we start as I've already done with a copper and a nurse and,' Inga glanced over at DS Nicky Scoley. 'Alopecia we reckon we know.' Nicky confirmed with a nod.

'Interviewing her this afternoon'll be seeing her from a different perspective if this is all true.'

'Bet I get the Trans,' Jake joked. 'Still in bold,' made him shrug and shake his head. 'But there's no asylum seeker I notice.'

'Or illegal immigrant just off a boat,' Raza offered.

Inga pretended to consider what they had contributed and as her team chatted on she gazed around the room.

Perhaps Morgan Hallam had not included an asylum seeker on racist grounds and wouldn't want to dirty his hands with the very people he most probably wanted rid of.

'Remember,' said Jake. 'Hallam bought and sold cars all over the county and beyond. "Hello young lady and what do you do? A nurse eh. I've got a lot of time for the NHS and the brilliant work you do. I'm sure we can manage to offer you a couple of hundred pounds more for this tidy little motor of yours."

'Makes his task easy.'

'But,' said Inga. 'Who walks in and says, hi guys, I'm gay, looking to buy that black Toyota?'

'Hi guys would annoy me on its own.' After a moment's pause: 'Those with the rainbow scarf?' Nicky enjoyed slipping in. 'It specifically says lesbian but not gay.'

'Not bisexual then or cross contamination I hear used these days.'

'Doing what he did for a living Hallam could easy pick out the blonde, the disabled driver, foreigners are easy when they speak and the vicar in a dog collar. A policewoman would answer his question when he asks what she does for a living and get five hundred knocked off the ticket price.'

'So,' a smiling Inga uttered. 'We're going for this are we?' Time to sup the remainder of her coffee. 'Nicky will you organize Ruth to scout about through social media, just to see if there is anybody he'd made friends with lately who just might fit the bill of those we assume he ticked and bold ones he may have been lining up. This could so easily be one of these getting their own back for sexual assault, rape and goodness knows what else. The Chinese one, a footballer, disabled maybe and blonde, brunette and redhead for starters. Have a look too on the flower tributes left outside Curran's garden gate. You never know who or what you might spot.' Raza and Nicky got slowly to their feet, with the latter taking her yet to be emptied mug with her. 'Jake,' Inga said as he too went to move. 'A word if you will.' He stayed put and took another Bourbon biscuit from the plate as Raza and Nicky departed. 'Might be an idea if we can discover how many coloured females he employs at his garages, in fact make it male and female. Raza's already been poking his nose into Brough Barn Motors, so allocate to somebody else they won't recognise. Try somebody like Sam from downstairs.'

Jake took a bite of biscuit before he went on. 'The more I hear about this bastard the more I'm thinking maybe somebody did the world a favour getting rid of him,'

Having looked at Frances Hallam's social media pages just out of curiosity, Jake had seen for himself the public image she was projecting. As far as he was concerned there had to be a divergence of social groups. How on earth had they as a couple chosen pairs to satisfy both their needs?

Jake waited for the office to eventually clear and Inga looked at him as if she expected her Detective Sergeant to follow suit.

'Said you wanted a word.'

Her finger went up. 'So I did,' she responded and looked at her notes. 'Can you get one of the PHU people to pop along and have a word with Lizzie?' who operates HOLMES 2 the Home Office Large Major Enquiry System. 'Ask her if when she has a spare five minutes if she could do us a big favour and load in something about previous sexual assaults, rape and stuff like that on the disabled, the blind, ballet dancers. Whatever,' she raised and lowered her shoulders. 'Make a list for her. Ask her to try nuns and dwarfs first maybe. Sorry, those of restricted growth and religious order. See what she comes up with. Shot in the dark, but you just never know.'

'We have got this right have we?' her Detective Sergeant asked. 'This is not just some offbeat list of people he hoped to sell cars to is it?'

'If it was, why are the blind on there, and remember some disabled folk can't drive and would one of restricted growth reach the pedals?'

'Just been thinking how I'd feel if say my sister had something like Cerebal Palsy and he seduced her purely so he could give her a big tick in one of his boxes.'

'That's a clear motive. Remember, people have been killed for far less.'

'Think I'm getting too sensitive in my old age. Used to take thoughts on some cases home with me in the early days. Now it's got to be something pretty nasty or a child maybe. This is one of them. Not the actual killing although he was a bit of a mess, but it's all this other business.'

'We're actually more concerned about possible victims rather than the actual ones.'

'Partly because we have no idea who any of them are.'

'Trouble is of course, they'd have no idea they were part of his master plan. A sort of bucket list.'

'You mean bedding a transsexual and a Sikh rather than climbing Kilimanjaro on a pogo stick or hiking across the Sahara with a bottle of water?'

'If the list is up to date he certainly managed quite a few.'

Goodwin had made some progress with the case files without until that juncture, having any ground breaking news the red tops would give their hind teeth to gather in. This list of course was now new information and he'd had to go on line to ascertain how this should all be described, in a way CPS would in time find easy to comprehend.

18

Enhancements from the in-house forensics team had started to dribble down to Inga Larsson's PC on her desk, and with the basic PM results in mind she was able to move on, now she knew the names of some of those who had been in the property.

Shockers she went for first.

Larsson had prepared Nicky Scoley to interview Morgan Hallam's wife Frances. In addition she had DS Jake Goodwin searching for her family connections which turned out to be easier said than done. Chestnut-haired Ruth Buchan in her social media searches had come across Frances Hallam in between the usual bragging such sites are frequently home to. She spotted Facebook messages from a 'friend' gloating about how far back she had managed to research her family tree.

In truth Nicky Scoley had done the same for her own family at one time but had never felt the need to sing her own praises.

The DI agreed with DS Scoley's preference to keep this interview low key. Under normal circumstances she would have conducted it herself. These were as yet not normal times. Inga's career was littered with memories of having to trespass into people's personal lives to interview grieving family members of a now deceased love one.

Each time it had got no easier and the focus of feelings had remained with her. The initial sense of grief she knew her Detective Sergeant faced would no doubt be truly tangible.

With Nicky and Jake heading up this sordid case for their boss she was to head up the ghastly task of talking to floundering loved ones, the act had left behind.

The blonde Detective Sergeant hoped she would be able to help put the heavily pregnant woman at ease, not just because of her condition but in the vain hope she could well be more forthcoming with her answers as was often not the case.

110

DS Nicky Scoley eased the tall woman slowly into the conversation by spending time discussing her pregnancy, without relating some of the trials and tribulations Larsson herself had encountered prior to Terése being born. What Nicky had discovered by taking that caring and comforting route initially was, the baby was due any day.

Scoley was throughout the process, aware how such an interview conducted not only whilst the woman was in the later stages of pregnancy but also as it happened within a short time of losing her husband could have a negative outturn.

Pregnancy and grief both threw up warning flags and she'd got them combined in one package. This was not at all like interviewing a street scrag who'd got herself up the duff by some scruffy smelly hoodrat she didn't even know.

What the young woman and her colleague Ruth Buchan didn't need right now was being held responsible for this woman aborting with the likelihood of suspension and a lengthy enquiry process all that would inevitably lead to.

The fairly new-build home in Osbournby was huge compared to Nicky and Connor's homely dwelling back up in Lincoln. Had to be at least five bedrooms and with what looked like a Granny Annexe as well.

This Hallam had even arranged for coffees each and a few biscuits on a plate. The weather was good although rain was threatened for later, and sitting out on the patio would have been a no-mask opportunity, but no.

'Have you seen Kirsten Wroe?' she asked when Nicky hoped they'd finished with all the maternity talk, which the boss would have been much better at.

'Who?' amused Scoley.

'The woman who discovered your husband's body,' she said tentatively. 'I believe Family Liaison did explain the situation.'

'Why would I?'

'Just wondered,' she was reduced to.

The maternity dress this Hallam was wearing screamed designer. Navy blue enhanced by a series of white and silver stars of differing sizes. Scoley had been pleased to see her wearing elegant Chelsea boots in black rather than the heels she'd no doubt normally prance about it.

It was so annoying to have to change subjects, when she really wanted to ask a crucial supplementary. Hallam could easily have been to the new home out at North Carlton with them being friends on social media. Too risky bearing in mind her condition to be verging into the realms of a pucker tape-on interview complete with lawyer.

Plus there was DNA she was desperate to ask about, but under the circumstances daren't unless she was planning to be at the scene of a child birth.

Instead Scoley went for something much simpler and less confrontational. 'I'd like you if you would, to send me an email in the next couple of days or so detailing all your activities from the week leading up to Morgan's disappearance right through to you being advised by us of his untimely death.'

'Everything?' she gasped.

'Pretty much. Everywhere you went, what you did, who you met,' said the detective. 'Word of warning,' she added as her mood changed perceptibly. 'Chances are my boss will be checking.'

'What?'

Coffee means all things to all people, and some go in for those little cups of Espresso they swig down on their way to work, others take their time with a milky Latte so many allow to go cold, but they all are supped for a reason. As it was for Frances Hallam that day in her big kitchen. She obviously was in need of a boost she had hopes a good caffeine giving her.

Not being an expert on décor Scoley only had her own opinions to lean on but the kitchen to her mind lacked colour. It had all the elements in fact a centre island and a table and chairs it was that big. Just light wooden units she knew looked like pine but were probably not. Grey ceiling, walls and tiled floor.

Her deep dyed auburn wig had been lacquered to within an inch of its life, and both Scoley and Buchan wondered if the ability to be able to remove your hair was a distinct advantage in preparing perfect locks. Her make-up, even the DS with a flawless complexion would admit, had been beautifully applied with vivid red lipstick and matching long nails. Too long to be entirely practical.

Nicky was sure she'd be the sort, full of her need to promote her perceived status, with a cupboard full of handbags.

'CCTV, ANPR and a whole bag of tricks our eTeam and forensics guys have up their sleeves in this day and age like NAFIS and PWITS.' Was hogwash but Hallam didn't know that. 'And on the subject of fingerprints I'd very much appreciate it if you could pop in some time to give us your fingerprints, in order for us to officially eliminate you.'

'Why?' she snorted.

'Statutory procedure.'

'If you must,' she sighed in a voice dripping with complete disinterest.

'Under the circumstances, and please remember woman to woman I have your feelings in mind. It would be easier on you if you compose a precis of what you did rather than put you through another lengthy and intrusive interview with us probing into every aspect of your busy life.'

'If you insist.'

'We have found fingerprints inside the property which don't belong to Mr Curran or his partner Kirsten Wroe or any of the workmen and friends he employed. Be very remiss of me if I didn't check whether they are yours.' Scoley pulled a face. 'Sorry about that, needs to be done.'

'What about the people who lived there previously, you checking theirs? I bet you're not,' she tittered.

'Of course.'

'What's all that business about?' Frances answered the question with one of her own which Buchan noted. 'Why keep on moving? Why don't they just buy something decent to start with for goodness sake?'

Probably because Kirsten is just a working woman without an overweight sugar daddy living at home with her.

'Progressing up the property ladder in stages as they can afford it I assume.'

'Makes a change from claiming they can't afford the deposit,' neither copper dare comment on. 'We finished?' Frances asked and glanced at her gold watch. Scoley had never been impressed by gleamingly obvious watches telling the same time as hers.

113

Finished? It had only just begun. Had it really been necessary to task things so gently? There had been no signs of grief and not one tear at all.

'What we are doing Mrs Hallam, is going through our normal elimination procedures. Questions I need answers to are very simple, but first we need to rule you out and for instance rule out the new owners of the property and a few people who worked with them for a few days. And…' she sipped her warm coffee to ramp up the tension. 'Your fingerprints. Do they match those found in the house? Got to say if they prove to be a match it's a clever trick, if as you say you've never been there,' she chuckled.

The risk of all this being too much for a heavily pregnant woman had weighed heavily on Nicky Scoley's mind and she decided there and then to leave it at that. Her question about DNA and probing into her relationship with Kirsten had been pushed to one side under the circumstances. Hallam's pregnancy would not last forever and there would be other opportunities. Her reluctance to plough on would simply delay their processes, not halt them entirely.

'If we could just arrange for when we can take your fingerprints, that'll be it for now.' the Detective Sergeant said as she golloped down her coffee and got to her feet.

'Don't you normally do that to people you've arrested?' Frances asked up.

'If you were being arrested,' the DS returned softly as she leant down towards Frances. 'You'd have probably been in handcuffs long before now and sat for hours in a smelly little room with a tape recorder running.' Frances smiled weakly at. 'And no decent coffee.'

DI Larsson walked up to Nicky Scoley and from the back swept her arm around her shoulder.

'I saw sense,' she admitted up to her boss 'That DNA business I decided was too much under the circumstances.'

'I worried she might ask how we got it.'

'Didn't give her a chance. One good thing is she says the baby's due any day.' Nicky's look turned serious. 'Don't overdo it boss, please. Think of Terése, we're onto this.'

114

'Thanks, but I can't ask any more of Adam. He's had such a bad time through the pandemic.'

'When we got there, two aspects were at the forefront of my thinking just as we chatted about. Pregnant and grieving.' She sniggered. 'Pregnant yes, unless it was a cushion, but grieving? Not a sign of it.'

'Just sorry you're getting lumbered with all this. Others are becoming more and more involved which helps, but constantly delegating is never easy.' She grimaced. 'You know what I'm like. Hallam, how was she?'

'To be honest I just blustered on about other things to fill the time once there was no blubbing, but at least she's aware she's not completely off the hook yet which was the main thing, plus of course we're getting her finger prints if she turns up.'

'Ruth found her blowing her own trumpet on social media about getting her father's DNA tested with one of these genealogy DNA sites on the web. Understand it'll be a close enough match to prompt us if the need arises, to get a sample from her father.'

'Check the prints first.'

'Few people have fallen foul of that. Given their DNA freely to one of these private firms, might as well give it to us while they're at it. Good one,' she patted Nicky shoulder. 'Don't want to do that yet. Think we need to be sure whose it is the lads discovered. Now we need to find out how her father might be involved. My guess is she's too pregnant to have been actually caught up in it all. But you never know, could be her alibi.'

'There are theorists who suggest this testing your own DNA business is a government conspiracy?' made Inga look at Nicky. 'There are those who reckon in the grand scheme of things this is the government attempting to have all our DNAs on a database.'

'Make life a lot easier,' she responded. 'I'll get Ruth to go back and see who she's been in touch with.'

'Just something she mentioned,' came to minds for Nicky. 'Do we know anything about Kirsten Wroe's parents?'

'Not as yet.'

'Social media, electoral roll, council tax, open source search here we come, or rather here you go.'

19

Kirsten

So, this is thirty something womanhood is it? I was just thinking that to myself this morning with all this business going on.

Further down the line, sometime after I had succumbed to the intimacy with Morgan, I'd been persuaded to attend a school's end of term theatrical production of *Les Miserables*. The daughter of a work colleague had a starring part in the musical. Afterwards with a glass of cheap wine in hand my colleague Esme – our very good Deputy Head of Business Support I rely on a great deal, introduced me to one of young Harriet's teachers: this guy called Freddie Curran.

That was how we met. I've always had a thing about learning and with him being a teacher it seemed to me how it could well be the perfect fit as far as I was concerned.

Few months later we moved in together into a very cramped two bed terraced house down Shakespeare Street. All part of this master plan Freddie had in his mind of doing-up this tatty house and selling it on at a profit. Of course as you know, it didn't stop at that and we've certainly moved up in the world. We're not these silly social climbers but in effect is what has happened over time. We're also not part of the Now generation either, waiting for everything to be handed to us on a plate.

Always find it slightly unusual how some people put so much credence behind insisting they live in the right area. That of course is only their opinion. I know people who live in very fine property I'd not give a second look to.

Knew somebody at one time who bought a good pre-war semi with a Monkey Puzzle tree in the front garden. Then discovered it is illegal to cut them down as they are endangered. It now blocks their view.

Another couple I heard about bought what they told people was the perfect location with easy access to all parts of the city and beyond. Except that is it was near traffic lights and getting out of their cramped drive was an absolute nightmare anybody else would have spotted a mile off.

"Better class of neighbour don't you know" is just the sort of tripe Freddie's mother would roll out.

I made no mention of the episode with Morgan Hallam or the spotty lad I snogged in a hay barn in the summer holidays when I was fifteen, as there was no reason to. Freddie to his credit had never approached the subject of any previous serious relationships and lovers I'd been involved with. Having said that I had probably unwittingly given him the distinct impression I had been so work orientated for several years, romance had been furthest from my thoughts. To some extent it was of course very true.

What my period of all work and no play meant was, I had built a good sum in the Building Society initially on my boss's advice. I was therefore able to add to our combined fortune to buy an even better property next time around, and so the sequence had begun.

There was a slight glitch as it turns out some time back when Freddie said he'd been asked for advice about buying a new car by a colleague at the school. The two of them set off one Saturday morning and I never gave it a second thought.

I had to bite my lip and be very careful what I said when he returned home a couple of hours later chuntering about their car buying experiences. Amongst episodes he wanted to recall in some specific detail was a visit to a Brough Barn garage his friend Laurence had insisted on. The tale was all about this pompous disagreeable salesman I immediately recognized, to bring the whole sordid experience flooding back.

As I said, I'd never suggested to Freddie I'd not had a series of lovers as some tend towards these days and to be fair to him he never asked me outright. On the same token he never said or hinted that he might be inexperienced either.

To be fair I'm not at all sure it's a big deal with him, but my worry is it might be. If he were to be told he'd married a harlot and if my virginity meant a great deal to him as it does some men, how would he react? Would the love of my life consider I had lied to him even if I'd done nothing of the sort?

I know there are feminists in this day and age who would make a big issue out of me having just once been out for an expensive meal with Morgan, who when we went to a hotel room had been satisfied with just once, I was now being unwilling to admit to a mere man.

Trouble is Morgan knew I was a virgin because his beloved and understanding Frances told him I was. Reckon Freddie might well have assumed I was that sneaky weekend two months after we met, when his parents were off to Rome for three days.

That's another thing. Freddie parents Dick and Penny are very religious, well at least she is. You know the sort, off to church at the crack of dawn on a Sunday, she'd attended a convent and their three children had all been to Catholic schools. Penny had been to Lourdes about three times over the years and always attended late night Mass at Christmas. Catching the Pope's speech at Easter is a must and following his trips out and about places on the news. Even went across to Ireland a few years back to see him in person at a distance.

My guess is Penny would most certainly have been virgo intacta on her wedding day, I'll put money on that. Was it exactly what Freddie expected of his woman? What if he wrongly assumed and had I put him straight about Morgan, my guess is there was a fair chance it could have been the big goodbye.

I know it shouldn't count in this day and age when so many women young and old just move in with whoever and before the year is out have moved on to foist themselves on some other poor sucker. Is it five lovers they reckon everybody has in their lifetime these days? In that case why do I worry what will happen should I ever come clean?

Freddie Curran and I are partners, we work together, play together and love together and we are truly building a life together literally brick by brick. Would a confession destroy all that, move me back into a one-bed flat or bed-sit on my own? I can't chance it, put my whole being at risk of destruction, so I have to back Frances in what she wants for her life and for her marriage.

Who would I be with now and what comely young lass would my Freddie have latched onto if I'd confessed the error of my ways?

20

A day later the ruse with Bill Knapp pretending to be an Amazon delivery driver using his brother's old van worked a real treat.

A canny mature copper from PHU downstairs more used to run of the mill acquisitive offences, the burglaries and shoplifting side of policing work proved to be an excellent choice.

The eTeam had become involved in providing a specially adapted hand-held receipt of goods machine for the customer to sign.

Bill had driven up to the house, still with grubby greying net curtains drawn at every window, jumped out with a parcel all carefully packaged in the Amazon style and walked up to the house.

No reply when he banged on the door. No knocker, no bell he could see.

Bill knocked hard three times and was considering walking round to the workshop when a man in a thick checked shirt, dirty jeans and filthy old trainers suddenly bounded around the corner. Whoever he was had a tanned gaunt face and close cropped thick dark brown hair.

'Thought nobody was in,' Bill told him. 'Parcel for Rumbold.'

'I'll take it,' said the man and made to grab it, but Bill yanked it back. Past his 50th birthday but this heavy knit slightly overweight copper was more than a match for this scamp, whether he was forced to produce his martial arts experience and skills or not.

'Not so fast fella.'

'Just give it 'ere.'

'Is nobody in round here?' Bill nodded towards the door.

'What's it to you?'

'This is the address,' said Bill as he tapped the label and nodded towards the front door. 'More than my jobs worth to hand it to some stranger. You Rumbold by any chance matey?'

'Course.'

'First name?'

'What?'

'What's your first name?' said big Bill Knapp and gestured to tap the keyboard.

'What's it to you?'

'Need it fer the machine. No name, no parcel squire, easy as.'

'Whas all this? Drivers give a knock and leave stuff.'

'New procedure, post Covid. Name?'

'Dez. Er, Derek.'

Bill tapped in that name only, handed over the machine as instructed, asked him to sign which was nothing more than a squiggle, then handed the parcel over and returned to the van. The man had quickly scampered back around the side of the building out of sight.

Bill spotted the Shogun he'd been told about by Sandy and back in the borrowed van wondered if he could have done more to gain access, have a butchers inside the place.

Then a mile along the main road back to Lincoln he stopped to call Sandy MacLachlan back at base.

'Sandy. Delivered your parcel okay, signed for by somebody calling himself Dez or Derek, except this one wasn't at all how you described the one you met. In his mid thirties probably, clean shaven with full head o' dark brown hair. No answer at the house at all and curtains all drawn just like you said.'

'Well done. Did he actually take hold of the machine?'

'Sure did. Now in an evidence bag, and he didn't want me hanging around, almost snatched the parcel off me and scooted round the back.'

'Recognise him at all d'ya ken?'

'No. Certainly not the one you described. Too young for starters and he fumbled over his name when I asked for it.'

'Thanks pal. See you when you get back.'

121

DI Inga Larsson got it all chapter and verse from the eager Scotsman but took no action or made any positive comment until she had spoken to Bill on his return to the fold.

Her first action was to ask if anybody had come across the mystery man Bill had encountered out at the house

'Green light from the boss,' was the news Sandy MacLachlan was waiting for but had wrongly assumed would not see the light of day. 'We're going in. Uniforms two-up with a van. You, Jamie, Jake and two of the lads from PHU with the big red key I suggest. Boss is speaking with HMRC to keep them on board with what we're doing, and he's suggesting you let Phil's dog Rory tag along for the ride just in case.'

Jamie Hedley had over recent years become fit enough to be a match for any gym bunnies he came across who fancied their chances, and with self-defence tactics as an add-on he could be a real handfull.

When some of her team spend a great deal of their time with their heads down often stuffing Haribo Starmix, Smarties and chunks of chocolate into their mouths Inga Larsson knows it is precisely when she needs to jolly them up a bit and is frequently the reason why she had always set demanding time limits on some actions.

Nicola Scoley had always been different. A family trait, something inbuilt into her DNA meant that no matter how pre-occupied she might seem, how long she'd sit staring at a screen, coffee mug in hands, there was nothing to worry about. No need to chivvy her along no matter how quiet she is vocally amidst the hub-hub of a murder inquiry. Scoley is working. Working flat out.

Yet not too involved not to perceive an issue with Jamie Hedley. Was he, she wondered, still trying to deal with not being the father of the child he told himself was his.

His partner Kerrie had dumped him for another but with the bait of being able to see his daughter had persuaded Jamie to fund her lifestyle with her new man. His friends being on good terms with both had made life for the DC more than a trifle difficult at times.

DNA testing had subsequently provided evidence the child was not his.

Next morning just after briefing Inga could sense by the look on her Detective Sergeant's face as she scurried towards her office, this would more than likely be good news, this was what the intense concentration had produced.

Stood with just the hint of a smile on her lovely face the butterscotch blonde looked down at her boss, took in a breath, licked her top lip and came out with it.

'Frances Hallam,' she said. 'According to my social media sources, she and our friend Morgan had an open marriage.' Inga said nothing just looked up at the DS. 'In that we're not talking orgys, wife swapping or dogging on the Fens apparently, just one to one meetings for how's your father. According to my sources Frances and Morgan told each other who they were actually going with. Most of the action on his part never took place in their marital home, and,' she stopped to grin. 'They approve or disapprove of who the other is having sex with. A sort of embargo.'

Larsson sat there with her mouth slightly open. Whatever it was she had expected from Nicky's announcement this was not it. 'Like the Russians using their veto at the UN?' was all the DI could muster so bemused was she by the revelation.

Inga knew she had no reason to query what she was being told. This dedicated young woman would have checked and double checked her facts. In addition she'd produce any evidence required to back up whatever it was she had to reveal.

When her Detective Inspector screwed up her face and closed her eyes, Nicky chuckled. 'Same principle I guess,' she said.

'The baby,' Inga gasped, hand to mouth. 'Jeezus! Whose baby is it? Is that what this is all about? She got herself pregnant by some...' she laughed and shook her head as the line remained unspoken.

'How about she broke the moratorium, chose somebody not on the approved list?' Nicky struggled with as she sniggered.

'Not another list!' the DI almost shouted. 'A list of whatever you'd call it and now a list she approves of for him?'

'How about he has a list she's not happy with, the nasty one we've seen, so she comes up with a list of family and friends who'll give him a good time when she's got a headache.'

'Really?' was expelled with a breath of a sigh. 'Do we have to take all this seriously?' Inga sucked in her breath noisily. 'But that's all askew. He would have done her in if that was the case, not the other way round, surely to God.'

'Unless Frances decided she would prefer to have a child by some rampant trendy young thing with a better class of DNA rather than an overweight forty something balding bore. He said no way not all that dirty nappy shit, you'll need to get rid. Gave her the number of a clinic and in the melee she smacked him round the head with a coal shovel.'

'Sit, down, sit down,' Inga urged as she chuckled at the scenario depicted with her brain running amok with ideas. Pictures of this pregnant woman giving this nasty piece of work a good bashing would have been good to see.

'Just get my coffee,' said the DS and was out to her work station and back in moments to sit down, cross her legs and sip her drink.

'She's due anytime,' said Inga as she sat forward to rest her arms on her desk. 'That means a baby coming our way very soon. Wonder what our chances are of getting a warrant to test the new born for bloods in order to identify the father.'

'Whoever it is could be the one with the coal shovel!' she joked. 'You think we can?'

'Been done before apparently, used the umbilical cord so I'm told in a paternity case some place down south.'

Nicky looked aghast at thoughts of the procedure required whirling round her head. 'Whoever the father is, the DNA could well belong to him. With luck be one of the two currently unidentified at the Curran residence.' Inga sat back shaking her head. 'You clever girl you.'

'Working on another bit too, but its early stages.'

For a moment Inga thought her young detective was going to keep it to herself as she tended to from time to time.

'Come across a woman who somehow or other discovered her husband was one of those on Frances Hallam polyamorous sex list.'

124

'She's got a list too?' the DI gasped planting both hands on her head as if about to rake through her hair.

'Not sure one actually exists. Anyway, as a result this woman is going for a divorce, naming Frances Hallam apparently and out to get as much out of her and her family as she can. This Olivia woman also reckons Frances has a brother, but that's as far as I've got.'

'Add this woman's bloke to the list, and a brother? Could easy mean another one handy with a shovel!' Made them both laugh.

'One minute we've got nobody at all and we're wasting our time knocking on workshop doors, and suddenly we have them lining up.'

'Social media for you.' Nicky took a drink from her mug. A new one Connor had had made for her with three of his best photographs printed on the side. 'Sandy got the green light for his mission?'

Inga glanced at her watch. 'Saturday morning is the plan.' She then drank more coffee and sat with her red mug clasped in both hands. Rather him than her. It was a showery day and Saturday was forecast to be worse. 'All this info you've got, this just on things like WhatsApp and Snapchat and sites like that?'

'Not entirely. Facebook for example because of their greater coverage gives me the first lead in, but when I worked up with the tech guys if you remember, they introduced me to this sort of advanced dross version of social media, where there are no holds barred. Took me an evening or two to get back up to speed but that's where I came across all this info about the Hallam relationship. Not the sort of stuff you'd want made public but provides a decent if warped platform for people to show their interest and concerns about what she'd got herself into.'

'Are any of these trolls suggesting any names?'

'Not so far, but Ruth'll keep a look out.'

'We don't get much chance for a chat these days,'said the DI. 'Let alone a fika. Everything alright at home, you and Connor still moving forward?'

'We're fine. But I'm not sure Jamie is.'

'How d'you mean?' Inga asked.

'Seems a bit down to me. Just wondered if his old problems have returned.'

'That's all done with surely.'

'Alright if I have a word?'

'Sure,' Inga responded but was concerned how she'd changed subjects the moment her man's name was mentioned.

'And Connor?'

'Not planning to buy a dump and knock it about like the Curran bloke, but we're thinking perhaps we could do with moving on,' was good news.

'Problems with your place?'

'Not at all, but,' Nicky stopped a moment to grin. 'Please don't read anything into this, but where we are as you know is not really ever likely to be our forever home and renting is such a pointless exercise. We're currently teetering on the idea of maybe pushing the boat out and going for a family home.' She saw the look in Inga's eyes. 'No,' was precise and unequivocal.

21

Kirsten

I can't for the life of me understand why Frances had put up with being treated the way she had been by Morgan. Did it mean nothing at all to her when she knew for a fact he was meeting me in London that day? What about all the wining and dining at a sumptuous restaurant and then making love...no sorry, having sex with me in a big king size bed with fresh cotton sheets and a lovely breakfast thrown in?

Talking of breakfast, it amazes me there are enough pompous fools about to eat the sort of nonsense the breakfast menu offered. Dry toasted seaweed is the one I always remember off the menu.

I bet there are millions of women with wondrously happy memories of the important moment when they lost their precious virginity and the one thought I'm left with is being offered seaweed for breakfast!

I guess it must be difficult when your father is the joint owner, silent partner in the car business. That was how they first met apparently when her dad became involved with Morgan and his stack 'em high sell 'em cheap string of showrooms. Somewhere down the line I'd been told Charles Pritchard actually owned a little over 50% of the shares in the group, Frances and her mother owned 10% each, leaving Morgan with the measly amount left over, of a business he purported to own.

Anyway I guess she enjoyed the lifestyle, and I have to assume she enjoyed the sex with these other men, a hand selected number of good men oneI assumes. Perhaps Frances was willing to put up with him pestering her from time to time in order to gain her satisfaction with others she enjoyed a great deal more.

By the time we got down to breakfast at least the worst was over, that and being bored senseless with his need over our evening meal to relate the story of how his grandfather had started the business from a barn on a mate's farm near Brough.

What about the blackmail, would it have been best if I'd admitted the whole shebang to Freddie one day sat together in bed with a glass of wine? Told him how Frances had threatened to tell on me with her being desperate to deal with her own issues involving Morgan.

Would that bring our relationship tumbling down? I do have to say, never any mention of marriage from my Freddie has always worried me. Forever there in the back of my mind, the thought that I live with a man who is not fully committed into what we have at all, apart from property that is.

On the other hand would my Freddie just go round there and smack Morgan in the mouth, get himself done for assault and if his temper was really up, finish up being put away for violent unprovoked GBH? Could easy be a few years stuck on my own.

Next on my list of matters to cause me concern was that Scoley policewoman. Why was she making a big issue about me spending a great deal of time at work, especially on that Monday morning? My guess is, according to her I should have stayed out near Branston holding hands with Penny and drinking her weak herbal tea. Freddie of course was running around re-organizing everything for the property and apologizing to all and sundry for the change of plan.

People I've spoken to reckon cases like mine are normally dealt with by higher ranks than just some bit of a Sergeant. Maybe they don't think I'm worthy.

To be honest and I know it's a funny thing to say, but work has in a way become my home. You see, both my parents are sort of devout Jehovah Witnesses. I say sort of because they follow a Fellowship a kind of breakaway ultra-group far more intense than the run-of-the-mill sad door knockers most people come up against or hide away from. They see me as the black sheep of the family a pariah they now shun totally. I'm sure I've been disassociated or as some of the brethren deem it, lawless. Had my name promulgated no doubt as such at meetings.

Not something I talk about most of the time to be honest.

I found it liberating when at the end of my first year at university I denounced their nonsense in much the same way as a good few of my friends have in recent times dumped the Labour Party. Moving away and no longer living in such a meagre world was set against all their constant talk of this paradise my parents believe in.

I suppose in the end the crux of the matter was me not feeling comfortable with the way in which women are treated, with far too much talk in this day and age of men heading the household.

At university being asked my opinion on a whole range of subjects and beliefs over the early months had become tiresome as I desperately knew I had to somehow find my loyal answer in a text somewhere I'd once been taught.

I had to pretend to know about bands, be able to reel off all their big hits. Claim I'd seen films, what they were about and who starred. This was all without ever having been to a live gig. visited a cinema or been in a pub before the start of my second trimester. This was just part of the embarrassment hurled at me by so-called Christians I had to suffer.

This of course was nothing new, having been embarrassed at school particularly when new Harry Potter books came out. I'd no idea why my parents and their cohorts banned them because of the witchcraft and wizardry. I had no idea what my classmates were on about when they spoke of Dumbledore and Hogwarts. Quidditch they enthused about just sounded very odd if not baffling and characters such as Hermione Granger and Newt Scamander were just names to me I heard constantly.

It was all part of an awkwardness I suffered from. Having been cloistered by religious bigots and knowing far less about the real world I was subjected to than the vast majority of students. I had to find a new friend.

Google came to my rescue and was quite simply my closest companion by answering a bevy of questions I had to pose on matters all the others were completely au fait with, or so it seemed to me.

My family have tumbled out all the excuses in the world to avoid seeing me, unless I promise to return to their chosen fold and go back to knocking on people's doors to thoroughly annoy them.

Here's a thought. Was all that been stopped by Covid? Are they back to knocking on your door these days? Do they wear masks? If they do, who in their right mind would answer? Interesting. What about their limited Sunday gatherings, how would they have been organized?

I do sadly have a sneaking feeling my mother would welcome me back without a promise to return to their religious fervor, but is scared to death how the head of her household, my father, would react if she did so.

I've always found it screwy how so many so called Godly folk have a dark side to their nature. You'd expect them to be all sweetness and light, caring and compassionate and very docile to a certain extent. Yet there appears always to be violence and discrimination between rival faiths. I wonder why they always see it as some bizarre competition.

My guess is it has always been there, certainly as far back as the Crusades and more than likely well before that I guess. Christians with Protestants and Catholics. Muslims mainstream and Islamists, secular Jews and ultra-Orthodox, the Sikhs and Bah'ais are permanently hostile along with the likes of Rangers and Celtic so I shouldn't be surprised by the way my own folk are with their silly little church behave. Just very sad at the intolerance of their own child.

I've never understood why they can't just get on with praying and fawning to whoever or whatever they fancy, if that's what turns them on.

Of course my stupid parents have always avoided birthdays, Christmas and Easter which my kindly work colleagues never do. I often wonder why nobody in authority seems to understand such action must amount to willful child abuse.

Apart from Freddie of course, my work mates even the real geeky ones are my new family, and to a certain extent I've grown up with them.

They're the reason I work hard as I tend to treat one or two close colleagues just like the family I've never really had. I often wonder what any God would make of how my father and mother treat people, as from what I understand from their version of the Bible in a way their God never did.

I cannot imagine my father would ever be able to understand how I felt when I stepped up to be awarded my degree. Stood there quite alone that day in the midst of all those happy families.

There are no photographs of me in my gown, throwing a mortar board into the air. I have absolutely nothing I can frame and give pride of place to in the permanent home I'm looking forward to moving into one day.

What about my friends at uni, I hear you ask? It was never their fault or their concern that I was all alone at a time like that. They had other priorities, their friends and families and it was beholden upon them to fully enjoy the moment with those who had made the sacrifices for their son or daughter, to be with those who truly cared.

I was with those who truly cared for me: I was the one stood all alone.

22

They'd knocked hard on the black front door of the detached white Eau House in front of the Rumbold workshop without any response on Saturday morning.

Sandy MacLachlan knew he'd probably spent far too much time in his career chasing drug gangs and scumbag beasties. Even so, waiting for this was light relief from the desk-bound drudge and they'd all got themselves well prepped.

It was a bad and good day news wise, with the Taliban taking more control in Afghanistan and GB gaining more medals in Tokyo.

DS Jake Goodwin, a DC from PHU and two kitted-up members of the Roads Policing Team had quickly skuttled round to the rear workshop past the Shogun and Rumbold's van.

Using the big red key Jamie met with a degree of resistance at the front, but the wood then buckled under the strain of the brute force and toppled inwards into a small pantry like room with white doors immediately left and right. The left one caved in under a single strike at the handle as he heard raised voices behind him.

Sandy and Jamie side by side shoved the damaged door to the floor, before stepping carefully into a fully-fledged professional workshop complete with a silver Volvo up on a ramp as two men in dirty grey overalls tried to rush their escape but failed as Sam and Ged from PHU joined the pair.

'Shit sake!' the big Scot uttered in disbelief at what he'd discovered. Bulky tall DC Alexander MacLachlan was gobsmacked and momentarily speechless.

'Down,' he heard a shout from outside. 'Get down now!' was then the roar of Jake's unmistakable voice. Not at all the calm polite man you'd meet normally. 'On your stomachs, now. I said now!' was screamed.

'Taser, taser, taser!' Sandy heard and when he turned and exited he spotted Dez the guy in his late forties he'd met before, fall down and end up squirming on the ground. Surprised to see him on a Saturday morning.

Tall bearded Phil had another middle-aged portly prone man having handcuffs fitted to his wrists behind his back with Rory the dog barking at him close by.

'These two just came tumbling out round the back,' Jake told him.

'You seen what's cracking off in there?' Sandy asked excitedly and pointed back into the house. 'Have a quick gander,' he told his Detective Sergeant colleague. 'Can't bloody believe it.'

'Bugger my boots,' Jake uttered as he stepped in turned left and looked all around at the set-up. 'Would you soddin' believe it? Crissakes how long's this been going on d'you reckon?'

'God knows. Years by the look of it.'

'Merit mark for you this week my son, what a cracking bloody find.'

'Get cannabis as well, I'll be the teacher's pet,' the Scot chuckled.

'Dog's got one of the shits. When your luck's in like this, anything could happen,' Jake laughed, as he slapped Sandy on the back ignoring someone moaning about being bitten. 'We'll need another van or two for all this lot. I'll sort,' said Jake as he stepped outside, headed off down the drive and stepped into the van uniforms had parked out of sight.

Back in the main house Sandy just had to have another butchers at what they'd discovered. Three scruffy foreign mechanics were by this time sat in a row in identical dirty bumfie uniforms next to what would have been the living room fireplace, handcuffed.

'We got one,' said Sam Johnson pointing. 'Pleading his innocence with a distinct eastern European accent. Another no speaky de Englaizee,' he chuckled with.

'I didna come up the Clyde on a banana boat.'

'Black guy's gone dumb,' was a reference to one chap all trussed up sat on the floor.

'If they ken what's going on, tell them this is Brexit in action.'

DS Jacques 'Jake' Goodwin eventually couldn't resist the temptation to call the boss back at base and explain by way of a victory speech exactly what they had discovered. She agreed to organize a CSI team and inform the dark boss in case he wanted HMRC involved in all the shenanigans.

Jake explained to her how they were waiting for more vans to cart the low life away and Inga suggested maybe it would be a good idea for her to join them to feast her eyes on everything he was babbling on about.

'What you're saying is,' she said to Sandy half an hour later stood together with Jake in the main workshop with the untouched silver Volvo above them. 'It looks as though they could well have nicked this one and are in the process of changing its identification to sell on at a profit?'

Jake was shaking his head. 'This one is actually a hire car which a…'

'Glaikit,' grinning Sandy came up with.

'Learnt a new word,' Jake joked. 'Never returned the car apparently.'

'Hired in Huddersfield two weeks ago,' Sandy added. 'So we're told.'

'What's the chances the hire company will have CCTV?'

'Ruth's already on it back at base,' said Jake. 'Sam Howard is currently down the far end,' he explained pointing at one of the PHU guys sat at a small desk who had worked with the team before. 'He's running number plates we've come across through DVLA and the ANPR Data Centre.'

'What's the betting plates are all linked to Volvos. Crafty bastards.'

'We reckon by all the stuff we've seen, they remove everything such as the registration plate, change the chassis and VIN numbers and anything that makes this high end vehicle unique. They then replace it all with info from another smashed up vehicle they get cheap.'

'Or another Volvo, to make it appear legit.'

'Can I just say,' said Jake. 'Remember Jethro Bennettt said he followed a van with a Lexus loaded onto a trailer. What if that car'd been written off say by the insurance company, which this bunch of rag bags bought off them for next to nothing? This bunch didn't have to go to all the trouble of repairing it. They simply take the data from one car and hoist it onto the new one they've nicked and bob's your uncle.'

'Stealing cars to order, but for themselves,' he translated for the boss. 'Our guess is they steal cars to suit the smashed up one they've already got their hands on,' she suggested. 'Or a legit car ANPR will ignore.'

'If they buy the old one legitimately they'll get all the documentation then transfer that to an identikit car they nick off some poor soul. Sort change of ownership through DVLA and they're tickety boo.'

'Did you say there's another workshop at the back?' she asked when Jake failed to explain his peculiar expression.

Jake and Sandy winked at each other and grinned. 'Wait there', she was told. 'Our pièce de rèsistance,' Jake announced in good French as the pair of them walked to the far wall pulled large bolts free down the left hand side and together pulled, pushed and shoved the soundproofed wall which moved slowly at first but they soon were able to ease it back like an enormous floor to ceiling door to reveal the other smaller workshop at the rear of the building hidden behind it.

Jake spotted the ffs expression on the boss's face and struggled to retain his composure. There'd be some Nordic naughty words going round in her head.

'That's what the photos of cars is all about,' said Sandy. 'It's a false wall, but the pictures on the other side give the impression it's a proper wall.' He went to the false wall now back against the bricked side and pulled it back slightly so boss Inga could get a look at all the racing cars plastered from top to bottom. 'Local people bring their cars in the back here,' he indicated. 'While these foreigners are working on the real money maker in here with the wall closed off.'

'I sometimes wonder why people who have the brains and ingenuity to think of all this, don't run a legitimate business.'

135

'When I came here first time, guv,' Sandy said. 'I didn't understand what those three oil barrels were doing just stood in this big space.' He wiggled one. 'They're empty, part of the charade, they just fill the space, and when they need to open it all up to bring a stolen car in or take one out, they're moved to one side, just as we've done and its free run in and out.'

'Money,' said Inga Larsson stood there arms folded gazing all around. 'That's what it's all about, and HMRC will just love all this.'

'Sell that four month old Volvo on the continent has to be worth a lot more than fitting a new tyre for some housewife down the village.'

'Here's a thought,' she pondered. 'Has Charles Pritchard also got his grubby mits in this pie I wonder? Got money in Brough Barn, but does it include all this business?'

'D'you think this is a vital ingredient of what's been going on?' Jake asked. 'Somehow, this is the reason Hallam had to be got rid of?'

'Did he get cold feet?'

'Canna imagine with all his bluster,' was suggested by Sandy.

'Seriously worth investigating though or is it sheer chance this fraud was going on at the same time as putting his lights out was being planned by others?'

'Looks as though the three foreign guys we found could well be living upstairs,' said Jake. 'Not sure it's any of this slavery business but turn right in the front door leads you to the stairs.'

'Probably better than being on the streets or living in a tent some place near Calais, came across in a dinghy which is possible if they're illegals. We also think Rumbold the older guy might well kip up there sometimes as well.'

'CSI are on their way, they'll get to the bottom of who was here,' Inga advised them. 'Asked their boss Shona Tate to consider this just might be where Morgan Hallam was done for. Maybe not the actual killing but was this where his body was kept?'

'No kitchen of course as such,' Jake advised. 'Apart from the cooker and washing machine we saw next door,' he pointed back to the main workshop. 'That must have all been ripped out to make more room in there, but upstairs there's like a communal room with a sofa, armchairs and a telly in one room, a bit of crockery, cups and plates, saucepan or two. Plus four bedrooms and a grubby bathroom.'

'Not to mention a fridge in one corner in the main bedroom en-suite well stocked with grub.'

'D'you reckon Deliveroo come this far out?'

'And this their crib?' referring to hip-hop blather made all three chuckle.

23

'This whole business is all too ridiculous for words! We've got a serious person of interest already. Which at any time in a case such as this has to be good news. Of course that would be if he wasn't dead.' Inga Larsson walked over to the two white boards full of photographs Connor Mitchell the Crime Scene Photographer and Nicky Scoley's partner had taken. All of which the gathered throng had looked closely at before Inga began her Sunday morning briefing. 'Let's go through the alternatives one by one,' she said as she moved a few paces to a list of names on a separate board, where she pointed to the FREDERICK ANSELM CURRAN heading. 'What's his connection with Hallam's demise, apart from Morgan's body found tucked up in his bed?'

'For starters he's not on social media,' said Nicky Scoley. 'But then I understand teachers are encouraged not to if they have any sense. Keeps the trolls from making their lives a total misery and pathetic schoolgirls making all sorts of malicious accusations.'

When normally disciplined Jake Goodwin unusually left the room to deal with an incoming call on his personal phone during her briefing, Inga Larsson knew it would be important and made no issue of it. What that did tell her was this was far from the norm for him. His own phone was normally turned off at work and if he did message somebody she knew he absolutely refused to use simpleton's text speak.

'Unless I'm very much mistaken I don't see Curran being involved,' Inga responded to Nicky. 'If you think about it, what would be his motive and why? My feeling is, he's too involved in sorting another house out. Teaching full time and then going hammer and tongs at house conversions non-stop doesn't leave him much time to plan and execute a murder. Next,' she tapped KIRSTEN WROE.

'Wonder when it is he does all this period planning we get told so much about?' Inga ignored.

'Curran's partner and some sort of IT wizz which probably means nothing more than being a monitor monkey networking and glad handing. Does she appear to be more involved simply because she knows Frances Hallam through being friends on social media? Is that her only connection?'

'But denies it.'

'Exactly.'

'Trouble is,' said Michelle Cooper. 'Seems to me you can have so called friends these days who you don't know from the man in the moon.'

'Except,' said Ruth. 'Being in IT, would she just accept anybody d'you think? You always get an option to accept or deny a new friend. Think she'd be more fastidious than the average mobile moron desperate for a like. She'd know all the pitfalls of hanging your dirty washing on something like Twitter, WhatsApp or any of the other platforms to allow it.'

'You're probably right,' said Inga as she ran her finger down the names. 'Which brings us very neatly to this one.' She tapped the name FRANCES JUDITH HALLAM. 'Frances Hallam nee Pritchard, and this to my mind is where it gets interesting. Her father owns a large chunk of Brough Barn Motors Ltd.' The blonde looked across the room. 'Raza, if you will please.'

'Excuse me,' Jake at the door interrupted the briefing holding his mobile in the air. 'Frances Hallam is in labour. Went in during the early hours, more news as it happens.'

'Thank you Sally,' said Inga as if Jake's nurse wife could hear her. 'Raza, you were saying?' She now knew why Jake had not switched off his phone as he tended to, aware of likely news from his wife up at the County.

'According to Company's House, Charles Pritchard owns 52% of the business, his wife owns 10% as does his daughter,' he pointed in the general direction of the photographs. 'Frances. Which leaves a couple of fascinating facts. Morgan Hallam only owned 28% of the shares and interestingly his father, the

139

one done for fraud some time back owns none at all. At least not in his own name.'

'And we've not seen him.'

'Might have been banned from being a director or something when he was locked up,' Jamie suggested from behind his open laptop.

'The two Hallams and Charles Pritchard are the three directors.'

'Question is of course. Who do 28% of the shares go to now?' Inga threw into the mix. 'Pritchards now have control, but and it's a big but, what about all this?' she said as she pointed back at Connor Mitchell's photographs of the garage workshops set-up. 'Was this Morgan Hallam's little sideline? That why he was able to flash the cash? This where he gets his serious money from?'

'Is that easy money which meant he was able to throw his ill-gotten gains about to bring his fantasies to life? Why he was able to afford to buy sexual favours off all sorts?'

'Why the Nun is still on his to do list,' said Raza. 'What's the betting they'd not be impressed by him flashing the cash from his ill-gotten gains? Tell you what,' he put on a voice: 'Give you another couple o'hundred on yours, reckon that Pope fella is doing a good job,' produced a snigger or two.

'Which because she was kept out of the loop with no knowledge of this extra income or how he'd come by it, Frances knew nothing about what he did with it?'

'Pritchard probably thinks it's just a bit of a workshop out in the countryside, if he even knows it exists at all.'

'Here's one for you,' said Inga Larsson stood in front of her team, now with red mug in hand. 'Frances Hallam is until we hear different, still just about pregnant. Who could the father be?' she allowed that to hang before going on. 'What if all this has nothing whatsoever to do with nicking and cloning cars but everything to do with the father of her baby?'

'Accidents happen,' somebody piped up to amuse.

'Dating other men in what friends and family probably consider to be by all accounts a normal marriage, has to be risky,' said Inga. 'Did she get married in order to tie him down legally, to make sure he always came home? Is the Male 5 in

Operation Thanatos the father of the soon-to-be child, and he and Morgan obviously didn't see eye to eye.'

'Is a screaming baby good for your sex life in an open polyamorous marriage?' Jake queried. 'I bet it's not. Vine tomato dip and pink champagne while you're changing the baby's nappy? No chance.'

'Morgan of course would never let her go,' the Detective Inspector continued. 'Because where else was he going to find another woman willing to allow herself to be used in that way. Was she in effect prostituting her body in order to retain her married status in the eyes of her pompous friends and was he scared stiff she and her parents could vote him out of Brough Barn Motors any time they like? Showing off a grandson to her proud parents keeps him very much onside.'

'Thanks for making it easy boss!'

Inga smiled, took a final drink of her almost cold coffee and went on. 'Forget Frederick Curran and Kirsten Wroe. Instead let us concentrate on Mum-to-be Frances Hallam, remember we have her link to DNA in the cottage. Next we have the father of her child…Jake,' she suddenly butted into her own thoughts as she pointed at him. 'We need to know what men visit her in Maternity if Sally would be so kind,' he jotted down. 'Where was I? Oh yes. Male 5 and Charles Pritchard plus,' Inga emphasised by tone. 'Somebody we've not come across who was involved in cloning these vehicles who Morgan then double crossed to get more money in order to have a romp with a four legged, three-eyed green Martian woman!' She looked at Jake. 'Any other news?'

Jake shook his head. 'To be honest,' he said in a somewhat downbeat fashion. 'With all due respect to those present, we seem to have been turned into a branch of the Prisoner Handling Unit. It'll be shoplifting from Boots next. There's one or two of us looking at Rumbolds garage place, plus the Nigerian illegal and those two from Poland somehow involved in cloning cars they've nicked.'

'Could be they just nick them, stuff say a Jag in a container and ship it to North Africa, they reckon that's the hot spot these days.'

'That or stripping them down to flog the parts.'

141

'Easy be a chop shop? Chopping up cars and selling the parts?'

'Looked too tidy for all that,' Jake suggested then pulled a face. 'But having said that, how about we have a nosy around Brough Barn's parts departments, ask to see receipts for the whole shooting match?' Inga exhaled at the thought of the work involved.

'There's a link to Hallam,' she slipped in. 'It's his death remember we're supposed to be investigating. We have as yet no motive and certainly no other serious suspects.'

'Just out of interest Shona Tate the Crime Scene lady yesterday morning handed the house back to Curran.'

'Be difficult to sell it now,' Ruth suggested. 'Quite a lot of people are funny about buying a place somebody's been murdered in.'

'Not be anything like it is now when he's finished, I should imagine. I'd like to get a look at it when he's done, see what he's created, see how good he really is.'

'Who do we have now, apart from the three foreigners the Border Force seem to be taking a look at?' was Inga Larsson back on subject. 'What do we know about Rumbold himself for instance?'

'Derek Robert Rumbold,' Jake announced after bringing him up on screen. 'Actually lives in Middle Rasen. Married with two sons neither of whom just like him are on PNC, but our suspicions are he sometimes dossed down at the house. At least that's what CSI now reckon.'

'We thought that at the time,' Jamie confirmed looking left to Sandy who raised a shoulder in a tiny shrug of confirmation.

'We're having trouble with linking him to Hallam,' Sam admitted. 'Looks to me from what we know as though he just might be a front man. He's the one you see when you turn up with an oil leak.'

'According to folk in the trade around there he's a fully qualified car mechanic, but they doubt if he's up to date with all the electronics these days. Be fine with the basic petrol and diesel apparently.'

'Like what happened when I popped in there,' said big Sandy. 'He was the only one I saw.' He twisted in his seat towards Jake. 'Do we have any idea yet who the guy was who took the dummy parcel off Bill Knapp?'

'No,' Jamie responded. 'As you know he wasn't there when we bashed the door in.'

'To be honest,' said Jake. 'We can find no financial link to Hallam, and there's no limited company we can trace but according to the Land Registry the house is in the name of Morgan Hallam. So looks to me as though Rumbold is just a paid employee and front man. But...'

'There's always one!'

'But,' irked Jake said again. 'According to East Lindsey, Derek Rumbold and his missus are the only ones listed on the Electoral Roll at that address.'

'He on both?' Jamie popped in. 'Can the guy vote from Middle Rasen and Eau House?'

'And with Eau House being owned personally by the Hallams and not by Brough Barn, could mean the others are not involved. This is a private enterprise they ran as a sideline and he paid Rumbold to front it for him.'

'Think Rumbold's problem now is, Hallam would probably have lent him his solicitor, but now he'll have to get a threadbare one of his own.'

'How's Lizzie getting on?' Inga was asked by Jake. 'Has she come up with a serial killer of disabled women or female vicars or anything close?'

'Obviously individual ones, but all by different people, no link to one person going down a list like Hallam seemed to be.'

'Worth a try.'

Inga moved back to the boards and gestured towards a list of names. 'Thank you Ruth,' she acknowledged. 'These are names Ruth has come up with for people somehow linked on social media. Not people we can get onto Facebook about to track down, these are just names mentioned in passing. She tapped ROBBIE SIBBALD, JENKINS, JON-JOE, WARDY, PANTER and STEPHEN. 'Please keep these in the back of your mind like missing persons.' She sighed. 'Might well have no connection but the way this is all going, anything's worth a try,' she shook he head in a dispirited gesture. 'Best way to find the truth is to look for the lies.'

143

Nicky Scoley took an opportunity to offer Jamie Hedley a coffee and sat together in a quiet corner in town she broached the subject of his ex.

'You over all that business with Kerrie?' she posed and sipped and he blew out a breath.

'Guess so.'

'You don't seem too sure.'

'Think I got a problem with women,' was jaded. 'Could be not having a sister doesn't help.'

'In what way?'

Jamie grimaced and look around. 'Mate of mine from way back's been in touch. Wanted to know if I'd take Kerrie back,' he stopped to drink his Americano. 'Just don't understand and…not sure I'd cope. Being with her'd be good but,' he sucked in noisily. 'Cheated on me big time once, could easy do it again and there'd always be Victoria in our lives, that bastard's kid. Be like she'd be there forever as a reminder.' Nicky waited. 'D'you know what the worst thing is, why didn't she ask me? Why not get in touch, but no she asks one of me friends to ask on her behalf.' He sat there shaking his head. 'Still with that Joey Foskett almost as if she wants to cheat on him with me.' Jamie looked at his DS as if he was looking for reassurance he was right.

'Don't know her of course,' Nicky admitted. 'But can't see it working to be honest. If she was really keen, ready and willing to admit her mistake surely she'd be knocking on your door. Think you need to be looking elsewhere.' The look on Jamie's face spoke volumes. 'Go on.'

'Suzie Gough organized a sort of blind date.'

'What d'you mean sort of?' Nicky sniggered with.

'We went for a drink and she brought along a mate.' He grimaced. 'Nice girl. Only trouble is, this mate brought along a friend as well.'

'And?' was asked as he drank his coffee.

'Suzie's got a partner of course. This Lisa's quite nice, but it's her mate I really fancy.'

'And that's a problem?'

'I have no way to contact her for starters, except through Suzie. Will she get upset I've not chosen her friend, so I need to get her details somehow...and she's coloured.'

'Problem?'

'Not for me. No, but my mum's not at all happy with all these foreigners. Illegals coming over by boat and in lorries. Be her generation s'pose.'

'Have you spoken to her about this...?

'Ashley,' he filled the gap with. 'Haven't got in touch with her yet!'

'Not just arrived in a dinghy at Dover has she?' made Jamie smile. 'First things first. Speak to Suzie. She'll understand, I'm sure she will.' Nicky drank her cappuccino. 'Anything else bothering you?'

'Think that's enough to be going on with' he sniggered.

24

On the Monday morning with the Olympics over. Climate change had taken centre stage along with the torid Covid news once more amongst the headlines. Pubs and clubs thronging with drunks, and football crowds back, meant the pandemic had once more returned as a serious cause for concern.

In an attempt to gain background information about the car cloning business DCs Sandy MacLachlan and Sam Howard had been sent across to Middle Rasen to chat with Derek Rumbold's dainty wife Faye, in their post-war semi in the village.

On the way Sam couldn't help but go on about a story emanating from PHU where he was usually based, about a thief being jailed after being caught stealing a jacket on his way to court on shoplifting charges.

This Peter Dunn-Prone stole the jacket from Primark when he was on his way down to the Magistrates Court in Lincoln High Street to be sentenced for other shoplifting offences.

Derek Rumbold himself was out on bail, and on a whim the pair had decided to give his place a quick check over. In plain sight is often a clue to be missed.

Waiting in Sam's unmarked Escort for half an hour they then saw Rumbold leave home, get into a car which had pulled up and he was driven off.

Sandy had already checked out the property. It was Derek Rumbold and his wife on the deeds and according to the property history they'd been the owners for a little over fourteen years.

This was one of those cases where having already met her scruffy, unkempt whiskered husband they never expected a neat and tidy well groomed slim woman of some intelligence to meet them at the door.

To her credit she had made an effort with highlights in her pale brown hair and a pink lipstick. Not at all what either detective was expecting.

Sandy made the chatty conversation all extremely casual by stroking her ginger cat and suggesting as an essential component of the recently revised justice system these days, they were there in an attempt to understand his personal situation in order to keep the prison population down from record levels of the past.

By inference MacLachlan indicated to Faye of some foreign extraction, how her husband might well get off with a fine or a community order as the authorities felt he was not personally involved in cloning cars.

After ten minutes chat casually Sam asked the woman if he might avail himself of her toilet which she innocently agreed to and he trooped off upstairs.

Back in the Escort heading down the A46 for Lincoln they both knew Larsson's missing persons had not been hidden away there unless he or she had been up in the loft and there were no clues they could spot to suggest anybody else had been there of late.

There's not much CCTV out in the countryside, even so it is still mighty difficult to just disappear into thin air. Airports and docks the pair knew had been checked.

Back at Lincoln Sandy and Sam were settled back in the Incident Room when Jake Goodwin became the centre of attention.

The sequence on his phone went from an IT'S A GIRL text, to one saying GOING HOME TOMOZ AFTERS all courtesy of Lincoln County Hospital staff member the whole Major Incident Team knew well. DI Inga Larsson took it upon herself to make a note to call Mrs Hallam in a day or two to arrange another interview with this new mummy.

A message later was not the good news Inga was hoping for, as Jake's wife Sally reported to Jake how so far only Charles and Margaret Pritchard had visited their daughter up at Lincoln County Maternity.

Three days later, a tanned Margaret Pritchard was there fussing around her daughter in the huge barn of a place out in Osbournby on the outskirts of Sleaford. The big house proved useful as she was able to take Niamh Siobhan her new grizzly granddaughter, out into the objectionably large conservatory and leave DI Inga Larsson and DS Nicky Scoley alone with Hallam in the open plan dining area, sat at the big oak table.

A constant cause for concern for Inga Larsson was this current predilection for post-pandemic hugging. She had been brought up on the premise that a gentle handshake was quite enough but not now. Keeping your physical attraction to a minimum was always her way, therefore social distancing had never been an issue. She'd even seen her mother Christal take a step back if somebody tried to grab hold.

As far as the cheek kissing business is concerned, with the DI it is best not to go there, with it being a sure way to humiliate yourself in Stockholm. It was now even less prevalent with the French seeing sense at last and ditching the habit.

Inga is always happy with people being nice and friendly but Swedes are suspicious when people use doting words such as "love", "darling" and in Lincolnshire the "Pet" tripe she reserves for dogs and cats. It immediately tells the recipient you don't know their name and in essence you are fake, with all such nonsense you are trying to exude for some reason.

Fortunately for them both there had been no such gibberish in this case.

Was it really necessary Inga wondered to stick a white plastic conservatory monstrosity onto a delightful American style converted barn? She guessed with her need to remain on-trend with her fancy friends the Hallam woman'd most probably have needed to go for a woodburner and roll top bath rather than be original in her choices. What the Detective Inspector had managed to see so far apart from the white plastic barnacle, had unfolded so well. Maybe she had misjudged the woman.

Larsson had decided to undertake this interview almost purely due to her also being a new mum. She allowed the inevitable baby talk to last just about as long as she intended, without getting too involved in all the tediousness of it all some

148

tend to rabbit on about. Despite there being no suggestion of refreshment she decided there had been enough mundane talk of the torment of labour, graphic placenta detail and birth canals.

Nicky Scoley was particularly pleased when the small talk ran out of steam.

'Reason we're here Frances is to discuss the fact your DNA has unfortunately been discovered in the main bedroom of the new Curran house.' She managed to stop herself adding *"where Morgan's battered body was discovered"*. 'Are you able to explain how that could possibly be?' Inga Larsson knew this was in fact a familial DNA hit probably from a father or brother.

There was nothing to be gained in situations like that, by going into all the practical business of low template DNA, where each string of which has a particular marker to do with genetic make-up. Such technicalities of which the public generally like Hallam, are unfamiliar with.

No matter, the question still required an answer in order for their enquiries to progress. Larsson was fully aware this woman needed handling in the right way. She was sure to be wary of getting involved with the Police. Asking her to wear a mask would likely be a step too far in her own home.

'I've no idea.'

'What about your father?' blonde Larsson asked from the iPad aide memoire on her lap.

'Don't see the connection.'

'We understand your father is co-owner of Brough Barn Motors, so he has a vested interest in both the business and Morgan I would imagine.'

'What are you suggesting?' she scowled and looked away.

'We're not suggesting anything Mrs Hallam,' said Larsson giving out the thinnest of smiles.

'My father is a very successful and extremely busy businessman and Brough Barn is just one of many ventures he's involved in.'

'But it is possible he could have visited? We're talking familial remember.'

'Hardly,' she chuckled and Larsson doubted if she fully understood. 'He was on a cruise. In fact they arrived back from Singapore and Indonesia on that Sunday.'

'Alright for some.' It had not escaped Larsson's attention how this woman had slipped in name dropping rather than just saying they'd been on a cruise.

'I could do with a spot of that right now, to be honest.'

Dressed immaculately, fully made up there'd be no guessing she had recently given birth. Dressed to impress had to be her watchword.

Sat there Inga wondered if she'd used a doula, a birth coach who some claim can offer support during pregnancy. Be the sort of business someone like her would go for she decided by the look of her, simply in order to brag to friends.

When she'd first heard about this fad of a doula coach in the early weeks of her own pregnancy, Inga had tried to imagine how she'd need to turn up for training in the kit she planned to wear for the birth and after a jog round discuss tactics for the big event.

'To be honest, it was only found in the main bedroom according to my forensic people.' Larsson took the opportunity to look past Hallam out into the garden. The pristine look of the lawns and wonderful flower beds said they had a gardener. No way would she be out in garden shoes digging in the borders, mowing, raking or potting on seedlings in the greenhouse. With acres of land and a paddock Frances had told them about, maybe it was a team of gardeners.

'Where did you get my DNA?' Hallam said breaking the silence.

'How about Kirsten's parents then?' Larsson asked ignoring the question. 'What do you know about them?'

'Who?' Frances released with a breath and for once appeared slightly confused, by the answer.

'Are you saying you don't know them? The father and mother of a friend of yours, possibly for many years?'

'Why should I?'

'Because you've known her a long time. Because she's a friend you've more than likely met up with on a regular basis.

Her never having mentioned them does seem a bit strange I have to say.'

'D'you know, I don't think she has.' Frances was pondering that fact as she went to respond some more but Larsson hadn't finished.

'Or is this all just the same as the place out near North Carlton you claim to have never visited, but it has your DNA plastered all over it?' wasn't exactly true.

'Don't think she ever has,' lacked enthusiasm.

'Never has what, Frances?' now Larsson was struggling.

'Have you destroyed my fingerprints?' was most certainly off the wall.

'Not our department,' Nicky Scoley chirped in with. 'All part of the forensics remit.'

'Can we return to Kirsten's parents, please?' was Larsson's attempt to regain control.

'Her parents? Now let me think,' said Frances and took a moment or two before she continued. 'She might have mentioned them, but I don't remember. Certainly never met them. What did you say their names were?'

'You tell us,' said Larsson smiling. When there was no telling she moved on. 'Can we look at the email you so kindly supplied detailing your movements. We will need details of a few of the people you mention.'

'Why in God's name?'

'In order to quantify what you say, that you were indeed where you say you were.'

She only lost her poise for a brief moment. 'That's not fair,' Hallam insisted. 'Really it's not. There's absolutely no need whatsoever to involve these good people. Think I need to talk to my solicitor.'

'Your prerogative of course Frances, but at the end of the day you will still need to confirm to us who these people are and all their whys and wherefores that involves, including addresses and phone numbers.'

Inga was taking the opportunity to look at the sheer clarity of her skin and without prior knowledge realized it would be near to impossible to recognize she was wearing a wig. Her clothes cost an arm and a leg and she reckoned to herself the wig would certainly be a great deal more.

'It appears from what you detailed,' said Larsson when her Detective Sergeant had taken it all down. 'You have a very busy social life. Is it always as busy as it was over that period? Hardly a day went by when you weren't out for lunch.'

'I've always had a penchant for eating out,' Larsson knew was total nonsense. She'd gone from a three-bed downtrodden semi on what at one time would have been deemed a 'Council Estate,' to university which would entail not much more than pot noodles, alcohol and kebabs to her loss of hair which had fortunately for her elevated her into a world of fine dining with Morgan.

'Liberate,' said Larsson. 'Tell me about it.'

'It's a charity I've become very much involved in.' Michelle who had researched it for Inga had talked about auctions, dinner dances and afternoon tea events. Nothing as basic and tawdry as organizing a Bring and Buy Sale, running a cake stall or shaking a tin. 'We organize all sorts of events to raise funds to better the plight of refugees. We can't hope to deal with the homelessness and devastation they face, or the long trek to reach our shores. However, we are able to provide help in a good number of ways physically and mentally.' She took in a breath. 'And we're here to greet them.'

'No matter how illegal they might be?' the DI could not help but say. 'All about the plight of these economic immigrants, you mean?'

'Have we finished?' was the reaction of a defeated woman. It was as if she was working hard to keep a grip on her composure.

'Almost,' said Larsson. 'One last question. You told our Family Liaison officer you woke up on that Saturday to discover your husband had not returned home.'

'And?' she queried as she shook her head slightly.

'If Morgan was out and about here there and everywhere chasing these women, how would you honestly know where he was supposed to be at any given time?'

'Because of the basis of our relationship.'

Larsson had to bite her tongue. This was an opportunity to ask about her marriage, about the poly whatever it was business. About her sleeping with a whole host of different men and Morgan's penchant for his bucket list of conquests he'd never completed.

'I'd no need to check up on my husband, but I knew what he was doing. All to do with trust.'

'You really happy with him squeezing women's buttocks?' was wrapped in elements of sarcasm.

'Yes thank you. Absolutely.'

'And your daughter?'

'Fine,' was all Larsson decided to say.

'Make it my business. Know the enemy,' answered Larsson's questions.

'You see us as the enemy? Might I ask why that would be?'

'You need to look in the attitude and yesteryear mirrors. Not just you of course,' her eyes never left Larsson's. 'Your whole damn shooting match is in desperate need of a calendar for this year.'

'What do you imagine that would tell us?' Larsson's snigger was deliberately wholesome.

'You and your sort are completely out of touch, living in the past in a world that's moved on long long ago. Remember I know how you think, know not being successful hinders people like you and leaves you wallowing in yesterday's mire. Why otherwise would you still be laboriously arresting a few toerags for smoking weed when the whole damn world's using? It's all too ridiculous for words.'

'Frances…' she tried.

'Morgan to his credit was a strict disciplinarian. Believed children must be taught right from wrong. Should be seen and not heard. Stop bits of kids taking phones to school, they need to walk or bike to school because somebody has to stop that ridiculous school run business.' She stopped to chuckle. 'How many people have I heard chuntering on about climate change yet they still ferry lazy kids to school, block the roads twice a day and polluting the atmosphere while they do it.'

'But,' Larsson tried. 'To be fair some of them do live a good way from their school,' even though basically she agreed with the woman.

'So?' was shot back. 'Move closer to school it's not rocket science! Goodness me. We now live in a society where a large chunk of the population are feral and untamed. I'm sure you'll agree that was plainly obvious through that pandemic. It was those types who constantly broke the rules, who had to party and get drunk, wouldn't wear masks or socially distance. The very same group of menacing individuals and gangs who dial 999 for the Fire Brigade and then throw stones at them. Same shower who attack paramedics and their ambulances caring for the dying, who hassle nurses and doctors. Even heard about a gang of them chucking stuff at people in boats trying to rescue people from their homes during floods. Time to bring back the cane, stop all this mamby-pamby no smacking stupidity from these snowflakes.'

'Mrs…' Scoley tried to butt in.

'This,' she went on pointing at the DS. 'Has all come about since they stopped giving the cane and created ridiculously soppy rules about giving kids a good hiding, not because of it.'

'How do you think this is connected,' Larsson managed when she took a breath.

'Be some politically correct twerps making a fortune with all that utter nonsense. Sort of hogwash we've got from bits of kids getting half-baked psychology degrees who see it as a way to make an easy buck if they ever come off their phones. They've created a divided society we didn't have years ago when strict rules of behaviour was the way to bring up children. There were none of these stabbings and gangs of reprobates with drugs outside schools. Children need disciple and they respect it.'

'You think they attacked your husband?'

'Who else is there, who else had he upset? He was murdered for telling the truth.' It was obvious how Morgan had been the moving force Frances had constructed her life around.

'What evidence do you have?'

'Stop all this politically correct garbage,' was not an answer. 'And you lot can stop dishing out a slapped wrist as punishment.'

'Interesting ideas.'

'Dixon of Dock Green died you know, or didn't they tell you?' Larsson hadn't a clue who he or she might be.

'I'll send my condolences. Thank you,' said Larsson and was on her feet with Scoley following suit. 'Unlike you Mrs Hallam I know exactly which beautiful woman my husband's hands are stroking and kneading right now and where and how she will ultimately benefit from his personal one-to-one intimate attention. However, it seems to me you had absolutely no idea yours was even missing.'

'How do you make that out?'

'You just went off to bed with more tortuous thoughts of some lithesome buxom wench and what they were up to.'

'You have no idea what you're talking about,' said Hallam as the pair reached the door.

'Maybe not, but what I do know is, he was more than likely cheating on you with half the county. Thank you.'

In her car Nicky Scoley was just about able to explain who *Dixon of Dock Green* was, but only by checking with Goggle as a reminder.

'She's involved with the suffering of refugees,' said Inga. 'Just been thinking. Makes life a great deal easier for him if Morgan had one listed.'

25

'You look down in the dumps,' Inga Larsson suggested to Nicky Scoley sat chin in hands, elbows on her desk just staring at her monitor.

'Not the only one,' said slim auburn Julie Rhoades acting in a similar way opposite her.

'Anything I can help with at all?'

'Trying to discover anything we can about this Stephen Jenkins who appears to be Frances Hallam's brother.'

'Where'd that come from?'

'Ruth,' was good to hear. 'And to add to it, I'm still at ground zero hunting down Kirsten Wroe's parents.'

'Can ASBO throw any light on it?'

Some of her team bear fruit constantly, but some unfortunately don't. Scoley was one of those she could rely on to always produce a good crop.

'Just look at this,' said Nicky flicking fingers across her keyboard. 'This is him, except it isn't,' was just the basic silhouette Facebook use rather than a photograph when contributors fail to provide one. 'Problem is, one of ASBO'S sidekicks checked it for me and we finish up with an IP address in an internet café. They're onto Facebook for us but that'll take forever. Too busy dealing with racist abuse cases.'

'How about you kill two birds with one stone, ladies? Head off out to North Carlton and chat to Kirsten Wroe about her parents?'

'Unless she has something to hide.'

'Exactly, and then just mention Frances Hallam's brother, see what she says. Bang the door and see what ops out. I'm sure you two can make the whole thing very chatty and casual.'

'Unless they're dead,' Julie offered.

Jake Goodwin an observer on this occasion will admit he is very much old school with mobile phone use in the way he uses his device as he has always done. Just for urgent calls and texts. It was so obvious others felt much better if their phone was within touching distance rather than as in his case in his jacket pocket.

He had certainly never quite got the social media frenzied world so many live by, and is not even a late developer. Not for him life in less than bite-sized chunks for those claiming short attention spans.

He can never fathom why so many treat clips of complete nonsense on their phones as vital news everybody just has to view, as something he should be in the slightest bit interested in.

Knowing his in-built discipline Jake was of course also part of a gathering trend of selfie refuseniks. To him all that twaddle was all about recording life's important moments until you lose them all down the toilet or get it snatched.

When Inga Larsson had reported back with her conversation with Frances Hallam he had an opinion.

'Morgan was right to a certain extent,' was not unexpected from Jake. 'As a nation we're not disciplined enough and the main reason we had the most Covid deaths in Europe. Raves, an obsession with parties and getting drunk spread it like wildfire. Not to mention refusing to wear masks and socially distancing and don't get me started on refusing to shut the borders.' He stopped momentarily. 'But having said that, I'd not go as far as beating children. People like that tend to be very selfish, thinking only of themselves. Which I have to say is at odds with Morgan's predatory list.'

'Wonder if all this discipline of his came to the fore in their marriage?' was a thought from Nicky.

'Teachers beating kids with a stick is seriously not good news, but we do seriously need to become stricter,' Jake went on. 'Tyler has a set of rules he abides by, we have taught him right from wrong and I guess sometimes he hates me for it, not allowing the freedom his pals have, but in the long rung he will be the benefactor.'

157

'Discipline has to start in the home, and we need to punish these feckless parents for not doing their job properly.'

'He'll walk or bike to school,' Jake added. 'Because as we all know more kids are killed in accidents on the school run than biking or walking to school. It's a no brainer. And it'll be a long time until he has a phone.'

'Stop him being targeted by paedophiles or some of that Tik-Tok nausea,' Raza Latif with children of his own added.

'School run nonsense,' said Inga. 'Is a bit like millennium burglaries. Idiots leaving their car on the drive rather than in the garage and then are gobsmacked when it's nicked'

Two dirty vans, their target's orange Nissan Micra, Freddie Curran's blue Ford and a cement mixer meant DS Nicky Scoley had to park some way away from the garden gate in front of the house out at North Carlston.

She had phoned Kirsten to ascertain where she would be and to her credit appeared from round the side of the property as soon as they arrived, dressed in a rough dirty man's denim shirt, dungarees and old Doc Marten boots.

Scoley knew Shona Tate's CSI team had found nothing untoward in the garden, front or back. A crisp packet, fag ends and the inevitable drinks can. Hardly surprising bearing in mind who'd lived there previously and the lane petered out in another fifty yards or more.

They agreed under the circumstances it would be best for all concerned if they chatted in Nicky's Mini.

'How's it going?' the Detective Sergeant asked once they were comfortable and masked-up.

'Right now, plasterers are patching up the walls where they knocked connecting doors through to the new en-suite. Next they'll be filling in the concrete floor in the bathroom before that gets done.'

'You'll need a holiday after all this.' Kirsten just chortled slightly. 'Freddie alright?'

'Yeh, fine. Working too hard, but what else is new?'

'Sorry about disturbing you like this,' said young Scoley to the woman sat beside her. 'We're still trying to piece things together to some extent, and somebody mentioned you've not given us any details about your family. Your parents.'

'Any reason why I should?'

'To be honest, because of forensics. We have unknown DNA from in there,' she gestured. 'And we have fingerprints we cannot match to anyone.' When Kirsten failed to react but just sat hands clasped between her thighs peering out of the windscreen, Nicky went on. 'We're looking at people who might have possibly been here in the intervening period. We've covered Roger and Cynthia Teesdale the couple who previously owned the property. You and Freddie of course and his parents plus one or two others we've discounted and that leaves your parents.'

'No.'

'No what?'

'Not been here.'

'Never?'

'Never.'

'Can you tell me why?'

'Because they haven't, that's why.'

'Is there any particular reason?' Scoley asked as she turned in her seat to look directly at Kirsten just sat there peering through the windscreen. 'Live far away then do they?' Nicky noticed all the ivy encroaching on the front door had been cut well back.

'I assume you've told them what's happened,' Julie Rhoades queried from the back seat.

'No idea,' was mumbled without her looking up.

'Fair enough,' said the Sergeant. 'We'll return to that later. We had hoped to keep these visits as infrequent as we can with all the work you've got on, but there you go.' Scoley paused. 'Frances Hallam's family. Can we look at them instead, please?'

Wroe reacted immediately. 'Bastards are a bunch of Jehovah Witnesses, that what you wanted eh?' was spiky as her head spun round.

'Her family are?' Scoley gasped her question. Why had nobody mentioned that before?

'No,' was louder. 'My bloody stupid parents. That's who.'

159

Nicky paused for a moment. 'Your parents are Jehovah Witnesses?'

'That's what I said,' was irritable. 'Well actually they belong to this odd-ball Fellowship a sort of peculiar adjunct to the mainstream,' all of which explained an edge of bitterness to her voice.

'And is that why they've not visited?'

'They've not visited anywhere we've lived,' she responded. 'They've never even met Freddie for goodness sake because he's unclean and with us living in sin and us being non-believers in their Fellowship hogwash, we've got no chance. On their scale of ten we get nil point. Even Stephen Hawkings said there's no such thing as God or an afterlife. And he was hardly an atheist crank.'

'I take it you don't get on,' was an understatement.

'You can say that again!' she sniggered. 'Not seen them in years so they've got nothing to do with any of this business.'

'Thank you,' said Scoley and smiled gently when Kirsten's head turned towards her. 'How about Frances's family?'

'Fancy dan parents, bit cranky.'

'In what way?'

'Her really. Maggie Pritchard has got herself into a way of life which really makes little sense in this day and age. Well, not to me anyway. All done up to the nines all the time of course, swanking about, lunching with the Mayoress and silliness like that she can brag about. It's all pretence with her, and the truth is in reality she's as common as muck, so I've heard.' Kirsten seemed to have relaxed. 'Sorry I can't offer you a cuppa,' she said as she glanced towards the open front door past the cement mixer going round and round.

'That's no problem. We fully understand.'

Nicky now realized what had been bugging her since she'd first arrived. Something was different. The mullioned windows on the first floor had been changed she suddenly realized.

'Margaret Pritchard,' Wroe said returning to subject. 'One irregular thing about her is the way she shops. Everything does or buys is purely for show which you can do if you have more money than sense. Heard one time she wanted a new dishwasher,' she stopped to shake her head. 'Just for the two of them? I ask you. Anyway, she paid way over the odds for the very same one you can get delivered by people like Curry's any day at half the price, but had to get it from some little bloke out of town. Paid top dollar of course.'

'Why?' Scoley filled the gap with.

'According to her, better quality.' Kirsten giggled. 'Absolute nonsense of course, they're all the same, they all come off the same production line for goodness sake. Paid well over a hundred or more for a bloody kettle one time. It boils water just the same as mine does! Buys pumpkins to hand out once a year to kids at some charity she supports which is fine and good on her. Except not far away is the biggest pumpkin grower there is anywhere who supplies almost the entire country every year. Does she go to him and get a good deal for the kids charity? No. Had to go to this market gardener bloke in the depths of the countryside and pay top dollar because...' she grinned. 'Again.'

'Quality.'

'Exactly. It's like she thinks each supermarket has its own nursery, which we all know is just nonsense,' she said. 'My mother knew a man who worked for Smiths Crisps at one time. He told her he got people forever telling him the Marks and Spencer crisps were heaps better than Smiths, which thoroughly amused him. They were exactly the same crisps, just different packets, that's all. She's like that with everything and it's all this "pumpkins came from my dear friend Arthur Conn of course, you just can't beat quality" and half the time according to Frances she doesn't finish up with anything like a quality product, just pays through the nose all the time. Says apples from one store last heaps longer than others, when the chances are they came from not only the same grower but the same tree. But then she does go shopping with a Harrods carrier bag over her arm.'

'Brothers and sisters?' Scoley reminded.

'I was just going to say,' Kirsten went on. 'Her charity work really sums her up. Rather than raise funds for say the local hospice or sponsoring somebody in the Race For Life she spends her time raising money for a charity which is into start-up projects in Gambia.' She gave a wry smile. 'Thinks people are impressed I guess. There's pretentious and then there's Mary Pritchard.'

'Brothers and sisters?' was a reminder.

'Not heard of any. Why?'

'Still trying to puzzle who the DNA belongs to. What about a brother, Stephen Jenkins?'

'Never heard of him,' she grimaced slightly. 'Who's he?'

'A name we've come across, that's all. Wondered if it might ring a bell.'

'What gives you the idea she might have a brother and his DNA would be in there?' she said and waved her hand in the direction of the house.

'We've discovered a weak link to a brother on social media,' was no answer. 'What about yours?'

'Brother and sisters you mean?'

'Yes please.'

'One of each unfortunately.'

'Why unfortunately?'

'Never see them,' Wroe admitted and then she paused to gather emphasis. 'Saw Luke and Naomi just before I took my second year exams at university. By then I'd realized the life my parents had planned out for me was not at all what I wanted. Knew it would hold my career back. So, after the drudgery of Easter at home I headed off back to uni, bought my first ever Easter egg I gobbled down on the train and never returned. Feel sorry for my siblings having no Christmas or birthdays and no beer or chocolate,' she grinned. 'Been taken in by it all and no matter what their hearts might want them to do, there's no way they'd come anywhere near me. I'm the devil incarnate,' came out as a forlorn cry.

'I'm so sorry.'

'Kirsten's not my given name,' she suddenly admitted more softly. 'Changed it when I left Swansea.' Both detectives had to wait. 'Mary,' she gave a slight sigh. 'From the Bible of course, I dropped to stop people asking too many questions. Told people it was with it being too close to Mary Rose and people got confused by it and a bunch of lads called me captain all the time. Worst thing you can do is have a name nobody can understand let alone spell.' Made little sense to Scoley as surely it was the Wroe causing issues or was changing that a far more difficult process?

There was further discussion about works going on before they left, but they'd only seen one person at the cement mixer then taking bucket loads indoors. No sight of her Freddie though but guessed her had to be there with his car parked behind theirs.

'Changing her name,' said freckled Julie now sat in the front on their way back to base. 'She says was confusing?'

'Exactly what I thought, but I'm not sure that's quite what she meant. At least we know why we've struggled to find any background on her. Guess the Jehovah Joe shower answer a lot of our questions.'

'Was that to stop her father maybe tracking her down? Always possible there were stalking issues.'

'They do that? These religious groups.'

'No idea. Could always be a Jehovah Mob, I suppose. Spend their time hiding behind hedges to make sure you knock on enough people's doors to annoy them.'

'Little job when we get back. You need to feed her original name onto the system.'

Nicky had noticed when she'd first met her how Wroe was wearing a crucifix on a chain and had suspected a god-botherer until she'd come out with all that Fellowship business.

The detective assumed now she was C of E or Catholic and all this religious sect business was repugnant to her. In need of a spiritual connection as some do, she'd jumped trains to join the main line.

Nicky Scoley had hoped to delve into this Stephen Jenkins using her own initiative and information she had picked up during a period spent up with the eTeam to increase her skill set.

Part of her problem was, she was used to delving into her own family history and working within the limits set for the public in order to ensure individuals' privacy remained intact.

Time once more to brave the geeks and seek the help of Adrian (Adrian Simon Bruce Orford) generally known to all and sundry as ASBO. To glean as much as she could from the painfully thin and pasty faced chief geek with little or no dress sense. To remind her of systems to find, gather and analyze data from the web.

It was always interesting to see which of his vast array of slogan t-shirts he was wearing. That day it was a new black one, or at least one Nicky had not had the pleasure of before, with BITS, BYTES AND DATA ANALYTICSprinted in yellow.

To look at him in the street you'd have no idea Dr Orford possessed BSc Masters degrees in both Artificial Intelligence and Computer Science.

Once he got down to it Nicky began to recall past lessons when she'd spent months in the department and the boffins introduced her to more advance systems she would need. He initially provided her with a reminder of how she could bypass the golden one hundred year rule which excludes the public from all censuses since early last century.

Then it was an open source intel refresher reminding Nicky of her real-world skills, techniques and the tools she needed to scour the massive intelligence fabric strewn across the internet.

A couple of hours spent with the IT guru who was going through one of his bizarre eating and drinking stages. This time he was limiting himself to drinking just hot water during the day as he always did, but on this occasion chewing on sticks of liquorice.

Although she'd experienced it before, ASBO's behavior still had an effect on Nicky, with a constant nagging feeling she really should not have nipped down to the canteen for a cappuccino and a small pack of chocolate digestives while he was supping from a steaming hot mug of nothing much.

Starting with Morgan Arthur Hallam using the new formulae provided by her liquorice chomper colleague, she was able to track him down on the 2011 census, then transfer her search back to when Frances appeared on the scene. From her first appearance on a census with him it was an easy jump from their marriage certificate to her parents and her birth certificate and Nicky was, head down, coffee at hand onto a Frances Miranda but no brother.

164

Although ASBO had assured her what she was doing could not be traced back to her, in her mind she did query the statutory need for a court order he'd just chuckled about, in a way that said such authoritarian nonsense had no place in his world.

She ploughed on and census records showed only the three of them back in 2001, but from there she used another ASBO formula to look at marriage certificates. This gave her a Margaret Louisa Jenkins to make a simple leap to birth certificates as easy as falling off a log, and hey presto there was a Stephen Jon-Joe Jenkins.

Nicky quickly briefed Ruth Buchan on a task for her to keep her involved and called out loud enough for Inga Larsson to hear in her office.

'Found him!' she announced. 'Born April 1980 at the Croft Baker Maternity Home in Cleethorpes,' she read from her monitor. 'Got a son for Frances's mother born out of wedlock. Stephen. The name mentioned once on Facebook. Stephen Jon-Joe Jenkins,' made Jake Goodwin pull a face.

His own name had caused him all sorts of problems over the years and he always felt sorry with those stuck with silly gimmicky monikers.

'And there's more,' Ruth called out to an audience now all ears

'Stephen Jon-Joe Jenkins, did nine months in a young offenders' for TWOC and driving without insurance, in Grimsby in 1997. He'd be about 17 then.'

'Photo on PNC,' said DS Scoley feeling as pleased as Punch. 'Anybody recognize him? Was he one of those at the workshop?' she queried towards Jake and Jamie who both trooped over to have a peep.

She knew he wasn't, as Custody had photographed them all and the faces were on display on the boards to her right.

Nicky and Ruth sat back arms folded and waited while the room-full all linked themselves onto the system or switched focus to seek out the Jenkins profile.

There were suggestions from one or two about having an inkling they might have seen him about, but nothing at all of a serious positive nature.

Fifteen minutes later while Nicky attempted to unravel as much detail about him as she could, Jake Goodwin who had strode away from the Incident Room, returned.

'Guess what? Could well be our luck's in. Bill Knapp reckons he just might be the guy who took the bogus parcel off him at the garage. Much younger of course, but…' Jake pulled a face. 'Can't be absolutely sure. It's a good few years since his mug shot.'

'Hang on a sec,' was Inga Larsson at her door. 'I thought we got prints off the machine he took with him.'

'But we don't have his. Minor offence at that age, chances are they destroyed the prints after five years or so.'

'Let me get this straight,' said Inga. 'Margaret Pritchard nee Jenkins has a son out of wedlock…'

'Naughty, naughty,' Jake chirped in with.

'Before she married Charles Pritchard. Then later had Frances we assume with Charles.'

'Ma'am,' said Ruth. 'Why in this day and age do we still get all bothered about this wedlock business? Most kids born today arrive out of wedlock anyway.'

'They're still wee bastards.'

'Sandy!' was a rebuke from the boss.

'Yes she did,' said Nicky. 'Both names on her birth certificate at least. Got to say, Kirsten Wroe was telling us this Margaret is a silly pretentious cow, who spends her time wasting money just to show off to friends for some reason. Wonder how her fancy friends would view her if they knew of her past?' She turned round to look at Ruth. 'That's when wedlock comes into play, when we're dealing with some pompous bitch like her, who's no better than she should be.'

'Give them something to talk about over their Lapsang Souchong, and chopped shallot sandwiches!' Inga dropped in with a chuckle then allowed the silence to draw on. When she spoke again she was more positive. 'This makes Stephen Jenkins her illegitimate son,' she put her hand up. 'I know what you're saying Ruth, but it's true no matter how you look at it. Google the word and see what you get even now.' she turned back to her audience. 'And, it has to be him working for Morgan Hallam, we think?' Inga scanned the room for further reaction which was not forthcoming.

'Looks like it.'

'How does that work?' was Inga asking herself as well as her team. 'Morgan Hallam and Charles Pritchard are in partnership and they just happen by chance to employ Frances's half-brother her mother's bastard son. That what we're saying are we?'

'Or how about this?' Nicky Scoley queried. 'Margaret pleads with Charles to give her son a job. Been in trouble with us in his youth, out of work and on Universal Credit if he's lucky maybe. So, Charles takes the fella into his family and into one of his businesses. Am I thinking right?' Inga looked at Nicky and offered a smile of acceptance.

'But maybe this was all Morgan if Pritchard really knows nothing about the chop shop nicked motor business.'

'Stephen's father is who exactly?' the boss queried.

'Blank.'

'Brilliant!' she responded as a breath spread itself out.

'So far,' Nicky offered. 'But ma'am, 'she added. 'Stephen Jenkins never appears on any census as living in the Pritchard household, at least not at the time when the census was taken. In fact he is not listed on any at all I've come across as yet.'

'Just our luck he wasn't out there when we kicked the door in,' Jake was shaking his head and sighing with frustration. 'Fantastic.'

'What's the betting he's keeping his head down now,' Sandy MacLachlan suggested.

'Another thought,' was Jamie. 'Not on a census, but is he on Council Tax anywhere? HMRC got him?'

'Nicky, please keep checking him. Now you're our qualified nerd, if you find him and I'll buy you a slickepinne for Christmas!'

'Non comprendi,' she shot back and chuckled.

'Lollipop.'

'I thought geeks always sucked on liquorice!'

'Not good.'

'Why?'

'Diarrhoea and high blood pressure.'

'Nice.'

26

Kirsten

D'you know it's that sort of intrusion which seriously annoyed me about all this police business. This bunch just couldn't care less that they were just trampling all over our lives and it seemed at times, mine in particular.

Are they like that because the ones I've come across are female? Is this the new way because all this diversity business is getting out of hand? Recruit more women the world is asking for, but then the men at the top use them to inveigle their way in. They think maybe we'll not notice, not say anything because they're on side with our thinking? Certainly worth considering.

There is absolutely no way my goddam stupid religion locked parents would ever visit me anywhere. It had always been a serious case of don't darken my door again particularly with my father, but I cannot imagine that blonde copper Scoley could ever begin to understand.

To be honest as far as I'm concerned what has gone on between me and that pair over the years is absolutely none of their damn business. If I'd had trouble with parents from any other religion what's the chances there'd be some protest group backing me all the way. Not with the Fellowship crowd there's not.

I'd decided after a great deal of thought, if I don't tell them when they start poking their noses in again, they're going to make a real issue about it.

Why did two of them have to turn up at the house? The other one, whatever her name was hardly spoke a damn word. What's the betting she'd be the witness just in case I gave that blonde madam a good smacking?

I do have to say, up to then things had gone very quiet. Which to some extent was useful to us. We had been handed back the keys to the house by those forensic people of course and now Freddie had been able to get on with all the work he had planned. Several days late according his schedule, but some of the people he was dealing with such as sub-contractors were really extremely co-operative under the circumstances. Probably because they were short of work.

Moving back in was a relief even though dear Penny tried so very hard to persuade us to stay with them. Often have a feeling she is quite lonely.

Living on microwaved ready meals is not the best thing to do, but even that is preferable to being served vegan Yorkshire puddings and mushroom bacon rolls we'd had to put up with. Stupid woman's got a current obsession with mushroom and onion gravy. It's truly awful stuff.

We did however treat ourselves to a new bed from IKEA, and the old one Morgan Hallam had been dumped in we got the joiner to saw up and Freddie took it to the tip.

One of his mates suggested we claim off the contents insurance. I cannot imagine what he thought we could enter on the claim form about a dead body? The bed itself was still intact, it was just the thought of it, for me in particular of course.

Can you claim I wonder off your insurance for aura? The nasty feelings we might encounter or are they only interested if it snaps in half?

It meant of course we also had the expense of buying fresh bedding as most of it was taken away in bags by those forensic people. Can't imagine we'll ever see that again, but to be honest I don't know what the system is with evidence. Do you get it back eventually? If they ask at some point I'll just tell them they can keep it. Probably still got all his blood and goodness knows what else all over it.

Might be able to claim that though, whether we get it back or not.

What I'd give to one day settle on our forever home and take my time selecting paint colours, carpets and curtains.

Thoroughly enjoy matching shades, textures and materials of my choice, but that day still seems to be a long way off.

Freddie you see has this theory that if we paint each room plain white it is more attractive to potential buyers. This just at a time when I'd read how people now expect a decent big kitchen to be two tone with bolder colours. Also heard folk are going back to individual rooms but Freddie'd not even consider not knocking down walls.

I just feel something slightly more inviting and warming might just prove more acceptable to some, maybe not too bold as such. There are so many lovely tinted colours available these days, but no. White it has to be. White and white will be the only paint he'll be buying for this place. Only thing is he can buy it in giant tins which works out cheaper and they don't necessarily have to be branded.

We are no longer in the news, even this week's issue of the *Lincoln Leader* has very little and our names are no longer mentioned.

One day of course it will all come tumbling back and when the case comes to court which it no doubt will, then I guess we'll have to suffer once more.

Only trouble is, people I know have not pushed it to the back of their minds when I bump into them at places like B&Q. Just buying nails and screws and as I was the other day when choosing new disks for our sander, can become a labour of love with people seeming to hunt me down in the aisles to ask about what had gone on. Desperate for all the nitty gritty the media don't mention for fear of frightening the cosies who still read actual newspapers.

All a bit silly really as we can tell them very little more than they can scour on line. Sorry, but I'm never going to go into detail about the state of Morgan's face. I don't need reminding of anything from that evening and in particular the mess they'd made of him.

Have enough of that in the middle of the night when I wake up in a bit of a sweat.

One bit of news I did get in return when I was in Wickes, was bumping into Rhos Clarke who was eager to tell me Frances had had her baby. A girl she said but admitted she was no longer in the know enough to be aware what name she had chosen.

That was baffling too. Why did that copper not mention Frances's baby? Don't tell me they don't know.

Have no desire to speak with Frances under the circumstances, but she's lucky at least she has her parents to offer tea and sympathy and welcome the baby into their world.

Thoughts like that one tend to grip me when I'm feeling a bit down. When Freddie and I start a family, I'll not have that great pleasure. My parents will never visit or welcome one from us and be eager to meet their new grandchild.

I've had my fill of Frances for now. Guess I'd better send a card though or that cop will start asking more bloody stupid questions.

Still quite strange that Scoley female not mentioning the baby. Is that because it was woman to woman for some peculiar reason? She's not gay is she, without children? No of course she's not, somebody told me early doors they understand she's married and got a kid. Bet she's married to a copper. What they tend to do isn't it?

27

Talk over breakfast with Adam and in the office as soon as she arrived had been all about the tragic deaths in Plymouth.

A local man had shot dead five people on Thursday evening, including his own mother and one was an innocent local child.

Inga received more details at Lincoln Central the moment she got in, about hate-filled online rants about single mothers and his own mother.

What concerned her in particular was there being a suggestion it was indeed terror related, but in a different form. The murderer had made reference to Incels in his online rants. To a team dealing with major crime Incels, an online group of involuntary celibate men who blame women for their sexual failings were obviously a concern. In particular were their links to right-wing violent crimes around the world.

It was soon time to put that awful news to one side and return to their own issues, the death of Morgan Hallam and the interview that day with Kirsten Wroe.

'Would you care to explain to us Kirsten as to why you suggested to my officer,' Inga Larsson gestured towards DS Nicky Scoley sat beside her and behind the perspex screen. 'You hardly knew Frances Hallam? What was it you said? People can just get onto platforms like Facebook and you can't ask everybody for their ID. Can I just say, it seems to me to be very loose talk for somebody who holds a Degree of some sort or so you claim, roughly connected to information technology.'

'How dare you?' she said indignantly as if it were the key to the Holy Grail. 'What d'you mean claim? Of course I have a degree. A Masters actually,' she shot back. 'BSc in Information Systems as it happens.'

'The truth of course is, you and Frances Hallam have been good friends for quite some considerable time.'

'Hardly the same Inspector,' said her solicitor. 'Our generation tended to have more eye to eye relationships and as a result friendships, than the young are prone towards nowadays.'

DI Inga Larsson was amused by what had been said but also at how far too tight the solicitor's dark suit was. She was sure the buttons weren't supposed to be done up.

'I know I'm not looking my best today Mrs Sibthorp, but your client is actually older than me. We are both from a generation where friends meant a great deal more than passing fads and a link to a host of likes at best.'

'Millennials.'

'I'm sorry Mrs Sibthorp,' Larsson sniggered. 'But I really don't want to spend my precious time becoming involved in this kind of chit chat. I do not belong to any sort of cohort of fanciful media created nonsense.' She immediately turned her attention back to Kirsten Wroe. 'I ask again. Why exactly did you deny knowing Frances Hallam?'

'Not sure I did.'

'Please,' sighed Larsson in the stark colourless informal interview room. 'When you were asked about her you glibly suggested she might have somehow slipped onto your Facebook account unnoticed.'

'So?'

'She is the wife of the dead man found in your new home, not some unknown trollop you walked past along Clasketgate. Remember, he was the man you alone discovered, nobody else. If you were not involved in his demise why then deny knowing him and her? Why suggest the only known contact was your partner going with a friend to buy a car once upon a time?'

They all had to wait. 'Because,' Kirsten mumbled as she was idly tapping her forefinger and the next two on the table nervously.

'Sorry?'

'Because!' was much louder.

'Because what?' Larsson probed.

She made a creaky nervous sound in the back of her throat. 'Because it's embarrassing, that's why!'

'And why would that be Kirsten?' Inga Larsson saw her grimace slightly and allow her eyes to move to her left as if she was attempting to pass a signal. 'We've got all day,' the DI spinning her biro through her fingers added when nothing was forthcoming.

'I'd rather not say.'

'Might I suggest,' said Larsson in a kindly fashion. 'Saying no comment at this stage in proceedings is really not in your best interests. Would you like us to give you a few moments on your own with Mrs Sibthorp here?'

'No thank you.'

'Kirsten,' said chubby busty Sibthorp quietly with a plain wedding band tight on a fat finger. 'It is in your best interests to answer what in effect in the grand scheme of things appears to be a rather innocuous question.'

Wroe had her eyes closed when she next spoke to break what was becoming a tense atmosphere in the cell-like room. 'I had sex with him and she made me, so there.'

Larsson waited a moment rather than to be seen barging straight in. 'This Morgan Hallam we're talking about?' the reply was nodded. 'And his wife Frances Hallam forced you you say?' received the same acknowledgement. 'May I ask how she managed that?'

Kirsten Wroe sat up and rested her chin on her over lapping hands. 'Owed her.'

'Money?'

'No,' came with a shake of her head. Larsson waited. The man who made time had made plenty of it. 'Look, this is uncomfortable,' she said but the DI realized if what Kirsten was hinting at was her wishing to speak without her solicitor being present, it dare not come from her. It was too soon for a break, too early to have coffees delivered. 'I'm sorry Alice,' Wroe suddenly said to the woman beside her. 'But this is a very private matter. I appreciate you being here. I promise you this is not E-Quilibrium business, so if you don't mind.'

Nicky Scoley saw the fussy and clearly peeved solicitor out of the meeting room, arranged for a cup of tea to be delivered to her and returned to Larsson and Wroe.

'Talk to me Kirsten,' Inga Larsson suggested gently.

174

'Frances Hallam once saved my life,' she admitted and then went into a lengthy description of the circumstances surrounding the events of the fateful evening in the restaurant. 'Then out of nowhere she wanted to call in the favour.'

'Which was?' she was asked softly.

'To spend the night with Morgan,' she shrugged. 'Now I've said it,' she said sat back in her chair and shook her head. 'Well, not to spend the night exactly, just er do the business if you know what I mean, but that's how it turned out in the end in some swanky hotel down in London. The deal was to clear the debt, I had to have sex with him.'

Choosing the right comment Larsson found difficult as she realized the surprise on her face must have registered. 'The reason for all this?' and she was sure Kirsten cheeks had pinked-up in front of her eyes.

'I was a virgin if you must know,' was all she said and her eye balls peered up at the ceiling

Larsson so wanted to nudge Nicky Scoley but daren't. 'Not because he fancied you?' she offered quietly. 'Not because you and him had something going on behind the...'

'No,' was abrupt.

'Was being a virgin the all important aspect to him do you think?'

'Yes,' she admitted. 'There all night, decent breakfast next morning, but that was it. Just once, took my virginity and...' she hesitated. 'I've never been alone with him from that day to this.' Kirsten blew out a breath and shook her head. 'No bloody thanks!'

'Some women kill for less,' Nicky Scoley offered as an aside.

'Not me. That was all ages ago. I met Freddie sometime later and we've been together ever since. It's something I don't care to think about and haven't for a long time until all this business came up. Should have said no, but it's all to do with their ridiculous marriage. She did me a big favour by saving my life and it was difficult to say no to her request for a good deed in return. Thought I was saving her marriage. He had this list apparently of conquests I think you'd call it he wanted to...go with.' Kirsten Wroe sat up and bit her bottom lip.

175

'What sort of list?' was Larsson acting as innocent as she dared.

Kirsten took a moment to answer. 'Think at the time I was worried she just might try to stir up trouble for me.'

'In what way?' Scoley asked.

'Put it about how she had saved my life but in return I'd turned her down when she'd asked for a little favour.' There was a short edgy pause and when Kirsten spoke again Inga sensed more pronounced nerves. 'Knew if she did that I'd not be able to admit in public what the favour was or it all might turn nasty.' Kirsten shrugged. 'On my own with not having a family I could talk to made it all a great deal worse. Get into a public fracas on the net I could easy have lost my job if she'd brought the company name into it. Chances are if she dragged E-Quilibrium into disrepute, has to be a sackable offence, surely.'

'Could you not seek help from work maybe, explain what was going on?'

'You are joking!' she said leaning forward at Larsson. 'Tell my boss about a friend's fat husband wanting to screw me cos I'm still a bloody virgin?' She chuckled as she folded her arms. 'How d'you start with that one on a Monday morning eh? Go on tell me.'

Larsson sucked in noisily. 'See what you mean. Tricky. And all this is why you were unwilling to admit you knew Frances Hallam?'

'Yes,' sounded tedious. 'Please, don't try making out it was nothing much.'

'And why it's best if Mrs Sibthorp does not become aware of all this?'

'Yes.'

'Anything else you wish to discuss while we're alone together?'

Kirsten Wroe's mouth was back in action. This time she spent a few moments dragging her top lip through her teeth.

'Are you aware of their strange marriage? How she enjoys what she describes as the exact opposite of jealousy which in the end destroys so many partnerships by thoroughly enjoying the fact her husband used to go with other women?'

176

Larsson and Scoley were back to pretending.

'Not completely sure what you mean. You still talking about your episode?'

'No,' she chuckled. 'They both had other partners, usually people they both knew, they'd go to bed with. For kicks I suppose.'

'You're kidding me,' a frowning Larsson put on.

'Yet she doesn't consider it cheating. They had this set of rules they both abided by, according to her.' Kirsten stopped and looked at both detectives sat there waiting on her every word. 'If I'm perfectly honest I've had this sneaking feeling Frances did the murder because Morgan broke their code of honesty with regard to their open marriage. My guess is, he went with a woman Frances knew nothing about and she had recently discovered one of these other woman was pregnant.'

'Do we know…?'

'Hang on,' she insisted. 'He had this list I mentioned earlier. I was on that list remember, don't know how far down of course,' she smiled. 'I was the virgin right? But there were all sorts apparently. The woman who got pregnant could easy be someone a bit away from the norm.'

'What do you mean by away from the norm?' Nicky queried.

'Disabled, foreign maybe,' she shrugged. 'I don't know. Could easy be one off the list.'

'This an actual list?' was Larsson trying hard to think of suitable questions as if this was all news to her.

'Only what Frances told me, no idea if he actually wrote it all down like you do when you go shopping,' seemed to amuse her.

'Such as?'

'Job to remember now. Think Jew, probably Chinese and maybe disabled in some way.'

'Interesting.'

'This just religious?' Nicky managed to slide in but a shake of the head answered that.

'One major problem with your theory is,' Larsson suggested as she folded her arms and sat back as Kirsten frowned and put her head slightly to one side. 'She was heavily pregnant.

177

Somebody carried his body up your stairs remember and put him to bed. Even if she was able to kill him, I think in her state at that time you'll find she'd struggle from there on.'

'This pregnant woman,' Nicky said. 'What do we know about her?

Kirsten Wroe grimaced, shrugged, exhaled a breath and just allowed her shoulders to drop. 'Nothing. Just what I been told.'

28

Kirsten

To be honest, what else could I do? There's no way I could just carry on telling those police I didn't really know the Hallam pair. Was there?

I sometimes watch these drama things on television unfold and ask the women on the screen why did you do that, why did you have to admit it? Assume of course without that sort of reaction by the leading lady the story would in the end lack credibility.

I'll know not to do that in future. Truth is as I now know to my cost, being stuck in the midst of something like a major police inquiry is hardly a nice place to be. Plus that was Friday 13th of all days.

What if I had carried on saying I knew nothing about a woman listed on my Facebook page, or how about if some busybody told the police how they were in a restaurant one time when Frances saved my life?

Somebody at work I've had to discipline could easy get their own back on me, as most people there if not all, know how I nearly choked to death at one time.

Apart from that the police are not stupid, they'd suss it all out somehow. Anyway what's to stop Frances telling them to take the pressure off herself?

Don't really want to give her a call using the new baby as an easy excuse in order to discover how things are from her neck of the woods. But to be honest I would like to know what's going on. Wonder if she's getting the same sort of grilling I keep having to go through?

In the meantime my immediate worry is those two policewomen. Might be a silly thing to say but I've a feeling it would have been better if the coppers had been men. That one who interviewed Freddie on the Saturday I know riled him a bit, but he was very pleasant with me. A bit dour maybe and not a very exciting hunk, but agreeable enough all the same. Good looking though I have to admit.

Wonder why that Larsson woman has suddenly appeared? Been on holiday maybe, this time of year. Name's a bit odd. Hardly middle England is it, but these days there's plenty about with unreadable names who turn out to be British born and bred. See loads of them listed in the paper under all the people who've been had up in court.

I've begun to have this constant worry about those two chatting to all and sundry in the loo at the police station. You know what some of them are like.

One of the reasons I've not been into social media in any serious way is all this perpetual belittling of each other. You get nasty vicious loud mouths in all walks of life, but the internet just has to be the worst. I can just imagine a couple of those coppers getting together with a few mates over a glass or two and trying to outdo each other with lurid stories of things they've had to deal with. Be what they do at the end of their shift and head for the nearest bar.

What's the betting I'm the latest crew room gossip?

Be desperate to get their phones out and rush all the salacious toilet tittle-tattle onto Facebook before you can say bitches. Be all the rage I bet among the two I spoke to, gabbling on to all and sundry about what they found out about Morgan and me. I reckon nattering about people they come across is all a major part of their sad little lives.

Trouble is of course, they'll not keep it to themselves and I worry how long it'll be before I start to get funny looks at work, spot people nudging each other as I pass.

Might be an idea to look them up on social media, keep an eye on what rumours they're currently spreading.

Frances of course could easy have gone on Twitter and told the world how she saved my life which would've told the cops in letters a foot high we obviously know each other.

Can't afford to have my name dragged through the mud by a load of cyber bullies on their phones. Not go down well with

180

my bosses and one thing would lead to another and before long Freddie would get to know about me and bloody Morgan.

Be no use moaning to Freddie about the abuse. He keeps well clear of joining in on social media as the little darlings he tries to teach would use him and abuse him and as in many cases could so easily ruin his career.

Glad I'm off to Dumfries and Galloway for a couple of days this week for work, even though I know that'll give a good few of them right of passage to talk about me. What's the betting now they're no longer working from home that Becky Armstrong and Lucie Carr at work have me top of their gossip list every time they nip out for a fag break?

Nothing I can do about it now. I've made my bed and guess ironically I'll have to lie on it. At least it's no longer the one I found Morgan in!

29

Inga Larsson had been through the process herself of giving birth and then going home to all that entails as you try to come to terms with a new way of life. At times she felt as though it were a whole new world she'd stepped into.

A post-natal process the Swede could readily recall reading about, being told about and imagined, but one which as it turned out was never anything like she had expected. Early mornings, late and sleepless nights resulting in tiredness surrounding everything she did.

Suddenly there was another person in her life. A helpless infant, a brand new being, somebody else in your life, a little one you have to devote your whole being to. A devotion alongside this new responsibility she could remember had taken some time to get used to.

Inga could easily bring to mind how quickly she had become used to the very different new baby smell throughout her home and how she had coped with the sudden change in daily priorities.

One aspect had worried her for a time and she'd put it down to a link to post-natal depression they talk about. She'd wondered about her daughter's future. What would she grow up like, what would become of her? All fine and dandy with a great career ahead of her, marrying this caring handsome guy and producing lovely grandchildren for her.

That is until her mind suggested maybe Terése Danielle just might catch a killer virus, brutally murder some poor soul, become an alcoholic or a druggie and how could she ensure it didn't happen?

Giving birth and having a six-week old baby when the government announced the pandemic lockdown was not the best situation she'd ever had to deal with. Adam stuck at home unable to stroke women's thighs for weeks on end, was at least able to provide considerable assistance.

Fortunately her concerns were simply a passing phase and to some extent felt her role in life and statistics she was aware of, had helped her over the dark times.

When Inga entered Frances Hallam's huge converted barn home down in Osbournby, it was as if nothing in her world had changed. A stranger stepping over the threshold would never guess there was a new born baby in residence.

Inga Larsson had chosen to visit rather than ask Frances Hallam to attend Lincoln Central in an attempt to offer up her caring face. Be on side with all the one mother to another guff she was able to offer under the circumstances.

On the way in she had seen Frances's Toyota parked rear end into the double garage and fifty yards or so away a blue Dacia outside what Hallam said previously was a 'granny flat' come holiday cottage.

This time there was coffee on offer in surprisingly cheap cups and saucers. The sort to stain each time you make tea. There was no sign of the child at all and as part of her mentoring process with some of the women in her team Larsson had taken the sturdy member Michelle Cooper with her on this occasion.

This she had done not only to add to her work experience catalogue but because Michelle was most certainly not a soppy slim Mumsy character, so many birth and baby websites are obsessed with.

Cappuccinos for Larsson and Cooper and for somebody in need of weight loss Frances surprisingly went for the Latte. All made by their host in her big expensive dull wood and grey kitchen using an equally unnecessarily lavish and expensive coffee machine.

As previously the detectives were masked-up but Hallam made no attempt. They went through the routine of discussing her health and that of the baby before they seriously got down to business.

'Why didn't you tell us you once saved Kirsten Wroe's life?' Frances looked more than slightly surprised at the

183

question, but as ever remained in control and unmoved. 'I ask again…'

'I heard you.'

'And?' Larsson pursued.

'She tell you that?'

'It was in the news at the time if you remember, and what goes on the web stays on the web.'

'Hardly relevant I shouldn't imagine, and anyway it was a long time ago.' Larsson watched a superior half smile playing on her lips. Top to tail in a mixture of fern and mint green, she reckoned the trouser suit could well be silk. Immaculate and pleat free.

'Very relevant I would have thought,' said Larsson. 'Particularly as you told one of my colleagues you hardly knew the woman. Truth is Frances, as a result of the incident you and her have been firm friends for quite some time. Am I right?'

'If you can call somebody a friend you just about remember to send a Christmas card to from time to time. Then yes.'

'What about this business of you asking your once-a-year friend if she would care to have sex with your husband?'

'What are you talking about?' she said and chuckled nervously

'How about you explain why you asked this Kirsten you hardly know, if she would do you a big big favour and tick one of your husband's sexual urge boxes for him?' Larsson having gained her undivided attention ploughed on. 'You ever pulled that stroke with any more of your friends? Friends of yours who are willing to romp in a bed with your husband when you have been otherwise engaged elsewhere with whoever. Somebody else's husband quite possibly. Maybe a magistrate, politician or a circus clown.'

'What's this all about?' she demanded. 'Where's all this nonsense come from?'

'You tell us. I think this is you being a dutiful loving wife and fulfilling Morgan's fantasies. Am I correct? Tell me if you will just out of interest, was a pregnant woman conveniently on the list you were also able to deal with personally?'

'I think it best if you leave,' said Frances uncrossing her legs and getting to her feet.

'Sorry,' said Larsson in the very annoying way she does. 'But I've not finished my coffee as yet.' She lifted her cup. 'Very nice I have to say.' *Crockery is cheap and cheerful, but you can't have everything.*

'Just get out!' she shouted and pointed towards the door.

'Might I suggest you sit down madam,' said Larsson up to her and actually sat back in the chair, cup in hand. The pair waited and in the end Hallam gave in and returned moodily to her seat.

'Do you mind if I have a look around,' said Michelle Cooper, thoroughly enjoying the experience of being with the boss on this sort of learning on the job assignment.

'Why?'

'Just to familiarize myself.'

'I don't think so.'

'A word,' said Larsson pointing at Hallam. 'Either Detective Constable Cooper who has experience in Family Liaison is afforded an opportunity to have a look round, or we exercise a warrant and I order up a CSI team to have them crawling all over this place. Choice is yours, and I know which I'd prefer because I warn you they most certainly know how to make a real mess.'

Hallam just sighed looked glum and shook her head as Cooper walked off.

'Now,' Larsson managed, then to further annoy sipped from her cup she then returned to its saucer on the table. 'Tell me about this polygamous marriage of yours.'

'Polyamorous,' she corrected.

'Whatever.'

Taped music had been there from the off. Great pop standards from decades past ushered softly from a hidden system somewhere.

'For your information as it happens, I never romantically dated other people which is the very basis of the relationship we developed.'

The Detective Inspector sat there slowly sipping coffee and listening intently to this well-dressed tall woman with over contoured make-up as she enthused about all the benefits she could muster regarding what Larsson considered to be a most unfavorable relationship full of obvious pitfalls.

'Thank you for that,' Larsson acknowledged. 'But to be honest, at the end of the day this was all about Morgan's list.'

'What?'

'Morgan had a list,' she shrugged. 'Still has I suppose on the internet. His list of categorized women he planned to seduce.'

'Don't be ridiculous. Morgan didn't need to seduce anybody,' she insisted. 'We have a wide range of like-minded friends and associates and will you please refrain from trying to make it all sound so grubby.'

'But Kirsten Wroe was on this list probably because she just happened to still be virginal?' Hallam pulled a face. 'I take it you were also on his list once upon a time.'

Blonde Larsson couldn't help but glance at her deep auburn hair. It just had to be a top quality wig and it would be difficult if not impossible for the average joe to detect her issues.

'How d'you make that out?' she demanded with a quiet chuckle, and Larsson knew she had to tread very carefully.

'Pretty obvious I would have thought,' she went for as an alternative rather than make mention of her hair. 'I was going to say we will need a list,' said Larsson getting to her feet. 'But this will do nicely,' she said walking over to a black laptop just fortunately sat there beside the pale blue bread bin.

'That's mine!'

'Even better,' said Larsson unplugging it and tucking it under her arm. The Computer Analysis Team (CAT) back at base would check it all for her especially young Dexter Hopwood.

'You can't do that,' she insisted. 'That's private property.'

'And this Mrs Hallam is a murder inquiry and not any old everyday murder investigation. This is us seeking the truth about the unfortunate death of your own husband no less.'

'I'll speak to my solicitor about all this, you mark my words.'

'You do that,' said Larsson as she audaciously simply returned to the wooden table and sat down, resting her hands on the closed laptop. 'Just out of interest,' she asked a very peeved

Frances. 'Is there anything in here,' she tapped. 'About your brother?'

'Brother?' was gasped and grimaced.

'Stephen Jon-Joe Jenkins also known as Neil Sands now and again.'

'Since when have I had a brother?' lacked a grin.

'Since you were born actually. True your embarrassed mother probably kept it all to herself in those days, but big brother Jon-Joe was running around well before you were born.'

'News to me,' she suggested without a degree of persuasion. 'Any other ridiculous questions?'

'I have one,' said Michelle Cooper as she appeared suddenly in the doorway. 'Where's your baby?'

'What's it to you?'

Larsson really annoyed the Hallam woman more by overacting her scanning of the room as if looking for any sign of the new born. 'Niamh is where exactly?' she asked and hoped she'd pronounced it properly.

'With Marie-Louise. Our nanny, child-minder.'

'That her car we saw as we came in?' Inga Larsson asked and considered asking her what she meant by the use of 'our' when there was only her.

'Go on, what's wrong with it? Tax out of date is it?' she shot out. 'Typical police.' Larsson took a sip of her coffee making sure she didn't drip a drop onto the laptop in front of her

'Just a couple more things if you will,' Larsson said calmly.'We could really do with the name of that woman Morgan managed to get pregnant recently and ...'

'What on earth are you on about now?' was shouted. 'This is all becoming totally totally ridiculous.'

'And our PHU team could do with...'

'Stop it! What you talking about? Got some woman pregnant? Crissakes. What are you on about now you daft bitch?' she shouted.

'Oh sorry, didn't you know,' Larsson smiled annoyingly at her and allowed her head to shake slightly. 'Whoops! Sorry about that,' with hand to mouth. 'Sort of slipped out. Meant no harm...'

'Who?'

'You tell us. We wondered what might be wrong with her. Idle curiosity to be honest, nothing more than that. Webbed feet's possible or bisexual maybe?'

Frances Hallam looked totally bemused and confused by the turn of events and a conversation she had wholly lost control of she could make no sense of.

'What on earth are you on about?' she demanded. 'What d'you mean what's wrong with her? You've totally lost me now,' was obvious and desperate. 'Do I really need to remind you how recently I've lost my husband?' She shook her head. 'Guess things like that don't matter to the likes of you. And I've got a new baby needing my constant attention.'

'Of course we appreciate your situation Mrs Hallam,' Larsson said after licking her lips. 'That's why we are here rather than asking you to traipse into Lincoln with your daughter and all that would entail. We do understand, but at the same time you do need to appreciate we are working on your behalf to solve this case and it is to that end our whole team are continuing to work extremely hard.' Larsson hesitated. 'Have no fear madam, we'll catch the baddie.'

'Now about this woman,' said Michelle Cooper who had appeared at the kitchen door. 'The pregnant woman we've been told about.'

'Just get out damn you!' the redhead screamed and sat there sobbing into her cupped hands.

'Before we leave, I need to remind you how this is your opportunity to tell us something.'

'Such as?' Hallam peered up with damp eyes.

'You tell me, and my advice is you need to make the most of this opportunity.'

'What are you on about now you stupid woman?' she shouted across at Larsson. 'Have you not heard I'm a widow now, I've not seen much sympathy from you. Miss the training course did we?'

'I'm not here for that,' said Larsson wagging her finger at her. 'I'm not the vicar, I'm not here to offer cheap flowers and sympathy. My job Mrs Hallam, is to find who sliced half your husband's face off,' made Hallam grimace. 'Or perhaps you would prefer carnations from the local garage. Thank you Mrs Hallam. We'll see ourselves out,' Larsson said being pleased with the reaction. She quickly drank down the last of her bitter coffee, got to their feet, squared her shoulders and walked out of the room followed by Cooper, and out of the big house in Osbournby.

Seemed an odd out of the way place for the likes of the Hallam to live, but Inga knew she could get up to Lincoln in no time which would keep everything buoyant.

'I'll drive past, you photo the car,' Inga mumbled the moment they were outside.

'D'you know,' said Inga Larsson ten minutes later driving her MG back the way they'd come in. 'My guess is she doesn't know anything at all about the woman he got up the duff a while back.'

'What?' Michelle asked and looked across at her boss. 'Up the duff?' she laughed. 'Sounds really odd coming from you.'

'Expression, sorry,' Inga chuckled. 'One my Adam explained to me, along with in the club and a loads of others.'

'There's plenty more where that came from.'

'Wonder why when talking about the nanny she said *our* nanny. Who makes her our nanny, rather than mine? This the child's real father you think she's linking with?'

'I'm having trouble keeping up with all this,' Michelle admitted.

'If we didn't know already. Would we have had any idea there was a baby living there?'

'Not me,' Michelle answered. 'Has anybody actually seen it? Smelt it?'

'Just between us. Jake's wife Sally has. That gives us proof positive of the child's existence.'

'Of course.'

'The nanny's car was outside that cottage place. That what she does? Farm the kid out to some nanny down in the holiday let. Out of sight, out of mind. And, I've got a baby needing my constant attention according to her.'

'More than likely with her sort.'

189

'Guess that way you don't get milky sick all over your silk trouser suit.' Inga Larsson drove on. 'Bitter taste of that coffee is lingering. Fancy something decent?'

'Cold would be nice.'

'Lincoln here we come,' she said as they slipped past Sleaford.'Got that Askew woman to see this afternoon.'

30

'We have her laptop,' said Inga Larsson back at base as she plonked it down on Nicky Scoley's work station. 'Job for you kiddo, take it up to CAT for me please and see what they can come up with. We're looking for women Morgan Hallam might have been with and men Frances Hallam bedded as part of this polygamous marriage of theirs. We jolly well need a suspect from somewhere and part-time spurned lovers is one option. Whoever he got pregnant is one likely candidate but even more so has to be the husband of whoever she was. Nice scenario for a good bit of jealousy.' Inga gestured to Michelle who reacted.

'There was a car outside the Hallam place parked up by what looked for all the world like a holiday cottage in the grounds. She said it belongs to the nanny.'

'I know, I know,' said a smiling Inga on hearing groans. 'We need more than Marie-Louise,' she quickly scribbled on the board. 'If only for elimination. Who is she, where does she live? You take that on Sandy, please,' and Michelle passed her phone to him.

'Photo of the car,' she told the Scot.

Inga then briefed her team on what had been said out at Osbournby about her claiming to not really know Kirsten Wroe and insisting she had no brother.

'Could always be a family secret ma'am,' Ruth offered. 'I've known people who were never told they had a brother or a sister, in those cases they were still born or died as infants or in the old days born to single women.'

'Possible he was a foundling ma'am.'

'Be all to do with keeping such matters within the close knit family, sort of for adults' eyes and ears only,' Nicky Scoley suggested. 'Come across it quite a bit tracing family trees for people as I did at one time if you remember. Know a woman who had no idea she'd had a brother and another discovered the man she thought was her brother all his life never was.'

'Why do we come across idiosyncrasies like this in major cases?' Inga queried. 'Why is nothing plain and simple?'

'Think that's because the world's no longer like that.'

'In this case we have this mystery brother for the Hallam woman and Kirsten Wroe has no contact at all with any of her family with them being religious nutters. Allegedly. Be a nice change if everybody could just be normal for once.'

'What is normal?'

'If Wroe has been driven out by her family of Jehovah whatevers, they'd say something about it being because she's a slave of corruption and would disassociate from her.'

'As I say,' Inga returned. 'Why can't these people just be normal?' Ruth Buchan caught her eye. 'Yes Ruth.'

'Know you've got her laptop; but one thread I've been following is a woman with a page on social media which I discovered is sometimes taken over by her husband. At least they have the same surname. He messages Hallam quite a bit, and wondered if they had a thing going.'

'Not got something wrong with her by any chance? Suffers with a trigger finger.' Inga chuckled at her own remark and squinted at the boards. 'Not on the list surely,' she jokingly asked and scanned the list. 'Thank goodness for that.'

'Not that I've come across so far, but not the sort of thing people mention every time they log on,' Ruth admitted. 'Want me to carry on poking my nose in or shall I leave it now we have the laptop?'

'Keep digging, you never know you might come up with another ticked box. Please,' she warned. 'Don't make contact or anything. Do we have a name?'

'Connie Askew known as Bonnie,' she gestured confusion at. 'Her husband is Grant Askew.'

'Ring any bells, anyone?' Inga asked. When nobody offered anything she gave Ruth the go-ahead to continue delving.

DI Inga Larsson decided to take it upon herself to deal with the women her team had come up with from emails on her laptop linked to a couple who had a serious social media presence.

Talking to mature women about their personal relationships, about their links to Frances Hallam and in particular the suggestion they might somehow be involved in this polyamorous business and Morgan's little list she felt was a one-woman job.

Communicating with this Connie Askew initially was Inga being ultra-cautious and taking on a bland approach regarding the sudden demise of Hallam. She talked to the woman in confidence and assured her this was simply part of the due process as she and Hallam had an association.

At the same time she was looking for signs of a disability or something which would mark her down as a likely prospect for the Hallam hit list. If there was something it was not clearly obvious.

People had done it before to Inga. Agree to meet somewhere they consider to be quite anonymous, then choose a place where anybody just might appear. Often with a dog in tow, or in some cases happen to be the one being towed.

She did wonder if taking the dog was used as an excuse to be out and about or did they see the mutt as their silent witness.

Been there before a few times with Adam and once she recalled for a secret meet she seemed to remember with a witness.

The sun was out, the weather was very pleasant but not too warm when Inga arrived first and sat outside the cafe in Lincoln's Hartsholme Park.

Chosen by Askew living in Newark and visiting a friend in Forest Park, it was a convenient place nearby as well as being out in the open air and no need for masks.

Inga Larsson was not quite sure what she expected when Askew appeared, checked she was talking to the right person and sat down opposite her. Tubbier that she had imagined, wearing glasses with fat cheeks, signs of a double chin and what Adam always called thunder thighs. Wide blue eyes with hair running to her shoulders. The black leggings as ever did little to enhance her look but obviously were preferable to white.

The Detective Inspector volunteered to obtain and pay for a coffee and a tea.

Once settled and after the pooch had invested in a drink of water supplied on site, they were ready for the off.

Inga Larsson explained carefully how there was a need in any major enquiry to speak with anybody who had even a passing relationship with the victim.

The hair of Askew was noticeably too black to be natural, but there did not appear to be anything physically wrong with her she could see.

Larsson placed her mobile on the metal table but assured the slightly dumpy woman it was there purely in case of emergencies. This was another female who wore clothes too tight, allowing her excess to be advertised, and as frequently happens with people of her shape the strappy red top was in her opinion a real must to avoid.

Askew thanked Larsson for not expecting her to visit the police station and offered to assist in any way possible, explaining at the same time how she and her husband had been long term friends of the Hallam couple.

'Close, but never in each other's pockets of course. Tends to be the way more and more don't you think what with the virus and all this modern technology?'

Larsson didn't bother to comment.

'Did you and your husband spend time together with the Hallams as couples, visit their home, go out for meals together, get away for weekends, that sort of everyday thing?'

As she shook her head, she spoke. 'Think I've been to their place maybe two or three times, but I don't think Grant has. Works long hours down in Derby where he's based which tends to preclude him from socializing in the evenings to a degree.'

'Grant does what exactly?' Larsson asked then took her first sip of Americano. The woman's phrasing suggested the faintest of traces of an Irish accent. Pity Jake was not there as he would have a better idea about where.

'In banking,' told her very little.

'That where you met, at work?' was Larsson attempting to establish her trade. A role off Hallam's list would have been much better.

'No. I worked in customer services that is until I met him. Now I'm the housewife. Grant prefers it that way,' brought seeking novel employment to highlight on Morgan's list to an abrupt halt.

'How did you and your husband first meet Frances and Morgan?'

'Be a long time ago now,' Larsson waited. 'Think it was through a mutual friend of mine I seem to remember. She knew Frances and think I was with her when they bumped into each other and one thing led to another.'

'You and Morgan?'

'How do you mean?'

'D'you see him at all separate from Mrs Hallam?'

'Just like Grant. He is what my daughter calls an add-on like an app,' she seemed to think was trendy. 'Frances and I meet up for coffee now and again plus all the social media ritual you need to partake in these days.' She smiled. 'Way of the world don't you find?'

'So, you've not spent time with Morgan?' was the way Larsson dealt with questions to which she wished to make no answer.

'Only as part of a foursome, and then very infrequently.' Larsson was pleased she'd not twigged what she was getting at as this Connie swiftly scanned the other tables and chairs, looked down to check her dog, lifted her tea and took her time sipping. 'Might I be quite frank with you Detective Inspector?' she posed quite softly. 'Don't wish to speak ill of the dead, yet my policy is always to be truthful in such matters. You see I'm afraid dear Morgan did have something of a reputation with...the ladies, shall we say.'

'That why you steered clear?'

'Little ripple makes a muckle,' totally bemused Larsson and there was just the merest twitch of a soft smile.

'I understand,' even though she had no idea and took time to sip and think. 'Am I right in thinking your husband also has regular contact with Frances Hallam?'

'Oh what a silly arrangement that is,' she chuckled, then dropped her voice in case the three other people each with a dog several tables away might be ear wigging.

'In what way?'

'Charles Pritchard, Frances's father-in-law you understand, has a lifelong best friend they went to school together or something along those lines. This man, his name escapes me at present, is in corporate banking, but Charles tends to think he's often offering him bad advice. Grant says this friend is used to dealing with major conglomerates and forgets the same rules do not necessarily apply further down the scale. Caustic is a phrase Grant uses. So, rather than upset his family friend he does business through Grant for many of his smaller deals,' and tapped her nose.

'And Frances deals with all that, is that right?' Larsson guessed as her team had told her about his email contact.

'Power behind the throne, you could say.' Time for another drink of weak tea. 'All part of the silliness, Charles has it all go through Frances, so if you like he can always claim to this friend of his it was not his decision, something he didn't know anything about.'

Larsson was struggling to pick up on anything she could follow-up and decided to go for broke before making excuses to leave.

'On a completely different tack,' she lied. 'We are also looking into another quite separate matter which appears to involve women of our age,' was blatantly untrue. Connie Askew had to be at least ten or twelve years older and certainly looked it. 'What does being polyamorous mean to you?'

Larsson had to wait for Askew. 'Not at all sure, don't really wish to make a fool of myself so I think it's best if I refrain on this occasion.'

'Rather than make a fool of yourself or for some other reason?'

'I don't honestly know, so rather than come up with something frankly stupid I'll refrain.'

'Are you saying you don't know people who have polyamorous relationships?'

'Certainly not,' was not at all what Larsson had hoped to hear. 'Why do you ask?' had her eyes screwed up in a slightly confused pose.

'Just came up as a possible issue in a case and I'm taking the opportunity when interviewing women to just test the water if you like, trying to see how widespread the practice is.'

'Which is what?' Askew then sat back and drank her tea.

'Polyamorous so I understand it, is where both husband and wife have other partners they date and are intimate with on a fairly regular basis.'

'You being serious?' Connie Askew gasped after taking the cup away from her mouth.

'Very.'

'What's the idea of that?'

'You tell me,' Larsson sniggered.

'This only married couples you say? What about all those living together as they do these days?'

'Not sure, but my guess is the same applies. To my mind people like that very often are not fully committed so I cannot imagine this business would make much difference.'

'People really live like that?' she asked. 'In somewhere like…Lincoln?' Larsson nodded with a smile. 'Seriously?'

'Apparently.' Larsson allowed her shoulders to rise and sag back down. 'So we understand.'

'And you're investigating it. Is this business an offence then, this er…whatever?'

'Polyamorous. Not in itself no, as we have to assume they're all consenting adults. Just something which has reared its head during a particular investigation. Just wonder what people's attitude to it is, that's all.'

'Haven't got one,' Connie chuckled. 'Just didn't know what it was, but it doesn't sound very nice to me at all.'

'Nor me,' Larsson admitted.

'Haven't spoken with Frances since all this has been going on you know,' was Askew needing to change subject. 'Sent her a message or two of course and a card when the baby was born.' She stopped to have another cursory glance about. 'You know she's in her late thirties don't you.'

'Yes, we do. Why, is that a problem?' Askew shrugged and Larsson told herself there was probably a cut off age people should abide by in her world.

'You probably can't talk about it, but Grant and I simply cannot fathom why she's waited all this time to start a family and can't imagine how according to the media this other couple became involved in all that business with his body turning up like that at their place at at…' she never finished.

If the woman expected Larsson to reveal all she was very much mistaken.

'We're still investigating the whole case, and today has just been a small part of the whole.' Inga downed the last of her coffee she forgotten to ask for an extra shot. 'Well, thank you Connie it's been most interesting.' Which it hadn't. 'Thank you for taking the time and trouble to see me.'

'Wish I could have been more help, really I do.'

'Helps me to put a face to a name and there are one or two more on my list I've yet to see. All a case of eliminating people in the main, as in your case.'

'Have you spoken to Sophie Smallman or Jayney Bidulph at all?'

'My team are going through a good number of likely names we come across, but they're certainly new to me. D'you have their details by any chance?'

Connie Askew produced her iPhone and skimmed down to reach the names of the two women, held it up to Larsson who made a note of their numbers on her tablet.

'Thank you,' she said. 'Appreciate that.'

'Good luck,' Askew offered as Larsson got to her feet, pocketed her mobile then bent down to pat the dog. 'Hope you manage to find who did it.' She shook her brown hair. 'Certainly a really nasty business.'

'Thank you,' said the DI again and walked off to find her car.

Women like Askew and her chums were never the sort Inga was used to dealing with.

Askew was a housewife and Larsson knew for a fact there was no 'housewife' on the bucket list. There was also no way Hallam had a tubby customer services woman on his list. Always the possibility she had an obscure hobby, but by the look of her it seemed most unlikely.

Back at Lincoln Central Inga had to admit she had found out very little from Connie Askew, but when she offered the two extra names to her team it turned out Jayney Bidulph was already on their list of likely candidates.

It had never been a priority task but Jamie Hedley had come up with info on Jehovah Witness splinter groups since their formation in the 1930s.

Back in 1951 a Goshen Fellowship had been formed and he discovered they even have a very intense Facebook page, the boss was able to have a look at. Other breakaways had appeared since the introduction of the internet with the appearance of people such as Lord's Witnesses. Inga decided it would most likely be this Fellowship which Wroe had mentioned her parents were devotees of.

'How easy would it be do you think Jake, to come up with a list of pregnant women with other side issues?' Her Detective Sergeant looked at her with a heavy frown.

'What d'you mean by other issues?'

'Would maternity records indicate if any of them are say blind or have lost a limb?'

'We back to Morgan's ladder?' one or two found amusing.

'Snake on a ladder,' Michelle popped in.

'If you put it like that.'

'My guess is their general medical records would state serious disabilities, but I'd have to ask if there's a separate list anywhere linking pregnancy to whatever it might be. But,' he said to stop his boss's follow up. 'I'm not at all sure it would have black written across your notes in capital letters in this day and age or vegan or left handed. Disambiguation or Clubfoot or…'

'Now you're just showing off!'

'As I was saying Clubfoot or even being one of twins might be included but I shouldn't imagine notes would record people as a Vicar or a Traffic Warden. Probably all written down if you're from Venus though. Why?' accompanied his grin.

'As I was saying earlier, it turns out Kirsten Wroe more than likely was the virgin off Morgan Hallam's hit list. She reckons she's heard about a woman who Hallam got pregnant and according to her that was why Frances was planning to divorce him because he broke the cardinal rule of their polyamorous marriage. Just wondered what it was attracted him to some woman. Can't just be sex surely. He was getting more than his fair share by the sound of it.'

'I'll ask,' said Jake.

'Thank you.'

'But I'm not at all sure there's a general list of pregnant women with all they might be incapacitated by, but religion could well be listed, especially something different.'

'Fine. Just see what you can do. Ruth,' she said as she headed back to her office. 'Any chance that woman you're researching is pregnant?'

'Nothing mentioned so far.'

'Here's an off-the-wall thought,' the DI said at her door. 'Hallam missed one off his sex list. There's no Jehovah Witness,' she suggested with a flash of a smile. 'That is unless he counted Kirsten Wroe who is lapsed.'

'Could easy be another where he doubled up maybe.'

'Quick thought,' Jake popped in. 'Pregnant Jehovah Witness could well have the stupidity of no blood transfusion on her notes.'

31

When Inga Larsson arrived for work mid-morning on the Saturday she was fascinated and slightly amused by Jake who had somehow discovered three white boards in addition to those already in use. He was studiously writing names and details in a variety of colours, of all the people involved in the case, from a sheet of paper to hand in clear capitals across all boards.

By the amount already entered on the boards it was obvious he had been there for some time.

Everybody from Morgan Hallam and Neil Sands, from Penny Curran to Faye Rumbold. Each person had been allocated a number and against them were links from one to another, their background, previous convictions, location, alibis and sources of the known data.

On Thursday there had been those Plymouth murders and then on Friday something closer to home had erupted out of nowhere.

A call had gone out the previous afternoon for volunteers to help in a major search.

An eight year-old girl had gone missing and when the call went out she joined in with house-to-house door knocking. Unbenown to Michelle, earlier in the day a scumbag nasty piece of work in a drunken rage had beaten up a homeless man in a random alcohol fuelled attack over a debt on the edge of town.

When she knocked on the badly painted black front door of a scruffy semi needing to ask if anyone had seen sight of little Catelyn, she was not to know who lived there. Totally unaware of what the sole occupant had been up to earlier in the day, was prone to violence and had a potty mouth.

The door opened suddenly and as she held up her warrant card this scum in a dirty t-shirt took two steps and head-butted her. As she went down and he began to kick her on the ground

Michelle knew why. 'No fuckin' girl's bloody arresting me!' he hollered.

She'd taken a good battering before the PC talking to a neighbour next door could get to her aid and with a colleague they cuffed and arrested the low life.

As it turned out the whole episode was all quite unnecessary, as the child was found safe with a friend's family who invited her to stay for tea but had failed to notify Catelyn's mother.

Thoughts of Michelle Cooper were still with her and Inga planned to visit her at home later in the day having been released from the A&E department at the County Hospital.

Rather than disturb Jake, Larsson got on with briefing Nicky Scoley and Ruth Buchan about Michelle's condition provided by her mother and the interview with Wroe. She asked the DS to contact Sophie Smallman and a Jayney Bidulph, the names given to her by Askew to arrange informal chats as soon as.

'Are you watching the new drama *Absent Without Leave*?' Jake asked at her door when he had finished his task.

'No, but I think Adam is.'

'What I'm about to say,' he said loud enough for all to hear. 'Is a spoiler, so if you don't want to know it's time to cover your ears.' Inga got up from her desk and joined him out in the MIT Incident Room.

'We watched that *Deceit* about that Rachel Nickell murder and the undercover work going badly wrong.' Inga sighed. 'Why do they do that, why when people have tuned on to watch a police drama about a murder do they come on with all that silliness of warning viewers about scenes some people may find disturbing. It's an horrific murder not a kid's tea party.' She shook her head. 'The floor's all yours Jake. This'll be interesting.'

'I've watched the first four episodes of *Absent Without Leave* and unless we're not very bright, Sally and I assumed all along it was about somebody going missing. Then the other night my clever clogs nurse suddenly had this bright idea half way through. Sally reckons it's not a person missing at all it's a missing fact, it's the absent link. Work that out and you can solve it.'

Inga scanned the room. 'Don't look at me, I've not been watching it.'

'Think you're probably right,' said Ruth. 'We've never been told it's a person, no names, nothing.'

'That's why it's so damn confusing.'

'Exactly,' said Jake as he walked back to his boards. 'Somebody's playing mind games.'

'Thanks,' said DC Jamie Hedley shaking his head. 'I had the young doctor down for it.'

'In our case we have everybody including the latest few women you've spoken to or are about to,' Jake said to an intrigued Inga. 'By putting them all down like this on a big sheet one below the other it's not the facts we have uncovered which stand out, it's what we don't know. The gaps.' He tapped three blank spaces. 'These are all absent without leave. Look.

'Jon-Joe Jenkins aka Neil Sands. What do we know apart from the fact Frances's mother gave birth to him before Frances was born and obviously years before she linked up with Hallam and this lad Jon-Joe was in a bit of bother as a kid. On CCTV hiring the Volvo and he pretty much matches the guy Bill saw when he handed over the parcel. Since then, what?'

'Nothing.'

'Gone to ground. Absconded.'

'Don't look at what we have on him, look at the blanks. The bits which just happen to be absent without leave. Has anybody we've spoken to ever mentioned him? No,' Jake tapped a square. 'What's his address? Blank. Phone number. Blank. DNA, sort of blank because we have two male samples we so far haven't been able to link to anybody. We assume DNA profile discovered at Rumbold's garage place is him and some found in the bedroom alongside Morgan also matches. Truth is they could well be anybody, so if we remove the DNA link because we have no actual proof, that's even more blanks.'

'Just to break in please Jake,' said Inga. 'I had a coffee in Hartsholme Park with a friend of Frances Hallam, she of the polyamorous marriage. This Connie Askew who has known the pair for years hadn't a clue what I was talking about,' she hesitated. 'Is that also a blank? Ask your friends if they know what it means. Next couple I talk to should answer that, but if that is the case, what in God's name is it all about? And, why did Kirsten Wroe tell us that's what's been going on, if in truth it hasn't?'

'Throwing us off the scent.'

'Just my point,' Jake broke in. 'We're probably being told stuff that's all bullshit, like the telly programme is doing, leading us right down the path of nonsense. They've not told me it's a missing person but they've inferred it, made it out to be, hinted at it well enough for me to believe that for a couple of weeks. Is Wroe doing the same for some reason making up some cock and bull story about the Hallam's sex life? If so, why?'

'Never forget it was her bedroom he was found in.'

'And found by her remember.'

'Sorry Jake, but we might just have a few more blanks. Carry on.'

'Just that I feel we need to fill in these blanks,' he tapped three. 'It's not what we know, it's what we don't know.' He put his hands up. 'I know it's not easy.'

'Back to it team, and you heard what the man said,' Inga instructed before she and Jake began an intense conversation close to the boards.

After explaining from the outset their conversation was all part of the necessary due diligence they go through in such cases, the informal chat with this Jayney Bidulph woman went about the same way. To her credit she had made life easier for Larsson by suggesting she attend Lincoln Central during her lunch break. Working as she did on the rental aspect of an estate agent, Inga guessed she'd still tag her lunch hour on the end.

An ulterior motive quickly became obvious when Ms Bidulph admitted she'd never been inside a police station before and had certainly never been interviewed by the police. Probably her idea of an exciting time she could spout about on social media.

Claimed she had known Frances Hallam for years having briefly worked with her at the North Kesteven Council offices before Morgan came on the scene. Visited the big house out at Osbournby a couple times and knew Morgan.

Larsson guessed that was Frances showing off as usual. 'I appreciate this is a delicate situation and I'm sorry to ask, but has there ever been any relationship between you and Morgan at all?'

'Why would there be? What are you suggesting?' was fed within a snigger,

'Not suggesting anything at all I can assure you. What were you doing when you first met Frances?'

'Doing?'

'Were you in the motor trade for instance?'

'Worked in Human Resources before this.'

'Thank you Jayney,' and a disappointed Larsson checked her iPad. 'Just out of interest on a different subject completely, and to assist with another enquiry going on at the moment my colleagues have asked me to check with all ladies of a certain age I talk to.' Larsson took in a breath. 'Might I ask if you know what a polyamorous marriage or relationship is?'

'I certainly do,' she scoffed. 'Cheating by any other name.'

'You think so?'

'Can't imagine what my wife would say if I came home with that idea,' she chuckled as the DI sucked in what she'd said. 'Goodness me no.'

Larsson knew she had free licence to pose a big one. 'I know this is going to sound a rather indelicate question and if you'd rather not answer it I quite understand. Since you came out, have you ever had sexual relations with a man?'

'Not before or since.'

'Fine, thank you Jayney.'

'Might I ask why you want to know?'

'We frequently need to ask questions of the public but one of our major problems is, in the main we only get to ask questions of people who are here as a result of crime and our emphasis obviously has to be on other matters and under such circumstances we're unlikely to obtain a truthful answer. Frequently we get suspects lying about what they have been involved in and when you ask them a perfectly innocent irrelevant question with no connection they tend to lie about that too. Thank you for being honest with me, I appreciate it.'

'My relationship with Frances is all based around us being work colleagues for a while. Frances and I have kept in touch, but to be honest I'm not sure Morgan understands where we're at. Think to a certain extent the world was passing him by, which is sad.' She thought for a moment. 'He was very much old school and putting my orientation to one side he was never the type of man I would be eager to have just as a casual friend let alone anything more.'

Back at base Larsson headed straight for the crime board where they'd pinned up Morgan's wish list.

'Problem?' Nicky asked.

'No. Just checking. Lesbian's still in bold which if we've got this right means it's still a to do.' She looked at her DS. 'Just met up with that Jayney Bidulph, a friend of Hallam who I discover just happens to be gay.'

'Interesting.'

'Frances grooming them for him was she?' Jake enquired.

'We shall see,' commented Inga as she went into her office. 'Sorry to intrude again,' she said to Bidulph on the phone. 'Just one quick question. Does Frances know you're gay?' Inga heard a sigh then hesitation.

'Well…she's met the wife,' was almost whispered as if others might overhear. 'We had coffee with her one morning I seem to remember.'

'One last thing. Did Morgan Hallam know?'

'How would I know that?' a breath blown out was followed by 'Yes probably. Even in this day and age it's what people do with their, guess what tittle tattle.'

'Thanks, appreciate it.'

As it turned out the Sophie Smallman the girls had given to Inga was really no better. A Primary School teacher she had actually been given Frances's name by a teacher colleague when she was looking to change her car and these days their contact was almost solely through social media.

She was a white British brunette with her own hair and no outstanding features. Except a small tattoo on her arm just above the wrist. No limp, not even glasses and as she drove away from the meet as there was no teacher listed could only imagine she would only be on Morgan's list as his warped way of getting his own back on a nasty teacher from his schooldays. Sophie Smallman, another non-starter.

206

32

Quiet evening at home, Terése tucked up in bed, just the two of them waiting for something decent to turn up on the television they might be interested in. 'Do you know what polyamorous is?'

'Poly what?' Adam asked from his comfy chair.

'Amorous.'

'I know what amorous is.'

'What about if I said I'd be quite happy for you to have sex with any of the clients you fancy,' Adam let the Radio Times just fall into his lap, and offered his wife a grimacing look.

'I know polygamy is about marrying more than one woman. Not sure it happens the other way round, probably a male dominance thing I guess and didn't one of these religious groups practice it at one time?'

'Mormons.'

'I take it that's not what you're talking about.'

'Not the same as an open relationships so I understand. This polyamory business apparently from the case I'm dealing with, is all about being in multiple loving relationships.'

Inga off duty as always wore no make-up, aware she had no need to with her Scandinavian creamy skin tone.

'Don't see the difference. One's married, the other probably isn't I presume. Anyway, I thought you were working on that Hallam murder. All this poly business against the law now is it?'

'I still am. Polyamory is all about being totally honest about what you want and need from your love life.' Adam was all ears. 'It removes all the secrecy from your relationship and to that end there's no having affairs behind your partner's back.'

'Partners plural, and not that you'd know of,' he offered.

'That's the key,' said Inga sat with her legs pulled up under her, glass in hand. 'I'm beginning to think that's what happened in this Hallam case. Some say polyamory is a way to rid yourself of jealousy and in some cases sex is not even involved as it always is in an open relationship.'

'Rid yourself of jealousy. Be serious. How does that work? If you're not jealous now, your wife bedding the milkman'll not do you much good.'

'We don't have a milkman.'

'You know what I mean. Amazon driver then,' was offered with a smile. One of his great features she'd fallen in love with. 'What I want to know is, how on earth would you get involved in all this sort of nonsense?' Adam asked and Inga shook her head. 'Excuse me Madeline, d'you fancy going to bed with me? It's alright Inga knows, and anyway she's having a bit of a lie down with her Desk Sergeant this evening,' made Inga grimace as she sucked in her breath.

'Who might I ask is Madeline?'

'And you say this gets rid of jealousy? Woman in this week with an ankle issue as it happens. Wears stupid high heeled shoes day in day out but you can't tell her that.'

'Like you, I simply cannot image how you'd get started,' the Swede said and sipped her red wine. 'How would we for example approach Cheryl and Harry or Averil and Lewis? What would our opening gambit be?'

'Like we are probably. Just start talking about it.'

'But you'd need to choose carefully. From what I've been reading today love and emotional connections are pivotal, the driving force behind it all, so they say. In the case of the Hallams they had a block either of them could use to stop the other one jumping into bed with any toerag they came across. Be a form of veto to maybe stop Morgan Hallam' wife jumping into bed with the local Ford Dealer for a bit on the side.'

'I've told you what he was like,' Adam reminded her.

During the course of their investigations Inga Larsson had heard a good few tales of Hallam's misogynistic attitude which she had mentioned to Adam. Crude jokes in mixed company many had spoken about and his desire to always be the centre of attention. It still amazed her how such crass individuals were able to survive in modern society.

'Apparently these people sometimes get engaged to one of the other partners,' had Adam with his mouth slightly open. 'Different men bring different types of love into the relationship, so the women don't feel they're missing out on some love elements.'

'You're being serious aren't you,' Adam gasped before he took a drink.

'All the men and all the women have equal rights with each other. Being the husband gives you no particular advantage.'

'Thanks,' he snorted. 'You reckon that's what's behind it? Why he was killed?'

'At the moment it looks to be the only theory, except his body was found as you know out at the Curran's place on the outskirts of North Carlton, and as far as we have been able to ascertain those two aren't into this polyamorous business.' Inga sipped. 'Plus he's a teacher of course,' amused Adam.

He'd never understood why some people talk enthusiastically about their school teachers being there for them, from a lovely family, enthusiastic, encouraging and an inspiration.

From Adam's perspective they were just humdrum teachers. He knew nothing about them away from school and apart from one in his last two years who was a bully there was nothing in particular he could recall about any of them.

'You think he's gone with somebody she doesn't approve of or the other way round?'

'Broken the golden rules of total trust is my guess. Be anybody else and she'd be a prime suspect. Except our luck being what it is, she was heavily pregnant at the time, so that rules her out.'

'Why?'

'How she carry his fat body upstairs? Ask yourself that.'

Adam nodded. 'With his child I take it?'

'Who knows?' Inga shrugged her reaction and finished her wine.

'If that's the case the chances are one or more of them, but more than likely it was him, decided to break the rules and regulations they'd set up as the basis behind it all.'

'He went with somebody else because she was pregnant. Which I understand happens frequently.'

'Always possible at that late stage.'

'So, if you wanted your fancy man to pop round does that mean I'd be forced to go out,' Adam suggested. 'Or d'you get on with it in the bedroom with boyo while I'm sat in here watching the *Celebrity Masterchef*?'

Inga chuckled at the thought. 'Except in the perfect polyamorous relationship as I understand it, we'd agree it was rumpty tumpty night on Thursday and you'd head off out for a bit of slap and tickle with that young blonde you've been treating for her planter fasciitis.'

'If I started a relationship on the quiet with young Sara on reception unbenown to you, that'd be breaking the strict rules. That what it's all about?'

'Most certainly, bearing in mind we'd know each other's lovers, we'd more than likely be friends. You'd be doing it with Ruby Pickard for example.'

'Think I need another drink!'

Glasses filled and Adam joined his wife on the big sofa, placing a box of chocolates between them.

'How did you find all this out?' he asked after eating one.

'Good old social media think it was. Nicky came across it with a bit of help upstairs on the dark net they got from his laptop. Well, it's a list, and we assume. Big clues were boxes ticked for pregnant, red haired and Alopecia. All of which describe his wife.'

'Aha. And Morgan had these lovers as well, that what it looks like?'

'Absolutely. I'm convinced this business might very well be behind his killing. In theory this polyamorous nonsense is all about having a number of lovers, some say they're people you care for as well as just being sexual partners. One thing I read suggested you would for example explain to me why it was you wished to bed one of our friends. Why you hold them in such esteem. In the case of Hallam my guess is he stepped out of line. Broke the golden rule by going with someone outside the precious circle.'

'Somebody off his hit list,' Adam grinned with. 'I was going to say is it really worth killing for, but you'll tell me you've dealt with people who are doing life for far less.'

'The other thing is, we understand he got some woman pregnant.'

'D'you know who?'

'No,' Inga admitted with a shake of her head.

'Pity. Might be off the list.'

'Just imagine if this female wasn't part of the special in-crowd and has a partner, especially as Morgan's wife's recently given birth.'

'Whoops!' Adam chuckled and drank more red wine.

'Here's another question,' Inga continued as she chose another chocolate from the box. 'What if all this polywhatsit business wasn't going on. Why would one woman tell another it was?'

'Sorry,' Adam grimaced. 'I'm not with you.'

'We've been going through her close friends or at least those who she meets for coffee occasionally, one or two she has her ladies what lunch silliness with. None of them, just like you, knew what polyamorous is when we asked. Surely if this Hallam couple were well into it, their friends might have an inkling?'

'Even if they didn't join in you mean?'

'Exactly,' he had to wait as Inga popped the soft milk chocolate Champagne Truffle into her mouth. 'We'd know surely if friends of ours were into something a bit peculiar.'

'Unless it's all done with complete strangers. To us that is.'

'Be serious,' was uttered before more red.

'Can't see what's to be gained by telling someone you're into it when you're not. Like telling our friends we enjoy visiting others to enjoy basking in their hot tub on a frosty night, when we hate the very thought of it. Why would you do that?'

'For some it'd all be part of keeping up with the Joneses.'

'You think me being forced to sleep with Ruby Pickard is just a case of keeping up with the Joneses? Be serious!'

'This is all bad enough but at least its not wrapped up in all that Incel business they reckon is behind the Plymouth murders. At least I'm not dealing with extreme ideology...'

'What's this polyamorous then if its not ideology?'

'You know what I mean. Seems that's all pretty harmless where as with all this Incel coming from America it's a developing theme around hatred for women.'

'I know all about the need for equality, but I do wonder if some of the guff these odd-ball women come out with doesn't help. Sure having badly dressed women on *Match of the Day* gets a lot wound up on social media.'

'That back on?'

'Yeh. New season. Hoardes of supporters rammed into pubs and all without masks.'

'Sounds like a brilliant idea.'

33

Kirsten

You really have no idea how embarrassing it was to get a phone call from that Larsson copper when I was visiting a client. Fortunately Hugh Latham the CX had gone off to organize coffee when my phone rang and it was that daft bissum.

Asking if I knew any of Frances's friends who might be into this polygamous business she was into with Morgan. There's me stood in his office debating this mucky business with Larsson when Hugh walked back in with a young assistant carrying a tray.

In one ear I've got her asking me if I happened to know the names of people Morgan was shagging with Frances's consent, and in the other this bit of a girl asking me if I wanted bloody milk or cream!

I called her back once I had set off from Birmingham and stopped off for a break at the services and a decent coffee.

How on earth would I know who they were? Thought we'd been through all that. It was something I now wish I'd never mentioned and my fear is she just might turn up at the house when Freddie's there and start asking embarrassing questions about people's sex lives.

Told her I don't have a clue. Then next day out of nowhere came a really good example of what could easily happen.

I'd been giving Freddie a hand by dousing the kitchen walls in wallpaper remover in preparation for getting rid of the awful woodchip.

'You nasty bitch!' she spat out the words. 'What in God's name d'you think you're playing at?' was screamed in my ear, the moment I pressed my mobile having seen the name FRANCES pop up on my screen. 'Had that foreign bitch round again, asking all sorts of nasty questions. Musta be you told her about our special arrangement. Was it eh?'

Once again I did the wrong thing.

'I, er…' I mumbled when I should have snapped the phone shut.

'You rotten cow!'

'Frances,' I tried to remain calm as I walked out the backdoor away from big ears, away from Freddie on his hands and knees with this remover gunge. 'Listen to me.'

'Why should I? I thought we had an agreement. I scratch your back, I save your bloody life and you scratch mine. And don't take it I'm the sort who go in for all that shit about saving a life and being responsible for it nonsense. All I asked you to do was open your stupid legs you daft cow! And you couldn't even do that properly. Morgan said you weren't up to much.'

'Either listen or I'll turn you off,' I shouted, then realized I needed more space and walked on over all the rubble, piles of old floorboards and stuff accumulating in the back garden. 'You're not the only one. I've had them at me time and again. They know about some secret list Morgan had, do you know that? Asked me about it. What was I supposed to say when they quoted chapter and bloody verse? To start with I tried saying I didn't know either of you. That didn't bloody work, coz they found out somehow. Some sod musta dobbed on me to that bloody Larsson woman who's suddenly appeared. Couldn't be anybody at work coz they don't know anything. But she knew all about us. See, that's what comes of employing foreigners like her, got a twisted way of thinking them lot.'

'That's all her bloody guess work. There's no stupid secret list for crissakes! Never has been, d'you hear me?'

'You bloody told me about it and that foreign copper quoted from it. How she do that then?'

'What you on about?'

'List of Morgan's conquests.'

'She's lying, just making it up to see what you say. That's how people like her work, over-egging the pudding. When I told you he'd got a list I didn't mean an actual sheet of soddin' paper with people's names scribbled down. You really are a barmy dope at times, d'you know that?'

214

'She knew somehow. How would she know if it's only in his head?'

'I was talking metaphorically, not really. Not bloody written down on a notepad from friggin' Asda!'

'Well, they know now,' I told her as Freddie waved to me out of the backdoor as if tyo say he'd finished, and I waved back. 'Somebody musta told them. Even asked me if I knew of any others he'd been with. Wanted to know what sort, even asked me what's wrong with them. How the bloody hell should I know?' I turned away from the house, worried sick in case Freddie could see my reactions or tried to lip read.

'What about this pregnant woman?'

'Had all that from the bitch. Poking her damn nose in again and the big worry for me is they'll not keep their gobs shut. What's the betting all their nasty gossip will come out and friends get to hear.'

'Now they're asking about a brother…'

'Asked me the same thing,' I retorted quickly. 'Did I know your family? Didn't even know you've got a brother.'

'That's the whole point. I haven't. She's just making it up like this bloody list nonsense.'

'Somebody's gotta be feeding them fake news that's for sure. Otherwise why would they ask something like that?'

'Such as who?'

'How the hell do I know?' I tossed at her.

'Bastards took my laptop.'

'Cops have?'

'Yeh.'

'Anything on it?'

'Bits and pieces.'

'About us?' *I was desperate to know. What I didn't need was date and time of that crap shag in London.* 'Please don't…'

'Lovers,' made me prick my ears up.

'Your lovers, the ones you…?'

'Yeh,' she admitted. 'And his. My best friend's on there, her old man finds out there'll be bloody hell to pay.'

'Look, I've not told that bitch anything, at least nothing they didn't already know.' *Was I making the right decision at last, my mind kept asking as I gabbled on?* 'Denied all sorts to start with, then she came back saying she knew I was lying. Asked about me choking, about Morgan and me, then kept on about your family I've never met. What was I supposed to do?'

'What a bloody mess.'

'How's Niamh?'

'She's fine.'

'Sleeping through?'

'Not yet. Be why I feel so knackered all the bloody time.'

'What's happening now?' *Should I tell her what Larsson was asking yesterday?*

'God knows. They've still got my laptop and that's a real shitty thing to do. Bet they phone them all up, worse thing is if they knock on blokes' doors and their missus answers, shit'll hit the bloody fan then, that's for sure. Like I'm bloody piggy in the middle.' I heard Frances chuckle, 'Talking of piggy, any ideas how I can lose more weight?'

'Colleague at work swears by cakes and bread,' had to be the right decision.

'Eat them?' she gasped and probably prayed I'd say yes.

'No,' I sniggered. 'Cut them out, and anything like crisps and stuff. Easy as, she reckons.'

'Cops get onto you again, you let me know. Now you make sure you do,' sounded like one of my old teachers.

'Same with you. And if I hear anything I'll bell you.' *If I have to.*

I didn't need this hassle really I didn't.

Dealing with Freddie was bad enough. Last night we squabbled again about the necessity for a wood burner. He's still insisting we go for one despite me reminding him how bad it is for air pollution. What's the betting with all yhis climate change business they'll be banned along with gas boilers.

It's not as if this is about choice for us to enjoy. We plan to sell the place, so a decent gas fire compared with the possibility these wood burner things, now getting a bad press from the eco mob, will soon go out of fashion is a no brainer.

Same with a roll top bath I've always wanted. Freddie fails to see the attractiveness with according to him the public are still bathing and showering too frequently. To him a bath is a bath, and frequently reminds me about how his grandmother was washed once a week in an old tin bath in the kitchen, with hot water boiled in a kettle. Plus some guff about using Lifebuoy soap. He also cannot see the advantages of a bidet.

When searching for a forever home I am acutely aware how future proof it would need to be. The current project would to my mind be too remote for children and straddle us with all the school run shenanigans the eco warriors are dead set against, as I am to be honest.

The back garden I was stood in had certainly seen better days but was now all overgrown as if the previous owners had decided on the very day they decided to sell, to do no more. They'd even left an old mower in the shed. That's something else'll needing to be knocked down.

I know Freddie expects me to be more hands-on, but on the other hand if I get it wrong I know he'll make some cheap remark to embarrass me in front of these people he brings in. I could do that, knock that old shed down.

Borrowed shears and secateurs from his father and I trimmed that ivy right back at the front door. He didn't comment, but then that's Freddie for you.

Today it's a plasterer and once I've had a go at this woodchip paper all I can do is tidy up behind him and offer sustenance at the drop of a hat or in truth the moment Freddie shouts down to me.

Once she'd rung off I just stood there in the middle of all the weeds and detritus strewn all over. I was hoping to get a few saplings planted down the far end, but they just keep dumping rubbish for me to clear up. What I'd give for a nice Latte and a scrummy cake. Perhaps if I volunteer to go to Wickes I can head for Costa at the shops or use the new drive-thru.

Right there and then the best I could do was put the kettle on for another boring brew for five. One no sugar, three with one and that lanky acne kid has three spoonfulls.

That skip went this morning and I just hope it's coming back. We've still got all this rubbish all over the lawn or what's supposed to be a lawn needs clearing. S'pose I could do that when the skip comes back. If it comes back.

34

Detective Constable Alexander 'Sandy' MacLachlan had done as he was told and checked out both the car they'd seen at the rambling Hallam house and the owner.

An Azurite Blue Dacia Sandero he'd checked with DVLA and the ANPR team down in Hendon. Not on finance, owned by a Mary-Louise Bach, taxed, insured and she had no penalty points on her licence.

Checking her personally on PNC came up blank but DVLA had given him her name as the registered keeper, her home address which just so happened to be Drovers Cottage in Osbournby which a Google search confirmed to him conveniently was the holiday cottage in the grounds of the Hallams' property and the Land Registry confirmed their ownership.

He'd even then done a search for Drovers Cottage and this had come up as a holiday let. Described as being "within easy reach of the historical city of Lincoln". This delightful property it claimed is tucked away in a beautiful part of the serene countryside. Sleeps four with 2 bedrooms and 2 bathrooms he guessed they meant en-suites, but no pets. Last but not least just as you'd get a liking for it there was an Under Major Maintenance red notice obliterating the enquiry box.

Inga Larsson on receiving his news despite what she saw as progress, was not at all happy. Another outsider in the murderer candidate stakes could be eliminated. This Mary-Louise female had to be the live-in nanny.

The Detective Inspector knew they were on the brink of the culmination of all their hard work in discovering the whereabouts of this Stephen Jon-Joe Jenkins. Anxiously she waited for her second in command to return to the fold with confirmation.

She even had Adam on the phone explaining what his nose had led him to. According to what he'd read on-line the main foundation of the polyamorous business apparently is based upon the freedom to be able to be involved in a relationship that works for you. That is, rather than what the vast majority do if they have any sense, who these people claim, step blindly into monogamy because it's regarded as the way to behave.

It was time to explain to her man how she already had enough info and he could stop digging, but knowing how intrigued he was she knew he'd carry on.

Jake Goodwin was never one to make rash promises to rush forward with false emotion and is very unlikely ever to give anybody a hug when he meets them, and most certainly not these days

Some tend towards dour, but the DI was more interested in his dedication to duty, his experience and more and more over the years his loyalty. She was in no doubt his wife Sally had struck lucky the day he had appeared in A&E, having been hit by an idiot on a bike during the Lincoln 10K.

As Inga spied him in the corridor and watched as the door opened he gave no indication of the outcome of having nipped downstairs to seek out Bill Knapp once more.

The look on his face stood in front of her in the Incident Room was not that of a forbidding and gruff individual. She could see the good news in his eyes.

'Now we're getting somewhere ma'am. He's your man,' he announced to please Inga. 'The guy on the CCTV from Huddersfield hiring the Volvo under the name Neil Sands is the very same person Bill met at the garage who claimed his name was Dez, but we know Dez has to be short for Derek Rumbold the old mechanic guy we busted.'

'He's sure?'

'Got what Bill described as the clean-cut retro set.'

'Sorry?'

'How folk looked according to him before some wassock thought beards might be a good idea and all the thicko's wives got them to follow suit. This Sands is clean shaven, with loads of dark hair, long nose and by the look of him I reckon he'll be the sort of knob to wear shorts,' he chuckled.

219

'And flip-flops?'

'I wouldn't go that far! Unless it was raining of course, then he probably does.'

'And we already know the address he gave when he hired the Volvo matched his driving licence, otherwise they wouldn't have hired it to him.'

'Pretty obvious to me, our Jon-Joe Jenkins has more than one driving licence. One in his real Jenkins name has him living at Rumbold's Eau House and garage. Except,' he hesitated a moment. 'He's not on the current Electoral Register as living anywhere, nor on the 2011 census or listed for Council Tax. Not round here at least. And this Neil Sands purports to live at an address in Hull which we now know is merely one of these back street mangy forwarding address places and we know where all his mail is forwarded to.'

'To near Faldingworth and that Eau House specifically which we know is nothing more than a workshop for cloning cars.' Inga ushered Jake to sit down. 'All this means, the spare DNA cannot be allocated to him until we get a definitive sample.'

'Here's a thought,' he said back sat at his station as he crossed his legs. 'If we go back, we know from PNC how old Harris Hallam got done for VAT evasion and all sorts, but the world it seems is always of the opinion his son Morgan was legit. We been looking at this all wrong d'you think? Is it this Jenkins geezer who's up to all sorts? The one with a false driving licence and one we assume uses false insurance to be able to hire a car? This Jon-Joe is not the grandson of Harris, but is in fact the illegitimate son of the woman who later became his daughter-in-law.'

'Keeping it in the family,' Inga responded as she nodded.

'DNA matching results too and they're waiting on stuff from the Criminal Intelligence Analyst upstairs. Two sets of DNA profiles out at the Curran property remember, were documented as Thanatos Males 5 and 6 according to Forensics. We have Male 5 off a toothbrush and the bedding on a double bed at Eau House.' Inga pulled a face. 'Dare we stretch probability a tad and reckon it's one and the same if we suggest this Male 5 is in effect Jon-Joe Jenkins aka Neil Sands?'

220

They always hoped one of these profiles would by chance come up with a cold hit off the national DNA database. They had the profiles for the Poles, Mateusz Szynabski and Dominik Kozlowski, plus Waziri Abubakar all taken when they were arrested, but there were two more unknowns in that communal room and the toilet and a third not on databases they had fingerprints only for.

'And does that mean therefore he was involved in the killing of Morgan Hallam?' Jake queried seriously.

'But where was he kept for a week or more?' Inga asked and blew out a sigh of annoyance. 'Is there enough of Morgan's DNA back at Eau House?'

'Virtually none, I can ask Shona Tate what her data shows, but if he was hidden there, if he bled out there I think Shona'd have been shouting that sort of news from the rooftops.'

'At least we have a suspect.'

'After we've trawled through a good few.'

'We have a suspect, we think we have a name, we have DNA and probably fingerprints. Even had Nicky and one of ASBO's geeky lads finding an ISP for a laptop in Eau House which we never physically found.'

'He can delete his history all he likes but all the time we have an eTeam upstairs we have the means. Only thing we don't have is an actual person.'

'Thing I still don't understand,' Jake admitted. 'Is why he was dumped in the Curran property?'

'When the link to there is Frances Hallam and Kirsten Wroe.'

'Look at his diary,' said Raza Latif pointing at one of the white boards. 'Look at the initials Hallam used,' he said enthusiastically. 'Just come to me. NS could be Neil Sands.'

'Except,' said Jamie. 'That Jessica Cooke woman at his head office place would know him, surely. She said only one or two initials meant anything to her, stuff like HC for haircut she probably worked out for herself, but she didn't mention NS.'

'But,' said Inga. 'What if she knows him as Jon-Joe Jenkins? Do we have a JJJ on the diary?'

'But that's only for the two weeks he was missing.'

221

'Job for someone, Jamie. Go back to Brough Barn Motors and check the diary. Need dates and times for NS and JJJ.'

'Remember,' said Jake as Jamie got to his feet. 'His name's Stephen so you might find SJ.'

Jamie comes back with bad news, the diary had conveniently been deleted from their computer systems.

Inga arranged with Luke Stevens for two of his bright young eTeam things to head off down to Brough Barn and do one of their Digital Forensic searches of deleted items.

As it turned out it was not all bad. They came back with the news neither SJ or JJJ are listed, but NS appears seven times and they had downloaded a copy onto a USB stick to hand to Inga.

This meant Sam Howard and Jamie Hedley were back to the diary again. This time they had on the boss's instructions gone back a couple of weeks before his disappearance to carry out checks on the people Hallam had visited according to his diary.

Solicitor was number one on the list and they were for some reason immediately anti. Trotting out all the client confidentially nonsense when that was not at all what the pair were after.

Did Morgan Hallam appear to be his normal self, was he at all agitated or appear to have something on his mind? Did he mention anything or anyone which had at the time seemed slightly awry? Was their discussion of the sort they would have expected prior to the meet?

Next up had been a trip down to Huntingdon, where the owner of a small garage admitted due to ill health he was looking to retire before the end of the year. Robert Dickinson admitted it had been the second meeting he'd had with Hallam and they were in the very early stages of discussing the possibility of a take-over.

Such a move would have been Brough Barn's first venture outside Lincolnshire. Back at Lincoln Central they were able to check what Dickinson had said was true. Two weeks previous in the diary was indeed Hallam having the other meeting. Listed as RD at H fitted.

Accountant was up next and this was followed by visits to two of the Brough Barn premises in Mablethorpe and Boston. Neither of those were of any consequence, it was more part of his management style of making his presence visible on a fairly regular basis.

In fact the Boston visit had by chance coincided with it being the service receptionist's last day at work before she got married.

Morgan Hallam was soft enough to have remembered and as Sam and Jamie were advised by staff down there, he had turned up with a bottle of quality champagne and a bouquet of flowers for her.

'Please,' said a soulful Nicky Scoley when that was offered. 'Don't tell me he turned up out of the goodness of his heart acting the perfect boss with champagne and flowers.' Ruth's snigger said her thoughts were not hers alone.

'And wanted nothing in return?'

'Not in the days leading up to her wedding. Please tell me no.'

'There's no blushing bride on the list,' said Inga having scanned the boards.

'Thank god for that!' said Nicky head in hands.

The accountant was not very forthcoming initially but when Sam thought to mention to the partner how they had already visited Dickinson, he became more willing to reveal. The purchase of the Huntingdon garage had been the main topic of conversation at the meeting when he had visited the number crunchers.

The murders down in Plymouth had produced a flurry of activity on the system as a form of warning about the murderer's doctrine and aspects to be wary of. Inga Larsson sat reading through the info about these Incel people. Involuntarily celibate where people are united by their frustrations, injustice and anger over their inability to have any form of relationship with females.

There was a whole screed of information about what was listed as black pill ideology. An extreme and fatalistic faction of this Incel business that dehumanises women and spearheads the desire for male supremacy.

She'd just read about there being an element of acceptance that some Incels see themselves as ugly. She was smiling to herself when Jake walked in, having just read all that. She had no need to worry or check, she knew there was no 'Ugly' on Hallam's list.

'What if I suggest this polyamorous business doesn't exist?' Jake Goodwin looked at his boss with more than a hint of a smile. 'What if I ask you to come up with a good reason why Frances Hallam told Kirsten Wroe, this was the vulgar business they were into?' he grimaced up to Inga in anticipation.

'Seriously Jake? I've spoken to three women. Not one of them has a single trait I could suggest is off Hallam's nasty sexual conquest list. They are all very much what you'd expect from her friends. This tells us surely the same people who are ticks on his list are not part of this sharing group. All white, middle class, happily married with children and nothing I can see as being likely to give him a thrill.'

'But is his list actually connected to this partner swapping nonsense? Is this maybe just his own personal quirk?'

'No,' she admitted. 'I'm just combining the two aspects.'

'It's not suggesting it might not happen in reality. I've got a problem with why would she suggest to Wroe it was going on at all? If you sensed or knew your Adam was up to something like Morgan's tick box system would you tell anybody?'

'For the polyamorous to work it would mean Freddie Curran being involved.' She chuckled and spied out in the Incident Room Nicky Scoley waving a sheet of paper. Inga beckoned her in.

'Just pulled this off from the eTeam. More Hallam stuff hidden away on the dark net they've just managed to unravel. Four couples, and I've just done a quick check with Ruth. None of them are on our social media contacts list and more to the point also not on Hallam' laptop's basic emails.'

'We still got that?'

'CAT's got it.'

'We need to get it back to her before she starts kicking up a fuss.' Inga looked up at Nicky.

224

'That's where they got all this,' she said handing over the sheet of A4. 'They've been dealing with some big fraud business and all that Bitcoins silliness. Think we were at the back of the queue that's why it's taken a while.'

'Thanks Nick.'

Her Detective Sergeant was far from finished with her explanation. 'To hide on the dark net they use what is known as a privacy paradox. Means nobody can figure out who hosts a site, in this case Hallam. ASBO told me before how she has obviously created...'

'Hang on,' said Inga to stop her. 'She?' she almost shouted.

'Yes. Frances Hallam,' said Scoley as if it was obviously her. 'Says she's created her very own corner of the internet which unless you're a top notch geek like he is, becomes totally untraceable.'

'First thing,' said a concerned Inga. 'We saying this Frances is some sort of nerdy IT expert as well.'

'So it seems.'

'Who else do we know who just happens to be an IT expert?' was followed by a wry grin.

'She may well not be boring or socially awkward as they often are, but our Kirsten Wroe certainly ticks the overly IT intellectual box.'

'This puts a whole new...' They waited for Inga to surface from her thoughts. 'I was going to ask for your thinking on this polyamorous nonsense, seeing as nobody I've interviewed knew what it was.' She shrugged lightly. 'Even Adam got confused with Polygamy which of course is marriage to many spouses.'

'What's it called if you're not married?'

'In this day and age probably the same thing.'

'Is it the same for gays?'

'Goodness knows,' said a frustrated DI. 'Anyway this Polyamorous, the desire for intimacy with more than one partner is not to be confused with polyandry or polygyny. Give it a try, ask people and I bet they don't know.'

'This mean we've been chasing the wrong ones,' said Jake without any tendency to gloat.

225

'You thinking these four couples are the ones?' Nicky queried and pointed down at the sheet on Inga's desk.

'What's the chances Stevens can get somebody to investigate further for us? Don't fancy talking to four more which all turn out to be a waste of space.' Inga smiled at her blonde Detective Sergeant. 'You're his favourite, how about it?'

Nicky Scoley just stood there shaking her head slightly as she sniggered. 'Yes Guv,' she sighed softly. 'All right.'

'Well done. I want you to run with this,' the DI announced for all. 'Ruth can help. I want you to find these people and talk to them.' She hesitated a moment. 'Probably best if you tackle the women. At least at first eh?'

'This looks to me very much like a way of them hiding their hobby from the total embarrassment being found out would cause.'

'All a bit much if you've got to be terribly fertive about your hobby. I bet you don't get that with stamp collecting.'

'Maybe not Jake, but what about collecting Coke tins or lawn mowers. You'd not want to admit to that either.'

'At least if you go in for something offbeat, you'd not have to think about slipping into bed at night and lying there right where some other geezer you can't stand the sight of, has been all evening.'

35

Kirsten

What now? I asked myself when my phone bleeped. 'Yes,' was all I managed to say before...

'D'you know Jayney Bidulph by any chance?' a shouting and demanding Frances asked in my ear. 'Used to work at the council now with Barclays.'

'No.' Certainly not a name which came readily to mind and not being a customer of that bank had no reason to visit.

'Well, somebody's been blabbing. Hope for your sake it wasn't you,' sounded very much like a threat.

'What are you on about now?' The lads upstairs having knocked through from the two bedrooms in order to create a Jack and Jill bathroom visitors could share as their en suites, were making a real mess now they were plastering. Knew I'd just put the kettle on and in no time they'd come trooping down for another bevvy to have with their pack-up. Need another good tidy-up after them no doubt.

'Those shitty coppers have started ringing round my friends, and I'm getting sick and tired of all this.' She wasn't the only one.

'I don't know any of your lovers,' I insisted. 'So why ask me? What were they trying to find out?'

'Asking all sorts apparently and as you can imagine all hell's broken loose, they'll hate my guts after this. Friends of ours for years are all bloody upset and who can blame them, this is their private lives being trampled on. God knows what I'll do if it gets on line. What's the betting it'll go viral? Thought those buggers were supposed to be public servants working on our behalf. Always got to poke their bloody noses

227

into matters which don't concern them that's their trouble, and according to Isobel they're making it all sound quite vulgar.'

'What sort of thing?' I asked again, and daren't admit this polywhatsit business they'd got themselves into appeared somewhat quite crude and objectionable to me too.

'Things like, how often we associated with each other, where and what we did. Wanted to know the last time any of them'd seen Morgan. When was it and who was he with and all that sort of business. Really upset some of my dear friends I can tell you, got very intrusive and personal.'

'But none o'that's got anything to do with me.'

'Who says?' Frances shot back.

'I say. You know it hasn't.'

'Aren't you forgetting something?' she asked and I could picture her smiling. 'You knew about Morgan being in your bloody wreck of a house.'

'I did not, and you know that!'

'Oh is that right?' she asked in my ear. 'And just what do you plan to say if that Swedish cow finds out you knew exactly what was going on?'

'I never did!' I shouted then remembered where I was. 'How dare you!'

'You seem to be forgetting I've still got the key you had made. You'll need a damn good excuse when she drags you into the cop station.' I heard Frances laugh and had a feeling somebody was with her. 'Easy trace your credit card payment, they'll go through your transactions like a dose of salt,' she chuckled.

'You wouldn't dare!' I insisted as another rush of adrenalin shot through me.

'Just try me. Now you'd better start doing as you're told in future young lady, or there'll be trouble. D'you hear me?'

I conveniently heard movement upstairs. 'Gotta go,' I told her. 'Got new bathroom being sorted.' Freddie still reckons there's enough in the budget to go for a wet room for us, but I doubt it. All I need is somewhere for a good warm soak.'

'You hear what I'm saying? That key is your get outta jail card,' she chuckled about. 'Hear anything you make sure you let me know pronto, or there'll be trouble,' showed just how interested she was.

Had it been her having work done she'd have shouted it from the rooftops, bragged about how much it cost of course and woe betide anybody who didn't sound jealous and plead for a visit.

She'd be shouting Jack and Jill to me as if it was something she'd invented. Be all surface mounted matching washbasins and terracotta this that and the other. A riot of decadence and her claim to be immersing herself in a luxurious experience with state of the art materials encased in timeless style of opulence they in truth use once in a blue moon.

I'm sure the three lads could sense something was up with me when they trooped downstairs. Managed to make their drinks before I just had to have a wander out the back to collect my thoughts and stop the nerves eating away. Just lucky I was at home that day with Freddie having to go on some course for work. Told me to project manage for him, which in truth meant he'd drawn up a list of do's and don'ts and any of them who seriously didn't follow it exactly to the letter was likely to get their head in their hands to play with. Including me.

I knew I had to pull myself together before he returned as I strolled round to the front and looked down the empty lane.

Cannot imagine how I'd have dealt with Frances had I been at work, or out visiting a client. Knowing her she'd not have taken not answering as a hint that I just might be busy. She'd call me time and again until I'd be forced to connect. Then what? Could hardly stand in a client's office listening to her obscenities and shouting at her down the phone could I?

36

'Can we go through these interviews one by one, please ladies?' Inga Larsson had Ruth Buchan and Nicky Scoley with her in the office. Ruth's glossy chestnut hair that day was in an immaculate plait and must have taken her ages.

'To be honest,' said Nicky Scoley. 'There's not much to tell apart from Rachel Tucker.'

'Even so, let's start with her,' she glanced down at her tablet.

'Said her husband would report me to the chief constable,' Ruth came out with. 32 year old, divorced with no children, Ruth Buchan actually looked worried sat there all down at mouth. Her normal bright blue eyes were dull for once.

'He'll not do that,' said Inga sharply.

'How d'you know?'

'Because they'll not want this out in the open. They report this to our big cheese it'll all come out and if they've got any sense they'll know that. Unions'll get involved and before you can turn round it'll be trending on social media, papers will hype it up and remember in this day and age transparency is a big plus for the likes of us.'

'I told you,' said Nicky.

'Cheer up,' said Inga. 'Now what happened?'

'We decided to take it in turns,' Nicky admitted. 'Doesn't help Ruth if I take the lead all the time. It's fine sitting in and being there but when you've got to think for yourself at times like that, it's a different ball game.'

'Agree with that,' Inga confirmed. 'Looks like you picked a good one to start with,' she sniggered. 'So?' she posed to Ruth.

'Went through the usual opening business of introducing ourselves and then we got round as you suggested to talking

230

about Hallam, but it was the moment I mentioned this polyamorous business.'

'Be honest guv, she went ape shit. This scraggy old bint all dressed to the nines swearing and shouting like a ....fish wife.'

'She was on her feet effing and blinding at me,' Ruth confirmed. 'Telling me my career was over, how dare I go into her home and suggest such disgusting things, did I realize who they are, what position they hold in society,' made Inga pretend to yawn. 'Didn't I realize how powerful her husband is and all this blah, blah, bloody blah.'

Inga was amused but pleased at how Ruth had exploded to give their chat more grist, to make it sound real rather than some drib drab report she so often gave. There had always been two sides to Ruth, the good and bad and it was a case of never knowing which one would turn up for work.

'And her husband is who?'

'An architect,' said Nicky. 'Designed one of those crap university buildings.'

'Chances are he's also a Mason or somesuch, which he probably believes makes him important and be how he gets his jobs.'

'Sixty years ago maybe when folk were naive.'

'Self-important,' said Inga. 'He is valuable, but only in his own head. In the end he's like so many of them, just an important nobody, to my mind. To my Swedish mind.' Inga smiled at Ruth. 'Guess she never admitted anything at all.' Ruth and Nicky both shook their heads. 'That tells its own story, she's worried sick it'll get out.' Inga sat back in her chair. 'That's Rachel and...'

'James,' Nicky prompted.

'What's she like? '

'First thing to strike me,' said the blonde DS. 'Was her past shoulder length flop of corkscrew curls and her gums show when she talks, dressed in these denim dungarees with high heels,' made Inga grimace. 'Sort I bet who've just got to pull you into a hug.'

'Nice,' sarcastic Inga scoffed. 'Who's up next?'

'Emma Maalik-Taylor,' said Ruth as her boss's face asked the question. 'Just totally denied it, said she had absolutely no idea what we were talking about. Everything she said was part of a nervous laugh. Told its own story.'

'Same for the other two,' Nicky said. 'Had the feeling by then the word was out on the grapevine and they'd been tipped off. Sort of sensed it, totally denying the situation but behind it all was this feeling they'd been fore warned. Got to say, none of the rest were anything like as irate as madame Tucker.'

'Our guess is, it was probably her who phoned the other three,' Ruth offered. 'Felt as if they were part of some clandestine secret society almost.'

'What Connor calls hugger-muggers.'

Inga Larson was sat there with her fingers steepled. 'Think we can take it as read this tacky business really is going on, but as it's not a crime and all the time the participants are adult and willing there's not a lot we can do about it.'

'By the way the fourth one Olivia Willan has to be the one I told you about I was looking for, on social media they just say Olivia. Has to be her surely. She's the one if you remember who's divorcing her husband on the grounds of unreasonable behaviour.'

'It's that all right,' Inga offerred.

'You think it confirms what Kirsten Wroe told us was true?'

'Always felt it had to be, why else would anybody come out with such a story otherwise. Not just generally, but telling us as well. By suggesting this all went on and how she was personally involved in at least one incident she's admitting to. Why on earth would Wroe put herself in the firing line otherwise? What if she's not told Freddie Curran?'

'Don't you think she'd have to admit to him early doors?'

'Difficult,' said Nicky. 'Worry me sick I'm bloody sure having to tell Connor I was party to all that grubby business.'

'And if she hasn't, when she walked in on Hallam's body in their bed, surely she had to say something then.'

'Unless she knew.'

'Even so, if she hasn't then if it all comes out he might well not be best pleased with her. I've just been looking for a connection somehow between all that business and somebody killing Hallam.'

'A word,' was Inga Larsson stopping Nicky Scoley in the corridor. 'Is it me or do we see remnants of a change in Ruth these days?'

'Could always be the subject matter.'

'How d'you mean?'

Nicky stopped as someone walked past. 'Her relationship breakdowns.'

'Divorce you mean?'

'She in effect brought on herself.'

'Really? I didn't know that.'

'Been with her boyfriend, they were at school together initially, a good year or two. Then out of the blue this guy appears on the scene and she sort of capitulates and like a spider to the fly he drew her into his web. Boyfriend gets dumped just like that,' she clicked her fingers. 'She's with this new one, moved in with him which she hadn't done with the boyfriend.'

'He the one she married?'

'Yes. Within six months I understand, and then it all changed in no time at all. Utter control freak with a really nasty business of her having to write down every penny she spent and once a week sit down and explain to him why.'

'What?' The Inspector gasped. 'Explain why she bought bread and milk you mean?'

'He decided who her friends were, spent all their money on his motorbike and then by sheer chance she bumped into her old boyfriend.' Nicky stopped. 'Walked out on the nasty piece of work she'd shacked up with and he threatened her which she used to get the divorce and tried to go back to the boyfriend. He quite rightly didn't want to know after what she'd done to him and before you can turn round she was soon back home with her parents.'

'You think dealing with Morgan and the women and the poly business has had an effect.'

'Certainly more up for it with this case, than she usually is.' Nicky checked there was nobody nearby and dropped her voice. 'When she tried to get back with the boyfriend she only made contact through a mutual friend. Dave Mason a firefighter we happen to know as it happens. Apparently the old boyfriend's reaction was if she couldn't be bothered to speak to him face to face to apologize they had no future.'

'Absolutely right.'

'Still on her own, lives in that one-bedroomed flat off Hykeham Road.'

'Interesting. Thanks.'

37

Kirsten

There it was again, another interruption. The name LARSSON on my phone this time at work on Monday morning I decided to ignore for once. Then less than ten minutes later the Swedish name was back to haunt me once again.

It crossed my mind as I got on with my work how it might well be in my best interests if I admit having got a spare key made at Timpsons for Frances. Perhaps that'd stop all this harrowing business from those beastly policewomen. Come clean at last? Was that really a good idea, I asked myself sat peering at my monitor.

At the time I was working on the finite detail of our new Employee Employer Correlation strategy for a health authority in mid-Wales. To just put our system for supporting effective management to one side just to answer a load more of her annoying questions was just not on.

I knew of course, as I ploughed on, how making such a confession at this stage would throw up a whole host of other major complications. Not least of which of course would be Freddie. Do I dare admit to him before I confess to Larsson about how I'd allowed a woman he didn't know and had never met, to access our new property? Admitting to what I'd allowed to happen to his new obsession, could very well be absolutely disastrous.

What would that do to our relationship particularly if it turned out really bad and me with my own money invested in that ramshackle of a home?

'I'm at work. I'm very busy. I'll call you back,' was me giving in eventually at the fourth time of asking.

'This *is* work Kirsten,' was quick enough to stop me. 'Just a couple of quick questions. Do Brough Barn or Frances Hallam in particular happen to be clients of yours?'

'Don't be silly,' I chuckled to myself at the irrational suggestion.

'Why is it silly?'

'Look. I would imagine Brough Barn has a system of sorts. They're not main dealers so they'd not need anything too complex with links to the factory and other dealers nationwide. But, how au fait is Frances with IT and the internet?'

'Are you serious?' I couldn't help but snigger when I spoke. We're talking about the wife of Morgan Hallam, not the head of BMW or Maserati.

'Very much. What do you know about the Dark Net?'

'We tinker with it for a few clients who have a particular need of an added layer of secrecy, but to be honest our main strategies tend to be Cloud based.' *Which I'd like to be getting on with if you'll just leave me alone.*

'So, you're saying it is very unlikely Frances Hallam is a proficient user of complex issues such as a privacy paradox for example?'

'Now you are being silly,' I said to dismiss the idea but I have to admit was quite a complex issue she was quoting about. 'Can't imagine she's much past basic Word or Excel. Think she does what she wants on her phone.' Why on earth would this foreign bloody copper know about privacy paradox?

'Thank you,' said Inga. 'Sorry to disturb you.'

'Why do you ask…?'

The phone had gone dead and I just sat there looking at it in my hand now clearly with something else to worry my tiny mind about. Time to take a break and wander down to see Nabhaan to find out why some foreign policewoman would even have heard of the privacy paradox.

38

In the main this MIT bunch of cops only got together as a group socially when there was something to celebrate, usually other than a conviction. Birthdays, anniversaries and Christmas and that sort of thing. Never been a tedious once a week after work downing of pints of ale like the old uniform guys still brag about.

DS Nicky Scoley knew from talking to Inga Larsson she had little time for a pie and half a dozen pints and the inevitable relentless oft repeated anecdotes about long since retired cops. Tales of scallywags they'd all come across. Shouts they'd been on, the good, the bad and decidedly dodgy one's they'd served with. Scurrilous tales of coppers wives and what they'd been up to when hubby was on nights, and who with.

All that immature business of being forced to get a round in and taking the piss out of any poor soul not keeping up with the supping rate was not something Inga Larsson had ever been able to abide right back to her university days.

Coffee or tea and Swedish home-made cake was the usual offering back in the Incident Room. It was what both men and women enjoyed back home and what she was used to when she was back visiting family and friends in Sweden. Different world, different attitudes and lifestyles.

This was more like it. Sat deep and comfortable inside a Costa, doing things the Swedish way with a Fika. Coffee, cake, good company and a healthy chinwag.

Why she wondered was there not one single male there with a babe in arms, the norm in Sweden? Guys out socializing happily with their pals, but encompassing their fatherly duties at the same time?

'Look. I'll be honest,' Inga said once they were settled and had given the Taliban advance in Afghanistan a mention

237

'Reason I wanted a chat was, apart from it's been quite a while since we've got together to put the world to rights, I wanted to talk polyamorous with you.' Inga sat back and chuckled. 'The look on your face!' she laughed. 'Not like that, not suggesting we make up a foursome to try it out. Just needed someone to talk it over with.'

Nicky had puffed out a breath at the thoughts running amok. 'You think this is all part and parcel?'

'Every night when I get home Adam has another question for me. Mainly to be honest about how on earth you'd get started on all this business. Reckons he's looked at clients in a whole different way since I told him what had been going on. Wonders how on earth he would suggest to these women he deals with, there might be an alternative therapy,' made both women chortle. 'I've always wondered about swingers; how would it ever come up as a subject in polite conversation?' the blonde pondered.

'My big concern is trying to see our particular pair being involved. They're like chalk and cheese or were.'

'I never knew him of course, but from what people say I don't see it, because from what I've looked up, the talk on the net is all about love, not just sex and he was his own biggest fan.'

'He was his own bestie,' seemed to Nicky to be a most peculiar phase from the boss.

'Where'd that come from, some awful late night telly nonsense?'

'Exactly. Sort of thing we watch because we cannot believe anything that bad ever got past the first concept stage.' Inga took her first cappuccino sip, stirred her drink once more with the long spoon and sat back.

'Before long you'll be coming out with that bro nonsense. Innit!'

'Think that's a step too far,' Inga laughed then became serious. 'Frances Hallam is an attractive woman for her age to be fair, but what about him? Good looks some would say, but what about the rest of him, not to mention his personality or lack of? Are these other women looking for a bit of rough? Married say to an accountant or some boring office wallah, isn't

Morgan Hallam more exciting, more experimental, rough and ready maybe?'

'More experienced by the sound of him.'

'Something you tend to get with the media. Put forward the notion that some personality or sportsman is the new face, the one with a sparkling personality and charismatic...'

'When in truth they are absolutely nothing of the sort.'

'Women wetting their knickers over some oaf like Boris Johnson.'

'Just the type who are simply boring loud mouths, the sort decent intelligent women run a mile from in towns and cities countrywide.'

'Absolutely right.' Inga pulled her mouth in as she thought. 'They're looking for the excitement their marriage lacks with some boring fart they're got stuck with. Once a week, once a fortnight there's good old Morgan with his sexual antics to give their lives a boost.'

'From what I've read it deals with various sexual urges,' said Nicky lowering her voice as she scanned those sitting nearby. 'Woman has timid urges but has to deal with a partner who is a twice a night athlete.'

'And this business sorts it you think?'

'He finds, or more than likely the wife finds him a randy wench to visit two or three times a week to satisfy her hubby's lustful needs, leaving her in the missionary position on Saturday night once a fortnight but only in months with twenty nine days,' a suggestion they both chuckled at.

'Those women we spoke to off that dark net list of hers. Are we really saying they were rushing round to the Hallam household for regular frolics? Chairperson of this that and all the others. The Mayoress seriously gasping for it? Spend all day doing good deeds in a charity shop and rushing home for a night out with dirty mouthed rampant tubby Morgan?'

'Do the Townswomen's Guild have French knickers on their Easter tombola stall, they're all absolutely desperate to buy a ticket for? What can you get at Oxfam I wonder?'

'We got this all wrong?' Inga posed. 'This not how it is at all?' She sat forward to drink, and then licked the froth from her lips. 'This one who's pregnant. What happens there?'

'How d'you mean?'

'Forget who got her pregnant for now. Instead just think about her situation practically. Does she still go off out to spend a few hours with the other men in their group? How does her husband feel about other men having sex with his partner who's with his child?' Nicky Scoley grimaced at the thought. 'And what if he doesn't actually know who the real father is? What if he has doubts? What if he's not at all sure she's with *his* child? Will he be bringing up another man's baby as his own, and is the other man still getting his share?'

'Must be loads these days who face that dilemma.'

'Except, this is deliberate. Not casual bonking on the sink estates. His woman had sex with two or three other men with his blessing, one of whom just happened to get her in the family way.'

'Is that the crux of the matter?' Nicky asked sat there with white cup in hand. 'Morgan got one of these women pregnant and this is her old man getting his own back?'

'Demanding Morgan contributes to the child's upbringing maybe. And with Frances at that time also heavily pregnant says no way. Aware how she will likely react if he hands out say a grand a month to a solicitor or an accountant or a university lecturer.'

'Or the rag and bone man,' she chuckled at. 'Not always couples Connor read somewhere, in some cases its one woman and two men all living and sleeping together.'

'Enough now,' Inga put her hands up, then took a decent drink of cappuccino. 'What you doing about a holiday this year?'

'We've been looking looking at train holidays for quite a while. Maybe do the Dordoyne, based on Paris we could reach with Eurostar. Think Connor's also interested in the Rhine Valley.'

'That sounds good.'

'Not yet though. Find ourselves our there somewhere and it turns orange or red even. Might look for a cottage some place but prices have gone through the roof.'

'Be a day out at Skeg then.'

For a while the pair didn't talk much as they set about the cake, a major Fika ingredient. Banana and Pecan Loaf they'd both gone for and as usual they chatted about some of the women sat nearby and their antics. One delicately picking the centre out of a muffin to pop in her mouth in a strange manner to suggest she needed to avoid what she saw as the crust. The uncoordinated clothes some wore was always a popular and amusing observation subject for the pair.

A suffering these fools very gladly time.

39

'Looks like she's in the same boat as us,' Inga Larsson announced to the few in front of her back at Lincoln Central. 'According to Wroe she thinks Hallam is just an everyday basic with IT and we certainly never imagined she'd be into it all.'

'Do we know,' Ruth, deputising for Michelle asked turning to look at Nicky. 'If it was actually her on the dark net, or somebody doing it for her?'

'Like Kirsten Wroe, for example you mean?'

'Always possible.'

'I'll take ASBO a glass of hot water and a stick of liquorice. See what I can suss.'

'Except he'll not know if its Wroe working with Hallam or working for her.'

'With ASBO you just never know. He's always producing artefacts of note I can then continue with.'

'Here's a thought I had in the middle of the night,' said a smiling DI. 'Our Kirsten Wroe isn't married to Curran. Been doing a bit of checking. The house out at North Carlton is in his name only.' She heard two or three suck in a breath. 'Is it me or do we expect her to be more intelligent than that?'

'He pops his clogs and what's she left with? Nicky asked, and immediately answered. 'Bugger all.'

'Unless he's made a will.'

'Possibly not, which means she'll be in a whole heap of trouble.'

Some forces Inga Larsson knew had what were called 'set-asides'. Small comfortable areas where officers can discuss issues away from their particular departments full of big ears with specialist crime experts or the forensic guys, even with the likes of ASBO all over a hot drink.

Lincoln County were behind the times on a number of issues just like the county itself. Time enough Nicky'd been told and nipping up to see ASBO was such an occasion when just a quiet chat over a mug of hot water and a decent coffee might well oil the wheels better.

The Detective Inspector was not the only one using the knowledge Nicky Scoley had gained over time. The same went for Sandy MacLachlan and Jamie Hedley still doing their best to investigate the car cloning business with Sam Howard having been returned to PHU as things quietened down and the budget restraints once again came into play.

Sandy had never been a desk jockey or as some saw them, monitor monkey. He'd tried being behind a desk all day before he signed up. Being with MIT had been a good move as he was able to switch roles frequently as force numbers declined.

They were still looking at the Rumbold garage place, which with the aid of a little bit of subterfuge they had managed to access.

'We still have no Jenkins,' Inga Larsson said icily as her phone whistled with an incoming text. She read it and placed the silver phone back in front of her. 'Yes maybe being arrested did come as a shock to Rumbold's system, but now he's out surely there has to be some contact. The eTeam looked at his phone I'll grant you, but that was then, this is now. Sorry, but nobody's that innocent. Keep an eye on him but at the same time remember our primary target.'

'According to his missus he doesn't even go to the pub.'

With Derek 'Dez' Rumbold out on bail, in an attempt to satisfy the boss the pair had arranged for Ruth to drive out to the garage on a scouting mission on their behalf.

The far end was back up and operating as normal in as much as Rumbold was there on his own. Bonnet up, tinkering with a car. She could not miss the false wall she'd been warned about, now back in place it appeared with the magazine cuttings still intact.

From what Ruth reckoned it sounded as if nothing much had changed. It had the look to her of a cheap as chips backstreet lock-up but out in the countryside backed onto a nice big house.

DC Ruth Buchan playing the naive little woman made tentative arrangements with Derek Rumbold to have her car given a once over pre-MOT check the following Thursday, saying she needed to consult her diary at work and would call him to confirm.

Being a woman she had taken on board sights such as old chocolate bar wrappers lying about, the three barrels the lads had mentioned and spotting one empty Chelsea mug on the desk.

Rumbold appeared to be in no hurry to see her off the premises as they stood chatting and there were no signs of anybody else having been there of late.

Back at base the Sandy and Jamie duo's next assignment was to take Nicky Scoley's advice gained from previous experience in Cambridge, on how to ask the ANPR process to indicate alternative data by filing his car registration number with the known registered keeper details, linked to insurance.

Once the concept was all set up the pair simply had to wait for Rumbold to be spotted by one of the traffic cars or to make a hit on an ANPR camera somewhere. Initially, the pair spent some time in the operations room waiting and hoping but had to keep returning to their desks to get on with other tasks involving Rumbold's garage and the car cloning business.

Derek Rumbold never went past any camera or a car with the live system anywhere along the route from the garage to his home just outside Middle Rasen all morning.

It was as Faye Rumbold had told them when they visited. These days, her Derek just went to work and came home. Even stopped going to the pub of a weekend and just stayed put playing with his model trains. Stopped going for a pint during the pandemic and had never returned. Faye admitted she bought bottles for him when out shopping. She had no idea why of course but had also admitted there no longer seemed any need for him to doss down at work of a night.

A routine the boss doubted he would be capable of keeping to for very long, but neither of them were so sure.

Sandy and Jamie who happen to be MIT's biggest and fittest two guys guessed Dez would have set off to work in the morning. Later travelling around the back roads, home again for a spot of lunch via Faldingworth. At last the scruffy Mitsubishi was zapped by a patrol car and the timing told Sandy and Jamie he'd be heading home for lunch and a decent cuppa with slim trim Faye. That happened at 13.07 with all cars instructed not to intervene, not to pull over the vehicle no matter what.

Jake Goodwin was of the opinion Derek Rumbold had somehow been bullied or coerced into being involved in the car cloning. Now he had been caught up in the arrests he was convinced the canny fella was dutifully obeying the law, going to work and back home again. Probably how he had been prior to becoming involved somehow with all the nicked and cloned motors.

Then out of the blue when Sandy and Jamie were thinking it was pie time and reckoned Rumbold was having lunch with his missus, his vehicle pinged another on-board camera at 13.24. The alert was just seven minutes later through the integrated asset system he had been spotted by the ANPR camera in an unmasked police Skoda Lima November One-Two-Six which was heading south along the straight A15 towards Lincoln. With on-board cameras scanning every vehicle there was no escaping.

Impossible for Rumbold to cover that distance in that time no matter what he was driving.

Quick thinking by Jamie Hedley saw him call Derek Rumbold's mobile and arrange to take his car to him later as he was having starting problems. Rumbold admitted he was having a lunch break but would be back just after two but if it turned out to be anything serious it'd have to be next week before he would get round to it.

Hedley and MacLachlan didn't bother to actually visit the man at the garage for fear of being recognised, but they'd managed to get out nearby just in time to spot him turn off at Faldingworth heading the right way.

Five minutes later the Duty Ops Manager phoned Jake to advise how Derek Rumbold's vehicle registration had now pinged a static camera on the A1. At the same time others were checking what mast activations his phone had made.

In co-operation with South Yorkshire, a black Mitsubishi Shogun with false plates, was pulled in by a proactive Intercept Team and the driver arrested.

'My money was on the Dacia!' Ruth shouted the moment she heard about the arrest. 'One we saw remember, boss?' she called out to Inga Larsson. 'Had this feeling he might be driving the nanny's car remember. The one we saw when we interviewed Hallam.'

'And that has to be why you can't hire the holiday cottage at the moment,' the boss said at her door. 'When I last checked, the website said something about maintenance work.' She shrugged. 'Never mind eh?'

'What if,' Nicky joined in. 'What if this Jenkins has been holed up in the holiday home all this time?'

'The idea this guy and Morgan Hallam had a bust up keeps nagging away. Our big problem has always been us not having his DNA or prints.'

'We will now.'

'And they found three cocaine wraps remember and a drug swab done at the roadside proved positive.'

'He dealing as well?'

'Must have been sheer luck he didn't happen to be at the garage when we raided,' a smiling Jake offered.

'Or in the house with Frances when we called. '

'Unless he nipped out the back of course.'

'They're still using poor old Rumbold,' Inga offered in a sad tone. 'Put everything in that poor sod's name, even nicked his number plate now. He that desperate to keep his job or does he owe them maybe? Did something naughty a while back and this Jenkins and his sister are using him. Blackmailing him?' she wondered out loud. 'Did old man Hallam find out what they were up to maybe? Just has a bad reputation with his big sexist gob, but under it all he was a decent bloke. I've got a feeling he really did learn right from wrong when his old man went inside.'

'He visit him inside had a look around and decided not for him. Not at all his idea of a home from home as some bad lads do.'

'But as far as I can see Rumbold's not actually done anything wrong. All he's doing is going to work, fixing folks cars and playing with his train set when he gets home.'

'Naughty,' said Raza. 'They're miniature railways they're not train sets. They're what you get for a five-year-old at Christmas.'

'Pardon me for living,' Jake pulled a face. 'It's the Shogun with false plates with no BS standard. Bet they got them off the net no doubt like all these dimwits do.'

'You'd not be able to do that in Sweden,' the Detective Inspector told her team for the umpteenth time. 'You can only buy number plates through the government and the sooner it applies down here the better.'

'Some folk love them,' Raza offered.

'It's because you can buy number plates which mean absolutely nothing to anybody except the pillock who paid a small fortune for it. Only way people like this shower of skanks can get away with it. Our lads can never spot that Shogun and think hey the number is a lot older than the car, when it could easy be the initials of the scrote in a vest.'

'What?' Jake gasped. 'Surely you're never suggesting we make it illegal, and stop the misfits trying to make up stupid words?'

'Or create something daft only they know what it is'

'Which is exactly my point. What if,' a grinning Inga crossed her fingers she held in the air. 'His DNA and prints they'll be taking downstairs in a while, match that on the parcel receipt machine, and the spare DNA at Curran's place and on the bedding?' She saw the look on cautious Jake's face. 'Perhaps not eh?'

'Have we ever been that lucky? Because if we are I'm off to do the Lottery!'

The two DCs, Jamie Hedley and Alexander MacLachlan were as pleased as Punch stood anxiously waiting for the Shogun driver who'd had the cheek to offer the arresting officers a driving licence in the name of Derek Rumbold, to be brought into custody.

When the pair first caught sight of him all handcuffed up, it was not quite the image of the person they were expecting to see. It was clearly and obviously not Derek Rumbold although the driving licence claimed he was.

247

This was as it turned out, Stephen Jon-Joe Jenkins aka Neil Sands but did not instantly fit the CCTV images they were used to seeing of him hiring the Volvo in Huddersfield.

What had made them look twice was the fact his head had been shaved, gone was the chunk of dark hair and he was growing a beard in an attempt to disguise himself, which was fine to a certain extent except without his mop of hair and added whiskers, he looked nothing at all like his fake driving licence.

Charged with the car theft, cloning, drug driving, driving with false licence and subsequently no insurance, plus being in possession of other false paperwork they were able to hold him in custody awaiting further enquiries and carry out a Buccal swab for DNA and get his prints.

'His Shogun's gone to the lab,' Jamie advised Inga back up in her office. 'They're looking for anything connecting it with Morgan of course.'

'Had a good valeting since then I imagine.'

'Could always be one they've cloned too.'

'Serial number on the engine block'll confirm it.'

'Old Morgan was taken to North Carlton somehow remember, and according to the Crime Scene Team we know he didn't die in situ. If he died in the boot it'll mean we're making good progress.'

As it turned out his real driving licence and valid insurance for the Shogun were in the name of Stephen Jon-Joe Jenkins with Eau House as his home address. The licence in the name of Neil Sands had Drovers Cottage as his residence and Sands was in addition a named driver on Rumbold's insurance. For imitating Rumbold it had him residing at his house in Middle Rasen on a totally separate policy.

Remanded in custody suited the team down to the ground. Had him where they wanted him while all the murder scene forensics was double-checked down in Leicester to make absolutely certain.

While all this was going on Nicky Scoley had got Ruth Buchan to start a search in an attempt to discover exactly who the original Neil Sands had been.

40

Tuesday morning and Inga Larsson was in her car when she made the phone call. Ruth Buchan who had never met Frances Hallam, was parked up in Osbournby just before the church. Close enough to the American style barn on the eastern outskirts of Sleaford, to be able to see who was coming and going from the property with Nicky Scoley wearing Connor's baseball cap pulled down over her eyes, sat alongside her.

'Larsson here. Know its short notice Mrs Hallam,' Inga said when her phone was answered. 'But I'm going to be in Sleaford around ten, wondered if we could meet up at the Riverside Café for a bit of a chat?'

'What for now?' Hallam sounded so forlorn.

'Just tying up a few loose ends. Box ticking we're lumbered with these days.'

'Must I?' Hallam sighed.

'That or you'll need to come up here. Happen to be down in your area this morning, thought it'd be an ideal opportunity.'

'Where's here?'

'Lincoln Central. Yes I know all this business is a pain, but I promise we'll be able to leave you in peace after this. Quick chat over a decent coffee, be better than one from the canteen in our dreary interview room don't you think?'

A sighed 'All right,' showed she was more than a tad reluctant. 'That the one at the craft and design place you mean?'

'That's the one. About ten then?'

'Yeh, okay.'

'I'll get them in, what's yours?'

'Latte.'

'And a scrummy cake suit eh?'

249

Larsson then called Nicky and explained the trap had been set and twenty minutes later Detective Constable Ruth Buchan sat waiting in Osbournby watching Hallam pull out and zoom past in her Toyota.

Ruth followed at a safe distance and eventually let her go and parked up in Silk Willoughby. The pair sat there just to see if by a piece of bad luck Hallam had forgotten her phone, or had an urgent message to return home.

Inga had been into the National Centre for Design to familiarize herself with the layout and exhibitions, and to check what was on offer at the Riverside Cafe Bar.

Places like that always worried her. The current exhibition in the main gallery according to a leaflet was described as being by an interdisciplinary artist weaving technological principles to bring a sense of the human touch to technology.

Back outside, Inga Larsson waited until she saw insouciant Frances Hallam striding towards her from the direction of the car park.

Inga Larsson had always wondered if the insufferable snobs of this world such as Frances Hallam were bred that way. Was being obnoxious an attitude she had been born with, inherited or taught. In the presence of such women the DI knew to behave or be considered as uncouth by a hypocrite.

'Nicky,' she said into her phone. 'She's with me now. Do your best.'

As the pair met with a gentle fist bump Hallam forced, there was to Inga one clue. No make-up plastered on or not would ever hide the dark shades under her eyes, a new baby's mother had to endure.

Ruth Buchan scooted back to Osbournby High Street, past the church and turned into the big property. She carefully pulled her car up close to the granny flat come holiday cottage just across the way from the big barn conversion. She and DS Nicky Scoley who'd dumped Connor's baseball cap walked up to the door masked up and knocked.

It was opened within thirty seconds by a mid-twenties lovely looking slim long haired blonde woman dressed stunningly in a pale pink vest, white shorts and gleaming white tennis shoes.

What was the most stunning look about her as well as her red bra straps on display was her left arm and shoulder covered in a whole whirl of amazing coloured tattoos.

'Yes?' she said.

'Hello Marie-Louise. We represent newborn health, an arm of the NHS. Your usual post natal visiting nurse has unfortunately been called away on urgent family matters. We're doing our best to cover as many new mums as we can. As we were in the area we thought we'd just pop in see how Niamh is getting along.'

'Elese was here last week.'

Nicky couldn't take her eyes off this black and grey ivy climbing up, round and all over her arm with rose buds and some in full bloom in stunning oranges and reds. All of which detracted from the on trend scruffy look of tucking a few front inches of the vest into her shorts.

'This is just a quick check, we're just popping our heads into as many new mums as we can, see if they've got any issues, trying to save Elese needing to rush around catching up when she's back.'

'Our role,' said Nicky. 'Is just to cover the general care of mother and baby and look for any danger signs post-natal. One of the new services introduced in the Health Budget earlier this year as you probably know.'

'I'm not the mother, though.'

'We did tell Frances we would be calling sometime to help Elese out. It was her said we'd find Niamh over here.'

'She didn't say,' she sighed and stepped aside. 'S'pose you'd better come in.' Marie-Louise scouped up a pale blue mask from a unit beside the door.

'Where is she then?' Ruth gushed the moment they were inside, rubbing her hands together like an anxious aunt.

'This is lovely,' said Nicky looking all about the very clean and tidy holiday cottage. Pick this up and plonk it by the sea someplace or in the Lake District it'd be perfect. 'This where you live?'

'Yeh.'

'Delightful.'

'Frances, I mean Mrs Hallam lives over in the big house and I do a bit of nannying for her. Had to rush out a bit earlier, so I've got her over here for now.'

When they were led into one of the two pretty bedrooms both detectives went through the bill and coo business to create the right atmosphere. They didn't touch the baby or suggest they make any kind of examination.

'Well, I've got to say she does look fine,' said Ruth. 'Sleeping well?'

'Most of the time.'

'What a lovely baby, Frances must be so happy. Tired of course which is understandable, but she's an absolute delight.'

'Just a courtesy call really, doing our bit to help Elese,' Nicky offered. 'Ticking boxes for her.'

'Is there a problem?' Marie-Louise Bach asked.

'Family business,' said Nicky. 'All we've been told I'm afraid. Haven't asked and we don't want to pry. Just trying to make life easier for her when she gets back.'

'Everything's fine,' said Ruth 'Have you got any problems you wish to discuss at all?' She prayed for a negative.

'No.' Her lengthy hair waved as she shook her head.

'That's good then.'

'Gonna be a nice day,' said Nicky looking out of the main window as they returned to the lounge. 'Good chance to get her out in the fresh air.'

'Thanks for that.'

'Oh,' said Nicky and stood still. 'Would you mind awfully if I just borrowed your loo? Been a busy morning and we've a good way to go next, with having to make these extra calls.'

'No probs,' said Marie-Louise and gestured to the bathroom.

'What a lovely place this is. Never been out this way before,' said Ruth. 'Better than some of the places we have to visit I can tell you.' The pair stood chatting casually until rubbing her hands together Nicky Scoley appeared.

'Thanks for that.'

'Good to meet you Marie-Louise' said Ruth and followed her to the front door.

'Thanks a lot,' said Nicky as she followed Ruth out. 'Grimsby here we come,' she chuckled with and the pair walked to the car without saying another word.

'I'm thinking it's not real when she opened the door,' said Nicky once they were back onto the road. 'All those tatts.'

'Get anything?'

'Bloody tempted to nick the toothbrushes but there was hair on a hairbrush and bits on a comb in a cupboard I've bagged up. Beard trimmer looks new so I've emptied that plus a load of man stuff. Made a note of a couple,' she said and pulled out her notebook. 'One called Kiehl's anti-perspirant and deodorant and an Acqua di Parma stick. Bet they're covered in prints.' Nicky put her notebook away and turned to look at Ruth. 'D'you remember what was on Morgan Hallam's hit list we've just seen?'

'No. What?' Ruth asked as she headed off up the A15.

'Tattoos, and if I remember rightly it was ticked. Well, not in bold anyway on Hallam's list. She the one you reckon?' Nicky posed.

'Could well be.'

'The bastard was shagging the nanny?' Nicky Scoley paused for a few moments. 'What d'you think of tattoos.'

'They're okay,' Ruth admitted. 'Not at all sure I'd want all that lot covering my arm and across my shoulder.'

'And goodness knows where else,' was sniggered.

'Bit of a passing fad seems to me all this business, bit like beards. Fine until you fancy a change but at what, mid-twenties is she, she's stuck with all that forever. Be fine now but look ridiculous when she's sixty, and somebody's granny.'

'Thought we'd catch a coffee,' Nicky suggested back on the A15. 'Place I've been before with my mum is Blanchard's Coffee Shop this end of town. Do scrummy cakes, You good?'

'Get behind me Satan!'

'Take the Sleaford road. Park at the windmill.'

Hallam's arrival for her meet with Larson was exactly as the DI had expected. Pink ankle grabber trousers were of high quality but as ever the woman simply lacked style in abundance.

Larsson on the other hand has an unaffected friendly air synonymous with those of Nordic heritage.

Larsson as part of the subterfuge and with a need to act as normal as possible made a point of suggesting she and Frances view the current Exhibition. After their culture fix, they headed for the Riverside Café for baby chat. There generous Larsson paid for two Lattes and a crumbly biscuit each. Somewhere she'd not been to in ages, and knew she'd need to keep an eye out for future exhibits, alone or with Adam.

Blanchards was doing good business by the time Ruth and Nicky reached it, but the pair managed to find a free table. Ordered cappuccinos and although there was an array of good food on a menu board they saw meringues dipped in chocolate they could not ignore. A delight they'd keep to themselves.

They were soon sat together looking around the cafe and out onto Boston Road

'Any news on Michelle?'

'Popped round the other night,' said Nicky. 'Reckons she'll be back in a week or so.'

'Shows, you just never know what's round the corner.'

'Or behind a door.'

After the coffees had been brought to their table and they'd both remarked and wondered how the boss was getting on with madam Hallam, they had their first sip.

''Sort of thing I thought about doing,'Visiting different coffee places. Get away from the norm of Starbucks, Caffe Nero and the rest but steer clear of the pompous places.'

'Like this you mean?' she suggested looking around. The familiar and delightful smell of coffee and baking filled her senses with a welcome aroma. 'Boss'd love this. Nobody here selfishly hogging a table with laptop, phone and a cold coffee. Something she simply cannot abide you know.'

'This is fine. Just somewhere different, away from the bog standard offerings. I could get used to this.'

'Why don't you?' Nicky asked but then realized there was already an answer. 'And the problem is?'

'Not really moving in the sort of circles where people I know would go along with it.'

'Why not? Seems a nice idea.'

'Not just…' Ruth shrugged as she stirred her cappuccino. Delightfully delivered as two separate items of milk and coffee in order for the customer to create a drink to match their taste buds. 'How my friends are I'm afraid. Plus there's all the baggage that comes with them.' Nicky remained silent. 'See,' Ruth eventually managed. 'I was the innocent party but it seems I'm the one who needs to change her life. Seek out new friends, visit pastures new.'

'What's the problem then?'

'People I'm still friendly with from back in my days of matrimony are still in touch with Marty and I get the feeling they're sort of spying on me and reporting back. Might be a stupid idea I've got in my head but it appears his name always comes up in conversation. Forever being told how well he looks, how successful his new job is, what he's doing, where he's been and who with. The gigs he's been seen at. And…'

Ruth stopped to take a small sip of her coffee. She didn't need reminding how her mother had told her more than once she needed to rebuild her life. Something she'd done nothing about so far, as once more the memories were invading her senses.

'Carry on.'

'Stupidity. Things like being told his old boss was pleased when we split up because he was never entirely happy with him being married to a copper.'

'Do what?' Nicky sniggered.

'Said it was like being spied on by the enemy. '

'Enemy?' Nicky gasped, cup in hands. 'What do they do then, cultivate cannabis?'

'No,' responded Ruth shaking her head. 'All to do with his old boss's attitude towards us, all about the traffic lads stopping drivers. Had a thing about him paying our wages and police should be looking for real criminals, not checking people's tyres, stopping dibbos for false plates or doing thirty two in a thirty and all that nonsense you get.'

'As if a drunk driver is not a criminal or one drugged up and the knuckleduster in the glove compartment is the sort of useful thing everybody needs to carry with them.'

'Exactly.'

'But apart from that?'

Ruth blew out a breath. 'Been told I need to rebuild my life and I often wonder if maybe somehow I've gone down the wrong path. My mother cooks every meal from scratch, hardly ever uses the microwave and most of what she serves up is fresh.'

'Different generation,' Nicky offered as she struggled to make the link.

'I know, but if I mention to friends what I've eaten or am planning to cook, the attitude of some is almost shock, horror.' She smiled. 'One friend last week when I said I was making macaroni cheese asked me why I bother. That's why Deliveroo was invented, he said.'

'Not sure the boss has ever had food delivered, but maybe in Sweden it's different.' Nicky drank down more coffee. 'Anything else bothering you?'

'This polyamorous business has got to me a bit,' made Nicky take notice. 'Just wonder if living what I regard as a normal life is the right thing these days. We've had all that business and recently I've been reading about a woman who confessed to her wife she'd been unfaithful, who then in return admitted the same thing. Now she's in a relationship with her wife and her girlfriend and her wife is exactly the same with her and some other woman and to make things even more tangled the two girlfriends are also in a relationship as a couple.'

Nicky Scoley just looked at Ruth as her brain attempted to take it all in. 'Why do that? It's not clever. Why make your life so bloody complicated? What's wrong with just being happy with someone?'

Was this she wondered what had been behind the break-up of Ruth's marriage? Were tales she'd heard about Martin just a smoke screen to cover her mental anguish over her sexuality? Had that been the real reason behind the break-up?

'And apparently they all ask and answer intimate questions from and to each other, as if that's the way to behave.'

Nicky had to drink her cappuccino and tuck into the meringue. 'And you think…?'

'No chance!' she sniggered. 'Just appears I'm not in a relationship because what I want is no longer the norm. I probably live the life I do because my parents set an example. Never do any of the daft things you hear about. Like the women I just mentioned or dressing up as brides to go to celebrity and royal weddings. Seems more and more what I value and enjoy, other people have no time for. Is that really what's going on and I have to adjust? Open an account with Just Eat, become all bohemian and drink cocktails which I've never done.'

'I bet there's an app for all this,' said Nicky shaking her head.

'Think they call it non-monogamy.'

'Be nonmog.com or something stupid. Go on moggy.com and you'll find cats! The mind boggles it really does. This real life or fiction you're talking about with these woman?'

'She says it's real.' Ruth looked all about. 'This place is absolutely fine, especially this,' she tapped her glass.

'Connor and I don't try to conform to some particular latest trend scenario. But, having said that we do know a couple who have two bathrooms because she won't share.'

'Sorry?'

'Friend has two bathrooms and always uses the main one because she won't use the en suite because her husband has been in it. I'm being serious.'

'And he can't use the main one?'

'Exactly.'

'Why ever not?'

'Do you use male toilets?'

'No.'

'That's her reasoning,' said Nicky and laughed.

'But he's her husband and they live together, surely…' Nicky answered with a smile and a nod.

'Bet plenty of folk come in here for coffee who wouldn't normally step foot in the place. Wonder how many of these are in some illicit affair with goodness knows who.'

'Or refuse to wash their husband's pants!' made them both chuckle. 'Just could do with a couple of pals I could meet for coffee at different places like this and not have to worry about Marty coming into the conversation every time,' she sighed and grimaced. 'Used to eat with a plate on our laps all the time,' and smiled. 'Sod sold our dining table to buy a stupid gaming chair.'

'You still do that?'

'No, no. Eat in the kitchen.'

'Same here,' Nicky admitted. 'So you're not living a different life from everybody else,' she was told. 'My mum knows a couple who formally dine every evening. She sets the table ready for when he gets home. They both get changed, have a starter, main and pudding with a clean white tablecloth, serviettes in serviette rings and all the cutlery. Drink fine wine, white or red depending on what the main course is and have a brandy after.'

'Just the two of them? At home?'

'And twice on Sundays,' Nicky added with a snigger as Ruth sat glass in hand shaking her head.

'This all fine dining they go in for?'

'Apparently not, just normal food. None of that snail caviar nonsense. So you see, you're not really living the wrong life. The other people are.' Would be nice to know if she did have sexuality issues but as having gay friends had never been an issue, Nicky let it go. 'Tell you what. Keep your eye open for somewhere different where we could meet up. Used to get together with the boss fairly regularly, for what Swedes calls fika. Coffee, cake and chat. Trouble is now she's married and got Terése not sure she needs a girly chinwag so much these days. Or got time.'

'But you've got Connor.'

'Doesn't stop us meeting now and again, and I've got a couple of pals from the hockey who I think are at a bit of a loose end from time to time. I'll have a word, see what we can fix up. Could be fun.' Nicky took a good drink and spied an improvement in the normal wan look Ruth carried. 'Anyway who says blokes can't come along? Boss told me once or twice about coffee houses being frequented by fellas often with their kids, even babies where she comes from.'

'Always the risk the coffee might not be up to much some places though.'

'Think as you say just going somewhere different would in itself be refreshing rather than the bog standard lot.'

'Darke boss can certainly sniff out a fresh cuppa.'

'He's also a bit of an expert you know,' Nicky advised as she sat back. 'Knows one from another, even recite the history of coffee back to the 17th century. Can tell a Café Misto from a Flat White just by the look, knows where it was first invented and has a great deal to say about what some of these pretentious places who according to him, get coffee seriously wrong.'

'We could invite him!' Ruth sniggered as she relaxed to please Nicky Scoley.

'You on the lookout for a fella?' produced a shrugged gesture.

'I'm not about having a plan as everyone always seems to me has a different plan to the one I think we have.'

'Here's a tip. Let it happen, someday out of the blue things will change for the better. Take me. All I did was go up to see the Crime Scene photographer and hey ho,' she sniggered. 'Could have been anybody the boss sent. That was it. One minute I'm staying in with my mum watching the *One Show*, next I've got a date.'

'Dating apps seem all the rage,' Ruth gingerly offered.

'Please no. Too many are scams, take it from me. I've done work with the e-Team on fraud cases like that and all the reverse image business. You'd be amazed what some are up to. My tip? Steer well clear.'

'So I just wait do I?'

'Not exactly, but relationships happen in the most extraordinary ways. Take the Darke boss.'

'Didn't somebody say he married his Sunday school pupil or something a bit odd?' Ruth asked as Nicky drank.

'Not exactly. In his teens he was a Sunday school teacher and Jillie was a pupil, but they were never an item as far as I know. He joined the police and married a nurse. His young wife got killed when this HGV idiot on his phone ran into the back of her car.' Nicky stopped and took a drink. 'Sorry,' she said. 'Just gets to me. One minute she's driving home from the hospital and an hour later she's back there in A&E being pronounced dead.' She stopped again, before she blew out a breath of emotion. 'Years later he was back home visiting his mother and he went along to a social function a summer fayre or something at the local church she went to. Just by sheer chance he bumped into Jillie. First time he'd seen her in probably a decade.' The smile had returned to her face. 'Married now with a daughter.'

'What did she do, she in the force?'

'No. Worked in London back then, some big banking executive apparently.'

'Guess we'd better get back.'

'You're right,' said Nicky as she downed the last of her drink. 'Time to go me thinks.'

Ruth checked her Fitbit she'd bought to encourage her to exercise and lose weight. With no fella was there any point, and anyway walking back to the car would be exercise.

41

'Some people would describe her as a self-made entrepreneur, brought up originally on what used to be called council estates. Luck was on her side when her mother managed to hook her claws into Charles Pritchard and then a bit later it looks as though the alopecia came to her rescue with Hallam.'

'All those years married to her and the poor sod probably had no idea what she was really like or what she was getting up to all the while.'

'To be fair,' said Jake Goodwin. 'We all know what he was like. Spent his time seems to me swanning about chatting up anything in a skirt and all the while she's running the place, backed by daddy's money of course.'

'Suited him no end.'

'Don't think you're quite right there,' said Sandy MacLachlan. 'From what we can make out so far, Morgan Hallam was his usual boorish self. But in the past six or seven years she let him get on running Brough Barn Motors on a day to day basis in his own inimitable style. She on the other hand somehow had convinced him to let her brother join the firm, albeit on the understanding he just ran Rumbold's place. What I reckon Morgan didn't know was they were running the illegal car cloning business from there.'

Sandy was taking a break by standing up with his can of Irn Bru opened on the shelf beside him. Could do with a poke of chips but there was no chance.

'I bet he just saw it as something to keep Jon-Joe happy.'

'But what if Morgan found out somehow what Jon-Joe was up to and it brought back memories of his old man being sent down and he wanted it stopped?'

'And as unscrupulous a person as he was, he was at least trying to run a legit business.'

261

'What about Charles Pritchard?' Inga Larsson probed. 'What's his involvement, is he just an honest to God dyed in the wool businessman?

'I shouldn't imagine so.'

'Time will tell.'

This was an extended break time in MIT with the whole team detailed to examine every aspect of the whole case to add grist to the mill of the CPS in bringing a case of murder and looking for something serious they could pin on Frances Hallam.

'She got her way all the time because in exchange for her taking control of his business he was very happy being in a marriage where he could have other women and the stupid woman even helped him with that God awful bucket list.'

'We assume.'

'Morgan could see his business going bottoms up when he found out, but worse than that doing time inside he knew would mean he'd not be able to go down his bucket list.'

'Not unless he added cell mate or Prison Govenor!'

'D'you think that was why she agreed to all that business?' Ruth asked sat at her work station mug held in two hands. 'Keep him happy running car sales while she dealt with the rest?'

'Certainly to her advantage to have him running the place, it did two things. Kept Morgan out of her hair and kept him onside with whatever she had planned.'

'Even if he did suss something was going on, why change anything?' was Nicola Scoley. 'Why spoil a good thing? He was like a pig in clover and she was making money hand over fist with the help of Jon-Joe her half-brother.'

'Keeping it in the family.'

'CPS seem to be of the opinion how in the end he'll plead guilty,' said a serious Inga Larsson sat at Ruth Buchan's desk. With most of the enquiry having calmed down she had been allowed to take a few days leave owing.

Drifting from good to bad, from total concentration at times to days when she appeared to have little interest, Ruth Buchan's name was one Inga was thinking about if another round of government cuts started to bite. More police on the streets as popular as it sounds often turns out to be a broken promise. Put more in uniform for Joe Public to see and reduce those solving crime was the most likely scenario.

'Could be he'll just take the rap, get a reduced sentence for pleading guilty and when he's done his time with loads off for good behaviour he'll come out, move back into Drovers Cottage probably, and Brough Barn will still be up and running.'

'You don't think perhaps all the publicity will do for them?' Raza queried.

'Quite the opposite,' said Inga immediately. 'She appears for all the world to be the innocent widow. What has she been charged with so far?' the DI asked her crew. 'Nothing.'

'We know full well who is about to receive his chunk of shares, and when her parents die who will get theirs as well.'

'All that socializing business, the flash motor, the clothes and jewellery was all a smoke screen,' Jake reminded the team. 'Like a magician she had people looking at her left hand with all the glitz and social media nonsense the world is obsessed by, when all the time it was the right hand doing the deals and skimming off the illegal profits.'

'Which have gone where?' Sandy asked.

'Being looked at for us. Given time Mason Lundy of the Economic Crime Team will find their stash some place no doubt.'

'Seems to me, the truth is, she's just a hard-nosed business woman who used people to her own ends,' was Jamie's opinion. 'One of the self-made sort they go on about which of course none of them ever are; the cornerstone of the Brough Barn business but doing it all behind the scenes.'

'Mention Brough Barn and everybody you speak to has tales to tell about glaikit Morgan Hallam,' Sandy suggested after a swig, as he unwrapped a Twix he'd taken from his pack-up box.

'Do wonder if his reputation was in fact a successful marketing tool. People went to Brough Barn out of curiosity maybe. Was it true what people had to say about him?'

'Truth is she was the driving force,' Sandy said. 'The one with her foot hard to the floor steering it on. Why wee half-brother was in the business and it was her who decided to include him in the illegal shenanigans not Morgan.'

Inga put her mug down. 'She was building fiction by the look of it, as a sort of smokescreen. A way to hide what she was really up to. Which is all well and good, but as CPS keep reminding me so far we have absolutely nothing we can pin on her. Financial audit lads could well come up with all sorts. Yes there's her one solitary fingerprint at the Curran property. What does that prove if she says the Wroe woman invited her over?'

'It'll be low template DNA,' Jake advised and went back to his black coffee.

'Transfer from Jon-Joe I would think.'

'Forensics say that by the way,' Inga confirmed.

'My fingerprints are probably all over Tesco,' said a grinning Nicky Scoley. 'But if it gets done over this afternoon it doesn't mean I went in there all guns blazing.'

'Be too late,' Raza suggested. 'My guess is that Curran will have painted over everything by now.'

'Grey is no longer on trend we're told.'

'Long way off that Raz. It's nae a wee hoose.' Sandy advised. 'Knocked walls down, had an RSJ going in, new bathroom all sorts before he opens the Dulux can.'

'You can imagine what her brief would make of it. Be all about the transfer of print business which it probably is anyway, if we're honest.'

'Can't wait for CSI results from the Hallam place.'

'And the holiday cottage,' Nicky slipped in. 'With the bits and pieces I managed to get combined with their findings we'll have him banged to rights, to coin a phrase,' she sniggered at her own remark.

'Tell you what has gripped me from day one,' Inga mused. 'How did Jon-Joe get into the place taking dead Morgan with him? Yes, she knew Kirsten Wroe, so there is a link no matter how tenuous, but there was no sign of forced entry.'

'He must have had help, surely.'

'That Bach woman could have helped, but the chances are it was our Polish friends from that Buslingthorpe place.'

'Or they forced that Abubakar guy to give them a hand.'

'Isn't this where the average crims show their lack of basic intelligence?' Jake got a look from Inga for using an American word she hated. 'Having got in undetected wouldn't you,' he looked left and right. 'Pretend to have used a jemmy or whatever to force the door open. Isn't leaving it all pristine a dead give-way?'

'That Curran'd been well pleased if they had!'

'It was an old wooden door, been there from day one looked like,' was Sandy providing on-site information from his co-ordinating position at the crime scene. 'Easier than the PVC monsters you get these days.'

'How about it really was set up between Frances Hallam and Kirsten Wroe?' Inga threw in the ring with a wry smile. 'I know we've mentioned this in passing before, but what do you consider to be the reasons why not?'

Nicky Scoley had taken a good dollop of coffee before she made her comment. 'What was in it for her? For Kirsten. That's what I can't fathom if she really was involved. Bearing in mind if that was the case surely she'd realize what a mess it'd make to his plans.'

'Have a feeling that Curran could be a right nasty bastard at times.'

'Something going on we've not sussed?' Nicky asked. 'Some hidden reason why Wroe was happy to disturb Curran's plans. She had enough of it all maybe?' Just couple of half-hearted nods was the disappointing total reaction. 'Fed up to the back teeth with living like that.'

'Surely to God, Frances didn't ask her if she could just borrow her bedroom while she was away, as somewhere to dump a body.'

'I've come across more ridiculous ideas than that, let me tell you,' Inga slipped in.

'How about Curran has bitten off more than he can chew financially with this new place and they're a bit short? What would he say if Frances offered Kirsten a couple of grand to borrow it for this caper?'

'Sorry no,' said Nicky. 'That Saturday night when I interviewed her she was in genuine shock, she was horrified. Just kept on about what she'd seen and I thought once or twice she was going to be sick in the car. She was seriously devastated by what she'd found.'

'So,' Inga sighed. 'She didn't know. But the partner Freddie Curran I'm not so sure about.'

Jake was shaking his head. 'You've not met him ma'am. He's a schoolteacher remember and he'd know how all his plans would be shot to pieces even for a few thousand and that's what bothered him more than anything. Sod Morgan Hallam dead in his bed, all he'd be bothered about was when he could get the plumbers in.'

'I've not met him of course,' said Inga 'But I'm not entirely convinced Kirsten Wroe wants to move anymore,' said Inga looking at Nicky. 'Think from what some of you have said Freddie Curran will carry on ad infinitum. Think she's fed up. Good idea to start with, but not now.'

'Same as me,' Nicky added. 'Think she's all for settling down and starting a family.'

'You think she mentioned it to Frances about how she was fed up with all that business, all the moving and living in one room for months on end. Trying to hold down a decent job at the same time, and by chance the one person she tells just happens to be looking for somewhere to dump dear old Morgan?' Inga shook her head. 'Not so sure.'

'Could be he was already dead and by sheer chance they were looking for somewhere convenient to hide the body.'

'Sorry,' said a sniggering Inga. 'I don't think so. Kirsten could easy be implicated in all that and how do you imagine she explained it to Freddie? Just what are the odds somebody mentions to Frances they'll have an empty house next week just a few hours after her half-brother has smashed her husband's face in?' Inga laughed.

'Bet365 are offering 100-1.'

'Sorry no, too much of a coincidence.'

'Not to mention too convenient.'

'What are we left with?' was the Detective Inspector posing a question she already knew the answer she was looking for. 'Apart that is from somebody we've not come across, somebody they used.'

'They used poor old Rumbold enough.'

266

'What about polyamorous? Has that business been staring us in the face and we've tried to ignore it, treated it as an amusing sideline but never seen it as providing solid evidence?'

'But the couples we managed to track down deny it all. Vehemently deny all knowledge of it.'

'Except that Olivia Willan woman might be a weak link,' Inga reminded Nicky. 'She's the one we suspect might have been pregnant by Morgan and currently seeking a divorce citing unreasonable behavior.'

'Denies she's been pregnant remember,' the DS was adamant. 'Told me her time for all that business is long gone.'

'Sounds like somebody making mischief.'

'Which is what the web's all about.'

'When we spoke with her,' Nicky continued. 'She'd not go into all that poly business in detail, but my guess is this was all about the grass being greener. Involved in the poly business at her husband's insistence I imagine. These other relationships emphasized how much better these other men were. This...' she peered at her iPad. 'Eric has the classic signs of a control freak, seems to me. Sort who refuses to admit when he's in the wrong, thinks he's the only one who can put a shelf up and all that nonsense.'

'Plus she admitted he's tight with money,' Raza slipped in.

'Told me she has to note down every penny she spends and report to him weekly,' added a grimacing Nicky. 'That's unreasonable behavior if you like,' she said and looked at her boss who winked her acknowledgement.

'Anybody fancy trudging round the abortion clinics to discover if by chance she was pregnant for a few weeks?' Inga asked. Blank looks were the answer. 'Thought not.'

'What about blackmail?' Raza offered and Inga looked at him for more. 'Was say Hallam looking to buy another place to add to the Brough Barn group and one of his polyamorous lovers is married to their accountant or solicitor and somehow between them used sordid insider information to give him a good deal?'

'That's a bit convoluted.'

'How does that involve Frances and Jon-Joe?' the DI wanted to know. 'Surely they'd side with Morgan not act against him, kill the accountant who wants too much for his client and probably a back- hander as well.'

'Think blackmail is an obvious route,' said Jake. 'Being involved in something like they were, does make you very vulnerable and open to all sorts.'

'If we're all done,' Inga Larsson sighed and downed the last of her luke warm coffee. 'Think we need to get back to it before something else comes hurtling around the corner,' she required of no one and everyone. 'Interesting ideas, but if anything else comes to mind we can always talk again. Thank you.'

42

Kirsten

To say I was shocked was an understatement when I turned up for work and three people were at me from the very outset. I'd not even had a chance to grab a drink or get myself all set-up for another day. I knew I'd be working on urgent contract management solutions for a client by looking at his monitoring processes. I still had my shoes on.

Don't know why but I've always worked with my shoes off. I usually kick them off under my desk as part of my settling in process when I know my day is monitor driven, but my pals with my best interests at heart were at me so quickly I'd not really settled down.

The *Lincoln Leader* website had a reference to it, but following the implicit instructions of my workmates I switched to an on-line news platform who for some reason always seem capable of delving deeper and quicker into some stories than most of the tabloid sites.

A suggestion that Morgan Hallam's murderer had been arrested was not entirely fresh news. What was a shock to me and my system that morning was who he was.

This Jenkins had been in court again in Nottingham the previous day with a date set for trial. Stephen Jon-Joe Jenkins meant absolutely nothing to me. I had assumed and so had Freddie when he was first arrested, he had to be some scurrilous toerag who in some way must have had connections with Morgan and Frances. The former rather than the latter probably.

Freddie of course claimed he wasn't at all surprised the Hallam's would be mixed up in something untoward. His opinion is of course shaded by his one and only brief encounter with Morgan. But that's Freddie all over.

269

My mind asked the question about sub-judice but then I realized people identities were usually known to the public in advance anyway these days.

Another shock I read sat there in full glare of colleagues was, this Jon-Joe Jenkins they claimed was Frances Hallam nee Pritchard's half-brother.

With Frances of course being the daughter of Charles and Margaret Pritchard and that horrid woman apparently is nee Jenkins. Of course I knew about them and had to smile at the thought of her closely guarded secret background being revealed to all and sundry across the internet. From what I've been told of her, that hoit-toity bitch is perceived as being patronizing and to a degree frequently disrespectful.

Blow me down, the stupid bitch was up the duff. That supercilious old windbag had a bastard son before she got her claws into Charles. Well, well how the mighty are fallen.

In this day and age with all the nastiness on the net, when you're down you are seriously down.

It was next day before I received the inevitable phone call. I'd managed to put off answering a few times but knew in the end I could end up with Frances phoning me at home with all the consequences of Freddie asking questions and what that might lead to.

I wandered off out mid-afternoon to that scruffy hot food caravan place I'd met her at before, just to get a bit of fresh air, remove myself from big ears and clear my head before she started at me. I knew what was coming right enough.

'You took your bloody time,' she shouted at me down the phone when I was sat on a rickety old white garden chair with a plastic cup of mangy coffee I'd bought from Doddie the owner.

'I'm at work and we're very busy.'

'You been opening your gob to Rachel Tucker?' She asked me. Fat Doddie had his arms resting on the caravan counter pretending not to, but quite obviously trying hard to listen in.

What else had he got to do? I'd asked colleagues what sort of name 'Doddie' was, and been told Dod or Doddie is a Scottish diminutive for George. I'm still trying to fathom. All Google had to offer was a nickname, but not why except for something about being used to disambiguate people with the same name.

'I don't know any Rachel Tucker,' which is true. 'But I see your brother's been in court,' I enjoyed slipping in. 'Thought I might phone your mum, tell her the secret's out.'

'What you talking about?'

'Your illegitimate brother was in court yesterday, bet by now the story's gone viral.'

'I've not got a brother,' Frances insisted. 'How many more bloody times?' she barked.

'Not what the press think.'

'Who told you this rubbish?' Frances spat out, so loud Doddie must have heard. 'It's just the usual fake news.'

'Social media told them I guess.'

'They're not allowed to...'

'Why not?' I broke in.

'Part of the case, you can't just speculate and tell lies before it comes to court. That's how it's always been.'

'Who says its lies?' Maybe it was, maybe he was not her half-brother after all, but I was only going on what I'd read.

'I do for crissake!' was firm enough.

'Sorry,' I said. 'But it looks to me like the on line community's already made their mind up and latched onto to it, as they do when there's mucky stories about.'

'Like I told you, I've not got a bloody brother. Time you started listening to what I'm telling you,' sounded like my mother. 'They're not allowed to publish lies about people, our solicitor will sort that out don't you worry.'

'He's going to stop the whole internet being awash with what the trolls think is he? Best you can hope for is damage limitation I should imagine. You happy with that?'

'With what?'

'Your brother killing Morgan.'

'Don't be ridiculous! I've told you before I've not got a friggin' brother,' I knew to be her default position. 'Happens all the time in cases, people getting their knickers in a twist. Just goes to show what a complete dibbo that foreign bitch Larsson is, coming up with some cock and bull story about us being related.'

'We'll see won't we, when it comes to trial. Remember, truth will out.'

'She'll get a right bollocking when it all falls flat on its face in court. You mark my words.'

'Time will tell.'

'What about Emma Maalik-Taylor?'

'Emma who?'

'Emma Maalik-Taylor. Some nasty snitch's been spreading downright lies about us to her and she's very upset I can tell you. If it was you opening your big mouth here's a word of warning. You'll be in serious trouble if they find out it was you. Her husband Mikael's a magistrate and I don't rate your chances when you come up in front of him,' she laughed.

'Number one,' I said slowly. 'I have absolutely no idea who this Emma woman is, was or might be or whoever else it was you mentioned and I'm not planning to go to court. So think on!'

'When I tell Larsson you got me a key cut, your feet won't touch, you stupid cow!' her laugh ran through my mind for ages. 'You're up to your fuckin' neck in it.'

'What about your crooked father-in-law, dead husband and this bastard brother facing a jury?' I sucked in a breath noisily for her to hear. 'I can just see how it's going to play out on Twitter. Trolls'll bloody love you, you shitbag!' I smiled to myself as I waited for her reaction but Frances had ended the call.

Frances and her intrusive questions could get stuffed.

What stupidity. I chastised myself and told the sensible me to pull myself together as I strode off back to work. She wouldn't put her own name in the frame with the cops. This was just another of her loathsome idle threats, and I just never imagined she'd one day turn out like this.

Knew if she as much as hinted to Larsson about the key all that'd do is drag her right into the mess and with her brother already facing years of slopping out I know she'd not seriously contemplate such a thing.

Also knew I shouldn't have lost my rag, needed to stay calm but it was all becoming too much to cope with at times.

You could say my biggest mistake was simply going for that meal in a restaurant and ordering Carbonara. If we'd gone for a Chinese none of this would have happened.

Looking at it sensibly that was sheer bad luck, so what else can I blame for my predicament?

There's Frances of course and me stupidly agreeing to that experience with Morgan. Was that part of a plan I wonder to put me at a disadvantage, place me in a position where I was then not able to say no, refuse her future requests.

Looking back now with good old hindsight it should have been a seriously advanced loud no. Having told her in no uncertain terms I should have stuck to my guns.

I never did drink that awful coffee and when I got back to work I made a dreadful mistake. I looked up the name Mikael Maalik-Taylor.

Difficult to concentrate after that and even worse later having to pretend to Freddie I'd had a good day at work. Slapping white paint on the bedroom walls was the best the evening could offer.

No matter what happens I can't risk losing him good or bad. There is just nobody else in my life I can ever turn to for help, guidance and advice. No family there to love and hold me or give me a warm hug.

43

The Major Incident Team had over time got used to the seriousness or not of issues by the choice of involvement by the boss and as in this case her decision over who would accompany her for a vital interview.

They all knew this time it was significant but it took on a new importance the moment they realized their question had been answered. Detective Sergeant 'Jake' Jacques Goodwin would be joining the DI in the grim dank room.

Jake Goodwin is the sort who'd be hard to faze. Facial expressions and visual reaction are never his strong point until he's face to face in a square room with them.

From the outset Inga Larsson had felt the need to up the stakes slightly and had imposed an attitude by threatening to arrange for a car to collect Kirsten Wroe from the E-Quilibrium offices. Not exactly blues and twos, but it'd be obvious to all concerned and to Wroe in particular.

The response was sharp, curt and to the point.

'I did suggest you could bring a friend with you,' Larsson reminded Wroe sat before her in the stark grubby interview room. A grey table in the centre and matching tubular chairs they were all perched on. 'Girlfriend, parent, Freddie maybe if he's not too busy.'

The feeling amongst Larsson's team was split evenly on the subject of the likelihood of more house renovations by Curran. Even if they did sell up and do the same one more time to find their perfect home, there were those convinced his obsession would make him carry on. Freddie Curran a few had decided, might easily go back to square one. Buy another rundown terraced place, do it up, flip it and move on to build a pension pot.

'I'm fine, thank you.'

'It's true you're not under caution, but if you want to phone a friend.'

'I'll be fine.' Kirsten Wroe knew she had nobody to ask. Not Freddie for fear of what might get mentioned and anyway he'd not be best pleased to be dragged away from helping his joiner pal fit a new door on the en-suite they'd built. Who else was there? Only nosey parkers from work who'd then gossip to the world everything they'd heard. Her eyes moved between the two detectives. 'You recording this?'

'Not unless you decide to confess,' was half joked. 'As long as you're sure.' From within a brown folder, Detective Inspector Inga Larsson pulled a plastic see-through Evidence Bag. 'Do you recognize this?' she asked but kept a finger on the bottom of the bag.

'This is looking to me like the harassment people talk about. After all we've talked about already I can't imagine what's left.'

'The bag?' was louder.

Kirsten shook her head. 'Only seen them on the telly.'

'Not the bag, what it contains.'

Kirsten Wroe had to lean forward and look closely to see anything. A key, a front door key. Made her lick her lips.

'What does this fit?'

'No idea.'

'How about your front door?'

'Does it?' Wroe shifted uneasily in her seat a slight movement Jake Goodwin spotted. Silent but all eyes and ears.

'Freddie got round to painting it yet?'

'Having a new one.'

'Did you kill Morgan Hallam?' A bolt from the blue. Where in God's name had that come from? Why were they asking her?

'What?' Wroe gasped with her breath, her face contorted and remained that way.

'This is the key to unlock your door so his body could be easy taken upstairs and placed in bed. In *your* bed,' Larsson emphasized.

Maybe it might have been a good idea to have got Freddie to go along with her after all. Confess all, tell him why, explain even plead a little if necessary and bugger the consequences.

275

Anything had to be better than this. Yeh, he'd go bloody lairy, but this was truly awful.

'No.' Where'd they'd got the damn key from as if she didn't know? The fucking bitch!

'Maybe you didn't actually kill him stone dead, just organized his death, with the key and your new place being nice and conveniently empty?'

'Accessory to manslaughter you think?' Goodwin spoke.

'What you on about?' was agitated. 'What you take me for eh?'

'Your idea was it, when you were looking for somewhere?'

'No it bloody wasn't,' Kirsten answered Goodwin.

'We think you've been put in an unenviable position and you realized how the only way you could ease the pain was by co-operating in the death of a man you yourself admit you've had sex with. Not just the everyday sexual frolics of the sort everybody takes part in, but in a major London five star hotel bedroom after a slap up meal and before as you've already remarked, a sumptuous breakfast.'

'Does Freddie know about the key?' Jake Goodwin asked. 'Maybe he got it for you, did he?'

'This ficticious key,' Wroe just managed and prodded the bag.

'Not fiction my dear,' the DS said. 'This is real, it exists,' he said and pointed to the evidence bag.

'Word of advice Kirsten,' said Larsson. 'You can play as many games as you like, but deep down you know we'll never stop digging. We have all the time in the world.'

'You only have twenty four hours.'

'After you've been arrested,' was a white lie. 'Have you been arrested?' Goodwin asked her, then turned to his boss. 'Have we charged her, I don't think we have have we?'

'No we haven't so far, Detective Sergeant,' Larsson replied. 'Well, not yet anyway.'

'Would you like to be charged? Charged maybe with murder, start at the top eh?'

'Don't be ridiculous.' Were her eyes glazing with the onset of tears Jake wondered?

'You sure you don't want Freddie here? Your father perhaps, we can come back to this. Have to hold you overnight probably, but we do offer breakfast.'

'Not as swanky as London I guess, but it'll fill a hole.'

'What's Freddie got to do with anything? I'm not his chattel.'

'But it seems to me you're not happy living like a gypsy.'

'We have a master plan.'

'Think that should be in the singular,' said Goodwin. 'Your Freddie has a master plan and you handing over a key to the front door of his current pride and joy and I emphasize, *his* pride and joy I don't think would go down too well. That why he's not here is it?'

'That could be anybody's key,' Wroe offered desperate for something to say and move away from Freddie.

'That fits your front door.'

'How d'you know that?' she demanded.

'By trying it,' he had not actually lied but what he inferred was untrue. 'Not exactly difficult.'

How on earth had they done that? They been creeping round at night trying the door while they were asleep upstairs? Was that legal?

'And?' was all she managed as her mind struggled to cope.

'You could save us a few bob,' said Larsson sat there elbows on the table looking at Kirsten's sad face. 'Just admit you were behind this killing, your job was to get a key made,' she pointed at on the table. 'A key we will be checking for fingerprints,' she lied about. 'Once that comes back from forensics as positive it'll be a certain Freddie Curran sitting where you are.'

'You do realize when this goes to court you'll probably have to sell up to pay your legal fees,' Goodwin slotted in. 'Just imagine how pleased your Freddie will be with that scenario. Back to a two up two down if you can even imagine it,' was his sarcasm. 'Or renting.'

'We're quite sure you see Kirsten, you didn't do this on your own.'

'I know you look fit, but I don't see you hauling Morgan Hallam's body upstairs and putting him to bed. Freddie Curran

277

just has to be part and parcel of all this. He's the one who took a dislike to Morgan Hallam as you said yourself and he even admitted as much to me. Your Freddie even identified the dead body before any of us.'

'Nothing to do with him,' was offered. 'He'd just bumped into him one time. Like loads of people looking for a car.'

'So, it *was* you.' Larsson grinned her sense of achievement. 'Going to tell us why or will that come once you've been formally charged?'

'Just tell me, why on earth you think I'd do anything like that,' she struggled with.

'Because you somehow got yourself well and truly mixed up in his sexual perversions.'

'I did what?' Wroe shot back and laughed nervously. 'Don't talk wet. What gives you that idea?'

'You were embarrassed and knew it could, if it all came out as it most surely will now, easily put your career at risk. Especially if E-Quilibrium ever find out what you've been up to sourcing women for him. Your family will no doubt want to help you but even they in this day and age will suffer untold abuse on line.'

Wroe snorted at the thought of it. They were seriously barking up the wrong bloody tree there if they though the Fellowship would lift a finger.

'It's always possible,' Goodwin took it up. 'You were recruiting sad souls for Hallam and even running his bucket list maybe.'

'What d'you mean…bucket list?' she demanded.

'Surely you've heard the phrase. It's a list of things people want to do before they die. Before they kick the bucket.'

The confused woman sat opposite the pair went to speak but was beaten to the punch.

'And remember Kirsten. Now it has all come sadly true. Morgan Hallam has kicked the bucket and it will all land on your doorstep. Another thing Freddie'll not be too happy about'. Even Larsson had to snigger at.

'Is there anything else?' said a heart thumping Kirsten Wroe as she somehow managed to get to her feet even though her legs wobbled a bit. 'I don't have a clue what you're talking about. None of this makes any sense. If you're not going to charge me with something really serious like buying a key I think it's high time I left.' With that she headed for the door praying as she did so. She turned back. 'What's the charge? Shoplifting?' she laughed pushing down the handle and was gone.

Outside Kirsten released a breath and staggered along the corridor as if she was drunk.

'What d'you make of all that?' Inga Larsson was sat hands on head leaning back.

'Not at all sure it's what she was expecting, but by the looks on her face every question seemed to be a massive surprise.'

'Scared stiff if you ask me.'

'Wouldn't you be?' Goodwin scoffed. 'Means that's one out the way, unless you think different.'

'Without fingerprints or even a partial what can we prove? Could be a million and one people bought that key, and we don't even know for sure it fits the bloody door.'

'What's Hallam playing at?'

'Certainly begs the question though,' was a conciliatory Larsson. 'If Frances really wanted to drop Wroe in the mire, why did she wipe the key clean before she shoved it in the jiffy bag?'

'Because it had somebody else's dabs on it. Choice was leave them all on or take them all off something that small.'

'Exactly, but it worked. I actually thought she'd crack and we'd get something we weren't expecting like we did before.'

'Not a confession?'

'No, just some useful snippet.'

'Like the mystery pregnant woman?'

'They sure about that are they?'

'According to CSI's Shona, the DNA on the jiffy bag is not known to us, but matches some found at the property and on Hallam, and helpfully it's a female match.'

'And fingerprints don't match our recently departed?'

'Exactly.'

'Thought she just might come up with a name we know nothing about, who'd match the dabs.'

'Such as who?'

Jake just shrugged and grimaced. 'Don't ask me,' he chuckled. 'Kirsten Wroe then. What about her? Certainly got some balls to just walk out like that,' Jake admitted.

'Scared stiff by the look of her.'

'Next question is if it's not her it certainly lessens the field, but who does it point towards?'

'Sure she was involved in some way, but as yet we don't know how. If the key came from madame Hallam without a link to Wroe what's that all about?'

'And why? Does she think we know who was involved but in fact we don't?'

'Push Wroe into the long grass and we'll look at the next prospect. Another why question is, why does she not want that Freddie Curran involved?' Inga posed to her colleague as they sat there together arms folded. 'That creaky round the edges you think? If that was me I'd have Adam down here like a shot.'

'What about him? Is he just not bothered, knows she's got us lot chasing her time and again and he's just swanning about with his tin of emulsion.'

'Why do we always come across these misfits?'

'Because the sensible law abiding decent people are never anywhere near us, not in our line of sight.'

'Is that a good enough reason to start to look more closely at Curran?'

'We've been over this before. Apart from that one time years ago he's had no contact with Hallam that we're aware of, certainly doubt he knows Frances.'

'Apart from a lack of motive.'

'Except his partner having sex with him.' Jake looked carefully at his boss. 'It was mutual consent I suppose.'

Inga sucked in her breath noisily as she pulled a face. 'It's more than likely he was at school teaching around the time the killing took place and you need to ask yourself would Freddie Curran of all people give somebody a key to his pride and joy with him away on holiday. I think not.'

44

Inga Larsson was sat at one of the spare work stations, red mug of coffee in front of her and on the adjacent desk an open tin of biscuit assortment she'd brought in with her.

Sat there with her team discussing the Taliban's take over of Kabul, it was as if she had introduced a top copper magnet to the Incident Room. For no sooner had they began to chat than the door opened and in walked Detective Superintendent Craig Darke.

'Got a nose like a...' Jake Goodwin muttered.

'Morning sir,' said a bright and cheery Inga Larsson. 'Coffee?'

'Not why I called in,' he said and Inga saw Nicky Scoley's face and found it difficult not to chuckle. 'But if you're asking.'

He just plonked himself down behind a desk, cheekily took two biscuits and the coffee Ruth had got for herself she slid along to him.

Having been through such intrusions on many occasions Inga knew not to allow his presence to phase her. She had nothing against him basking in their Operation Thanatos reflected glory.

After all the best he could hope for nowadays was a dutiful thank you for another successful speech to the local Women's League or the Soroptomists,

'Know what I often think?' she posed getting back to business. 'When the balloon goes up we have absolutely no comprehension of what it will eventually lead to. That Curran guy just dialled three nines to say there was a body, in his bedroom. Any other day it could have been a Code Red done and dusted in no time. In most cases these days it'd be a domestic, burglary even or easy be some dosser'd broken in, snorted way too much and overdosed his way to oblivion.'

'Or in some of the big cities another stabbing or organized crime monsters.'

'But no, we had what was virtually an empty house in a small community in that state. We then came across that crazy list on the dark web, not to mention bizarre marriage arrangements I still can't get my head around, and to top it all we stumbled across cloned cars. Almost at times as if we have absolutely no idea what's going on in the world, until we just happened to turn over a stone.'

'PHU clear up rate musta gone through the roof.'

'Sam downstairs reckons that bunch of toerags could be linked to car thefts in three counties.'

'Waziri Abubakar the illegal Nigerian is being lined up for deportation, so I understand,' Craig Darke contributed.

'After he's been inside I hope?' Jamie asked.

'Brief is going down the slave road apparently,' the Detective Superintendent suggested. 'Reckons the two Poles forced him somehow and with that as an excuse CPS are coming down on the side of just packing him off home to cut the numbers. But to be honest it didn't look like it. As we know all four bedrooms were being used and I'm sure Shona Tate and her team know full well who was sleeping in which bed. Just the lawyer trying it on.'

'From what I could see,' said Sandy. 'Looked like the two poles had one room together, there were two single beds. Maybe Abubakar had a rough deal being allocated the small box room.' He nodded. 'I'm with you, sir. Reckon he's trying it on.'

Craig Darke was sitting drinking coffee there listening in the knowledge this team of hers had Inga Larsson's DNA running through it. For a year or two he had still seen himself in some of their systems and actions, the way they worked but now Darke was willing to admit it was as if he had never been party to this united gathering.

'Rumbold dossed down there as well sometimes, remember,' said Jake. 'Bear in mind all this time he had a wife out near Middle Rasen. My guess is he probably kipped there from time to time if they had to work late, had a rush job on. Car heading for Morocco, lorry turning up first thing.'

'Looks like she's another one who didn't know what was going on. According to that Faye Rumbold woman she just saw him as a mechanic obsessed with his model railway and visiting exhibitions.'

'Had a few bevvies I bet, when they were done fixing the latest one they'd nicked and daren't risk being stopped so he'd just kip down there for the night.'

'Who was ever going to employ old Dez if he refused to play his part and got himself kicked into touch? Nobody else local to him is ever likely to offer a job.'

'Too many young mechanics about these days could easy do his job, except they'd not put their name to anything dodgy. Name on the deeds, had his Shogun registered at the garage but Jon-Joe's false ID he registered in his own name but at Rumbold's Middle Rasen address. Same procedure with the licences. One at one place, the other with Jenkins photo on as Neil Sands where his half-sister was.'

'They knew Rumbold was always as sober as a judge. More than likely he's never even tried drugs, van taxed and insured and full driving licence with nil point. Safe as houses, and he knew his job was safe as long as he obeyed the rules madam set.'

'His hobby meant he was always in need of extra cash which full time employment guaranteed him. You seen the price of these model trains these days?'

'Something I've thought about doing from time to time,' Jake admitted. 'Building up a model railway. Then when Tyler came along that buggered using a spare room with Sally insisting we need the third for visitors.' Jake pushed a breath down his nose. 'One helluva set-up though to be fair.'

'You could do what he did and use your garage.'

'Not with a wife who has to house her car you can't.'

'What'll they do him for?' Ruth asked.

'Next to nothing. He's got a genuine licence and insurance. He's not the one got it off the net.'

'What's happening with that Marie-Louise Bach woman?' DSup Craig Darke asked suddenly. 'Something I've been meaning to ask. Heard a rumour or two about her solicitor having something to say about a couple of women pretending to be nurses. What d'we know about that?'

'Anything to do with you?' Inga asked Jake.

'First I've heard of it. I'll ask Sally if she's heard anything.'

'As far as that Bach is concerned,' Inga hurried into. 'We know she's been living in the holiday cottage, looking after the baby seems to me. Attractive young woman to be honest, except for all that rubbish down her arm apparently.' She looked over at Darke. 'Got all these tattoos down her arm so we understand.'

'Across her shoulder,' Nicky added. 'Like a creeping ivy someone described it, and we can only guess where else it goes.'

'Poison Ivy.'

Keeping a straight face was almost impossible for Nicky by the look on the dark boss's face as he tried to picture this ivy creeping down and down.

'How d'you know?' was Darke immediately.

'Somebody said,' Nicky shrugged. 'Can't remember who now.'

'Plus of course this Jon-Joe was living with her.' Inga sighed and just shook her head. 'And to think when I visited Frances his bloody Mitsubishi was probably in the cottage garage.' She shrugged. 'Never mind eh? You can't win 'em all,' she sniggered and looked to Darke. 'Anyway. Our subjective guess is Morgan Hallam made a play for that Marie-Louise with all the tattoos and looks as though he may very well have succeeded as tattoos is crossed off his list,' she said pointing towards the white board. 'I'm guessing Jon-Joe found out somehow. Probably around the same time as mummy Frances discovered her husband had got one of her group of friends outside her precious poly group pregnant, possibly on purpose.'

'What's the chances that would have angered and embarrassed her?'

Jamie Hedley listened to all this aware his time with the Major Incident Team was all but up once more. It'd been good working with them through that ex-copper Mackenzie murder.

And he'd hoped all the work he'd done over in Gainsborough would have done him some good.

Although things had improved, a big government knife had over the years cut through the staffing like butter and whenever there was a major case, extras were called in pro tem.

This had been another such case. He'd been recommended by his boss down in the Prisoner Handling Unit and it had certainly been a real experience being away from the dross of life downstairs.

Time would be up in a few hours and he'd back to the knobheads and wasters he dealt with on a daily basis. All the shoplifting, the domestics, the users, pushers, loud mouths and con men littering and spoiling people's lives.

'I've come across cases in my time,' Darke suddenly offered, cup in hand. 'When one person in a partnership is the well-known gregarious one. The person folk know of and gossip about, when all the time the real criminal is the quiet unassuming partner. In this case it was the social climber who in some circles was even better known than her husband. The one people assumed was the show-off spendthrift all of which was probably nothing more than a smokescreen of opulence.'

Why did Darke do this Inga wondered. Pretend he found it difficult to understand the minutiae of a case when all the time he was obviously had his finger on the pulse of every strand.

'This was all,' he continued after putting down his cup. 'To cover what she was really up to, with her absolute desire to use her husband and outwit him to the extent she allowed herself to be used and abused by him.'

Inga was pleased Craig Darke had not as yet asked difficult questions about the polyamorous business. When she'd explained it to him she was not at all sure he fully comprehended what she was telling him. Was that him again taking this diffident stance?

'It would seem whoever it was, decided to have an abortion. It had to be that or face the divorce court.' Inga lifted a hand as Darke inevitably went back to supping coffee. 'I know, I know. We'd have hell on trying to work out which one might have been pregnant enough for anybody to know,' was aimed at Nicky Scoley and Ruth Buchan both anxious to comment.

'Guess that seriously puts doubt on the on purpose theory. And the only innocent one we're left with is dear Frances. No husband, half-brother heading for nick and probably pretty soon no nanny. Now we just need to tie all the loose ends.'

'But she'll have an empire all to herself with daddy's finances behind her.'

'There's a motive if we ever needed one,' Jake offered.

The telephone rang in Inga's office.

'Spoke too soon,' the Detective Inspector said as she reluctantly eased herself to her feet and trundled through to her office as the team members and boss Craig Darke continued to chatter, drink coffee and eat her biscuits.

From inside her cramped working space they could hear her reactions. 'In God's name that's all we need!'...'When d'you say this was?'...'Where d'you say?...'Say that again!'...'Really? You are joking!'

'Here's another, what's the betting,' said Jake watching Inga's reactions and Darke checking his phone. 'We need to remember this moment,' he grinned and bit off half another custard cream. 'Friday morning, sea of calm tranquility for a change. We're all here having our morning break going over recent events with a mountain of paperwork in front of us to keep CPS from knocking the door down. We're back to fairly normal hours after that mess with yet another strange bunch. Then wham bam thank you ma'am, here we go...'

'Why does nothing surprise me,' said a strident Inga Larsson in pale mauve blouse and navy blue skirt stood with both hands perched together on the top of her blonde haired head. 'If I offered you all a big fat bonus you'd never come up with this one. That was Control. Time to down our coffees, put the lid back on the biscuits and get back out on the road.' She stopped to take her hands down as she shook her head grinned, chuckled and was far from finished. 'Guess what?' she posed stood hands on hips. 'We've only got an unexplained but not unknown.'

'Least we know this can't be Jenkins.'

'Unless he's escaped.'

'Please, no.'

'Who's into gardening around here?' a grinning Inga tormented them with. 'Think garden centre,' she said as Darke pulled a face at what he was reading on his phone. 'Think about those enormous giant terracotta plant pots they have sometimes.'

'Go on,' Jake sighed loudly and sagged.

'Sort you wonder how the hell you'd get it home?'

'Need a forklift at least. Big buggers I've seen I'd never get through my back gate.'

'Exactly,' said the smiling blonde Swede. 'But bigger. Advertising gimmick for a new plant pot section at...Silk Willoughby. At least six foot tall I'm told. Apparently there's this customer making his way in from the car park just happened to go up to one and on tip toe peers inside, just outside the front door. Guess what?' She paused with a smile on her face. 'It's only Frances Hallam would you believe! Dead inside.'

'Serious?' Nicky gasped. 'You having a laugh?'

'What did I tell you,' said Jake as he got to his feet and scouped his phone into his pocket.

'Crime scene please as soon as,' Inga told Scot Sandy sat there looking dumbfounded.

'A reet jobby!'

'No peace for the wicked,' said a smiling Craig Darke as Nicky Scoley went to slip the lid on the biscuit tin. 'You get off, I'll look after them.'

ACKNOWLEDGEMENTS

I have to admit the circumstances surrounding that final sequence was not entirely my own work. The idea for the body location was suggested by good friends of mine once when we were casually sauntering around a garden centre. Thank you Eddie and Shirley.

Brough Barn Motors is a name I have conjured up, and none exists as far as I am aware, least of all in Lincolnshire. My very good friend Mr Google told me there was no business of that name when I was editing the final draft. If by sheer chance there is, I'm sorry but I did my best to use an anonymous brand.

It was suggested to me one day that if somebody upset me for any reason, I always had an easy way to get my own back. I could use their name as an objectionable character in one of my books. For fun I put this idea onto social media and a friend of many years got in touch and offered her name. I did explain she may well not turn out to be the most pleasant person in the world, but she was willing to go with it. I sincerely hope Frances Hallam enjoys her few hours of fame as people read about her – in name only. Thank you Frances.

In much the same way as Brough Barn Motors, the Lincoln County Police do not exist. Although all the characters including police officers are figments of my imagination it is obvious some readers are likely to conclude they are from the real Lincolnshire Police. Please understand, whilst they have very kindly answered questions over the years neither the organization nor their officers have any affiliation with this book. Any errors are all my own work and I'll claim they are made in the interests of the story.

To discover exactly what it is Inga Larsson and her team become involved in next, read on...

PREVIEW

Early morning milky coffee was always a login to the boss's heart, and with her start of day briefing having been precise and to the point without any serious actions, Nicky Scoley had decided to take her boss's return to her office as the perfect moment to strike.

Then just as she was about to slip in and have a word she saw DI Inga Larsson grab her phone with undue haste. It was as if she too was bored senseless by the monotonous stream of reports, dealing with endless CPS pre-trial queries over the double Hallam murders, expense claims and notice of yet another seminar somebody thought she should attend.

Then as Nicky watched out of the corner of her eye she spied the boss sleeve her jacket and in no time she was out and gone. Enquiring looks, a gurn or two and shrugs littering the Incident Room as the statuesque blonde swept past her team.

Larsson's reaction appeared to be based purely in response to an urgent call. DS Jake Goodwin was not the only one to check the system for a clue to the boss's sudden disappearance and he passed on his findings with just a frown and another shrug, as the copier continued to churn out a forest's worth.

In Detective Superintendent Craig Darke's absence at some conference to bore the guy senseless, she knew he'd absolutely hate, DCI Stevens had been nominated by the powers that be as her next up the line contact. A standby line manager in effect.

Luke Stevens is the smoothie, the urbane one with a great past record of complex crime solving, who had been running the now ever expanding Computer Analysis eTeam. Dealing increasingly with all manner of digital forensics and intelligence gathering very successfully, and Inga was not the only one to expect him to be moved on any time soon to pastures new.

Within fifteen minutes Nicky watched as her boss still obviously in a hurry, literally trotted back to her office to scoop up bits and pieces from her desk, whisper briefly to Jake Goodwin, tug at Raza Latif's arm and in no time the couple were scurrying along the corridor and away.

'Thought it was all a bit too quiet,' said Nicky Scoley sarcastically. Not really complaining but there had been no real excitement since Operation Themis and the dead copper Mackenzie plus the murders of both Morgan and Frances Hallam recently.

'Alyson Allsop apparently,' said Jake once Larsson had disappeared out of sight with swarthy Latif trailing in her wake.

'Rings a bell.' Nicky clicked across her keyboard switching actions and subjects. 'Oh,' she sagged. 'Oh no, not that stupid bitch again! What on earth's she got to do with us?'

'Dead, that's what.'

'You're joking!' DS Scoley exclaimed across the hubbub of chatter. 'Dead?' was louder. Her tittle-tattle news would have to wait.

'On your bike Sandy, CSI already on the move and they've called a pathologist. Off Carholme Road.' were Jake's instructions as the big man was another gathering his things together. 'Rest of you wait for word from the boss, but get your Code Red procedures up and running in case.'

'Name rang a bell, but I couldn't fathom it,' said the Detective Inspector, as she slipped her nippy quartz grey Mokka SRi out of the car park with DS Latif strapped in beside her. 'Just had Stevens going on about treading carefully along with platitudes about us having to protect the innocent and warned the injunction might still be in operation and all that business.' Larsson blew out a breath. 'Alyson Allsop,' Inga said with a slight glance left. 'If you remember she's the woman who wouldn't let her husband have access to their daughter for getting on seven or eight years. You must remember her and all that bloody fuss in the media?'

'Few years back certainly.' Raza suggested as he tried to bring it all to mind as the boss hurtled towards Carholme Road.

'All in social media and didn't she get injunction after injunction?'

'Absolutely right,' she responded. 'There's an injunction to protect the daughter, and that's what Stevens and the powers that be are worried sick about. Going to be hell on to keep her mother's death quiet, though. Neighbours will know who she is and social media'll go into melt down. Again.' The Swede banged her fists on her steering wheel. 'This is all we need. Get a few minutes to catch our breath, then we get this!'

'Trouble is Stevens knows we've not a live op so I reckon that's why we've been lumbered,' and why he had been virtually grabbed by the scruff of the neck and tossed in her car.

Craig Darke the big cheese had told Larsson he wanted Latif out and about more, with as much public face time as possible. The idea was to cure his abrupt and blunt attitude with the public which was once again highlighted in his assessment. Raza could investigate and analyse as good as anyone from in front of a computer, sat on his own delving, scrutinizing.

'Tell you who's just crossed my mind,' the DI said. 'The obvious candidate. Surely to God this can't be her husband can it? Would he really be that stupid?'

'Too obvious by far. But it'll be a good starting off point.'

'But they often are aren't they? Part of what keeps us in employment, people being thoroughly stupid. Ex-husband now of course,' she corrected. 'Name in the frame as they say and he's the poor sod who's had to put up with all her nonsense for years. Must have driven him round the bend which is a good motive to begin with.' Inga glanced quickly at Raza and grinned. 'Known people kill for a lot less, that's for sure. If my memory serves me right he's been to court dozens of times costing him a small fortune. Which leads us nicely onto another motive of course.'

'We're building up a good case against him and we don't know for sure yet what's cracked off,' swarthy Raza smirked.

'From what I can remember the kid in the middle of all this nonsense probably doesn't know anything about what's been going on. What's the betting the kid's been told her father wants nothing to do with her? Poor little sod's been lied to all her life, by that bitch of a mother.'

'Can't be him, can it? He's not your average skurk.'

'Well done,' she responded to his use of her Swedish. 'Too cut and dried to be him.' Inga hesitated to watch the traffic, took the corner at speed and headed west. 'Could well have got fed up to the back teeth with it all and just snapped I'll grant you...oh no.'

'What's up?'

'Just remembered somebody mentioned O'Connell's away. We'll have that dickhead Hellingworth. He's all we need.' Blonde Inga shook her head at the thought of him. 'Got it wrong again. Stevens asked if I wanted the boss recalled. Not much point as he's due back in the morning, I thought. Wrong. Could do with him to kick Hellingworth up to speed.'

'What's the betting he calls him anyway?'

'Don't be so sure. Stevens might well be looking to solve this one quick while Craig's away and get himself a few more Brownie points.' Inga had to slow as she approached a line of traffic. 'Give Jake a call will you, tell him we need everything he can find on this Alyson Allsop woman and we'll need the husband's info soonest if not quicker. And you can just check if he's got Sandy on standby ready to co-ordinate in case we need him. With a bit of luck and the husband's confession, we can have this all wrapped up in no time.'

'That'll mean handing more points to Stevens while we're at it though.'

Inga Larsson knew parent manipulation of children can be so exceptionally harmful. Using children to suborn the flouting of court orders was extremely damaging and to her mind was close to child abuse the courts were condoning.

Situations such as these when all the purveyors of all that's wrong with the world seem to have fallen asleep, were always a concern to the Detective Inspector. There had been whole days over the years when she felt real concern for how strange her world of work had become.

Sat about at a desk, leading a team of trained professionals all of whom were doing little more than waiting for somebody to be murdered, seriously assaulted or attacked. If everybody in the county went about their lives in a decent orderly manner she and all those gathered round her would soon be redundant.

Inga Larsson and her swarthy DS Raza Latif both wearing suits arrived at the house in an avenue off Carholme Road near where the old Lincoln racecourse used to be. It was Latif's brown eyes who noticed it, parked with two wheels on the pavement between two traffic cars; on the slosh as the yokels would say. Sighting Home Office Pathologist Dr Bronagh O'Connell's Volvo was really good news.

The pair made their presence known, signed in and then donned all the blue and white suit paraphernalia CSI dished out from their van down the street, before entering the house.

Alyson Allsop a woman probably in her late thirties was on the floor beside a dark green sofa covered in an imitation corduroy throw. Dr O'Connell on her hands and knees wearing her own hooded pale blue tyvek CSI suit and Connor the photographer were the only people in the room with the techy forensics guys busying themselves in every room but, or so it appeared to the new arrivals.

'Good morning Inga,' said the doctor without really looking. 'Not really making much sense. She has the look of having suffered a myocardial infarction.' She just peered up. 'On the other hand, this could be reasons unknown until we get the lab tests and bloods done. Think she may well have digested something. There's some evidence of laryngeal oedema that can be linked to a severe asthma attack. I've asked CSI's best man to search out any medicine. An inhaler would be a useful clue.' Bronagh pointed specifically to an abrasion on the neck for photographer Connor Mitchell to take intimate close-ups. 'This'll keep you off the streets,' she chuckled.

'As if I haven't got enough on,' Inga sighed. 'Still dealing with CPS over the Morgan Hallam's murder.'

'Remember that writer chappie?'

'Darragh Kennedy better known as Scott Casey you mean?'

'Reading one of his books,' Bronagh admitted. 'Half way through *Withered Rose*. Quite good I have to say, got some of the procedure a bit wrong time wise though.'

'That's what our Jamie Hedley was saying. How he got to know him,' Inga released a breath. 'Back to the here and now. Room's in a bit of a state,' Inga had observed.

'Suggests she was fighting for her life is my guess,' Bronagh offered up.

'Got it from every angle,' said Connor and offered Inga sight of shots he'd taken when he first arrived.

The plain wooden coffee table was upside down, the Radio Times and three cushions, two maroon and one purple were on the floor. If this was just a tragic accident or natural causes then it was good news. That would cut down the chances of a whole lot of hullabaloo over the court cases, her ex-husband, her young daughter and all that injunction business.

'And the daughter?' Inga asked when she came to mind.

'With the next door neighbour apparently,' Bronagh advised without looking up from her work. 'She had a sleepover at a friend's house so I've been told; this morning the girl's mother dropped her off. Poor kid walked in and found her mother like this and ran next door screaming.'

'Need to tread very carefully,' said Inga quietly as Bronagh carried on with her examination. 'This is Alyson Allsop apparently. She's the woman all the fuss has been about for years. Wouldn't let her husband see their daughter. Ignored court order after court order. Whole lot of nastiness in the media.'

'And social media,' Raza added.

'Name rang a bell. You're right, now I think about it. Thanks for that.'

'Press'll be all over this like a honey pot. Kid needs protecting. Think you'll be told to keep a lid on her name, pretty sharpish.'

'Ann Other will do for now.'

'She can join the queue. We've already got an inadequate Joe Bloggs at your place somewhere.'

'Not be anything here for you today,' said Bronagh as she sat back on her haunches and looked up. 'This will take time, unless CSI come up with something specific.' She smiled. 'How's Adam?'

'He's just fine thank you.'

'You know he sorted my hip.'

'So he was saying.'

'Good man you have there.'

'You and your family?' Inga enquired.

'Pretty good thank you. You two must come round for a meal sometime. Been a good while.'

'Thank you, that'll be lovely. Just text me.' Inga peered down at the body again. 'We'll leave CSI with all this, got people coming down, think it best politically if we set about looking after the girl.'

'Thanks Inga,' said Bronagh, as she pulled a notebook from her pocket and started to scribble and called for Connor who was by then in the kitchen. 'And Craig?' she asked just as Inga and Raza Latif were about to leave her to it.

'Conference in Coventry, back in the morning apparently.'

'Been sent to Coventry? Interesting,' she suggested with a smile. 'Think him and I will be talking,' she said with a slight grin.

Inga ushered Raza out into the back garden and phoned smarmy Detective Chief Inspector Stevens who was more concerned about release of the identity of the girl, than the state of the body. She spoke with him at length and he agreed to organize a family liaison team along with social services to handle the matter with utter discretion. She shut her phone.

Raza was on his, calling Jake Goodwin with as much information as they had gathered so far. Once all noted the pair just spoke with CSI and then hung about waiting for the arrival of chunky DC Sandy MacLachlan to act as Crime Scene Manager before the pair of them were able to head off back along to Lincoln Central and upstairs to MIT.

BITTER END

A *NEW* INGA LARSSON NOVEL

Coming your way in 2022

SACRIFICIAL LAMB

Detective Inspector Inga Larsson is enjoying a spot of retail therapy, sipping a cappuccino and relaxing on a bright Sunday morning in Lincoln when her idyll is shattered by an alert to attend a major incident.

She quickly discovers what stated off as a simple suspicious death is, in fact, murder. As she delves deeper in to the circumstances surrounding the young woman's death and the events leading up to it, she realizes the Gubber family has been hiding secrets for generations.

There are torid lies hidden beneath the benign appearance of Martha and Esther, the successful sisters. Inga is aware other people are lying to her and her team and there is a nasty undercurrant of bad practice, illicit trading, theft and corruption, into which she must dig deep to uncover the truth.

To make matters worse, her young assistant stumbles upon an extraordinary family twist known to only two living people.

After this, visiting a farm shop will never quite be the same again!

AN INGA LARSSON NOVEL

IN PLAIN SIGHT

'Back here soon as you can, there's an issue with DNA,' said Craig Darke.

'How d'you mean,' Larsson queried.

'If I tell you you'll not believe me.'

'Try me.'

'DNA found at the scene belongs to a woman who's been dead eleven years. More than just plain old-fashioned dead,' Darke said. 'She was murdered.'

Back in 2006, Christine Streeter went missing. When her blood was discovered in the flat she shared with Thomasz Borowiak, he was jailed for manslaughter, even though her body was never found.

Streeter remains missing, presumed dead, and Borowiak, who never admitted to her killing, is still languishing in jail.

Then, in October 2017, after an anonymous tip-off, the police find the body of Mindi Brookes in a house in uphill Lincoln, together with fresh DNA belonging to Christine Streeter.

In Plain Sight reveals hideous secrets of the past, deadly crimes today, and will pit one woman against another.

Printed in Great Britain
by Amazon

69743801R00172